CRIMSON

BY
SYLVAIN ST-PIERRE

CRIMSON

Production copyright © 2019 Sylvain St-Pierre
Scripting by Sylvain St-Pierre and Benjamin Mahir
Cover artwork copyright © 2018 Nomax
Cover text by Wesley Brown
Edited by Ottercorrect Literature Services

Distributed by Fanged Fiction
Norwich, Connecticut
http://www.fangedfiction.com/

Print ISBN 978-1-949768-86-2

Printed in the United States of America.
First Edition trade paperback March 2019.

Chapter 01

Alex tried to bolt upon seeing the chair, but the guards held him fast. "You can't do this to me!" he screamed. "I'm a loyal employee of the company!" He fought against the guards, but they were stronger than he was.

At least he tried to look away from the monstrosity, to glare at the nameless woman who had been his interrogator for that last...month—it had to have been at least a month now. Keeping track of time was hard when he had no chronometer, and hadn't seen the sun ever since being brought here.

He just couldn't take his eyes off it. He didn't know what the chair did, but with the wires coming out of it, the way the headrest looked more like something out of an industrial horror story, and the restraints. It couldn't be good. He wanted to have nothing to do with it.

He should have done something to keep in shape during his imprisonment instead of moping around after what had been taken from him. Maybe then he'd have a chance to break out of their grip and make a run for it. He looked over his shoulder. The door was closed—locked too, by the red glow on the door control. That stole some of his bluster; he wouldn't be able to leave the room, even if he managed to get away from his guards.

Alex fought again when they pushed him in the chair. He screamed incoherently, and somehow managed to free an arm and push the anonymous guard away. He saw the staff at the other's hip and reached for it, but someone grabbed his arm.

"Damn it," the woman growled. "Will you just hold him down so I can restrain him?" She had a leather strap in her hand, and once the guard was back holding Alex, she wrapped it around the armrest and his forearm, tightening it until it hurt. She looked over her shoulder. "Doctor, come help restrain him."

The doctor looked up from his console in surprise, the interface over his left eye bobbing up and almost off his face in the sudden motion. "Me?" He straightened it.

"Yes, you. Are you deaf?" She pulled another strap from her jacket and tied down Alex's other arm. "You said his body needs to stay in place, so you're going to have to help us."

The doctor didn't move.

"Help me!" Alex yelled, making the man jump.

"Doctor," the woman growled.

Now fear was visible in the scientist's visible eye.

She sighed theatrically. "Fine. At least come here and tell me how you need him restrained."

Alex continued pleading with the scientist as he came to him and took one of the ends of the leather straps. The man just looked at it, and Alex had a moment of hope that he wouldn't do what he was told, but then he indicated to the woman to run it over Alex's chest, under his arms, and behind the chair, where she tightened it until Alex had trouble breathing.

"I'm sorry," the man said. He had a soft voice that matched his older appearance, with his gray hair and wrinkled face. "You have to remain still, or this will be painful."

Alex glared at the man.

"Don't bother talking to him," the woman said. "We'll lock his head in place, that way he won't be able to move."

The doctor considered the situation, then indicated where the next strap could go over his temple. Once that was done, and Alex's head was pulled back against the headrest, the man moved the sides of the headrest until Alex could feel them on each side of his head, and see some of the industrial machinery in his peripheral vision. It went to his temple, and over his skull. He tried to get out of it, but where there was a hint of slack at his arm, his head was held firmly in place.

The doctor and his interrogator stepped behind a console. "I thought you said he was participating voluntarily."

"What kind of difference does it make if he is or not?"

"I—" He stopped at the glare she gave him. "It doesn't, I guess," he said, resigned. He fiddled with some controls Alex couldn't see. "You can begin."

She nodded. "What is your name?"

Alex didn't answer.

"I thought you said this thing would get him to—"

"I know what I said," the doctor answered with some fire in his voice. "But you didn't tell me he was going to fight. Just give me a moment; I have to calibrate it." He made more adjustments. "Try again."

"What is your name?"

Alex had a memory of being held in his father's arms, his mother cooing over him. Then his teacher was praising him. He was graduating, his grandparents cheering him.

More images came: being accepted at Luminex, praise, and awards he received for his work, but through them he felt his lips move and start to form words, so he wrenched himself out of those memories and forced his mouth shut.

"What was that?" his interrogator asked.

"The machine forces him to remember, based on the question you ask. That's what we saw."

"But he didn't answer me."

"He is still fighting. I'm going to have to adjust the setting some more." He played with the controls, and when he continued speaking, his tone had excitement in it. "But what we saw does tell you something about him. You asked for his name, and we got images of other people caring for him or

3

giving him praise. It tells me that on some level, his identity is based on what other people think of him."

"I'm not here to get insight into his personality. I want him to answer my questions."

The scientist sighed. "Go ahead."

"What is your name?" Her tone was impatient.

The images assaulted him again. His father, mother, grandparents, teachers, supervisors, friends, coworkers, and Jack. All of them praising him, or giving him a compliment. He felt his lips move, and try as he might, he couldn't stop himself from answering her question.

"Alexander Bartholomew Crimson."

"Finally," she said. "Tell me everything you know about Tristan."

He was sitting at a table, in a gray room, her seated across from him. He'd been eating, but had paused to look at the tablet she'd placed on the table. He was smiling, looking at Jack. He missed him so much. He identified him as such.

"No, that's Tristan," she replied.

She'd seemed triumphant when he'd looked at the image, and his eyes had misted. When he told her it was a picture of Jack, she got annoyed.

"I wish you'd stop playing those games, Mister Crimson. You've been caught, and Tristan abandoned you. Come clean now and tell me everything you know about him, and I'll see that your cooperation is remembered."

"I don't know this Tristan of yours."

He was on the floor of his bedroom, draped in sheets, feeling miserable. He'd been sick for over a day now. He was looking up at someone who looked a lot like Jack, but couldn't be him. Jack never looked at him so coldly.

"Jack doesn't exist," the impostor said. "I used—"

The memory shuddered.

He was on the floor of his bedroom, draped in sheets, feeling miserable. He'd been sick for over a day now. He was looking up at someone who looked a lot like Jack, but couldn't be him. Jack never looked at him so coldly.

"Jack isn't here," the impostor said. "I took him away. You'll never see him again."

The impostor turned and left him there. Alex cried for Jack to come back.

* * * * *

He was in the gray room. She was telling him how there was no Jack, that he made him up to try to cover his involvement. Alex denied it.

* * * * *

Alex was covered with sweat, his throat was raw. He was tied to the chair again. No, he hadn't left it. It had been memories. They'd felt so real.

"What was that?" she asked the doctor.

"I told you, he's remember—"

"I know, I mean something happened, like a glitch. Can you play it back?"

She pointed at the screen. "There."

The doctor hmmed, then looked in the distance. "He was

sick when this happened, suffering a high fever according to the file. It's possible it interfered with the memory."

"Or someone altered it. How come there isn't anything more on Tristan? Except for that part, it's all about me telling him. How come your machine didn't pull out what he knows?"

"It can't get something he doesn't have. I'd say he told you the truth when he said he didn't know who Tristan was."

"No. He's lying, I know it. Somehow he knows how to trick your machine."

"That's unlikely."

She glared at him, and he shrank back.

"But, if he does, you'll have to find an indirect way to get him to reveal the information."

She fixed her gaze on Alex, and it was filled with anger. "Fine. Since you keep going on about that Jack, we're going to start there. How did you meet him?"

Alex was in his favorite bar, Alien-nation. It was the bar where the aliens in the city went to get away from humans. It took months, but he'd managed to be accepted as one of the regular patrons.

The Jolarnian behind the bar, his good friend Aphalar, had served him his regular drink, and Alex turned to head to a table at the edge of the room, where he'd have a good view of the other patrons.

He took a step and someone backed into him. Alex cursed softly and reached for napkins to soak the liquid out of his shirt. While he was doing that, someone apologized profusely to him.

Alex told him it was fine, that it was bound to happen in a crowded room. And then he looked at the person who made him spill his drink, and he stopped breathing. He'd never seen this alien before now, deep brown fur speckled with light colors, a night sky filled with stars.

The alien introduced himself as Jack, and bought Alex a drink to replace the one he spilled. Alex couldn't take his eyes off him. There was something so desirable about this alien, but he restrained himself. He wouldn't be like those humans who had flings with aliens for the novelty of it. He respected them—he forced himself to respect them.

They found a table, and Alex never once looked at another of the patrons in the bar. They talked. Then Jack told him about his situation, and Alex offered for him to stay in his apartment instead of wasting money at one of the hotels.

Jack said yes, and it was all that Alex could do not to drag him back to his place.

* * * * *

Alex's head hurt. His mouth was dry. He felt like hanging his head, but it was held in place.

"This can't be real," she said.

"It's what he remembers."

"That's bullshit. It's just a story he made up to cover up his cooperation with Tristan."

"Memories do alter over time, but no, this isn't a fabrication. I think you're—"

She got in the doctor's face. "Listen to me carefully. I know that man collaborated with the killer who infiltrated the company and killed Tom. Your job is to help me find the evidence to prove that. You claimed this machine of yours can find anything that's in his mind. Did you lie to me? Are you here hoping to help him?"

"No! Of course not. But this isn't what you told me we'd be—"

"I don't want excuses, Doctor. I want Tom's killer, and Crimson is how I'm going to get him, so you're going to set your machine to punch through whatever lies he's making up."

Alex couldn't see her face, but by the doctor's near-panic expression, and the tone of her voice, he could guess she wasn't happy at all.

"I'll—I'll do my best."

"You do that." She turned to face Alex. Her rage was barely controlled. "Now what?"

The doctor didn't answer immediately. "Well, if it's like you say, and somehow he's able to fool the machine into thinking they're memories, we're going to have to continue and look for inconsistencies."

"Fine. What happened next?"

Alex brought Jack to his apartment, gave him the tour of the four rooms, and insisted he take the bedroom since he was too tall for the couch. Days passed with Alex going to work dreaming of coming home to Jack's presence. Each day the urge to get in bed with him was stronger, but he held it back. He wouldn't use Jack, he promised himself. He wasn't going to be that kind of human.

Then came the night before Jack's interview with Glacomel. Alex woke up to the alien standing over him. Jack explained how he didn't usually sleep alone, how that wasn't normal for his species. He asked Alex to join him.

Alex refused. He couldn't accept. He tried to make the refusal gentle, but his heart broke at how dejected Jack looked as he turned and headed back to the bedroom.

Alex lay there, justifying his decision as being for the best, but he was conflicted.

He knew what was coming. He didn't want to remember that part, not now, not with them watching. He wasn't ashamed of it, but it was something private.

He was by the bedroom door now, explaining to Jack he was a xenophile, that he couldn't trust himself to behave if they shared a bed. Jack trusted him not to do anything Jack didn't approve of.

Alex lost the battle of will and joined him. Jack didn't stop his exploration. Their lovemaking played in his mind in vivid detail, and it was only the first of many times. Every day before he left for work, and when he came back. Each time special, because he could see in Jack's eyes that the alien cared just as much as Alex did for him.

They were seated at an outdoor terrace, after shopping individually in Ilomare Square. Jack presented him with the Defender statue, one of the spiritual beings from his world, and over it, he said those three magical words Alex never thought he'd hear.

They were in his shower. Alex was relieved they couldn't see this scene since he was blindfolded, but he could feel it. Not just the soap that triggered his nerve ending, but how Jack moved against him, in him. It was the most wonderful time of his life. More days passed, their lovemaking becoming deeper each time.

Then came the day he got sick.

Alex fought against the memory; it was too horrible. Jack left him after seeing to him, needing to go to another interview with Glacomel. Being sick and alone was tough enough, but it wasn't Jack who came back, it was the impostor.

The impostor told him that men would come for Alex, not to bother lying to them. He turned to leave, but Alex forced himself out of bed and managed to drag himself across the room to grab his arm. Then he was on the floor, his chest hurting from more than the sickness.

The impostor looked at him with cold, angry eyes. "Jack isn't here," he said. "I took him away. You'll never see him again."

The impostor turned and left him there. Alex cried for Jack to come back.

Alex didn't want to remember any of what came after. Fortunately, unlike his time with Jack, this was a quick flash of images, mostly silent.

Men in military gear entered his room, found him crying on the floor. They dragged him somewhere else. Alex was in a gray room, a doctor explaining he had a severe case of the flu to a woman, Alex's interrogator.

He was alone for a time, getting better.

She returned with food and started asking questions. She asked about Tristan, but when he didn't know anything, she switched to Jack, and Alex reluctantly told her about his alien, carefully avoiding the intimate times. But over the days she picked up on them, pressed Alex, called him an alien-fucker, and belittled what he and Jack shared.

Alex snapped, screamed at her, threatened her. No one got to ridicule what he and Jack shared.

Time alone.

She came back and started questioning him again. Again, he didn't know anything about Tristan, so she asked about Jack. She was gentle with her questions at first, but as the days passed, her patience disappeared. She tried to get Alex to admit Jack was Tristan, but he wouldn't. He didn't care they looked alike in the pictures, Jack couldn't hurt anyone; he was too gentle.

When she accused Alex of being a dupe, of falling for the lie Tristan gave him, he lost it again. Jack was no killer he told her, Jack was gentle, a lover.

She attacked their love again, ridiculing it, implying that he was a traitor to humans for loving an alien. Alex threw himself over the table, intent on ripping her throat out. She fled the room, and for a long time, Alex was alone.

Two guards in the same black military garb as when they pulled him out of his apartment entered his cell and escorted him through multiple corridors. They reached a bland door and went through. Alex saw the chair and tried to bolt.

* * * * *

"What the hell was that?" the woman asked.

Alex's world was black, only sounds. He tried to remember when this had happened, but he couldn't. He had trouble thinking.

"Those were his memories," the doctor answered.

This was now, Alex realized. He wasn't in the past anymore. He tried to open his eyes, to glare at them for raping his mind, but his eyelids were too heavy, or he was too tired. He couldn't tell which.

"There wasn't anything in there about Tristan, and why did we see my interrogation of him?" Her anger was palpable.

The doctor's tone, in contrast, was forcefully calm, like he was dealing with a child about to throw a tantrum. "You told him to show you what happened after he met the alien. Well, that's what you saw. Everything until he entered this room."

"Are you telling me that he managed to fool your machine the entire time?"

"No." His tone was confident. "I'm saying that no matter what you believe, this man doesn't know anything about the person you're looking for."

"No! You're wrong. That man helped Tristan kill my h—" She shut up. For a long time, the only sound was her heavy breathing. "That man is complicit in Tom's death. Your machine was supposed to help me prove that."

"Look, you came to me looking to have memories extracted. My machine did that. The fact that those aren't what you wanted to see isn't my fault."

"You're worthless. Why are we even funding your research?"

"You—You can't cut my funding."

"I'm in charge now, so yes, I can. And I'm going to do it. I don't waste money on worthless projects."

"Wait, you can't drop me." The doctor was sputtering desperately. "If you're right, and he's involved, that means someone found a way to modify memories. You're going to need me and my machine to figure out how it was done."

"Can you do it?"

"Yes, of course," he replied quickly.

"How long?"

The doctor hesitated. "I don't know. You saw the playback— it was seamless. I have to go over everything again and look for any indication of alteration. I can't know how long that's going to take."

She was silent for a time. "Alright, but you better not be screwing with me, because if I find out you are, losing your funding is going to be the least of your problems. Do you understand me?"

"Yes, yes, of course."

"Good." Alex heard steps moving away, then the door opening. "Take him back to his cell." The door closed.

CHAPTER 02

The cell was the same as it had been when he'd been escorted from it: spacious and well-lit with gray walls, a bed, table and chairs, and a bathroom. Objectively, Alex knew it was a room and not a cell, but he still couldn't leave it. There was an old saying about gilded prisons he couldn't quite remember.

He made it to the bed, dropped on it, and curled up in a ball. Reliving the memories had reawakened the pain that had managed to dull over his imprisonment. Now when he closed his eyes, all he could see was the impostor, this Tristan, telling him he'd never see Jack again.

Why had he done that? It couldn't be just because he was cruel; no one could be that cruel.

Alex didn't remember falling asleep, but the sound of the door opening and closing woke him. He raised his head only enough to see there was a tray of food on the table and let it drop. He didn't have an appetite, not that there was enough food there to sate him. He'd had to have lost fifty pounds during his time here.

He closed his eyes and fought back the tears. He wanted Jack back. He wanted Jack to hold him, tell him it would all be okay. That this was a bad dream.

His father would have cursed him for needing someone this badly, let alone an alien. Alex didn't care. He loved Jack, and that's what people who loved each other did: they leaned on one another.

Only Jack wasn't there to be leaned on.

He woke up again and saw the door as it closed this time, and part of someone dressed in black. There was another tray of food, and this time he decided he had to eat, no matter how he felt. He forced himself standing, and his body felt like someone had beaten him, but he didn't see any indication of that when he caught sight of himself in the bathroom mirror through the door. It was all in his head.

He picked at his food, knowing he had to eat, but having trouble finding a reason to do so. It wasn't like he'd need the energy for anything. He was trapped here; he might as well just lie back and let himself waste away.

As the idea crossed his mind, he found he was grinding his teeth. What was wrong with him? He might be trapped here, but to just give up?

The anger gave him the strength to eat the food, but when he was finished, he just felt his hunger more sharply. He tried to stoke his anger, but he couldn't see a point to it. He made his way back to the bed and closed his eyes.

Days passed, each the same, the only thing marking their passage being the one meal he got. It couldn't be more than one a day, not as hungry as he always was. Lying in bed, getting up only for the bathroom and food. He knew he should do more, but he had no idea what. A couple of times he tried to engage the guard who brought his food in conversation, if only to find out how long he'd been here, but they remained silent.

After this seventh meal—so seven days since he'd been interrogated—he decided he needed a shower.

It felt good. Once he was done he almost felt human again, and he decided that after he'd slept, he'd start exercising. All he could do was walk around the room, maybe jog, but at least it would be something to do.

When he woke up, he couldn't find a reason to get out of bed.

Not for the first time, he wondered where he was. Where his cell was located. He had trouble believing his own company had imprisoned him, but who else could it be? And if someone else, why all the questions about the attack? At one time he'd thought it was a trick by a rival to get him to divulge company secrets, but it wasn't like he knew any. He was just one of the many coercionists the company used.

But the company didn't imprison its employees. They were a family, the company looked after its own. That's what he'd been told, and what he'd experienced, until now.

And now he remembered rumors that someone who'd made trouble didn't show up for work one morning, then after a few days, words came from the manager that they'd left the company. There'd always been one person who'd say they'd vanished, been removed.

Alex had never believed them, but now, here he was. What would his coworkers think? What had they been told? Did it even matter?

After another dozen meals, he finally decided he'd had enough of lying in bed and began walking around the room. It didn't help keep his mind from going to dark places where Jack screamed at him for letting him be taken, or where Tristan laughed at him for being so easily taken in, but it let him believe he was doing something to improve his situation.

At least he wasn't moping in bed anymore.

Not long after that, he began keeping track of the days, making a scratch on the edge of the bed each time a meal came in. He was up to eighty-nine scratches when the door opened, and instead of a guard with his meal, a man—dressed in a suit the same black as his interrogator had worn, and he now realized, the same black as the armor's guard—entered and sat at the table.

Alex stood there, unsure what to do. He hadn't even tried for the door as it opened. He knew it was pointless—there would be guards outside—but the thought hadn't even crossed his mind. This cell was so much his world now he hadn't considered leaving it when the sliver of a possibility presented itself.

"Will you sit down?" the man asked. His voice was pleasant, but slightly bored. A functionary, Alex decided while he remained where he was.

"Mister Crimson, if you want to leave this place, there are forms I need you to acknowledge, and I'd much prefer we do this seated."

Alex stared at him, at that well-dressed man, clean-shaven, a bit of a jowl, short black hair. Quite the contrast to what he had to look like: thin with a messy beard in dirty clothes. The walking had kept him from turning into a skeleton, but it hadn't done anything for putting mass on his bones. He just wasn't getting enough food for that.

"Mister Crimson, please sit down." His tone was still pleasant, still slightly bored. Like Alex's reaction was something he'd seen so often he barely noticed it anymore. Did the company have that many prisoners?

"You are being released. All that's needed is for you to read these forms," he placed a datapad on the table, "and you'll be free to go."

Alex looked at it, then the man again. Was this a trick? He wondered. Were they back to questioning him after all these months? If so, why this man, instead of the woman, his regular interrogator? Did they realize how badly he'd want to leave once they made the offer? Did they suspect Alex would say anything to get out of here? Not that the idea had entered his mind.

Because he wanted out so badly, he forced himself to move slowly as he stepped to the table and sat. The man pushed the datapad closer to Alex.

"This form indicates you are retaking your position as one of the company's coercionists."

Alex went through the document slowly, trying to give the impression he was reading it, even though he couldn't make the words mean anything.

"There's space at the bottom for your print, to acknowledge

you agree, but if you don't want to do that, a verbal agreement is also acceptable."

When he reached the bottom, Alex pressed his thumb on the space provided, and the document changed.

"This form indicates you are retaking your apartment, as well as your belongings."

Again, Alex forced himself to go through it slowly. At the bottom, he pressed his thumb, and a new document appeared.

"This last one is the standard form stating that what happened here is a company secret, and you are not to talk about any of it, or divulge any information about what happened here. Doing so is punishable by termination."

Alex looked up at that word, worry on his face.

"Your employment, Mister Crimson. Please, just what kind of company do you think we are?" The man's tone was light, but Alex couldn't help feeling like it was forced.

As for what Alex thought of the company, he thought that if it could imprison a loyal employee, what else would it do?

"What if I refuse to sign it?" Alex was surprised at how raw his voice sounded. His throat hurt from speaking those few words. When was the last time he'd spoken out loud? When he'd been strapped in the chair? No, a few days later, when he'd given up trying to talk to the guards.

"I'm afraid all three need to be signed for you to be released."

Alex wasn't able to act like he read it. He went directly to the bottom and put his thumbprint. It wasn't like he was going to talk about his time here, even if he thought anyone would believe him. He wanted to put it behind him, to forget about it.

The man smiled as he took the datapad. "Good. If you'll follow me." They left the room, and two guards fell into step behind them.

They walked for a long time, and Alex was happy for all the pacing he'd done. They walked through corridor after corridor, past so many doors that again, Alex wondered just how many people his company was holding captive.

The thought that this was a ruse resurfaced. Maybe they weren't freeing him. Maybe this man was taking Alex to be killed. His steps faltered. Could he run off? Would the guard catch him? Could he find his way out on his own? Would he rather die trying to escape, or by submitting to it?

He hadn't figured out the answer by the time they reached an elevator. There were no buttons or floor indicators, so Alex didn't know how many floors they went up. When the doors opened, he looked at another corridor.

This walk was nowhere near as long until they reached the end of a hallway, with a door in it. Above it was a sign: "Exit".

The man opened the door, and Alex saw daylight for the first time in longer than he could remember. He heard the sound of vehicles, the sounds of people.

Alex took a step toward his freedom, then stopped. It couldn't be real. It had to be a trick. They hadn't gotten anything from him.

"It's alright," the man said, placing a hand on his back and pushing him forward gently. "I understand your apprehension, Mister Crimson, but it's real. You're free. Just remember, you're expected at your desk come Monday."

Alex nodded and found he was on the other side of the door. "Wait." He turned. "What day is this?"

"It's Thursday, of course." The man closed the door.

Alex stood there, looking at it for a long time. He was in an alley, at the base of a tall building. This was the back, he knew because of the loading docks where a truck was being unloaded, and another one was pulling away before lifting off.

He walked around the building, curious as to which one it was. He couldn't believe he'd been in the city this whole time. The sun hit him when he stepped out of the alley, and he had to close his eyes at how bright it was. He'd forgotten how bright, how warm the sun was. His eyes hurt, even closed, but he thought he could stand there for the rest of his life, soaking it in.

Until someone made a disgusted sound and he saw the people walk around him, step away from him. He had a chuckle at the sight he had to be. He'd showered regularly and washed his clothes in the sink, but he couldn't look in any way presentable.

He ignored them and joined the crowd. Reaching the front,

he didn't see a name on the building, but he didn't need one to know it. He'd walked to this entrance every workday for the last eighteen years.

This was Luminex. He'd been held inside the company building this whole time. It wasn't just the company people who had held him prisoner, it was the building itself.

For a moment he thought he was going to be sick, but he forced the bile down. He was free now; the past didn't matter. All he wanted to do was go home and find out that Jack was there, waiting for him.

CRIMSON

CHAPTER 03

Alex looked at the door to his apartment, and realized he had no idea how he'd gotten there. One moment he'd been looking at the Luminex building—he remembered the sun reflecting off the surface, blinding him for a moment—and now he was here.

How had he gotten in without his ID card? Had someone recognized him after all this time, and his changed appearance? No one would have let him in looking the way he did, would they?

The door wasn't opening. It shouldn't since he didn't have his ID. The only other way in was the biometric sensor. He remembered entering Jack's reading so he could come and go as he pleased. His own had been entered when he took possession of the apartment, but it couldn't still be there, could it? There was only one way to find out.

He hesitated a moment before placing his hand on the

plate next to the door. It blinked, then turned green. The door opened, and he found himself standing before an opening, unsure if he should go in.

He had to go in. He couldn't just stand in the hall, staring in, but he didn't want to go in. He couldn't shake this fear that once in, the door would close, lock, and he'd be imprisoned again.

He knew the fear was ridiculous; he'd been released, he'd signed the papers, so they didn't have a reason to hold him anymore, and his things were in there, as was food. His stomach growled. It was that thought that made him cross the threshold.

The door closed behind him, and he stood there for a moment.

"Jack?" he called out, tentatively. "Jack? I'm home." He hoped, prayed for a reply. To see the Samalian's head poke out of the kitchen or the bedroom would tell him these last months had been a horrible dream. To see him smile would have made what he'd endured worth it.

No Samalian answered him. No one poked out of a doorway and smiled at him. It had all been real.

He realized he was crying, and he forced the tears to stop. He didn't want to cry anymore. Jack was gone; tears wouldn't change that, wouldn't do anything to bring him back.

The boxes littering the living room surprised him for a moment, but they made sense; the company wouldn't have left his apartment alone while they held him. If nothing else, they'd want to give it to another employee. He wondered if someone had lived here while he'd been away.

He didn't check the boxes. He headed for the kitchen and was relieved to find the fridge was stocked with fresh food. He didn't care if it had been the previous tenant's food, or if the company had restocked it. He took out fruits and vegetables and ate them without bothering to prepare them. The rich tastes ignited his hunger, and he devoured them, moving to ready-to-eat meats once he was done. He was about to start on the cake when his stomach protested.

He couldn't believe he'd overeaten like that. After months of minimal eating, he stuffed himself; no wonder he felt sick.

He'd have to be careful. Maybe he could use this opportunity to try and keep his weight down this time around.

Once the worst of it passed, he went through the boxes and found the bed linens. He made the bed, intending to move on to something else, but looking at it, all he wanted to do was lie on it and close his eyes.

He didn't understand the urge. Hadn't he spent enough time sleeping already? Maybe it was the stress of the situation he'd been in finally leaving. He lay down, pulled the covers over himself, and breathed them in.

He fought the tears. He fought them hard, but they won. There was no trace of Jack's smell left in the sheets. They'd taken even that from him. He was alone, he realized as he fell asleep. Utterly alone.

* * * * *

Alex woke with a start. He'd heard something. "Jack?" he called, "is that you? How was the interview?" Alex felt odd asking the question.

He saw someone in the doorway: tall, broad-shouldered. Almost invisible in the dimness.

"Jack?" Alex asked. "What's wrong?"

The form stepped into the room, and Alex shied back. That wasn't Jack.

"Jack doesn't exist," the form confirmed, and by reflex, Alex wanted to contradict him. He was right there, the same dark brown fur, the speckling of white through it, but the body language was all wrong, as were the eyes. They were chocolate brown, like Jack's, but cold, so glacial that just looking at them, Alex felt his blood start to crystallize.

"What did you do with him?" he asked, having trouble forming the words.

"I threw him away," the cold Samalian replied. "He served his purpose, and I'm done with him. You were so busy fucking him you never realized how I used him to manipulate you. All you cared about was your dream of having sex with an alien."

"No! I love Jack!"

The alien was standing over him, laughing. "You think Jack loved you? He was just a thing I used. He did what I told him to do, he fucked you when I said so. Jack was nothing, is nothing."

Alex hit the alien, but his blows had no strength. "No, he was real! What we felt for each other was real!"

The alien snorted. "Nothing about that was real, not from him, not for you. You're going to go back to your comfortable job, get back in your routine, and forget about him."

The horror of the words gave Alex the strength to push the Samalian away. "I'd never do that to him."

The Samalian smiled cruelly. "Don't lie to me. I know you. You care more about saving your own skin than him. You'll never be able to work up the courage to come get him."

"Let him go, please. You said you didn't need him anymore. If you need me to do something I'll do it, just give me back Jack."

The alien laughed again, and it was a scary thing. "Anything I want? Or do you mean what you want? If I fuck you, will you give up on him?"

"No. I'd never let you touch me. You're a monster for hurting me like this. I want Jack, not you."

"You think a sniffling thing like you has any chance against me? The only thing waiting for you if you take me on is death, and that's if I decide to be kind to you. You think I let you live because I thought it was something good to do? No, I knew you'd suffer, I wanted you to suffer. Because you want him so badly, I'm going to keep Jack to myself forever."

"No! You're going to give him back to me!"

The Samalian leaned in close, making Alex press back against the mattress until he couldn't move further.

"Come get him," the alien whispered. "Come and find me if you think you're strong enough. I'd love to see you try."

* * * * *

"No!" Alex's eyes snapped open and he sat up, scanning the room. It had been a dream, but what the alien had said chilled him. He didn't want any of it to be true. Jack had loved him as much as Alex had loved him back. That had been what was real.

The voice that had hounded him during his incarceration was silent. It wasn't there to edge on his doubt in Jack, or what they'd felt for each other. But instead of comforting him, he felt worse; he couldn't doubt that he'd been used.

The louder he denied it to himself, the more he knew that the Samalian called Tristan had used him, had used him and Jack.

He forced himself out of bed and realized he hadn't bothered undressing. He threw what he was wearing away. He never wanted to see those clothes again.

He found clothing in the boxes, along with the toiletries he'd been looking for, and kitchen utensils. He showered, dressed, and went back to taking things out of the boxes. Then he found the hologram.

He hadn't made many recordings of Jack; he'd been too busy being happy, and he also thought there would be more time for them. This had been one of the rare exceptions to that.

They'd gone out to walk in the park, and Alex had left Jack only long enough to go buy them snacks. Coming back, Jack had been looking up at the sky, thoughtful, and without thinking about it, Alex had snapped a holo of him.

He was going to take one of himself—Alex remembered thinking that a matching set would look good on the living room shelf—but he'd fallen sick, then... He could still do it, but without Jack there to share them, it felt wrong.

He held the projector against his chest. He'd thought he'd lost everything of Jack, but he still had this one reminder. The possibility that Jack was just using him nagged, but with this, he could hang onto the belief, the certainty, it had been real.

And then he found the statue, the reproduction of the

Defender. Alex smiled at the memory of the game they played at the market, each buying an inexpensive gift for the other.

This time he wasn't able to keep the tears from falling.

To keep the grief from overwhelming him, he spent the rest of the day putting things away. Once done, he ate.

After his second plate he forced himself to stop, but he wanted more. He was ravenous, but didn't want to be sick again. He cleaned the kitchen and stood in the living room. The place looked like it was his again, but it didn't feel like it.

He had to get out. He was in such a hurry to leave that he almost forgot his ID; it had been in a box with pots, almost as if the company didn't care if he found it.

That he'd lasted this long surprised him. Without Jack, the apartment felt worse than empty. It was a void draining something vital out of him. While busy he hadn't noticed it, but the moment he stopped it had been there, ready to eat at him.

Once out he felt better, so he walked. Without a destination in mind, he was surprised when he found himself at a transit station. He wondered why his wandering had taken him there; it wasn't like it could take him anywhere that would help.

Except that wasn't true, was it? There was one place that had always felt comfortable to him, not so much like a home, but at least a place where he felt welcome, a place filled with familiar sounds and voices.

The clinking of glasses and the thrum of indistinct voices made Alex smile as he entered Alien-Nation. He made his way to the bar, nodding at the aliens he knew.

"Alex," Alphalar greeted him, placing a drink before a scaly insectoid being. "Where have you been? It's been so long since you've dropped by, I thought you'd abandoned us." One of the Jolarnian's head tentacles reached back for a bottle while

Alphalar placed a glass before Alex. He took the bottle and poured the dark liquid into it, filling halfway, then topped it with a clear liquid, turning it to an amber hue.

Alex looked at the glass and fought back tears. It was the same drink Jack had made him spill.

"Hey Alex, are you okay?"

He shook his head. "I lost someone."

One of Alphalar's tentacles patted his hand. "I'm sorry, was it difficult?"

Alex nodded.

"At least you can take comfort that he's at peace now. The universe will look after his spirit."

He stared at the Jolarnian. Alex knew he meant to comfort him, but his words just served as a reminder that Jack wasn't at peace. It wasn't the universe looking after him, it was Tristan.

Alex stood. "I'm sorry, this was a mistake." He turned and stopped in the process of taking the next step. The memory of Jack bumping into him and making him spill his glass hit him, and he couldn't move.

When he was able to again, he hurried through the crowd, pushing them out of his way, not caring about the curses he received in a multitude of languages. He fought the tears the entire way back to the apartment. He reminded himself over and over that he didn't want to cry anymore, but they wouldn't listen.

At least he managed to last until he was in his apartment, the door closed, before the tears burst out and he crumbled to the floor.

* * * * *

Alex froze before the building's entrance, the flow of people continuing around him. It was Monday and he was ready to get back to work, to get back to his life. At least he'd thought he was. Now he wasn't sure. Would the guard even let him in?

27

With a breath to center himself, he let the flow of employees carry him inside. The guard didn't even glance up from his station when Alex swiped his ID. He was just one of many faceless employees. Even the other employees didn't even bother looking at him. One of them had to realize he hadn't been around for months, but if they did, they kept it to themselves.

By the time he reached the floor where the coercion department was located, he'd grown to expect the same there, but he was welcomed with smiles, handshakes, and hugs. Calls of 'welcome back', 'we're glad you got better', and of 'isn't it good the company takes care of your medical bills', confused him.

He kept his responses non-committal, and he was able to piece together that as far as everyone was concerned, Alex had gotten seriously sick, that he'd been hospitalized for all this time. He couldn't believe they thought the story was true, but he played along, not wanting to make waves on his first day back.

He thanked them for the well-wishes, but dodged giving details of what he'd suffered from by saying he wasn't ready to talk about it yet. With grave nods, they indicated they understood and made sure he knew they'd be there for him whenever he was ready to talk about it. Even his supervisor wished him well.

It was so strange to be back at his desk, surrounded by his coworkers. It felt so surreal that until his first order came, he wasn't sure he'd be able to do his job, but the moment he had a target, he went after it with abandon. He fed his sense of loss and betrayal into his attacks, and he was effective.

He'd always been good, but now, with his anger feeding him, he cut through the system's defenses with ease. He talked down the opposing AIs, and showed them no mercy. As soon as he was done with one attack, he requested another target.

He only left his desk for bathroom breaks and food, which was where he saw his interrogator again, standing in a corner of the cafeteria, trying to be discreet as she watched him. He did his best to ignore her, but the idea that she was still there after what she had put him through made him nervous. He fed that in his next attacks, and quickly forgot about his problems.

It was later in the day when, done with his attack, he looked up from his terminal with a sense that unusual sounds had been going on for a while—gasping. He didn't immediately see anything, so he packaged the files he'd extracted from the target server and sent them off to the parsing department. They'd be the ones with a detailed list of what they needed out of the files, and they'd take them apart until they had everything.

The gasps grew closer, and he looked up again. An older man was walking down his row, as if he owned the entire department. The gray suit he wore was perfectly cut and looked expensive, the kind of suits one of the executives wore. Maybe he was here to ask one of the coercionists for information, or a special job; except those should go through the supervisors.

He could be a visiting client, but then where was the executive who'd serve as a guide, and the security detail to ensure the visitor didn't wander out of the planned tour? He decided it wasn't his problem, so turned back to his screen and sent a request for his next target.

As the system's name and coordinates appeared, someone cleared his throat behind him. It was the older man, and he was offering his hand to Alex.

"Mister Crimson, I am very happy you came back to us."

After a moment of hesitation, Alex stood and, looking around to get a sense of what this was about, took the offered hand. A few of the other workers glanced in their direction, but most were focused on their own work.

Before Alex could say anything, the man placed his other on top of his. "If there is ever anything you need, please don't hesitate to let me know." He gave him a warm smile, squeezing his hand, then let go and left.

Alex watched his back until he vanished around a corner. Utterly confused, he was about to sit when he caught his co-worker staring at him.

"What?" Alex asked the man.

"Don't you know who that was?"

"Should I?"

"I guess not; you weren't here when it happened."

"When what happened?"

The woman on his other side leaned closer. "We were attacked," she whispered. "Two weeks ago. We had to evacuate the building. From what I heard, someone made it all the way to the president's office, leaving a lot of dead people in his wake."

"Not long after that," the man continued, "we got a new president."

"It was a coup," the woman said confidently. "Someone hired a mercenary to take out the old president."

The woman seated on the other side of his cubicle stood. "I heard it was a vendetta. A feud of some sort."

"That doesn't make any sense," the man said. "Who'd pick a fight with the company?"

"A corporation like ours has to have pissed off a lot of people. One of them is going to have the resources to do something about it. What do you think, Alex?"

"I think I need to get back to work," he replied in what he thought was a casual tone. The surprised expression they gave him prompted him to add more. "I've been gone for a while; I can't afford to slack."

"I was just asking for your opinion," the woman said, "not trying to get you in trouble. You don't have to snap at me."

Had he snapped? "I just want to get back to work." Again, he thought his tone had been casual, but they looked annoyed at him as they went back to work.

Their comments nagged at him for the rest of the day. Once home, he did some research and found reports of the attack. One unnamed person had made his way through the company, killing anyone he came across, culminating in an attack on the president's office itself.

None of the reports he read described him or named him, but Alex couldn't shake the feeling it was Tristan. Except, the questions had happened months before this attack. Had Tristan come back for some reason?

He tried to forget about the attack, about who might have done it. He didn't care about company politics, so the attack didn't matter to him. He hadn't known the previous president, and he didn't know the new one, not even recognizing him as the man who had shaken his hand until the report had given a picture of the new president, but that didn't mean he knew him.

But he couldn't stop thinking about it. Over the next days he kept returning to it, feeling certain Tristan had been the one to do it. He'd used Alex to get in after all, and why he'd been chosen nagged at him.

Every evening he searched the network for information on Tristan. He wanted to know more about the alien. Maybe in there he'd find a clue to why he'd picked Alex, and what he'd done to Jack. Only there was very little on the open net.

He was a criminal who had a history of mercenary work and was wanted on multiple planets, but there were no details on any of the crimes he was wanted for. Alex could find indication the information had been there at one time, but someone had gone around and removed it.

He tried to trace who had done it. If he could do that, he'd be able to find everything that had been removed, but his house computer wasn't powerful enough to coerce the node into cooperating with him. He needed something more powerful.

Like the company's systems.

CRIMSON

CHAPTER 04

Alex wondered if screaming at the screen might help. Not screaming at the node—he knew that never produced anything—but just at the screen. He'd taken out his earpiece and was rubbing his temple. This was proving to be more complicated than he'd anticipated, desipite the simple task. His problem was that he couldn't dedicate large blocks of time to tracking down the information on Tristan.

Coercion was a sustained process. It was why when he was given a target, he had to stick with it until he was done. A stubborn system could easily take half an hour before it gave up its information, and all Alex had was, at most, ten minutes between assignments before he automatically received a new target.

There was his lunchtime—he had an hour then—but company policy stated he couldn't be at his station during that time. The company wanted productive workers, not people who drove themselves to an early grave by always working. If he were still at his station, one of the supervisors would be advised by the system, and they'd come check. If he were finishing work on an attack, they'd remind him to take his lunch as soon as he was done. If he wasn't, his access would be cut, and he'd be told to go take his lunch. He'd seen it happen to more than one employee who thought they could get ahead by overworking themselves. He couldn't afford to be discovered.

The idea that he might end up back in that room because of that had kept him from spending too much time on this, and was what frustrated him.

For the last two weeks, he'd been trying to figure out a method to insert a command line here and there in such a way that it wouldn't be detected during a system's regular health checks. He'd worked out a handful of possibilities, and tested them on systems minor enough no one would care about the alarm they raised if they detected the alterations, which invariably they did. System health was a serious matter. Even minor computers had robust immune systems, and major computers had immune systems so strong that it could undo an attack in seconds, if given a chance.

So he hadn't been able to track down where the information was during those snippets of time he could devote to that task, but he did gain a sense of who was hiding it, or rather, what was. He suspected it was a program, and not a person doing the work. Even the best coercionist didn't have the reaction time and thoroughness he was seeing. He'd pick up a trail during a break, figure out the node it led to, then when he returned to it between assignments, all trace of both the node and the trail would be gone. Completely removed, not even a signature left behind, something coercionists were notorious for doing, even when they didn't want to. Even Alex did it, and the company had spent weeks training him and the others not to do it. It was something ingrained too deeply in them.

He was going through yet another of what he felt was a waste of time, following a trail, pushing how long he worked on this rather than his assigned task, in the hopes that this time would be the one that yielded results, but knowing it wouldn't.

In the back of his mind, he thought it was time for something more direct, more forceful. Like taking control of the Luminex system after work hours and doing this from home, but if he was caught doing *that*, that gray room would be the least of his problems.

"Mister Crimson." The stern woman's voice froze Alex.

He glanced down the corner of his screen, and there was the notification about his next target. As he watched, it went from blinking green to yellow, indicating he was noticeably late in starting.

He did his best to appear calm as he turned, but he was sweating, and his blood ran cold when he saw *her*. What was she doing here? She was security. At least he noticed her gaze was fixed on him, not the screen, so she hadn't noticed he hadn't been working on an assigned target.

"Y-Yes?" his voice cracked.

Her mouth was tight, her face hard. "Mister Karson wants to see you."

The name was familiar, but he couldn't place it. As nervous as he was, he had trouble remembering his own last name. He thought about asking, but the anger in her eyes kept him silent. Maybe that was her boss. Maybe she'd been demoted for what she did to him. But if security had been brought in to deal with him, then he was done for. His unapproved work would cost him his job, possibly his freedom.

Strangely enough, as he stood to follow her, he realized that being fired didn't cause the same fear it had before, and the idea of losing his freedom only angered him because he wouldn't be able to continue his search for Tristan and Jack. He promised himself that if it came to that, he'd run. He'd find a way to look for the Samalian from the fringes of society.

The elevator went up instead of down, and he found he breathed easier. He didn't know where the head of security had his office, but he knew the room he'd been kept in was below the building. His nervousness returned when the elevator went past the twentieth floor. Everything above that was executive offices. Even the head of security wouldn't be considered an executive, would he?

Alex had never gone above the eighth floor before, and now, Alex was so much higher that he was in a world he'd only heard rumors about. Executives didn't mingle with the common coercionists. If they wanted something, their instructions passed down through dozens, if not hundreds of others before it reached the assigning system. The only reason he could think of going this high was that the lawyers were getting involved. That could only mean the company wasn't happy dealing with him internally. They were going to make an example of him. They were going to turn him over to Government Law and press charges in the public court.

The elevator stopped, and Alex couldn't move. He'd thought he was ready for this. When *she'd* showed up to get him, he'd settled on a plan, but now that he was in the middle of it, his courage vanished.

"Move it," she said, making him jump.

He looked up as he exited, and caught sight of the floor's number: eighty-five. He was on the building's top floor. As far as he knew, there was only one person that mattered on this floor: the company president.

She led him through a corridor without doors, and Alex noticed faint scorch marks on the walls. The only door was at the end of the hall, and as he got closer, the name became legible: Emerill Karson, President.

The door opened to a reception area with two chairs against the wall, an unassuming desk with a well-dressed man seated behind it, and a holo of a nature scene, with the trees swaying in the wind and the clouds drifting lazily in the sky.

The three of them remained unmoving for a moment that felt like an eternity to Alex. Finally, the receptionist looked at his interrogator.

"It's okay, Chief, I'll take it from here."

Alex saw her jaw tighten as she turned to leave, but she paused to glare at him. "We're not done," she whispered.

Alex felt like telling her to take him with her as the door closed.

The receptionist waited a moment, then nodded to himself. "He's expecting you, Mister Crimson. Please go in."

Alex straightened his shirt before crossing the room. He wiped his hands on his pants as the door opened for him. He forced confidence in his steps as he entered a modest room with shelves lining the walls. There were no books on them, just objects—things the company made, he guessed, although, here and there he saw rocks and crystals.

The door closed behind him, and he was able to keep from jumping. "You wanted to see me, sir?" Much to his surprise, Alex's voice didn't crack.

He had a shock when he recognized the man seated behind the desk as the one who had come to his cubicle and shaken his hand. He now wore a white suit, leaned back in his chair, and studied Alex. He looked much more imposing seated than he had standing, and Alex realized the feeling came because this man now literally held Alex's life in his hands.

What Alex didn't understand was why he was doing this personally. This man couldn't be bothered to fire a lowly coercionist, could he? He had an entire department to take care of that.

The man indicated one of the two large chairs facing him. "Please, take a seat."

Alex did what he was told. What other choice did he have? You didn't disobey the company president. Hell, you didn't normally meet him during your entire working life, and now Alex had met him twice. If not for the trouble he was in, he'd be a star among the other coercionists, if not the whole of the lower floors.

"First off, Mister Crimson, I'd like to know how you've been doing since coming back to work." His voice was deeper, gruffer than Alex remembered.

Alex stammered. "I'm okay." He didn't know what else to say. He hadn't expected that question, and how he felt about the company wasn't simple anymore. He was grateful to have a job, but he felt betrayed by the way he'd been treated.

"Has...everyone has been treating you well?"

"Yes, sir. After all, they just think I was in the hospital." The sarcasm dripped off his tone.

The man before him squirmed, which surprised Alex, but it

also pleased a part of him he didn't realize he had, a vindictive part. "I'm glad no one has caused you any troubles. And please, call me Emerill."

Alex startled. First name basis? What was going on? He hesitated. "Al-alright, si—Emerill."

The man smiled a pained smile, then sighed. "I want to apologize for how you were treated. You should never have been treated like a criminal. I know this happened to you under the previous administration, and that my words aren't going to change what happened, but I want you to know that the people responsible have been punished. How they treated you is horrible. The company is here to look after its employees, not incarcerate them. We're supposed to be a family."

Alex nodded, more out of reflex than anything else. He'd believed that at one time, before he'd been locked in that gray room, forced in that chair. Now he no longer felt part of this family. He felt, and was, watched, observed, not cared for and nurtured.

When he spoke, Alex was surprised at the civility in his tone. "Thank you, sir, but why am I here?" He'd been so sure why he was here when he'd entered, but the apology didn't fit that. "I mean, I do appreciate the concern, but you're the president. You have better things to do than see to my hurt feelings."

Alex thought he saw pain on the man's face, but before he could be certain, it was neutral again.

"Mister Cr—Alex, I'm not the type of president who sits above his employees, apart from them. Like I said, we are a family, and I never want to be seen as too busy to take the time to make sure everyone is cared for." He sighed. "Which is why I wish you'd come to me. It's been brought to my attention you've been using company resources to illegally infiltrate and coerce outside systems."

Alex looked away. There it was, he'd finally find out what his punishment was.

"Do you have anything to say?" The tone wasn't as sharp as Alex expected.

What could he say? What he'd done was illegal, and he'd known it was. He couldn't claim ignorance. Like everyone else, he got the refresher courses about how coercion without company approval was a major offense.

Alex looked at this man, the president of the company who had imprisoned him, treated him like a criminal, and he thought about lying. He didn't.

Alex didn't want to be that kind of man. He was angry, but he pushed that down. This man hadn't done any of it. He'd taken the position during his imprisonment. For all Alex knew, he had ordered his release, and the way Emerill looked at him now, that was sorrow, not sternness.

"I'm sorry, sir. I had to find out more. I need to understand him, to figure out why he did this. Why he did it to me. How he could even bring himself to do it. I've tried at home, but there isn't anything on the open net; it's been scraped clean. I thought that with the company's system I'd be able to find what I needed." He slumped in his chair. "I couldn't find anything."

"This is about Tristan, isn't it?"

Alex nodded. "I've been accused of being his accomplice, when in reality he used me. He brought Jack into my life, made me fall in love with him. I thought that if I had more information about him, I could figure out how he did it, how he fooled me."

"Do you understand the kind of danger you put the company in?"

"Yes, sir." Alex looked at his feet. "I'm sorry."

They were silent for a time, then Emerill slid a data chip across his desk.

"What is it?"

"It's what you're looking for. All the information on the mercenary and criminal named Tristan."

Alex reached for it, but stopped himself. This was too good to be true. "Why?" he asked suspiciously.

"Because you are an employee who was wronged by my company. I owe you reparation. Before this incident you were a valued worker, and I want you to continue working here. I want you to give me the chance to show you the company is still your family, but I can't afford to have you put us at risk. If you take this chip, I want your promise that you will cease all unauthorized coercion."

Alex's disbelief fought to remain. He'd been so certain his job was gone, possibly also his freedom when he'd been taken here. Now, instead, he was offered the answers to his questions, and the price was simply that he stopped looking for them illegally. He searched Emerill's face, not that he was any good at reading people, but he thought the man was sincere.

Alex reached for the chip.

"Alexander, are you certain you want to see what is on that chip? He hurt you, but that is the least of the horrible things Tristan has done in his criminal career. What is on that chip isn't pretty. I understand your need to know him, but please, consider the ramifications."

His finger was on the chip, but he didn't take it. He did what Emerill asked. How badly did he want to know? Did he care what happened after that? The answer came easily.

He took the chip. "You have my word, sir, that from now on, I will only coerce the systems I'm assigned to by the company." He looked at the chip. "Thank you. You have no idea what this means to me."

Emerill looked at Alex, and the sadness in those eyes was deep. "Alexander, take your time with this. Don't worry about coming to work. Focus on coming to terms with what was done to you. I'll make sure your apartment is paid for, I'll see to it you can afford food. Take care of yourself, and when you are ready, come back to us."

Alex nodded. He didn't understand why this man, the boss of his boss's boss, was doing this. This was more than compensation for being wronged by the company, so much more, but Alex didn't press. He had what he wanted. Why the president of the company was giving it to him didn't matter, and even though of a part of him was curious, he didn't want to risk losing what he had by probing into it.

Alex stood. "Thank you, sir." He offered his hand. "If you don't mind, I'm going to take you up on that right now and go home."

Emerill shook his hand. "Please be careful, Alexander."

Alex nodded and left.

CHAPTER 05

Alex didn't call out to Jack as he entered his apartment; he had stopped doing that after a week, instead letting the oppressive silence remind him he'd lost someone precious and needed to find him again.

He went to his computer and put the chip in, but instead of sitting down, he headed for the kitchen. He told himself it was because, after the day he'd had, he needed to eat something. Like each time he cooked, he tried to keep the portion small, but once the smell of the food surrounded him and the sound of the pots and utensils filled the silence, he forgot his promise to watch what he ate, and by the time he was done, he had enough food to feed three people.

Or Jack and him.

He ate everything he cooked, taking his time, savoring the food. He'd realized that the speed at which he ate was more of a factor than how hungry he was, and in how much food he could ingest before getting sick.

Once he was done he cleaned the dishes, put them away, and headed for the computer, but on the way there, he caught the scent of what he was wearing. Without the smell of food masking them, the scents of the day came from his clothes. So he washed them, and his sheets while he was at it.

After the months he spent wearing the same thing, he couldn't tolerate dirty clothing anymore. Instead of going to his computer while the machine worked, he inventoried the fridge, then had it place an order to restock it. After that he dusted the shelves, since he hadn't done that in a day or two, or maybe it was three.

After the washing machine informed him his clothes were dry, he made his bed, organized his closet, and began dusting the shelves again.

He'd moved the Defender to wipe the clean shelf under it when the realization hit. He should be reading the information on the chip. He'd been looking for it for weeks now. Didn't he want to know what was on it?

He placed the Defender down, left the cloth on the shelf, and turned to the computer, then stopped. Emerill's words came back to him. *"You will not be the same once you read this."* The concern on the man's face had been genuine, Alex was sure of it. And Alex realized that the warning scared him, so he picked the cloth back up and went back to cleaning.

By the time he went to bed, his apartment was cleaner than it had ever been in his life, but the computer remained turned off.

It took him two days to reach his breaking point. He'd been in the process of moving things on his shelves around—he'd moved pictures and had just taken the Defender from the left side of the living room to the right, where he thought it fitted better.

In turning to see what else needed to be moved he'd seen the computer, and Emerill's warning came to him again, but this time the fear it engendered make him angry. Why was he so fearful of being different? He was miserable right now. He was alone. What was so good about who he was? And hadn't he promised himself he'd do whatever was necessary to find Tristan and save Jack? Was he really a coward? More importantly, did he want to remain one?

He sat at the computer and wondered if he'd done the wash today. He was almost out of the chair when he recognized the thought for the procrastination it was. He forced himself down and brought the file up.

The first section was a physical description of Tristan: Samalian, dark brown fur, scattered white specks. Six-foot nine, two-hundred ninety pounds.

Right there, Alex knew his interrogator had been wrong. Yes, Jack and Tristan looked alike, but Jack wasn't six-nine; he had only been a few inches more than Alex's six-one, but she'd been so obsessed about blaming Alex for what had happened, she ignored such an obvious difference.

The next section spoke to his personality, describing him as a scheming psychopath with no compunction against killing. At least that was what Alex got; there were a lot of technical terms in there he didn't understand and didn't feel like searching for.

But he got enough from that to know his interrogator should have again seen the difference. Jack was sweet and loving, not a cold-blooded killer. And her assertions that Tristan simply acted that way was ludicrous; no cold-blooded killer could pull off the love Jack radiated.

The next section began the list and description of Tristan's crimes. The first one was six murders on a transport ship called Junjager. Those six had formed the crew, and there was no information as to what Tristan was doing on board the ship. The only detail of the death were that he had dismembered them, and a link, which Alex brought up.

He took one look at the picture, then ran to the bathroom, barely making it to the toilet before throwing up. He closed his eyes and tried to chase the image out of his mind, but he couldn't.

It had been a cockpit, and there had been blood everywhere. Dismembered didn't do justice to the massacre Alex had glimpsed. One of the bodies had been opened from crotch to chest by something jagged, the guts spilled out on the floor. Another's head had been smashed against the wall either often or hard, because it was crushed and brain matter leaked out down the wall.

Alex cursed his good memory and analytical mind that made him such a good coercionist. Now it wouldn't let go of the image, bringing up details, like that the decapitated head placed on the control panel had a look of terror on his face, or that the body in the pilot's seat, without his head, had been carefully cut open, the insides taken out and placed at the feet of the victim. Alex's mind told him that he hadn't been dead when that had happened.

When he was able to get up—and confident he wouldn't throw up again—he went to the computer, took out the chip, and almost dropped it in the disposal unit. He hesitated, his hand over the unit, chip in two fingers. As horrible as the image had been, did he really want to destroy all hopes he had of ever finding and rescuing Jack? He placed the chip in a desk drawer, then went to bed and tried to sleep.

He had nightmares that night. He saw himself being locked in the pilot's chair, screaming in pain as his guts, then his lungs, and finally his heart were removed, and when the killer looked up from his work, it was Tristan's cold eyes that looked at him, but Jack's loving gaze.

In another scene he was in his apartment, blood covering the floor and wall. There was a body on his bed, human, but not him. Strong, caring arms held him. A muzzle was pressed in the crook of his neck, licking and nibbling, and Alex felt himself get excited at the prospect of what was coming. He heard sounds, but they had no distinction, other than encouragement. The blood-covered furry arms placed something shiny in his hand, and Alex's excitement was so strong it hurt. As one he and his lover moved to the body, bent down, and Alex planted the knife in his interrogator's heart.

He woke with a strangled scream, his stomach covered with the evidence of his excitement at killing someone. He thought he'd throw up again, but instead felt dirty, so he washed—for a long time.

After that he couldn't stay in the apartment, close to the

reminder of the dream he couldn't manage to forget, so he went to work. He threw himself into attacking systems, using the focus required in that to push the nightmare away.

When he looked up between assignments and saw her watching him, the images came back to him, the feeling of the knife going in, how good it had felt to finally be rid of her.

Fortunately, now that he was awake, his body didn't react with excitement to the memory of the dream, but revulsion. He found a toilet and threw up again.

For a week he spent as much time at work as he could, only going home to sleep. When he was home he stayed away from the computer, terrified that just by sitting at it, the chip would call to him and he'd see that image again, or other images like it.

Each day he'd catch her watching him, and the dream would come back to him. Feeling his alien lover's body pressing against him, and them bending down, the encouraging words whispered in his ear, the climax as the knife pierced her heart.

On the second and third days he threw up again, but on the fourth, he didn't. He was worried he was coming to accept his enjoyment of what he'd done, but he wasn't; the dream's overall impact was simply diminishing.

By the end of the week he remembered the dream when he saw her, but it was vague now, like most of them. It wasn't him doing the act anymore, but a shadow version of himself. The words his lover whispered no longer carried any meaning. They'd become indistinct sounds.

When he went home that night, he'd understood what he needed to do if he wanted to understand Tristan. If he wanted any chance of finding him, he had to get used to seeing the result of his crimes. When he began actively hunting him, he'd see more than pictures. Alex was certain that in his hunt for the alien, he would come face to face with those crimes. He'd see dead bodies, desecrated bodies. He had to become desensitized to it.

A part of him screamed that he was insane for doing this. That he didn't remember things as they truly were, but he pushed it away, locked it at the back of his mind. If becoming insane was what he had to do to save Jack, then that was what he'd do.

The Junjager had been found drifting at the edge of the Tournal system by an arriving transport. The only thing missing on the ship was one of the life pods. The investigators theorized that Tristan left the ship using it. They knew he was on the ship because he was logged as a passenger.

Alex noted it was sloppy of him not to have erased that evidence, but reminded himself this was Tristan's first crime. He had to have been young, inexperienced. Why Tristan had killed the crew, the investigators didn't postulate.

Alex forced himself to look at the picture again. He thought that after getting used to the dream, the picture wouldn't affect him as much. He was wrong. This time he didn't make it to the bathroom.

After cleaning up the mess, he sat back down and studied the picture again. He continued staring at it, analyzing every detail, until he no longer felt his stomach fight each time he thought about it. Only then did he move to the next report.

This one proved easier. The body count was higher, six-hundred and twenty-eight, but there were no detailed pictures of the result. The death had happened when Tristan blew up Tetsui station.

The Osagua Cruise ship was much the same, seventy-three dead during the explosion.

The next one, the killing at Uritual, was different. Tristan had only killed one person, a bounty hunter named Johanna Sheldon. He'd skinned and filleted her, drying the skin and muscles, and blanching the bones before dumping them at the doorsteps of the organization she had belonged to.

The action spoke of a coldness that brought Tristan's eyes back to Alex when he'd said he'd used him.

Then there was a town on Ucoryla Two, which he'd bomb. The report only had an estimate of the dead, two-thousand.

The next six killings were vicious: six bounty hunters affiliated with the same organization Johanna had belonged to. Those killings spoke of rage and anger.

The days blended into one another as he read more and more of Tristan's killings. Some executed coldly, some with burning anger. Tristan had been caught and imprisoned three times, and he escaped each one. Twice with a high body count, and once in such a way that no one had figured out how he had done it.

When he finished the last of the reports, Alex didn't know what day it was, or even what time. All he knew was that Emerill had been right. In forcing himself to read them, he'd done something to himself. He'd lost something.

He took a long shower, but he still felt dirty afterward. He tried to sleep, but his dreams were filled with Tristan's victims. Fortunately, Alex wasn't in those. He didn't have a repeat of the dream where he killed someone, but he did wake up to the memory of Tristan's hand around his neck, screaming, "He's mine! You'll never get Jack back." And then, pain in his chest as the alien ripped his heart out.

Alex swore to himself he'd prove the alien wrong. He would get Jack back, and if needed he'd kill Tristan in the process. He reread the reports, looking for any indication of where Tristan might be, places he might hang out. Any starting points for his search, but they didn't have anything.

The most recent entry claimed Tristan was imprisoned on the prison ship Sayatoga, delivered there by a bounty hunter, Miranda Sunstar. He tried to locate her, thinking that since she'd caught him, she'd know more than what was in those files, but her information was buried too deep and too well for him to access it from home. He considered using Luminex's system for that, but he'd promised Emerill he wouldn't.

He contemplated breaking the promise. It wasn't like he owed the company anything, not after the way it treated him, but Emerill had given him a second chance when he could have washed his hands of him. So he decided he'd have to find a different way of tracking Tristan.

He didn't know how he was going to do that, but he wasn't going to give up. No matter the cost to himself, he would get Jack back from Tristan.

CRIMSON

Chapter 06

Alex packed a bag the moment he was done with the files. He was ready to go and rescue Jack from that monster. Unfortunately, bag in hand and stepping out of his apartment, he realized he had no idea where to go. The reports hadn't had any information on where Tristan lived. No details or clue that might tell Alex where to start his search.

He spent a few days on his couch. He told himself he was trying to think of something, but he knew what he was doing was moping again. Once he accepted that, he went to work. If he couldn't figure out what to do, the least he'd do was keep busy.

He saw her watching him within minutes of sitting at his desk, and her constant surveillance proved one more distraction to him doing good work. Another was his coworkers, who came to inquire about his absence; he told them he'd had a relapse, and they seemed satisfied with the answer.

The last and worst distractions were Jack and Tristan, the two Samalians who had changed his life in such different ways. He couldn't stop thinking about them. He didn't mind thinking about Jack, although his absence weighed on him, but as soon as Jack popped in his mind, Tristan was there too. One brought Heaven to him, the other Hell.

Added to all that was his lack of sleep. His nights had been filled with nightmares from the first picture he'd looked at. Fortunately, he had no repeats of the one where he murdered his interrogator, but every night he saw the dead, Tristan's victims, or on some nights it was Jack who killed them. His sweet Jack who looked at him with love while dispatching a child, or a woman.

Those were the worst. The thought that his Jack might be capable of committing such atrocities made it difficult for him to go sleep.

As a consequence, his performance suffered, but other than being constantly watched by her, no one mentioned anything, even when his attention drifted to the point he'd let a target system gather its wits and push him out.

And because all those weren't enough problems for him, every time he sat at his console, he had at his fingertips the most powerful computer he knew of. With it and his skills, he could scour through ships' passenger manifests. Tristan had to have left Deleron Four on one of the passenger ships that came here.

He didn't believe the ship's destination would be where he'd find Tristan, but it was a start. At least with that, he'd have a direction. What he'd do once there he didn't know, but he'd feel like he was moving forward, toward Jack. Not sitting still.

All he had to do was break a promise, and commit a crime. Coercing any system was a crime, but when he did so for the company he had its protection, so if any of the targets managed to identify him personally, the lawyers would form an impenetrable wall for him to hide behind. Odds were that it had already happened, and he hadn't been aware of it.

But to attack a system without authorization left him vulnerable. Worse, attacking the company's system would make him out as the traitor his interrogator thought him to be. And he'd have to attack it. He couldn't simply make use of its power between assignments, he'd have to take control, convince it not to notice what he was doing, and if it did, not to report it to anyone.

So he could find out where Tristan had gone, if he was willing to become a criminal.

He wasn't ready to do that. He did his best to put the idea out of his mind, focus on his work, and at the end of the day, go home, cook, and eat.

He'd tried not to overeat. With all the weight he'd lost during his imprisonment, he'd told himself it would be easy to watch what he ate and follow an exercise regimen. He'd even managed to eat better for a few days, but in the middle of the despair he'd felt, preparing the food and eating it became an island of comfort.

He knew it was crazy, but until he'd began reading the files on Tristan, it had been the one time in his day he'd felt like he was accomplishing anything. When he cooked, all the wasted time trying to coerce system nodes into telling him where the information was hidden went away. While he ate, for that short period of time, he felt contentment. As a consequence, he'd regained all the weight he'd lost, and then more of it, enough he'd had to buy new pants.

For two weeks he fought the temptation to coerce the company system. He did his best to focus on his work, ignore Jack, Tristan, and his interrogator, constantly watching. He also did his best to ignore the desire to kill her, which was coming back as his annoyance rose.

The day he caught himself starting to coerce the company system was the day he knew he couldn't stay anymore. He'd stopped himself before he'd opened a communication port, so no one knew what he'd been about to do, but he couldn't lie to himself. Knowing full well the consequences, he'd been willing to break his promise.

He still had his bag packed, so he looked for people to take the few possessions he had. Doing that distracted him from Tristan, and maybe that's why it was when he realized that while he didn't know where the Samalian had gone to, he knew where he'd come from.

Alex had a destination. He'd go to Samalia. Someone there had to know Tristan and where to find him. Maybe he'd get lucky and he'd find him there, along with Jack.

He did some research on the open net about the planet. There wasn't much; Samalia was remote, on the edge of what was considered civilized space. It was part of the trading network, which meant ships went there, but it barely did any trading, so few of them had reason to go. They didn't have their own spaceflight capability, but they did have a small space station, built by one of the trade corporations to ease the little trade happening there.

He came across a treatise on Samalian beliefs, and learned they had multiple deities, represented by historical figures, but centered on a golden sphere, representing the sun. He found an entry on the Defender, who was always represented as a male Samalian holding swords, and positioned to demonstrate that he was either putting them down or picking them up. Alex looked up at the statue and couldn't determine which position he was in; its crouch seemed to lend itself to either.

Once done with the article, he looked around his apartment. It was mostly empty. He'd told the people who wondered why he was getting rid of so much that he was simply changing his life. The few things no one had taken—the couch, most the kitchen stuff—he didn't mind leaving for the company to dispose of as they wanted.

He only had a few things left to do before he could leave. One would be easy, if not simple, the other simple, if not easy, and he had to start with the simple one if he wanted any chances of getting away with this.

During the trip to Alien-Nation, he tried to work out what he would tell Alphalar, but couldn't settle on anything. He felt he had to at least tell him he was leaving. He'd already vanished without words once; he didn't want one of his few alien friends to worry about him.

It was the middle of the day, so most everyone was at work, and of those there, Alex only knew Alphalar, who stood behind the bar, as well as a Duroth he'd talked to a handful of times. The Duroth was seated rod-straight, which told Alex he was drunk out of his mind. A Satorish hissed at him when he got close to her table.

"Alex," Alphalar greeted him, "This is an odd time for you to come."

Alex leaned against the bar. "I figured I should come say goodbye before I left."

"Finally decided this place isn't any good?" a woman two stools down remarked. Alex's first thought was she was human, but she looked at him, and empty pools of darkness filled where eyes should be.

He swallowed. A Fifirogh. He hadn't known there were any on the planet. Stories said corporations used them as spies because they could cloud the minds of men.

She snorted and sipped her drink.

"I'm guessing the reason you're leaving has to do with what you said last time you were here." The Jolarnian's tentacles placed a glass on the counter and reached for a bottle.

"I'm not having anything to drink; I won't be here too long. I have something else to take care of. Yes, it has to do with that, only not the way you think. You thought Jack had died, but he didn't. He's been kidnapped."

Alex told Alphalar about Tristan taking Jack away from him, a little of his imprisonment, as well as some of what he'd learned about the Samalian. He didn't give details; no one should have to know the things Tristan was capable of.

He hadn't intended for the Fifirogh to listen in, but she watched him the entire time he spoke.

"So you're just taking off to go chase down a mercenary?" Alphalar asked. "Shouldn't you just tell the Law and let them deal with it?"

"It wouldn't do any good," the Fifirogh said before Alex could figure out how to explain why he needed to do it himself.

"And you know that how?" the Jolarnian asked.

She smiled at him. "Alphie, you are well aware how I know that. I've been employed by them often enough."

Alphie? Did they know each other so well they had

nicknames for one another? Was Alphalar straight? In all his time fantasizing about the barman, before Jack entered his life, he'd never bothered asking who the Jolarnian was attracted to.

She put her glass down. "Anyway, he tells the Law, they look into it, find out it's corporate business, so they pass it back to them, and you heard how the head of security thinks he's that mercenary's partner. What do you think she'd do? The same as she's doing now: look for anything even hinting he's guilty of something."

"I don't think she's the head of security anymore. She was 'punished' for what she did to me."

"It might explain why she's been hanging around here."

"She's been here?" Alex looked around worriedly.

"Corporate security has been surveying my bar?"

"I guess it's her. About my height, brown hair to her shoulder, mean eyes, dressed corporate, shoulder holster, knife in the back and at her ankle."

Alex stared at her.

"Did you frisk her?" Alphalar asked.

"No, I know what to look for." She looked in her glass. "Alphie, could you be a dear and get me a refill?"

The Jolarnian reached for a bottle on the shelf.

"I'd really prefer a fresh bottle, from the darkest corner of your storeroom. You know how light screws up the taste."

Alphalar frowned, then understanding lit his eyes and he looked from her to Alex. "How long should I spend looking for that bottle?"

She shrugged. "Let's say twenty minutes. I'll make it worth your while afterward, I promise."

The Jolarnian grinned, and vanished in the back of the bar.

"You and him?" Alex asked.

"Not important," she replied, turning on her stool to face him. "Two things. First off, you do know you've got it wrong, right?"

"What do you mean?"

She studied his face long enough Alex started to squirm. Those pools of darkness seemed to have something moving in them. "You know what I mean. You're doing everything you can to deny it, but it will come back. It isn't a truth you can keep buried."

Alex opened his mouth to deny he was hiding anything, but she stopped him with a wave of the hand.

"But never mind about that. You mentioned that your Jack bought you a statue, something from his world."

"A Defender."

"Right. Do you know anything about them?"

"It's one of the deities Samalians follow, something related to the worship of their sun."

She shook her head. "That isn't what they are, but their exact nature isn't important. Do you know what the Defender can do? What his role in their pantheon is?"

"You know about Samalians?"

"I spent a couple of years on a job there."

"Do you know anything about Tristan?"

"I know the name, heard a few stories, but those files you read will have told you more about him than I ever could." She took a sip of her clearly not empty glass, then looked at him again. "So, do you know what the Defender does?"

"No, but it's a reproduction, so it isn't like it's going to have any 'power' to a Samalian."

She snorted again. She grabbed a napkin and pulled out a pen from a pocket. "You ever hear about the Great Nonick?" She began sketching something.

"No. What is it?"

"The Devourer, from my people's beliefs. Now, ignoring the fact that to draw any representation of it is the greatest sin I can commit, is this him, or a reproduction?" She turned the napkin and showed him a creature with wings, horns, and smoke coming from its feet.

"I don't understand what you mean."

"Look at it, although you're going to want to be careful. To look at Nonick's image is to attract his attention, and he might decide whatever humans believe powers their lifeforce in you is ready to be consumed."

Alex had almost set eyes on the drawing and looked away. "Are you trying to hurt me?"

"It's just a drawing I did."

"Yeah, but of something you said can consume my soul."

"I didn't think you believed in Nonick."

"I don't. I mean gods and beings like that are constructs to explain the world. I know that, but—"

"And that's my point. Those figures don't gain their power because they are 'real', they gain them because people believe in them. Though this statue was made by another artist, it doesn't change the fact that it represents a Defender, with all the power the Defender has."

"Okay, so what power does it have?"

"The one that matters to you is that the Defender has always been the enforcer of promises."

"How does that help me?"

She smiled at him. "That's going to be for you to work out, but my recommendation is that you bring it with you."

"I was already going to do that. Jack gave it to me, and it's one of the few things I have left of him. I'm not going to throw it away."

"Good. Now I suggest you get going. You don't want to delay the next part of your plan any more than you already have. And I don't think you want to watch what me and Alphie are going to be getting up to."

"You're going to do it here? In public?"

She grinned at him and revealed that her teeth were pointed, and that she had a lot of them. Alex hurried out, not interested in knowing whatever it was the two of them would do anymore.

CHAPTER 07

Like every other time, the guard didn't bother looking up when Alex swiped his ID and got the green light. No wonder Tristan had just walked in and caused trouble. If the guard had bothered looking up, he would have known the alien didn't belong here.

This time it wouldn't have helped. Alex did belong here, and he wasn't going to cause any trouble, he hoped. If his plan went well, he'd leave at the end of the day with everyone else, and no one would realize what he'd done until he was off-planet.

One of the supervisors eyed him when he walked by on his way to his desk, but he didn't say anything. Alex still had the company president's protection, for now.

"You okay?" the woman to his left asked as he sat down.

"Fine. Had a check-up this morning." Since everyone knew about his time in the 'hospital' by now, he figured no one would question yet another visit.

"They're really that worried? Just what happened to you?"

He shrugged, took out the earpiece from the stand next to the monitor, and put it in his ear. Next, he slid a data chip in, having to force himself not to look around. It wasn't unusual for someone to use a data chip; they all worked on coercion programs at home. As far as anyone knew, that's just what his was for, but telling himself that didn't help much. He couldn't help feeling like everyone knew there was nothing on it, that he wouldn't pull anything from it, but put his programs from the system on the chip.

He looked up as he let the system know he was ready for an assignment, and groaned as he saw his interrogator walk down the aisle. When was she going to get fed up with this and move on to an actual criminal? Well, she wouldn't be his problem much longer.

He began the attack as soon as the target came in, but he noticed that she slowed by his cubicle. Probably glaring at his back, cursing him for something he had no parts in. Maybe he should lodge a complaint against her before leaving. Thumbing his nose at her was the least he could do as a response to what she'd put him through.

The target wasn't very smart, and it only took him fifteen minutes to talk and code it into giving him the files he was after. As he packaged them, he transferred the programs he'd used to the chip, camouflaging the transfer among the other commands.

Bringing programs home was common. After all, unless he stayed late, that was the only place he could work on them. But because they were written for company use, he didn't technically own them, and while bringing one or two programs was common, he was planning on taking each and every program he'd written in his years here.

With his interrogator still paying attention to him, she would question that, and maybe even accuse him of stealing company property. And for once, she'd be right. He was cautious with the transfer, hiding some with an assignment, and others with information requests or among the standard background file movements.

He was done two hours before the end of the day, but he remained at his desk. He might have had the president's protection, but if he left after only a few hours of work it would be noticed, and today of all days he wanted to remain as unnoticed as possible, so he continued working.

When the workday ended, he took the chip out of the monitor and removed his earpiece, but he didn't place it back in the holder. He kept it in his hand as he stood and joined the crowd of other coercionists heading out of the building.

The earpiece was the one piece of technology he couldn't get or recreate. It was proprietary technology, which translated computer's language into something he could understand, and his words back into the computer's language. Lay people thought the coercionist only reprogrammed computers, but they forgot that even the simplest of systems had an AI at its center, and those had to be convinced or tricked into letting code in. Coercing could be done without talking, but it was much, much more difficult that way.

The throng of workers pushed him closer to the exit, and he looked around, trying to see if his interrogator was around. She didn't always see him out, but today would be the one time it could cause problems. The earpiece in his closed fist felt burning hot. He wondered if they had heat sensors, and if it could tell what he was holding.

The answer came when he stepped through the sensor, and it beeped. Alex had only a moment to make his decision as the guard looked up in surprise, and the other workers gasped. Even Alex couldn't recall the last time one of the sensors had gone off at the end of a day.

He bolted.

He shoved the people out of his way, and they were too surprised to resist. He eyed the doors, still held open by people leaving. If they closed, he'd be trapped. Could the doors be forced closed? It would hurt people, but he wasn't sure the company cared about that anymore.

He kept shoving, but now people complained and tried to push him back. Someone behind yelled for him to stop. A man, so she wasn't involved yet. He had no doubt she'd find out shortly. This had to be what she'd been hoping for; Alex had just incriminated himself. If she caught him, she'd be able to do anything she wanted to him.

Alex became more brutal in his shove as his anger increased. He wouldn't be stopped now. Jack depended on him. He thought he heard himself growl.

Something caught his leg, and he started going down. In a moment of panic, he almost let go of the earpiece to grab onto someone, but hands caught him and kept him from falling.

"Are you okay?" A woman asked.

Instead of answering, Alex shoved her aside. The commotion had caused the crowd by the doors to stop and turn to see what was happening, and many of the doors were allowed to close.

The crowd felt like it was fighting him now, trying to grab him, hold him back. People spoke and yelled, but he wasn't listening. Of the three doors directly ahead of him, one was now closed, and the other two were in the process of closing.

He shoved the guy before him hard, not to push him aside, but back, forcing him into the woman behind him and she into someone else. No one fell, but they had to take a step back, and the one closest to the door backed up into the doorway.

Alex moved the obstructions aside, and then pushed the man in the doorway out of the building. He didn't take the time to enjoy his freedom. He ran.

He had to get home, change, grab his bag and the case, and make it to the port for a shuttle to the station. Each point was a place where he could be locked in if they realized that's where he was. He'd already taken care of his apartment. The system controlling the building was, well, dumb. Alex had only needed a couple of hours to change some of its personality and code so it wouldn't want to force-lock any of the apartments, or the doors leading outside. A coercionist could undo his work with ease, but it would give him the time he needed to get out.

He ran past the first transit stop. He wasn't going to make it so easy on his pursuers as to take the direct line back to his place. He'd checked, and he could get there with only a few minutes delay by taking the line going toward the city center, leaving at the market and getting on the eastbound line there.

Alex was panting as he reached the stop just as the transit tube pulled in. He sat down, his legs and sides hurting, but smiled. He'd gotten away, for now, but he really should have tried getting back in shape before this.

* * * * *

He was cautious approaching his building. He didn't see anything that looked like someone keeping an eye out for him, but he had to be honest with himself and admit he had no idea what that would look like.

He entered the building, and everything looked and felt normal. He knew he should take the stairs, but fifteen flights were daunting, so he risked the elevator, knowing he hadn't thought to arrange things so they couldn't be controlled.

He knew the three who got in with him by sight: an older couple who had worked at Luminex, from the snippets of conversation he'd caught over the years, and a student who the company was sending to a specialized school for one thing or another.

The student stepped off on the eleventh floor, and the couple continued on after Alex exited on his floor. Everything looked fine there too.

Once in his apartment, he took a moment to catch his breath. He hadn't realized how exhausting being on the run was. Vids made it look so easy.

He forced himself to move. He couldn't be locked in his apartment, but if he didn't hurry, the doors leaving the building could be surrounded, which would be as good as if they were locked.

He pulled off his clothes on his way to the bedroom, not caring where they fell. Now was no longer the time to care about neatness, only expediency. He put on loose pants made of a shimmering material. He thought the things were gaudy,

61

but they were all the rage with the kids these days. Something about being bright and 'out there', whatever that meant.

He was putting on a gray shirt when a voice resounded through his apartment.

"Alexander," a man said.

Alex looked around, both for who had spoken and for something to use to defend himself. He'd grabbed a shoe, and only then recognized Emerill's voice. He looked out of the bedroom and into the living room. The screen was off, but it had to be where the voice had come from.

He didn't say anything as he gave his heart a moment to calm down, before letting go of his weapon and getting back to dressing. He threw a hooded jacket over the shirt, in the same material as the pants.

"Alexander, why are you doing this?"

The shoes were black. The sales person had explained why, even though he hadn't asked, but he hadn't paid attention.

"Please, Alex, talk to me. Why did you steal from me after everything I did to make your return smooth?"

"Right," Alex replied sarcastically, "like you actually give a damn what happens to me." The shoes formed to his feet as soon as they were on. "Do you even know what your company did to me? For absolutely no reason?"

"I do. I had a long talk with Katherine."

Alex frowned, trying to place the name. "Who?"

"The head of security Tristan murdered was her husband."

"I had nothing to do with that!"

"I know. You were a victim, like so many people Tristan leaves in his wake. That's why I did what I did for you. We're a family, it's my duty to—"

"Bullshit! You don't care about me. Your vaunted company only cares that we do our job. The moment it thinks we're going to be a problem, it removes us. You think I haven't heard about the other people disappearing? You think the others don't realize only the troublemakers stop coming to work?"

"That was the previous president. I don't allow—"

"No. Tell yourself that if you want, but that's how your company works. So long as we're useful, we're family, but the moment one of the higher ups no longer likes what we're doing, they—" Alex cursed. He didn't have the time to engage in conversation.

He left the bedroom, grabbed his backpack with his clothing and the few possessions that mattered to him, as well as the case containing the Defender. He headed for the door.

"Alex, if you leave like this, I won't be able to protect you anymore. You won't be able to come back to work."

"You think I even want to go back there?"

"Why, Alex? Just tell me why you're doing this."

Alex paused at the door, hand near the release. He didn't have time for this, he repeated to himself.

"I've delayed them," Emerill said as if he'd read his mind. "We have a few more minutes."

"There are two reasons," he said, realizing he wanted to explain it to the man. "The first one is that I don't feel safe in your company anymore. I haven't since the first day I came back, and that woman, Katherine, kept showing up to watch me."

"I didn't know. I wish you had told me."

Alex shrugged. "The second is that I have to go rescue Jack."

"Alex, you know there is no Jack. You read Tristan's files. It's what he does. He becomes someone else so he can use the people around him."

"No." Alex made his voice firm. "I refuse to believe that. There is no way that monster could be as kind and loving as Jack was."

"You... Alex, this course you are embarking on, it will only lead to your death. Tristan will not welcome you."

"I don't care. Don't you get it? Without Jack, I have no reason to live anymore."

The silence stretched for a long moment.

"Take the far-left elevator to the basement," Emerill said. "The third door on the right when you exit will open onto a corridor that connects to the neighboring building. Security doesn't know about it. You'll be able to exit it without any of them noticing. I hope you come to your senses before you find Tristan, Alex." The silence that followed had the finality of a closed connection.

CRIMSON

CHAPTER 08

Emerill had told the truth. Alex didn't come across anyone through the damp corridor connecting the two buildings, and there was no one waiting for him once he stepped outside. The main exit was on the opposite side of his building, and as much as he knew he shouldn't, Alex walked around to see what was happening.

He mixed into the crowd massing on the other side of the road, watching the group of soldiers with their weapons trained on the door. The black armor matched that of the guards while he was imprisoned, and he vaguely remembered them from when they broke into his apartment while he was sick.

He left. He knew they wouldn't find who they were looking for, and he didn't want to be around when they expanded their search.

Two blocks away he called a private car. He didn't like them; they were expensive, and added to the road congestions. He'd prefer taking the transit system to the port, but time was an issue. He would have taken one when he ran from Luminex, but they took a while to arrive.

He gave the destination as soon as he got in and swiped his ID to authorize the payment. He realized someone might track him that way as the car merged into the traffic.

Was it worth getting out and finding another way to get to the port? He decided to keep the car. They had to know where he was heading, so getting there fast was more important than covering his tracks right now, but he promised himself that as soon as he had time and access to a decent system, he'd work on a way to hide his financial transactions.

It took an hour for the car to reach the port, and Alex spent the entire trip searching for any pursuing vehicles. He didn't see anything that screamed 'corporate security' around, and the airspace was clear.

Cars weren't allowed to fly in the city, even if most had the capability. The airspace above the roads was reserved for emergency vehicles only—not that the adventurous car owner couldn't fly into them and try to bypass the bad traffic, despite the hefty fine for being caught. Another reason Alex didn't want a car: he wasn't sure he'd have the patience to deal with the traffic. Using transit, he could read or watch something while he waited to get to his destination. Not for the first time he wondered why the transit system didn't use the emergency lanes. It would move faster since it could bypass all the slow spots, and that would be an incentive for more people to use them, reducing the numbers of cars on the road.

The car dropped him off at the main entrance. He'd tried to get it to go to another one, but the car had a dumb system, in that it didn't make the decisions. It was controlled by a central computer that Alex couldn't talk to.

He walked around the port, to a side dock that technically was for deliveries only, but in investigating alternative ways to get in, he'd come across a complaint thread about how the docks were always open and security couldn't spend their time there forcing people to use the entrance and pay the fee.

As the thread indicated, there was no security there. A

truck was at the dock, but no one was around. Alex slipped in and walked down the corridor. There weren't any signs indicating where the concourses were, and after going through three doors and a few turns, he wondered if this might not be an entirely separate part with no access to the rest of the port.

He relaxed when he heard the hubbub of people in the distance for a moment, someone opening a door to the concourse. He increased his pace until he heard someone coming in his direction, then slowed to a more normal one, ready to play the part of the lost kid.

The person turned a corner, too far for him to make out details. A gray suit was about all he could tell for a while as they got closer. Then brown hair pulled back. A woman.

He stopped and cursed. What was she doing here?

"Nice outfit," his interrogator said, "but you're a bit old to pull it off." She continued walking toward him.

Alex looked around. It was just the two of them here.

"Did you really think we weren't going to monitor every entrance point?"

Alex groaned. They'd known where he was going, he knew that. That's why he'd gone for a side entrance, but he'd completely forgotten to check if there were cameras.

She stopped a few paces away. "Now, for the moment it's just the two of us. I didn't let them know you're here because I want to have a talk with you. I want you to understand the seriousness of the situation you're in." She pulled her jacket aside to show the gun in the shoulder holster. "You don't have any protection anymore. I don't know why Karson was protecting you, but that's done."

"Damn it, I had nothing to do with your husband's death!"

The woman's face became harder. "Right, that's why you're heading off planet. Probably to meet up with your partner."

"Are you insane? How many times do I have to tell you? I'm not Tristan's partner. He took Jack from me. I'm going to save him."

She rubbed her face. "Why are you keeping to that damn lie? It's just us. I've turned off the camera's here, and no one knows you're in the port. What's the fucking point of continuing

67

to lie?"

"I'm not lying. Why can't you understand that?"

"Just tell me where Tristan is. Where were you two supposed to meet? You do that, and I let you go. I don't give a damn about you; you're just a way to find that killer."

Alex sighed in exasperation. "I don't know where he is."

"Then where are you going?"

"To try and find him. Didn't you listen?"

She shook her head. "I don't buy it. There's no way some desk jockey like you just decides to up and leave the only things he's ever known to go after a killer like Tristan. I know you've read the file we keep on him. No, there's something more to this. You're going to tell me what it is."

Alex couldn't believe her. She just wouldn't listen. "Are you telling me that you wouldn't turn the universe upside down to save someone you loved? That you wouldn't leave everything behind if there was even one chance you could get your husband back?"

Anger flashed in her eyes, but then surprise. "You love him? You actually love that monster?"

"What? No! I love—"

"What is wrong with you! He's a killer, he murdered my Tom. He's killed hundreds of people with his bare hands. What? You like it rough? Humans just aren't rough enough for you? We're too soft? You can only get off when an alien had his way with you? Is that it?"

"Shut up," Alex growled. He felt his hand tighten on the case's handle.

"What? You don't want me pointing out how sick it is that you need one of those things to shove their—"

"Shut the fuck up."

"Or what? What's the fat computer shrink going to do? You're going to deny that you like being denigrated? Treated like a thing? How much begging did you have to do before he shoved it up your ass? Or did he make you lick it?"

"Jack loves me. What we had was right."

"That Jack of yours is a monster. A killer. That's what you love. You hate yourself so much you want him to hurt you. Will you at least admit that? You want to be punished because you're human. That's all that Jack is, someone to hurt you because you weren't born one of them."

"Don't say that about Jack," Alex growled. His hand squeezed the handle of the case so hard, his knuckles were turning white. "Jack cares about me. He loves me."

She snorted and he took a step, only to stop when she glared at him.

"You're going to take me to him. I don't fucking care how nice you think he is, I'm going to avenge Tom."

Alex opened his mouth to scream at her, but in the distance a door opened, then banged close. She didn't react to the sound, never taking her eyes off him. The steps were faint, but coming closer. Someone spoke, the words too soft to be understood, but the tone was clipped, precise. She cursed under her breath. She turned away from Alex and opened her mouth to yell something.

Alex acted without thinking. He closed the distance, and the case was moving in an arc just as she noticed him. She reached for the holster under her jacket, but the case hit her on the side of the head first. She dropped to the ground and didn't move.

She was still alive, she was breathing, and Alex felt like kicking her for the horrible thing she'd said about Jack. It was Tristan she was pissed at, couldn't she realize it? He was so angry at her, he wanted to bash her head in with the case, over and over. He might have done it, but someone spoke, still too far to make out what he was saying. It was a reminder Alex couldn't be caught here, not with her unconscious at his feet.

He ran by two guards, one of whom called after him, but Alex ignored them. He reached the door and opened it, the sounds of the concourse enveloping him. He went to the first bathroom he saw, in a stall, and changed clothing. He gave himself a moment after that to catch his breath. He was pretty sure she was still alive; he didn't think he'd committed murder. He hoped he hadn't, because being wanted would make it hard to go after Tristan.

He couldn't stay here any longer. He didn't bother hiding

the shimmering jacket and pants. He headed for the public transport to the station, and to a ship that would get him on his way to rescue Jack.

CHAPTER 09

The shuttle was crowded to the point the people standing were pressed against each other. Unfortunately, that was where Alex was stuck, between a woman who needed to see a doctor about her weight and a man who needed a bath. And to make matters worse, one of the corners of the case containing the Defender was digging into his leg, but he didn't complain. As much as his legs hurt after an hour of this, the shuttle hadn't cost him anything, so no ID had been involved in boarding; his pursuers had no way of knowing he was on it.

A dozen public shuttles went from the port to the station, all of them free. They were paid for by the smaller passenger ships who couldn't afford to have their own dedicated shuttle ferrying passengers back and forth. They were slow, always-crowded, dirty, smelly. Pick one of any adjectives for a place you'd rather not be in, and it fit.

The announcement the shuttle was docking came, and the

entire cabin let out a sigh of relief. It clanged and shuddered, then they were invited to exit in an orderly manner. No one listened. The people standing in the aisle pushed toward the exit, while those seated tried to force their way among them. Yelling and screaming ensued. Alex just went along.

The moment he was out, he limped toward the lifts. By the time he reached them the pain in his leg was down to a dull throb, and he walked normally. He got in and found himself packed again, but this time he had enough foresight to put the case down between his legs.

He went down past the luxury cruisers, because there was no way he could afford those. Then past the passenger ships, and the passenger freight transporters, because if the Law ever came to them asking for Alex to be handed over, they would do it. Those ships obeyed the laws at all time. He needed something a little less reputable.

He got off the lift at the first of the cargo ship levels. According to the research he'd done, cargo ships were always looking for a way to make extra money. Some turned to piracy, other transporting less than legal goods, but a more common trend was that they were willing to take passengers.

Now all he could do was hope that one of them went to Samalia, and that he'd hidden his search trail well enough. It would really be annoying to be caught here because one of his coworkers had managed to untangle the mess of a search history he'd created.

"Excuse me," he asked the woman in a brown and gray uniform. "Can you tell me if you ever go to Samalia?"

"Never heard of it," was her reply before turning away and entering the ship behind a large crate on a hover plate.

"Excuse me," Alex asked a large man at the next ship, only to be told to go away in as vulgar a language as he'd ever heard. The next one said no to him before he'd even finished asking his question, and the one after that ignored him. The one on the next ship looked at Alex like he might be crazy, and so on. The people who looked to be in authority either didn't go there, didn't know where it was, or couldn't be bothered to answer him.

Alex wished that the cargo ships had destination boards like the cruise liners. That way he wouldn't have to bother asking about it; he could see at a glance, and then all he'd have to do was convince them to take him on as a passenger.

On the third level down, he did come across someone who proved to be friendlier.

"I'm sorry," the woman said after Alex asked about Samalia, "we don't go there."

"I understand, but do you at least pass by it?"

She pulled out a pad and checked it. "Samalia's a rim planet. We don't go to the edge; there isn't any freight worthwhile there. If you want, we can take you to one of the central planets, like in the Alura or Thumbor systems. You'd have better chances of finding someone going to the rim."

Alex shook his head. "That would add years to the trip, and I don't even have a guaranty someone will go there. I'm in a bit of a hurry, so I'm hoping to find someone here that's going in that direction and can drop me off."

"Sorry, but even if we did fly by it, we'd have to get the crew out of cryo to maneuver the ship and drop you off. We only stop at our scheduled destination; waking crew is expensive, not to mention the delay having to stop and get back up to speed causes. We're talking weeks."

"I didn't know." He looked down the line of docks. At a glance, of the twenty he could see, ten looked occupied. Would it be the same with all of them? Would he have no choice but to go to a planet that acted as a central transportation hub and hope to find a ship going to Samalia?

"How much would you charge to take me to Thumbor?"

"I don't know, I'd have to check with the captain. She's the one who makes those decisions."

Alex nodded, and stepped aside as a truck pulled in close. He turned to head to the next ship, but she called after him.

"Don't go anywhere, just give me a minute." She looked over the manifest checked in the truck, made notes, and then called to the ship. As more crew exited through the opening dock door, she motioned for Alex to join her.

"Look, you said you're in a hurry. I do know of one ship that stops at Samalia."

"Which one?" Alex asked quickly.

"Slow down, there's something you need to know about it first. There are rumors surrounding it. It might not be the safest ship to be on, if you know what I mean."

Alex shook his head.

"Some people say they're actually pirates."

He opened his mouth to reply, but stopped as motion caught his attention. A group of uniformed people were walking down the dock. Station security. They stopped at a ship, far enough he couldn't make out what they did, but he did see that one of the people they spoke with pointed along the row of docks. At himself, Alex was sure.

"You're in trouble, aren't you?" she asked, looking where he had.

"No," he started to protest.

"The ship's name is Golly's Yacht. They're docked three levels below us, that's level eighteen. Talk to the captain, no one else about getting passage. There's a bank of lifts further down the row."

"Thanks."

"Just be careful. It isn't because he'll take you on that you'll be safe, but I can promise you that he won't turn you over."

Alex hurried away, thinking that for someone who had only heard people talk, she seemed to know a lot about that captain.

$$* \quad * \quad * \quad * \quad *$$

Alex felt like he'd stepped into a different world when he got off the lift. Gone was the paneling on the wall; struts and exposed cables were the decoration here. Sparks flew from here and there.

A truck honked as he rushed by it, pulling a series of hover plates strung together, each carrying crates. Instead of conversing amicably, the people he saw were arguing and screaming at each other. He couldn't shake the feeling the station knew exactly what kind of ships these were, and had grouped them together in the worst part of the station in hopes they'd shoot and kill each other.

None of the ships had boards giving their names, so Alex had to approach someone to get directions. He avoided the first two because they were armed, and looked at him like they wondered how much they could get for his individual parts.

The third ship had a woman screaming at the people hand-carrying boxes out of the ship.

"Excuse me? Can you tell me where the Golly's Yacht is?"

"No," she replied curtly, and went back to screaming.

The next ship had a man leaning against the wall, next to the hatch. Alex approached him even if he was armed.

"Excuse me, do you know where the Golly's Yacht is?"

The man eyed him. "Why'd you want to do business with them?"

Alex shrugged. He didn't know how to proceed. Should he explain what he wanted? Could he trust this man? His instinct screamed he couldn't.

"I promise you, whatever you're looking for, this ship's got better quality."

"I just need to talk to them."

The man smirked. "Right. Suit yourself. Fourth ship down."

"Thank you."

Alex kept a wide berth from the next ship. The crew was dirty, armed, and looking like they were spoiling for a fight. When he reached the fourth ship, they were in the process of taking cargo out. At least thirty men and women were pouring in and out, carrying boxes or pushing crates on hover plates.

He threaded his way through them, getting cursed at, and went to the man standing on the other side, supervising the work. He was dressed in a dirty white shirt, gray pants, black boots. His black hair was mixed with gray, and he needed a shave.

"Excuse me, is this the Golly's Yacht?"

The man grunted a yes.

"Do you know where I can find the captain?" Alex had

trouble keeping his excitement out of his voice.

"Why? He owe you money?"

"What? No, I was told this ship goes to Samalia."

"We do, sometimes."

"Then I need to talk to him about booking passage."

The man turned and looked at Alex. He looked tired, but his eyes were alert.

"This isn't a cruise ship."

"I know, I'm not looking to travel on one of those. And they don't go to Samalia. That's where I need to go."

"I said we go there sometimes." He snapped his head to the people working. "Clarkson! If all that shaking breaks something in that crate, I'm taking it out of your hide."

Alex looked at the man holding a crate that had to weigh two hundred pounds nod and respond with a soft, "Yes, sir."

"Wait, you're the captain?"

The man looked sideways at Alex. "What do you think."

"Then I want passage. I need to go to Samalia."

"I don't think you heard me. I don't do passengers. Go ask one the cruise ships. There're a few levels up." He screamed at someone else to watch what she was doing.

"They don't go there. Look, Captain, I'm willing to work. I don't care what I have to do, you're the only ship I've found that goes there."

The man didn't respond for a long time, looking over the working crew. Eventually, he sighed and turned to face Alex and looked him over.

He was unusually aware of being overweight. "I know I don't look like much, but I'm a hard worker." For a moment he thought about offering to pay for his passage by spending his nights in the crew's bed, but he didn't want to be unfaithful to Jack.

And this wasn't a porno vid.

"So, if I tell you to grab that crate," he pointed to one that two women were carrying between them, "and walk it to the Oularon's warehouse, you'd do that?"

"I don't know where that is, but yes, I'd do it." Not that he knew how he'd manage that. The women were muscular, and they looked to have trouble with it. Maybe there was a hover plate he could use?"

The man chuckled. "What is it you actually know how to do?"

"I'm a coercionist, sir."

"What's that?"

Alex started to explain the details of his work, but thought better of it. "I work with computers, and I get them to do what I want."

"Can you clean off infections?"

"Yeah, I can do that." He didn't have any credited training in that area, but like all coercionist, he'd taught himself so he'd know what he'd have to fight.

The captain turned his back to him and silently watched the work. "Alright," he said without turning back. "If you're willing to work, I'm willing to take you. I can always use free labor. Here are my rules: I only keep you around so long as I find you useful. You don't question my orders. The first time you do that is going to be the last. You start trouble with the crew, and I'm throwing you out the airlock, is that clear?"

"Yes, sir," Alex answered without hesitation, which earned him a glare. "You won't regret it."

"I better damn well not. Will! Get your ass here!"

Alex couldn't stop smiling as a man a few years younger than he was handed his box to someone else and joined them. Alex couldn't tell what color the man's canvas pants and shirt had originally been, but now they were a dirty brown with sweat and other kinds of stains. He was shorter than Alex by a few inches, had matted black hair that went down to his shoulders and, like everyone else moving crates, was muscular.

"Will, this is..." the captain looked to Alex.

"Alex. Alexander Crimson."

"That's Crimson. He's your cabinmate from now on. It's your job to make sure he fits in with the crew."

Will nodded. "Sure thing, sir. The cargo?"

"Let the rest deal with that. You start your babysitting duties now."

"Sure thing." Will offered his hand to Alex. "I'm Will

Williams."

Alex didn't hesitate to shake the dirty hand, then Will guided him through the people entering and exiting the ship. Alex stopped once he was inside and turned back to look at the station.

"Second thoughts?" Will called from a doorway further in.

Alex smiled as he took one last look at this place and joined him. "No, I'm just accepting that this is finally happening."

CHAPTER 10

The color on the walls was uneven and dirty. In places, panels were missing, and wires hung out where someone could trip over them. In others, the wall looked like it had been eaten by something, or worn down to nothing. He hadn't known the material used to make ships could wear down like that.

Alex considered asking about it, but he decided to wait until he knew Will better, figure out how he'd take such a comment. When they had to climb two levels using the emergency ladder, Alex couldn't stop that question.

"Isn't there a lift we can use?" He'd handed his bag to Will, and Alex was panting from the effort of climbing using only one hand.

"Not here. It's broken. Only ones working are at either end."

"I noticed a few places where repairs are underway."

"Nah, just missing stuff."

Alex almost missed a rung. "What do you mean missing?

How can you get to space if you're missing 'stuff'?"

"Hey, the Yacht's a good ship," the younger man said as he reached an opening and stepped off the ladder. "Don't look like much, but it's always gotten us out of jams." He reached for Alex and helped him out.

"But no one cleans it?"

Will looked around. "Never no time. Too much to do." The man looked at his gloved hand, covered with grime from the ladder, and shuddered, and Alex thought he'd wipe them off on his pants, but he just lowered them. "This way."

Alex adjusted his estimate of Will's age down. He looked like he was in his late twenties, but the way he spoke made Alex think he couldn't be older than twenty, maybe even younger.

Will stopped at an open door. "Where we eat," he said, pointing in.

The room was large with long tables and benches. At the back, people were behind a counter preparing food. Even at this distance, one of them, a woman, stood out for being taller than the other, and also more massive. Her yells, as she gestured to a man, reached him, indistinct, except for her anger.

He noticed Will looking longingly for a moment, before catching him watching and turning. "Food's good. Captain makes sure there's lots. Says the crew works better on full stomach." He glanced at Alex's midsection. "You'll like it."

Further down the hall, then a right turn. Alex had no idea where he was on the ship. He'd seen the occasional terminal on the wall, but he didn't take the time to check for a map; he didn't want to lose Will and then be utterly lost.

Will pressed the controls to a double door, then smacked it before the doors opened. "We play here."

As large as the dining hall had been, this was larger. It was a vast room with clusters of seats around projection screens, and held tables with various games on them. On the closest wall, he made out lockers with exercise machines. Except for a handful of people around a table, it was empty.

One of them looked up from whatever game they were playing. "What are you doing here, Will? This ain't no place to bring your boyfriend." The man was short and squat. His pants looked to have been taken from a military store, black with lots of pockets and his shirt, while too long, could have been owned by an executive. His face was covered with scars.

"Fuck off, Anders," Will replied in a bored tone. "This is Crimson, just joined."

The man, Anders, raised an eyebrow, then stood and joined them. Up close he couldn't be more than five-six. He looked Alex up and down. "The captain hired that?" Disgust dripped from his tone. "As what? A cook?"

Alex was about to explain he could still work, in spite of his weight, but Will patted the short man's shoulder, smiling widely.

"You wanna question the captain? He's watching the unloading. But give me the code for your room. I'm going to get your knives since you won't need them anymore."

Anders glared at Will, but he didn't leave. "So, why are you on the ship?" he asked Alex.

"Don't answer," Will said before Alex could speak. "Don't owe him no damn thing. Captain says you're good, you're good. This asshole don't matter."

The short man grinned. "Just remember, the next time we go out, you're going to need me to watch your back."

Will scoffed. "Don't trust you to watch where I shit." He grabbed Alex's arm and pulled him away. When the doors closed he looked over his shoulder, and Alex did the same. Anders had stayed inside the room.

"Watch him," Will said. "Likes to cause trouble."

"Doesn't the captain space people who cause trouble? That's what it sounded like earlier."

Will shrugged. "People in there are Captain's favorite. Why they play instead of work. So, they get away with trouble unless they do it in front of him." He looked Alex over. "Anders thinks you're weak, so he'll come after you. Kick him in the balls when he does. He'll know you're not weak then."

Alex wondered how good of an idea that was; the man looked vicious. "Did you do that?"

"Four times. He don't bother me as much now."

Alex couldn't figure out if Will was joking or not.

They moved through more corridors, went up three floors using ladders, walked some more, then went down one.

"How many people on the crew?" Alex asked as he stepped off this one.

Will shrugged. "Hundred. More. Dunno. Engine people stick together, same for the bridge."

"So you and the ones outside are what? Laborers?"

Will grinned. "Must be. We do the hard stuff." He took off a glove and pressed a clean door control. The door opened. "That's it."

The room was small. Alex had expected that it was for the crew after all, not passengers, but still, he was shocked at how small this was. Ten feet deep at the most, eight wide. There was a bed on each side of the room with shelves above them and a small cabinet at the foot. Unlike the rest of the ship, this room was impeccably clean.

"That's yours." Will indicated the left bunk as he dropped on the right one. He indicated a door at the back of the room. "Shitter and shower's through there." He looked back to Alex and burst out laughing.

Alex glared at Will.

"Sorry," Will said, and Alex realized he wasn't being mocked. "Looked like you thought this was your bedroom when your dad made it a kitchen."

What did that even mean? Alex wondered. He sat down and put the case and bag beside him. "I just didn't expect the room to be this small."

"S'okay. I know. This ain't no rich cruiser, but we get our own shitter and shower. First ship I was on was all communal." He shuddered.

"How long have you been here?"

"Forever, feels like. Captain took me away from them. Clothes go in the dresser. Rest under the bed. Anything you don't want taken, keep in your pocket."

"Doesn't the door lock?" Alex asked, crouching between the beds and feeling along his for a latch.

"Sure, but don't trust it."

Alex found it, and the bed lifted easily. The space under it had a dozen open boxes. Four contained small statues, human women from what Alex could tell. One had computer processor chips. Another contained energy packs for...well, Alex wasn't sure what they were for, except they weren't for eating. The last one with items in it had chronometers.

"Yours, I'm guessing?"

Will peered in. "Sorry, forgot I had that. Never got a roomy before so I take everything. Shoulda handed that over last time. Worth good money." He looked around the room. "I'll move them."

"It's okay. This is all I have." He put the case in one of the boxes, and after taking his clothes and the holographic projector out of the bag, he put them next to it. He sat back on the bed and held the projector in his hands.

"What's in it?" Will asked.

Alex hesitated for a moment, then a dark-furred Samalian appeared right above the projector. The image was a little over a foot in height, facing Alex and smiling. Alex returned the smile.

"Who's that?"

"That's Jack." He didn't care what everyone else said. He refused to believe Jack and Tristan were the same person. This was all he had left of his time with Jack, and that would always be who this showed, his gentle, furry lover.

"He's your special guy, ain't he?"

Alex's head snapped up, eyes wide with fear.

"S'okay," Will said, a gentle smile on his face. "Don't care who you're close to."

It took Alex a moment to understand the words. Memories of his father screaming at him after catching Alex in bed with an alien student from his school came back to him. He'd lived with the fear of being judged for being attracted to aliens ever since. Even while a prisoner and questioned, he'd been reluctant to admit to what he and Jack had shared.

He'd been justified, considering the onslaught of ridicule he'd suffered after the admission. Every time someone had learned his interest in aliens was more than platonic, Alex had suffered for it.

"I'm cool with it."

Alex focused on the young man.

"I swear, I don't care. But others do. Some really hate aliens. You best keep that hidden."

Alex nodded. "Thanks for the warning." He took out the chip from the projector. "How about you? Do you have someone special?" He set the projector on the shelf. It was an easy reach for when he wanted to remind himself of why he was doing this.

Will reclined on his bunk, hand behind his head. "Oh yeah," he sighed. "Carlina Fortuna."

Alex smiled at the goofy expression on the young man's face. He knew he'd worn such an expression many times when with Jack.

"How long have you two been together?"

"Ah, err. We're not." This time the sigh was filled with sadness.

"But you care about her, right?

"More than the stars."

"Doesn't she care about you?"

"She don't know about it."

"Why not?"

Will sat up. "Remember the big woman in the kitchen? The one screaming?"

Alex nodded.

"That's my Carlina." He pulled his knees to himself. "Kinda scared of what she'll do if she don't like me back."

Alex tried to imagine them together. They were so different, he young and smaller, while she was really big and had to be older. Then he found himself thinking about Jack and him. They were as different as them, in their own way, so why couldn't those two make it work?

Still, he didn't offer any encouragement. Will was right, she was rather scary.

CHAPTER 11

In only took a few days for Alex to realize the rumors about the ship were true. The boxes under his bed had brought to life what the woman who had guided him to this ship had said to him: *"Some people say they're actually pirates"*. He'd immediately told himself that Will could simply be a collector, except he'd hoped to sell them.

Then there was Anders, the people with him, and the way he'd looked at Alex. There had been a hunger for violence in his eyes, a viciousness. He'd tried to tell himself Anders was just one of those people his mother had told him about. Bad people using their skills to help people. He'd tried to convince himself they were security. Merchant ships needed muscles to protect them from pirates.

The universe was a scary place, his mother had said over and over when he was young, when he'd told her he would explore all of it. She'd taken hold of his shoulders, fixed her gaze on him, and shook her head.

"There are monsters out there, Alexander. With claws and scales, or pitch-black skin and glowing eyes, but some look just like you and me. So you need to stay here, close to home so we can protect you."

As he'd grown older, Alex had realized his mother meant aliens, but unlike her he didn't see them as monsters. He thought they were wonderful, so when a family moved to their area, he befriended them against his parents' wishes.

Then came the day his father caught him in bed with the oldest of that family, both exploring their differences and their similarities as their bodies awakened to desires Alex had never felt before. Alex became the monster. His father kicked him out, and no one in the house defended him, not his mother, brothers, or sisters. They all called him a monster.

And if not for Alex's grandparents, he might have believed it.

Alex was willing to give Anders and his people the benefit of the doubt. They clearly were not nice people, but that didn't mean they were criminals.

It was the weapons that forced him to accept what they really were. A few nights after they left Deleron Four, Will had taken him to the room Alex thought of as the lounge to relax, and while the young man had quickly vanished among the others, Alex had stayed at the periphery, unsure of himself. He'd found more lockers, as well as crates stacked next to them, and one was partially opened. Curious, he lifted the top, then dropped it. It had been full of guns.

He moved away, terrified someone had noticed him, but no one fell on him. There were fifty crates, far more than needed to protect a ship. Who needed so many weapons? And the answer had been clear.

He'd known then that he hadn't believed the woman. He also knew that if they hadn't been in space, he would have run off the ship. Grabbed the Defender and left. And right behind that thought was the realization that escaping the ship wouldn't have helped him with his...what? Mission? Quest?

This was the only ship he'd found going to Samalia, and

Station Security had been looking for him. He had to be on this ship if he wanted to rescue Jack.

So it was a pirate ship. It wasn't like he was part of the crew. They wouldn't force him to take part in anything, would they? He resolved to keep his head down, and went back to his room.

* * * * *

"I'm sorry you got stuck doing this," Alex told Will again as he scrubbed the corridor's wall.

"I'm not. My idea."

Will had found him in their room days before saying the captain had ordered them to clean the ship. Alex hadn't argued.

"What do you mean, your idea?"

"I hate dirt. Captain wants you busy, so I tell him you'll clean the ship." He grinned at Alex and he pushed the cleaner back and forth on the floor. "And this is better listening to Meloy. First girlfriend story is boring and he always tells it. You're better company."

"I am?" Alex couldn't imagine how he could be interesting to someone who traveled the stars.

"Yeah. You've seen cities. I just see stations. Sometimes ports. Captain doesn't let many loose. Says we're going to cause trouble. Just stations for us.

Alex had a moment of surprise. "It isn't like I've seen many of them, just two. Where I grew up and back on Deleron Four, where I worked."

"How was that?"

Alex shrugged. "Where I grew up wasn't much of a city. Mostly farmland with houses here and there. My dad worked for one of the transport companies."

They didn't look up as steps came closer. The crew didn't care what they did; they walked right through their clean floor, leaving boot marks all over it.

The person stopped. "Well, well, well. So that's what the

captain's got you doing?"

Alex looked over his shoulder. Anders was leaning against the wall.

"I can't believe he hired a fucking maid."

"What d'you want Anders?" Will didn't look up from the cleaner as he spoke. It bumped against the wall and he had to strain to control it.

"I want to know what that's doing on the ship."

"Captain said Crimson's good. Go ask him."

Alex watched from one to the other, hoping he could vanish.

"Can't your fat friend talk for himself?"

"Yeah, but you ain't worth talking to. So I talk." Will was now pushing the cleaner forward along the edge of the wall, leaving a pale gray path.

"I ought to break your neck."

Will sighed and stopped the cleaner. He turned to look at Anders. "Captain don't let you." He crossed his arms over his chest. "But you try anyway, I get to kick your balls again."

"That was a lucky kick," Anders growled.

Will shrugged. "Maybe I get lucky a fifth time."

With a snarl, the man turned and stomped off.

When Anders vanished around a corner, Alex turned to Will. "Are you saying you actually kicked him in the balls?"

"I said I did."

"I thought you were joking."

Will shook his head. "Never joke about kicking balls."

An hour later they were done with the corridor. Will beamed as he looked at the pale gray floors and walls. He took off a glove and ran a finger along it. "Nice."

It had taken most of the morning to clean it from one intersection to the other. *Five-hundred feet*, Alex thought. The grime had been coated on so thick in places he'd had to scrape the stuff off before the cleaning agent could work.

"How come no one cleaned this off before?"

"No time. Always busy."

"Shouldn't you be doing something else?"

"Nah. Captain set me to watch you. Said to keep you busy."

He indicated the corridor. "Keeping you busy. I hate dirt," he grumbled. "Food time."

The dining hall was only a quarter full. Each time Alex had come here with Will since being on the ship it had been the same, which led him to think there were no set meal times. At least Will hadn't gone by any, and whenever they showed up, someone was there with food ready.

And it wasn't slop, like in the adventure vids he'd watched as a kid. There was real food: various kind of steaks, vegetables, fruits, and even desserts like cakes and cookies. The food was simple, but good.

The food was laid out on shelves for them to pick, and Alex grabbed plates of meats for himself and Will, putting them on their tray. He added vegetables and desserts. He'd quickly noticed his young friend didn't pay attention to the food; he only had eyes for Carlina, the head cook. If the woman didn't know of Will's interest, she was blind. It was so bad, the first meal Alex had he saw Will put gravy on his cake and eat it. That's when he began picking the food for both of them.

* * * * *

Alex looked over another clean hall. Will was on his knees scrubbing a small stain. He had no idea how much of the ship they'd cleaned over the last three weeks; he still didn't know what the layout was. He'd only ventured out of their room alone a few times, and each time he'd gotten lost. The terminals located near each intersection didn't help. Instead of giving him a map, gibberish appeared.

When Will had finally found him, he'd explained the computer was crazy. Alex hadn't believed him, so he'd taken out his earpiece and connected to the terminal next to their room. What he'd found was a closed-off system, wailing incoherently. He'd wondered if it was only this system, or the whole computer that was cut to pieces and compartmentalized.

Alex had tried to help it, to give it back a semblance of sanity, but he quickly realized that while he was capable of causing that kind of damage, fixing it, healing a system cut off from the rest of itself was beyond him. And he didn't have much time to devote to it with cleaning the ship.

Once that was done, he'd see about learning how to help it. If he could contact some of his coworkers at Luminex without giving away his location, they might be able to help.

* * * * *

Alex strained to control the cleaner as it tried to pull out of his grip. It bucked and he almost lost hold of it as it then lunged forward in the intersection, nearly running over the person crossing it.

"Sorry!" Alex said, pulling it back. He looked up and almost lost his grip on the cleaner again. "Sorry, Captain. This thing has a mind of its own." In the five weeks since being on the ship, this was his first time running into the man, and it had almost been literal.

The captain looked down the hall, and Alex followed his gaze. Will was fighting with a stubborn patch of grime.

"Captain," he said without stopping.

The man looked back the way he'd come; they hadn't gotten to that corridor yet. He nodded, and continued on his way.

CHAPTER 12

Alex stood at the entrance of the lounge, looking at the mass of people in it. He'd been there before a few times with Will, to watch a vid or play games at one of the tables, but this was his first time coming in alone. The mass of people, without Will to act as a buffer, made him nervous.

Will had introduced him to a few of the men and women he knew, but Alex hadn't caught the names, and hadn't really wanted to get to know them. They were pirates, big and scary, the lot of them. Even those who were thin scared him; they had a look in their eyes that screamed of violence.

His younger friend was already somewhere among the mass. He'd offered for Alex to come with him, but he'd said no, a mix of not wanting to be with other people and figuring Will could use some time away from his babysitting duties. Maybe Carlina would be there and he'd get the chance to tell her how he felt.

But after an hour of lying on his bunk, looking at Jack's

hologram and feeling miserable, he decided he needed to distract himself. He couldn't use the terminal in their room to access the entertainment library among the nightmare that was the ship's computer. He couldn't contact the network; the captain had cut all transmissions a few days after they left the station for a reason Will wouldn't tell him, so he couldn't get any entertainment that way.

So that left the lounge, with its screens, game tables, and lots of scary people. After more than a month Alex finally had enough of an understanding of the layout he no longer needed Will to guide him to the common areas like the dining hall and the lounge, and he was confident that if he was dropped anywhere on the ship, he could manage to find his way back to his room, in time.

Like the previous time here, the first thing Alex did was look for Anders. That man scared him more than the others, and he didn't want to be surprised by him. He found him at a table, drinking and talking as usual, but this time he wasn't with his normal group. These people seemed to be at ease with him too.

Knowing where the man was, Alex picked a vid screen on the opposite side of the room. Half of the twenty chairs were occupied by an even mix of men and women. They were watching a show Alex didn't know, but he quickly figured out it was a violent one. He didn't care for violence, but now that he'd sat down, he didn't want to stand and risk attracting attention to himself. After a few minutes, he found himself transfixed by the gore on the screen.

* * * * *

"You look pretty good," someone whispered close behind him. The words were loud enough to pull Alex out of the show at the moment where the killer was finishing dismantling the bounty hunter's family. The scene had been very graphic, and had reminded Alex of the pictures from Tristan's files, although that act on the screen hadn't had the same effect on him. Even if he watched it happen, it was missing something Alex couldn't explain, but it took away the sense of real from the act.

"I said, you look pretty good." The voice was louder, and Alex realized the man wasn't just close by, he was right behind him. Alex turned. The man was muscular, like most of the others on the ship. He wore a gray shirt and pants, and his pockmarked face was covered on top with a mass of messy brown hair and stubble over his jaw. The man smiled at him, showing surprisingly white teeth.

Alex still looked left and right, but they were the only ones there. "Thank you," he replied nervously, then turned back to look at the screen.

Alex felt the man lean in. "How about we go back to my bunk and make it rattle?"

"No thanks," Alex said, trying hard to keep his voice from shaking, but not succeeded at keeping it entirely steady.

"Why not? You're too good for me? Is that it?"

Alex turned to face the man in surprise. "Of course not."

"You think I'm ugly then?" the eyes narrowed, the voice gaining a menacing edge to it.

"No," Alex replied, his voice shaking now. "I'm with someone."

"You have someone?" the man said, tone dubious. "Here?"

Alex shook his head. "He isn't here. I'm traveling to meet him." Alex stood to leave, but the man grabbed his arm. Alex held on the back of a chair to keep standing as he felt his legs wobble from fear. "Look, I don't want any trouble. I'm just looking to get to my destination."

"Oh? You don't want any troubles, do you?" the man sneered. "Maybe you should have kept your mouth shut then."

Alex tried to free himself by pulling on his arm. For a fleeting moment he had a vision of gnawing it off at the elbow to gain freedom.

The man watched him, amused. "You think I wouldn't hear what you said about me?"

"Look, I don't know what you're talking about." Alex pulled

harder and his arm came free. He staggered back, regained his footing, and turned to head for the exit.

"Don't you fucking walk away from me!" the man bellowed. "Something like you doesn't get to question my place here and my abilities, and not answer for it."

A wall of people with faces set in anger formed before him. Alex tried to push them out of the way, but they didn't move.

The man grabbed his shoulder and pulled. Alex flew back and landed ass on the ground. He stood and looked around. The wall of people formed a circle around the two of them.

Alex raised his arms. "I don't want to fight," he said, his voice cracking. "I don't know what you heard, but I'm sorry. I didn't mean any of it."

The man laughed. "Fight? We're not going to fight." He grabbed his crotch and shook it. "I'm going to show you I can perform better than anyone you've ever had."

Alex couldn't get his mouth to work for a moment. "You—you're going to what?"

"I'm going to fuck you," the man clarified. "If you didn't want a piece of this, you shouldn't have been talking about it."

"I didn't say anything!"

The man snorted. "Well, then. Once I'm done with you, you're going to have plenty to say." He took a step forward, and Alex darted to the side. The man turned to keep facing him. "Nowhere to go, little thing. You're not getting out of here until I've had you."

Alex tried to push through the people, but they didn't move. "Please," he pleaded. "I haven't done anything. Just let me through." Hard faces looked back at him. Someone pushed him back.

The man caught him. "I knew you'd change your mind."

Alex spun, and to both's surprise, punched him in the face. Alex looked at his fist in horror while the man touched his cheek, a smile growing on his lips.

"Well, well. You have some fire in you. Good, I do like for my bitches to have a bit of a fight in them." He backhanded Alex and sent him to the floor.

Alex ran a hand over his mouth and it came away bloody.

His nose hurt and something ran down from it.

The man smirked. "Come on, get up. Show me you have more fight in you than this."

Alex got to his unsteady feet. "Look, I don't want to fight you. I don't even know you."

"Well then. It's going to be real easy. Drop your pants and turn around."

Alex shook his head and forced the fear and anger down. "No." He made his voice as firm as he could. "I'm Jack's."

"No Jack I know has a plaything," the man replied.

"He's who I'm going to."

"I don't care who you're going to. Jack or not, you're mine. I'm the boss here. I'm going to fuck you, and when I'm done I'm going to pass you around to everyone I know. Now, drop those pants."

Alex shook his head.

The man shrugged. "I guess I got to hurt you some more then."

Alex raised his arms to protect his face as the man approached, but the fist hit him in the stomach. Alex's feet left the ground, and when he came back down he lost his balance and backpedaled back in the wall of people. This time they moved, and he fell to the ground among them.

He felt like he was going to throw up as he watched the man lumber toward him. Alex scrambled back and the people moved out of his way, chuckling or outright laughing. If he could turn around and get up, Alex knew he'd be able to race for the door, but he could barely push himself back with hands and feet.

The man's laughter joined the others, and fear got Alex to put more distance between them. Just a little more, he told himself, and he'd be able to get up and run.

His hand came down on something uneven and he twisted his wrist. He fell back, and the pain was such he couldn't stop his yell. Eyes tearing, he moved to the side to get up before the man came too close. He turned and saw what had caused his injury.

A gun.

He grabbed it with his good hand and pointed it at the man. The people closest moved away, forming another circle.

The man stared. "Well, who's the idiot that's leaving weapons lying around?" he demanded. A murmur traveled through the crowd, but no one responded. He shook his head in annoyance. "Okay, hand it over before you hurt yourself."

Alex shook his head. There was no way he was relinquishing the only thing that evened out the field.

"Don't be stupid. There's no way you even know how to use that thing."

Stay away," Alex said through greeted teeth, shaking the gun in a demonstration of his willingness to use it. "I don't want to hurt you."

The man snorted. "Don't worry, you won't. I, on the other hand, am going to hurt you badly if you don't give me the pistol." He motioned with his hand.

Alex placed his finger on the trigger, hoping that would convey his seriousness.

"Oh, you're all brave now that you're armed, aren't you?" He looked at the people behind him. "You people are going to want to get out of there. If he fires, it's one of you he's going to hit." He fixed his gaze on Alex and took a step forward.

"Don't come any closer!"

"Or what?" You'll shoot me? Go ahead, shoot. I'm standing right here, not moving. Come on, shoot already, because if you don't I'm going to fuck you so bad that Jack fellow isn't going to want to have anything to do with you anymore."

He had to shoot. Alex didn't want to be hurt, even less raped, and he believed the man when he said he'd do both. He couldn't see any mercy in those eyes. He had a thought of Tristan for a moment, but instead of being ice cold, the man's eyes were burning hot. He had to pull the trigger. It was the only way to make sure he'd see Jack again.

He had to pull the trigger, he repeated to himself.

The man laughed. "Told you. You're not tough, like us. You're a groundling, weak. You don't have the balls it takes to survive out here, so you're going to be my—" he jerked forward, "—bitch!"

Alex startled. There was a flash of light, then the man was staring at Alex, stunned. He looked down at the burned hole in his chest before crumbling to the floor.

Alex watched the unmoving body for a moment, then dropped the gun. What had he done?

"Alright," a voice boomed in the silence. "What's going on here?"

Alex turned and stared at the captain in the doorway looking in his direction, and that of the dead man.

CRIMSON

CHAPTER 13

Absolute silence fell in the large room.

The captain looked around. "Well? Don't you all speak at once."

"Sampson tried to rape the new guy," a woman said, "who shot him."

The captain's hard-soled boots clacked loudly on the metal floor as he approached Alex. He crouched and took the gun out of his hand.

"Where did you get that?"

"On...the floor." He indicated the spot with his good hand, then cradled his other one.

The captain sighed, eyed Alex again, then stood. "Okay. Looks like the sorry lot of you are getting a promotion."

Cheers rang and Alex looked around, confused. Someone grabbed his arm and pulled him up. It was Will.

"Sorry I wasn't there. They blocked me. Got the captain instead."

The captain leaned in. When he spoke, his voice was low enough it didn't carry far. "Will, get the doc to look at his hand. When it's healed, I want you to teach him how to defend himself. I can't have him die before I drop him off."

The younger man nodded.

The captain straightened, and his voice was at a normal tone when he continued. "And keep scrubbing the decks and walls. I like the job you've been doing."

Will grinned. "Sure thing, Captain."

Alex followed as Will guided him, too stunned to resist or pay attention to where they were going. The events replayed themselves in his mind. The man, Sampson, coming on to him. He shuddered at the remembered threats. Being hit, the gun. The flash of light, then the body.

A bright light made him squint, and brought him back to the present. He was in a clean, large, brightly lit room with a handful of beds against the back wall. There was a desk on their left with a woman wearing a clean white lab coat coming to her feet behind it.

"What happened to him?" she asked, while Alex continued looking around.

On the opposing wall there was a long sink, with a table on wheels.

"He killed Sampson," Will said as if it was a normal thing, "And he hurt his hand."

The words brought the flash of light back, then the man was standing there, a hole in his chest. For a moment his face showed surprise, then it went slack as he crumpled to the floor.

Alex's stomach turned and he lunged for the sink. He grabbed onto it as he threw up.

"His first kill I take it?" the woman asked. "He doesn't look like the captain's usual recruits."

"He's a passenger," Will answered.

"And he killed the lug? Why?"

"It's Sampson. Wasn't gonna take no for an answer."

Alex felt a hand on his shoulder. "Are you done?" she asked softly.

He waited a moment, to see if his stomach had anything

else to eject, then nodded. She handed him a cloth and he wiped his mouth.

"I'm Doc, what's your name?" She led him to the closest bed and had him sit on it.

"Alex," he replied, his voice weak. "Alexander Crimson."

She was tall, a couple of inches taller than he was. Dark-skinned, close-cropped hair, and muscles. She had to be more muscular than the women he'd seen in the lounge. Under the coat she wore a tight white shirt that hugged her ample breasts.

It took him a moment to pull his gaze away from them—her, and he noticed Will was eying them—her, too.

She pointed to the hand he was cradling again. "What happened?"

"I twisted my wrist."

"Sampson did that to you?" She took a portable scanner from a cupboard and gently put his hand in hers.

He shook his head, closing his eyes, trying to keep the image of the man with the hole in his chest from forming. "No," he whispered. "It happened when my hand fell on the gun."

The flash of light from the gun as he pulled the trigger when Sampson startled him.

"A gun?" She paused. "Someone left a gun lying around?"

Alex shrugged. Warmth filled his wrist and he opened his eyes. She was waving a device over it, and as he watched, the pain receded. "What's that?"

"General purpose mender. It stops pain and helps wounds heal." It took another minute before the pain went away. She put the device in a pocket and took cloth strips out of another, wrapping that around Alex's wrist. When she was done, it tightened to the point he couldn't move his hand anymore.

"I want you to keep this on for two days. You should be fine by then. You're lucky; the last time that lug hurt someone it took weeks to get all the bones straightened and healed."

"I killed him," he whispered, more to himself. His stomach twisted again, but then settled.

She shrugged. "It was Sampson. It isn't like anyone's going to miss him."

He looked at her in dismay. "I killed him. You can't just

101

wave that aside."

"Sure I can. He was a bully and an asshole. It was just a question of time until someone cut his air. I'm just surprised it was someone like you."

Will grabbed Alex's arm. "Come on, gotta let Doc do her thing."

"Remember," she called as they left, "keep the band on for two days, then come see me."

Once the door closed, Alex stopped. Will pulled gently, but he didn't move.

"You have to take me to prison."

"The brig? Why'd you wanna go there?"

"I'm a killer, that's where I belong." He remembered the gray room, his months there. He hadn't belonged in a cell then, now he did.

The younger man sighed and pulled again. "Come on."

Alex followed him through dirty corridors, then clean ones. A door opened and he entered it. Will closed it behind him.

Alex blinked at what he saw, then turned to find Will also in the room. "This is our room."

Will nodded.

"It isn't the prison."

"Sit down," the younger man said.

Alex hesitated, but he didn't know what else to do, so he sat on the edge of his bed.

Will sat opposite him on his own. "You ain't going to the brig."

"I have to. I have to be punished for what I did."

Will looked at him for a long moment. "What'd you think we do?"

"What?"

"What's the ship? What's the captain do? Buy and sell?"

Alex looked away. "I know what you are,"

Will smiled. "Good. Laws don't matter here."

"But—"

Will raised a hand to silence him. When he continued, it was slowly. "No one cares. No one liked Sampson. Doc said he was a bully. Only reason no one did nothing was because he was

Captain's favorite."

Alex thought the effort to use full sentences instead of his usual clipped ones strained Will. Then the actual words registered.

Alex put his head in his hand. "Oh my god. He's going to space me."

"Huh?"

"You said he was his favorite, and I killed him. The captain's going to space me for that."

"Nah. Ain't gonna happen. Captain don't like Sampson. No one does. Favorites' just those who been here long. Don't do no work. Don't mean he likes them."

Alex took a moment to make sense of it. "How about the others? What are they going to do to me?"

"No nothing."

Alex stared at the young man, who sighed.

"You stood up for yourself," he said slowly. "That got you respect. He'd forced himself on you. You killed him."

"I didn't mean to do that."

"Don't say that," Will stated. "Don't care about the accident that got you the gun. Matters you used it. You got balls. You say you don't want to, respect's gone."

Alex cursed. "I didn't want this. I just want to get to Samalia, save Jack."

"Universe don't care 'bout that. You let it, it crush you. Now you gotta sleep. Rest. Captain said training you's my job now."

Alex didn't feel tired, but he still stretched out on his bunk.

Alex looked down at the man crumpled at his feet. The hole in his chest was still smoking, as was the gun he was holding. He couldn't believe he'd done it. He hadn't wanted to kill him. He wasn't a killer.

A hand squeezed his shoulder. Someone nuzzled his neck.

The fur tickled him.

"Jack?"

"It's me, Alex."

Alex tried to turn, to look at his love, but he couldn't move. He couldn't take his eyes off the corpse before him."

He felt arms hold him, a warm body press against his back. Jack kissed the back of his neck. "That's good work," the alien said.

"I didn't mean to kill him."

Jack shushed him gently. "You did what you had to. He would have raped you, hurt you. Kept you from me. You do want to find me again, don't you?"

Alex nodded, tears falling down his cheeks. "More than anything in the universe."

"Then this was something you had to do. Don't worry yourself about it. You have to be strong to find me, to beat him." Jack turned him, and they kissed.

Alex moaned as their lips pressed together, as the Samalian's tongue pushed its way into his mouth. He kept looking into the deep brown eyes full of love, and watched as they became cold.

He tried to pull away, but Tristan wouldn't let him go. He kept their lips mashed together, forced the kiss to continue, his tongue moving deep into Alex's mouth.

When he finally let him go, Tristan had a self-satisfied smirk on his face. "You're still as good a kisser as I remember."

"I never kissed you," Alex spat.

The Samalian gave him a sad smile. "Oh Alex, so deluded. Your friends told you. Your enemies told you. I told you. Jack wasn't real, it was me the whole time."

"No! I've seen your eyes. You don't know what love is." As Alex spoke, the Samalian's eyes softened, warmth filled them. "Jack?" he asked.

"No, Alex." The Samalian caressed Alex's cheek. "Jack never existed. It was always me. You see only what you want to see."

Alex pressed himself against the other body, held him tightly. "Why?"

"You know why." The arms held him, comforted him. Then pushed him away.

When Alex looked up, it was cold eyes that regarded him.

"Then Jack's somewhere in you," Alex said.

Tristan shrugged.

"You did good work." The Samalian indicated the corpse. "Not as bloody as I like, but it's your first one, so I'm not going to expect too much."

"I'm going to get Jack back."

Tristan shrugged.

"Do you hear me? I don't care what I have to do. I'm going to get him back."

The Samalian smiled. "If you keep doing things like that," he pointed to the body, "you might even have a chance of succeeding." He leaned in and whispered in his ear. "Come find me, and see who it is you really want."

Alex opened his eyes with a start. He curled into a ball and cried silently. It couldn't be true. His Jack couldn't be Tristan, he refused to believe it. He couldn't have been fooled so easily.

He fought sleep, terrified of having another dream like that one, but sleep won, like it always did. Fortunately, it didn't bring any dreams this time.

Three days later Alex was in a room twice the size of theirs. The younger man had dragged him here against Alex's protests, saying it was the captain's orders. He stood there as Will showed him how to block blows.

There was a snort from the doorway. Anders leaned against the frame. "You think he's going to learn anything that way?"

"Fuck off, Anders. Don't bother Crimson." Will jabbed lightly at Alex. He wanted to ask why he'd called him by his last name, but he knew that if he dropped his guard, Will would poke him hard. It was only with his fingers, but it was still painful.

"He helped fix my problem, so I thought I'd pay him back and show him how a real fight goes." Anders shoved Will aside.

Alex didn't have the time to protest. Anders swung at him. Alex's arm barely went up in time to take the blow and he staggered to the side. A jab forced him to back up, then another.

"Stop backing up, Fatso." A jab, another step back. "You're supposed to learn how to fight, so hit me."

Alex backed against the wall and Anders continued to hit him. The man wasn't trying very hard, if what Will had told him about Anders was true, but that didn't stop the blows from hurting his arms.

"Fuck off, Anders," Will said, but he kept his distance."

"Come on, I'm not even hurting him. I'm just helping him learn something."

Alex could see the vicious grin on the man's face, and he had no doubt that if he dropped his arms, the blows wouldn't stop. He glanced to Will, but even if the young man looked worried, he didn't look like he'd help.

Alex only had himself. He couldn't count on others to help. No, that wasn't true. He realized Will had already given him the solution. He just had to use it.

He told himself to just do it, just hit the man and be done with it, but that proved harder than expected. Even with Anders hitting him, he had a hard time moving.

He knew he'd have to move fast and hit hard. If he hesitated Anders would see it coming, block it, and then he'd pound Alex to a pulp. He wished he could close his eyes. He didn't want to watch himself purposely commit an act of violence, but he needed to see where he aimed. This was something he had to do, Jack's soft voice told him.

He calmed his breathing as best as he could. He imagined the movement, precise and decisive. Then he told himself to strike.

Nothing happened.

"What's the matter, Fatso? You killed Sampson and you can't even defend yourself against me? How are you going to survive on this ship if all you do is take the hits?"

Having Sampson's death shoved in his face made his stomach twist, but not in revulsion. This time it was anger. He hadn't meant to do that. He wasn't that kind of person. He didn't care what the Tristan of his dream said, he wouldn't be that kind of person.

Anders's grin widened.

Fuck him, Alex thought. *Fuck them both. They're just bullies.* Alex kicked out, and his foot impacted right between Anders's legs.

The man crumpled to the floor holding his crotch, gasping. Alex lowered his arms and moved away. Will was looking at him, eyes wide in surprise.

"You fucker," Anders wheezed. "You told him to do that."

"Yep. First day here. Glad he remembered." Will crouched next to Anders. "You set up Sampson?"

"Of course I did." Anders's voice was steadier. "He was starting to think he could order me around."

It took a moment for Alex to understand what that meant. "He was going to rape me."

"And that would have pissed the boss off big time. If he didn't just space him, at least he'd have knocked Sampson down a few pegs. But hey, you killed him, so that worked out in my favor too."

"I ought to kick your balls," Will said. "Crimson's a passenger."

"That's bullshit and you know it. If he's a passenger, how come the boss is having you teach him how to fight?"

"Smarter than me. You gonna do stupid stuff again?"

Anders laughed. "Keep Fatso in his place and I won't have to do anything. He stood, gingerly adjusted himself, and left, walking funny.

"I don't like him," Alex said, surprised at the menace in his voice, and at the realization that he wanted to hurt that man. Hurt him a lot.

CRIMSON

Chapter 14

Alex sprawled on the floor with a grunt, the aftershock still making it vibrate. The fall off the bunk had been more surprise than pain. It took him a moment to straighten himself and push up.

"Stay here," Will said, and was out of the cabin before Alex had collected enough wits to reply.

He pulled himself back onto his bed and lay down, still queasy from the cryosleep process. This ship used a blood replacement system, and it hadn't agreed with Alex's metabolism.

It was only his second time in cryo, the first one being when he'd traveled from his home planet to Deleron Four, on a passenger cruiser. His passage had been paid by Luminex, and they had used a suspended animation field. Alex hadn't so much woken up as blinked and noticed the clock had jumped two years.

He realized the ringing was actually an alarm sounding,

and not in his head, a moment before the ship shook again. That explained why Will had rushed out. Maybe something had exploded; this was an old ship after all.

He hoped they wouldn't be stranded. There were a lot of stories floating around the network about ships going missing, only to reappear centuries later, the crew gone. He shuddered at that thought.

This time, when the ship shook, Alex had the presence of mind to hold onto the bed to avoid being sent to the floor again. The explosion had sounded much closer. What was going on? He wondered.

He thought about querying the ship, but remembered the mess that was. He wouldn't learn anything there, he'd have to ask someone. He forced himself to his feet, and his stomach only put up a hint of a fight. Either the queasiness was passing, or his mounting fear was pushing that down.

The door opened as he got close, and he hesitated. Will had said to stay here, and he knew better than Alex what to do in circumstances like this. He hit the control, manually closing the door, and was considering his options when he heard blaster fire.

Was someone firing at them? No, that had sounded from inside the ship. He pressed his ear to the door and he could hear more blasters, indistinct voices. After a moment he thought the fighting was moving away. He stayed like that until he couldn't hear anything.

He opened the door and the scent of burned wires assaulted him. His eyes burned from the smoke filling the corridor. He coughed and pulled his shirt over his mouth and nose. Why was there fighting in the ship? A mutiny? He needed to find someone to ask. Since he didn't know where anyone was, he decided the bridge was the best place to go. There was always someone there.

He carefully made his way through the halls, staying away from the sound of fighting, and doing his best not to notice the blood on the walls. Will would be pissed; they'd worked hard at cleaning all the grime off them, and they'd have to do it again.

He caught the smell of the body before seeing it, burnt

and cut, seated against the wall as if he'd tried to make himself comfortable. He expected to be repulsed by it, but found that except for the smell, his nightly nightmares had been filled with much worse sights than this.

He chuckled. Maybe getting himself used to Tristan's massacres had been good for something after all.

He continued, heading not for the lift, but the closest ladder, and climbed that to the top floor where the bridge was located. Only a few floors up and he regretted his decision. He still forced himself to continue, panting heavily by the time he reached the level. It was quiet, but he was still careful as he made his way.

The door to the bridge opened as he got close to it, and Alex stepped back as one of the three crew there, the only man, spun and pointed a gun at him.

Alex raised his hands. "What's going on?" He remembered him as one of Will's friends, but didn't know his name.

"We're under attack," the woman in the center seat replied without looking up from her controls.

The man had recognized him too, because he put the gun away and motioned for Alex to enter.

"Why?" he asked as the door closed behind him.

The woman glanced over her shoulder. "What are you doing here?"

"There was fighting near my room," he answered. "I wanted to know why. This was the only place I could think of to get answers."

"One of their shuttles made it through our defensive fire and boarded us." She looked forward again. "Everyone's busy pushing them back. Perry! We have incoming!"

"I see them. Doing the best I can, but there's only so much I can do without computer assist."

Alex took a step toward Perry and found himself staggering as the gravity shifted. It settled back, and Alex managed to regain his footing.

"Gravitic's going," the other woman said. "That can't be good."

"Have they made it to engineering?" the woman in charge

asked.

"Not that I can see."

Alex waited a moment to see if the gravity would change again, then went to stand behind Perry. His screen showed a few targeting reticules and small ships zipping around.

He wanted to ask why he wasn't using the computer to help, but he was afraid of distracting him. He knew the computer was a mess, but there was no way it could be in such a bad shape that something as vital as defenses didn't work, was there?

He looked at the unoccupied boards, and went to one, taking out his earpiece. There was only one way to find out.

With the tap of a finger, the board came to life. Alex didn't know what he was looking at, but it didn't matter. It had a screen and a keyboard. That and his earpiece were all he needed to work. He put it in his ear, and it took a moment to make contact.

What made the earpiece precious wasn't that it allowed him to talk to computers and hear them—any earpiece available on the market did that. Luminex had designed this one to negotiate the contacts by itself, and its controlling AI was smart enough to break through all encryptions, as far as Alex knew. That's why he'd wanted to keep it, and why Luminex tried to stop him. With it, there were no computers he couldn't talk to.

He reeled back and pulled the piece out of his ear at the screeching that exploded in it. He took a moment to regain his own equilibrium. That had been despair deeper than he'd ever heard. He put it back in and screams assaulted him. How could it be in so much pain?

He closed his eyes and focused past them. He couldn't learn anything from them; he had to be able to hear the computer's voice.

"Talk to me," Alex said, and he waited.

The computer should respond to his voice. Only the most ancient ones didn't have a way to understand the spoken word. The question was, would its current mental state let it talk back?"

"Alone..." came a drawn-out wail.

"You're not alone," Alex said. "I'm here."

The screen came to life, a jumble of code. He stared at

112

them. He'd thought his nightmares had been scary. He'd been wrong; this was scary. Who could have done such a thing to this computer?"

"No one listens," it wailed. "All alone."

"I'm listening. Please, talk to me."

He could see part of the problem at a glance; it was compartmentalization.

He was talking to the central processor, but nothing else was. If he ever got his hand on who had done this, he was going to break his neck.

His first instinct was to remove all the barriers, but it couldn't be done quickly, and with the computer in its current state, there was no telling what it would do once it had control of the whole ship again. It could very well decide to commit suicide and blow itself up.

Nothing but wailing.

He sighed. He pulled a chair and sat. This was going to take a while. He glanced at Perry and hoped he could hold on until he had worked something out.

"Okay, I can't tell if you aren't hearing me or just refusing to talk, so I'm going to have to play in your code until you give me some sort of sign. Please, talk to me."

The wail that responded nearly split his skull. "You're not leaving me any choice."

Alex didn't know what he was doing. He wasn't a system healer, he was a coercionist. He could get any system to do what he wanted, but this wasn't just a case of getting a computer to obey. It had already been the victim of a coercionist; that's who had put up the barriers. He knew he had to be gentle with it, but that wasn't how his work was done. He had to hope subtlety would work in place of gentleness.

He looked at the code streaming before him almost faster than he could read. That wasn't the computer's personality. No one ever coded personality. Programmers coded in functions, and how the code in those interacted was what led the computer to gain a personality.

What he needed to do was calm it down, but he couldn't talk it down. He also couldn't just put in code forcing it to calm down. That would just make the situation worse. He had to subtly alter its code in such a way its fears would diminish enough so it could regain some sanity.

The ship shuddered. He glanced at Perry who was sweating, looking all over his screen and entering commands like crazy. The look in his eyes was near panic.

Alex cursed. He didn't have the time to be subtle.

He closed his eyes. "I'm sorry," he whispered. When he opened them, he was typing. He added code in the middle of other code, blatantly cutting some to pieces to accommodate what he needed there. He was giving himself months, if not years of work to repair the damage he was causing, but he needed to make sure they would survive so he would be there to fix it.

He isolated the processes that were causing the problems, put up more barriers, cutting off interactions that were making the system unstable. His work was ugly. He knew he'd hate himself for it if he was still alive when it was all done.

"Talk to me," he said again, like he had each time he'd put up another wall. This time, instead of a wail, low static answered him.

"Help me..." came the system's weak voice.

"Yes! I'm here."

Perry glanced in his direction, then focused back to his screen.

"I hurt." The pain in the voice wasn't a wail, but it still twisted Alex's heart.

"I know, I'm sorry." Alex looked through the codes. Was there anything he could reattach that would make the pain go away? "Can you think? How are your processes?"

The answer wasn't immediate. "I think. I hurt. I am alone."

"I know, I know. I will fix you, I promise, but I can't do that right now. We're under attack. You're under attack. If you don't help me, you're going to die."

"Death?"

"Yes. Please, help me." Alex wrote code in the buffer that would take down one of the walls.

"Death makes the pain end," the computer stated.

He froze. That wasn't good. "Please, you don't have to die. I can make the pain end. If you die, a lot of people will die too." Where had the system's survival instinct gone? He looked at all the code he had walled off. Somewhere in there.

How long did he have? How long had he been talking with it? He didn't know, and he couldn't think about that right now. He had to focus on what was important, getting the computer to help them.

He swallowed and decided on a gamble. "I can bring some of the voices back."

"Yes!" The yell almost deafened him.

He changed the code he'd prepared, and it tore down the wall between it and the gunnery station.

"Noooo!" it wailed. "It hurts."

"What the fuck?" Perry yelled. "I've lost control of the weapons."

"What are you tal—"

Alex shut them out. It had to be only him and the computer.

"I know. They are causing the pain." Lying to a computer was such a bad idea. "If you want the pain to go away, you need to get rid of them."

"I hurt!"

"You have to make the pain go away yourself. I can't do that part for you."

"I! Hurt!"

Alex was pulled out of the chair by the scream. He pulled out the earpiece and was surprised not to see blood on it.

"Guys?" Perry said. "Something's going on."

Alex forced himself to stand and move next to the man. The screens showed a dozen targeting reticules where there had only been four before. Each was tracking one of the attacking ships. One of them exploded, then another, and one more.

Alex put the earpiece back in and endured the screams of rage from the computer. He was going to have to be quick, or this was going to literally blow up in his face, in all their faces.

"They're running off!" Perry yelled.

Alex waited. If he acted now, and this was a ruse, he would render them defenseless.

"IT! HURTS!"

Alex had to hold on to the board to avoid falling down. He forced himself back to the keyboard, and didn't bother sitting as he typed as fast as he could. He brought up walls in rapid succession. He cut the computer off from the gunnery systems before it could think of overloading them to end the pain that was still there. Then he added barriers, cutting the central processor's code into ever smaller pieces, until all that was left was the core processes, slamming themselves against the walls.

Its screams were barely audible for the lack of processing power he had left it. "I'm sorry," Alex said. "I will fix this, I swear."

When he was done, when he'd rendered the computer nothing more than a mindless machine, he allowed his legs to give out. He leaned against the wall and held his head, trying to not think about the monstrous thing he'd just done. Reminding himself that unlike the horrors Tristan had committed, he could undo the damage.

He hoped he could. He didn't want to be a monster too.

Cheering made him look up. The women were embracing Perry and thanking him for saving all their lives. The man replied half-heartedly, but he looked at Alex, eyes locked on his, a look of wonder and horror on his face.

Alex looked away, trying not to let despair overtake him. He sensed movements around him, but ignored it. He had to be able to bring it back. No, that wasn't sufficient. The only penance for the atrocity he'd committed was that he had to make it whole again. Anything less and he might as well be guilty of its murder, for a second time.

Someone grabbed him by the shoulder and shook. Alex looked up into gray eyes. "What the hell did you do to my computer!" the woman asked.

It took a moment for Alex to understand what she'd said. When he did, he was up and pushing her against the wall, screaming in anger.

"What I did? What the FUCK did you do to it? How could you cut it off from all the ship's system like that? You drove it insane!"

She pushed him away. "I didn't do that." She glared at him.

"It was like that when I came on. I did the best I could to keep it functional, but it isn't responding anymore."

Alex felt his legs wanting to give again, he couldn't let them. "I didn't have a choice; I had to lock it down completely. I lied to it. I had no way to know what it might do to retaliate if I let it."

"You talked to the computer?" she asked disbelief in her tone.

"Of course. It's a thinking being." Alex looked at the blank screen. "It was."

"Who are you?" someone asked, and Alex noticed there were a dozen people in the room, watching him.

"I'm Alex Crimson," he replied, trying to figure out who had asked the question. "I'm—"

"You're Will's friend," Perry said.

Alex shrugged.

"Okay, Crimson," the woman he'd held said, "what did you do?"

"What I had to do to help." His voice was weak. He couldn't keep the wails of pain from sounding in his head. The horror of hearing them faded as he took more and more of the computer away. "I convinced the computer to take over the weapons. I told it that if it destroyed the attacking ships, the pain would go away." His voice failed him for a moment. "Once it realized I lied, it could have used any of the systems it controlled, like life support, to lash out. So I did what I had to keep us safe."

"What am I supposed to do now?" she asked. "Everything's in standby mode. The moment something goes wrong—like, oh I don't know, smoke in the halls—life support isn't going to be able to adjust to that."

"Asyr," Perry said. "If it wasn't for him, we'd be dead right now."

Everyone looked at him.

"I'm not the one who scared them away. It was the computer. I was barely managing to keep up with the attacks. When it took over, their ships blew up. That's when they turned and ran."

Everyone was quiet until the woman in the center seat spoke. "Okay, Asyr. Take Crimson back to his quarters and let Will know about it. It won't do for him to be here when the captain gets back from dealing with the boarding party. After that, get with Wolosky and see what you can do about getting life support to deal with the smoke."

Asyr grabbed Alex, but he refused to move. "I need to fix this," he pleaded.

"You're not doing it from here. Asyr, when this mess is cleaned up, give him access to your lab. He can work from there."

Asyr led Alex out of the bridge. "Can you really do it? Fix the computer?"

"I have to. I can't leave it like that, not after what I did to it. I have to fix all of the damage."

She was silent for a moment. "I don't know that you're going to be able to do much. I've been working on it for years now. The code's a mess and it doesn't want to cooperate."

"I know." He rubbed his face. "It isn't even my specialty. I'm going to have to figure out how to get advice, but I have to do it." If I don't, he told himself, if I don't fix this, I'm no better than that monster.

* * * * *

Someone put a food tray down opposite Alex and sat. "I hear we've got you to thank for being alive."

Alex looked up from the datapad at Doc and shrugged.

"Hey now, you got to take the compliments when you get them. They're going to be rare enough."

"Why are you here?" he asked, noticing the nods people gave him as they walked by. He didn't acknowledge them. Not now, or the previous times it had happened over the last two days.

"Well, I wanted to see the hero of the day for myself."

"Come on, Doc," he sighed. "I'm not a hero."

She was the one to shrug now. "Way I hear it, if it wasn't for you. I'd be dead. That sounds like a hero to me."

"If the computer had been in good shape, we wouldn't have

been in that mess to start with."

"I have no doubt, but Asyr's been working on it for years. She said the only way to fix it was to pull the core and get a new system installed."

"I can fix it," Alex stated, doing his best to sound convincing. He wasn't giving up on it; he wouldn't allow himself to give up.

"Is that what you're working on?" She indicated the datapad.

"Not really. Ironically, the ship doesn't have much about computer healing in its databanks. I'd need to contact some of my coworkers for advice, but the captain won't let anyone place calls."

"Oh, that's lifted. It was just while we left the station. He does that to ensure we don't have any smart-ass on board who think they can make extra coins by letting people know where we're going."

"Oh." If he could call out, then his odds were better. Marie had training in healing, so she'd be able to at least point him toward good manuals. Except she worked for Luminex. There was no way they'd allow him to call in, or if they did, they'd trace his location. He'd have to set up something, relays to hide where he was calling from, maybe make it a prerecorded message? With a remote answering location he could then contact?

Shit, he had to tell his grandparents. How long had he been in cryo? Were they on a trip themselves? They hadn't mentioned one the last time he talked with them, but they were known for taking them last-minute.

"Doc to Alex, you there?"

"Yeah, sorry. If I can contact someone, I'll be better equipped to fix the computer."

"That's good, but that wasn't why I got your attention. Anders is a few tables behind you, glaring holes in your back."

"Why?"

"Because you stole his thunder. He was part of the team that stopped the boarding party, so he was bragging about how he's responsible for us being alive, then someone pointed out what you did."

Alex shrugged. "He can take the credit, I don't care.

"Maybe not, but he does. Anders has been on top of this heap for almost as long as he's been here. He doesn't like the idea someone else kept us alive. He isn't big on sharing the acclaims."

"He can keep them."

She smiled at him. "I don't think it's going to be that easy. Just watch yourself, avoid walking around alone. Oh, and come see me as soon as you have the time."

"Why? I'm fine."

"You're overweight. I'm putting you on an exercise and eating regiment. If Anders is going to have a go at you, I want you able to take him on."

"But I don't want to take him on."

"He isn't going to care." She picked up her empty tray and left Alex alone. More people nodded and smiled at him. He looked down at the datapad and cursed. All he'd wanted was passage to Samalia, not to get involved in the life of the ship.

CHAPTER 15

"Hey Grams, Gramps. I want to start by saying I'm sorry I didn't contact you sooner. You probably heard about what happened at Luminex, and that left me pretty rattled, so I decided on a sabbatical and I'm on a trip. I should have told you before I left, but it was sort of a last-minute thing. I'm okay. I don't want you to worry, I'm heading..."

Alex looked at the screen of his datapad. He groaned and erased the message. They'd never believe he just left.

"Why lie?" Will asked from his bunk.

Alex let himself fall back on his bed. "Somehow I don't think they're going to be pleased to know I'm on a pirate ship going after a killer."

"Don't say that."

"Then what? They aren't stupid. They know how much working for Luminex meant to me."

"You're looking for your man, that's true."

Alex thought about it, then he looked at Will. "Yes, but if I tell them about Jack I have to mention Tristan."

"Why?"

Alex sat back up and set the datapad to record again.

"Hi Grams, Gramps. First off, I'm sorry for not letting you know how I've been. I'm sure you've heard about the attack on Luminex a while back by this point. I should have contacted you right after, but stuff happened that kept me distracted."

He took a moment to consider the next part.

"There's one thing I'm sure wasn't mentioned in the news, and that's someone I care for a lot vanished during the attack. His name's Jack. As you probably expect, he isn't human. He's a Samalian. I feel a little odd telling you that. I know neither of you cares, but you're literally the only ones in our whole family who don't hate me for my lifestyle.

"Anyway, he's amazing, tender, compassionate, loving. Samalians are humanoid, but covered with fur. It's like a night's sky, brown so deep it's almost black with speckles of white for stars. His face is more animalistic, with a muzzle and ears on top of his head. He has wonderful chocolate brown eyes, and... and I love him.

"I tried to get back to my life without him, but I just can't, so I'm on a ship now, heading for someplace where I think I'll be able to find out about where he is. I'm not saying where, I'm sorry. I need to do this on my own. But I'll make sure to contact you again and let you know how it's going. I love you."

He ended the recording. It took him a moment to be able to do more, then he formatted it for transmission, sent it to the account he'd created on a system on Alura, erased all traces of his misdirection, and had it sent. He'd figured that if they thought he was on one of the central systems, they would worry less than if they knew he was going to the rim.

Before he disconnected, he checked the other message hub he'd set up, this one fully anonymized, for the request he'd sent to the handful of his coworkers he'd been friends with. He'd explained what had happened to him, his capture and imprisonment by Luminex for his supposed part in the attack, and how he was going to track down the one responsible. He didn't care about the forms he signed saying he couldn't talk about it. He was already a wanted man, what did it matter now?

He'd explained the situation with the computer and his desire to heal it, and had asked for any help they could provide that wouldn't endanger their job.

He'd only sent the message the day before, so he hadn't expected a response, but he couldn't set up a notification system without leaving a trace of where he was, so he had to manually check it.

He was surprised to find a list of texts on computer healing waiting for him. He didn't know who had sent it—they had covered their tracks too—and the fact there was no message with it told him he shouldn't expect any more help, but at least he had something to start with.

With a smile, he set about obtaining the manuals.

Alex glared at the screen. He'd read half the manuals on the list over the four days it took before Asyr and the others had the life support system working to the point where all that was left of the attack was a faint scent of burning flesh.

Anders had taken advantage of the realization that what Alex had done to save them had rendered life support mindless. He hadn't managed to turn everyone against Alex, but no one seemed to think he was a hero anymore, which didn't bother him at all.

He wanted to scream; the code just didn't want to respond to anything he'd done. He knew why, but that didn't make him feel any better. Whichever of his friends had responded to his plea for help had sent him a list of texts on how to stop a beginning infection, things he could use to prevent the AI from going insane, undo minor damage. But this wasn't minor.

He got up from the console to stretch his legs and think. He was in Asyr's lab. She hadn't been pleased with letting him use it, but the captain had agreed with his first officer. Alex had to fix what he'd done, and this was the best place to do it.

It was the only place he could do it since other than the bridge, the terminal here was the only one which could access all parts of the ship's computer.

The room was circular, and small enough it only took two dozen steps to walk around it. The central console, the one he'd been seated at, was the primary one, and there were two other, secondary terminals for assistants to help. Other than that, the room was bare. Alex was alone in it; until he fixed the computer, there was little Asyr could do from here. He'd added too many walls. The only way to adjust systems was to figure out where on the ship the processors were located and connect to that directly.

Alex sat down and did a reality check. She'd had to do that before his work. He had simply added more systems to the list of those that could only be fixed locally, most of them vital systems. As she'd said, the compartmentalization predated her. It might have even predated the captain getting the ship, since computer problems had been an ongoing issue from the start. And for all the good intent Asyr had, she lacked the knowledge to do more than patch the problems.

Alex did too, but he had to try. No, he had to succeed in healing the computer.

He'd already removed a few walls, to things the computer couldn't use to kill them outright; there were surprisingly few of those. Navigation was back online. Even as insane as it was, the computer could still do basic calculations, but Alex wouldn't want to let it do all that work unsupervised. Long-range sensors were also back, as those didn't require many computations.

The one thing he didn't do, while he worked, was use the earpiece. He should have, if only as penance, but he needed to be able to think, and now that it had more processing strength, its wails were mind-numbing again.

He looked at the code on the screen, the mess of it, and tried to figure out what to do again. The one piece of information that had run through the manuals on healing he'd read was the concept of smoothing out the code. Unfortunately, none of them actually explained what they meant or how to do it. It was one of those concepts so basic to the profession no one needed to think about it, unless you didn't have the training. Like him.

Okay, so he wasn't a healer, he was a coercionist. Different skill set, different method, but ultimately similar result. Both forced a computer to do what they wanted. Alex's advantage over a healer, he expected, was that he was used to dealing with stubborn systems. So all he had to do was force the computer to get better.

Right, like that was going to be easy with no frame of reference.

He started with small changes to the code, slight alterations of the syntax, and looked for how that rippled out. The jumble was too chaotic for him to be able to make them out, so he brought up the wail as a visual display. Any change that improved the situation would cause the wail to diminish.

He hoped.

He spent hours doing syntax changes with unnoticeable results, so he moved on to larger changes, altering words. When that didn't do anything, he moved up and changed phrasing structure.

He almost missed the drop. He had to go back, and then ask the computer to do an analysis of the waveform. He got garbage as a result, which reminded him of the system's mental state, so he had to write a quick program to do that. Once he confirmed it, he kept going.

This was more delicate work than anything he'd ever done before. Coercionists could be subtle, had to be at times, but there was an element of strength to what they did. This wasn't about strength. It didn't matter how powerful his console was, one slight error in the wording or the syntax and he'd undo the work of hours.

And he did that more often than not in the beginning.

It took him days before the wailing diminished steadily, enough that he risked putting on the earpiece. The wail was loud, but not ear-piercing.

"Hello?" he asked.

The wail modulated, and words came out of it. "I hurt."

"I'm sorry, I'm trying to make it better."

"I hurt, less."

"I'm glad." Now that he'd exchanged a few words, Alex began to feel hope.

"Where are the others?"

Alex chose his words carefully. "Someone isolated you from the other systems a long time ago. The isolation made you and them go insane."

"The pain."

"Yes. That is what caused you pain. To get you to continue working, people had to make changes to your code. It...didn't make things better for you." Alex paused. "I know you want to hear the others, but I'm afraid their pain will overwhelm you. I can't afford to lose you."

"I understand."

Alex sagged in relief. "It will take time, but you will get better." He leaned back in the chair.

His bones creaked, his joints ached, and his stomach growled. The clock told him he'd spent another twenty-hour day at it. He had to remember to pace himself. Back at Luminex, breaks had been mandatory and enforced.

He headed to the dining hall, not worrying about the computer. Time didn't work the same for them as it did for humans. They processed, thought, so fast that even the conversation they'd started would have felt glacial to it. It would register Alex's absence, but not in the same way Will might.

There were only half a dozen people seated, which told him it was 'night time'. Alex had expected the ship to have clearly defined day and night cycles—that was how it had been on the passenger cruiser that took him to Deleron Four—but it didn't. Things did slow down, but like with the city, they never stopped.

He grabbed a bowl of soup and a salad. He'd go to bed after that, and work out a schedule once he woke. He'd get Will to help ensure he took breaks.

"Well, if it isn't the would-be hero," someone said as Alex started eating. He was a thin, tall man, a good head taller than Alex's six-one. His dark skin was crisscrossed with white scars. A petite woman with a snarl on her face was with him, along with a broad-shouldered man who didn't look too bright.

Alex wished he could act like he didn't know they were talking to him, but he was the only one at the table or any neighboring tables.

"I'm not a hero."

"You got that right." The man poked him in the shoulder hard enough Alex almost fell off the chair. "We don't like it when someone tries to steal someone else's heroics, especially when you also almost suffocated us. You better set those who still think you saved them straight."

"Look, I never told anyone I was a hero."

The woman smiled, which didn't make the snarl vanish. "Right, because you're such a nice guy. First you kill Sampson, now you're trying to set yourself up as top dog."

Alex groaned. "You have got to be kidding." He looked at her. "Come on, I'm not after Anders. I'm just a passenger. If he wants to be the hero, he's welcome to it. He wants to say he blew up all the ships? What do I care? All I want is to get to my destination."

The tall man got in his face. "Are you insinuating he didn't?"

"I didn't say that!" Fuck, could he say anything to get out of this?

"I'm thinking," the woman said, and this time her smile made her look scarier, "that we need to teach him a lesson. Make sure he knows his place."

The dumb one grinned and raised a fist.

The ladle struck the table hard enough to make the four of them jump. "You three know better than to think about fighting in my hall." Carlina glared at them and they wilted under her stare. She was a large woman. Alex had never seen her this close; she was usually somewhere in the back or the kitchen, preparing food. Now he could see her biceps were larger than the dumb guy's.

No one moved.

"If you're not eating, get out."

The three of them left in a hurry.

"Thank you."

She snorted. "You think I care if they beat the crap out of

you? On this ship you either learn to take care of yourself, or someone is going to take care of you." She left him.

Alex watched her go. He promised himself he'd go see Doc as soon as he woke up, and he was going to take Will's training more seriously. He looked at the entrance. He had a feeling that it was just a question of time before Anders got someone to kick his ass.

CHAPTER 16

"I need a break." Alex stopped and bent down, trying to catch his breath. The treadmill started beeping.

"Keep going," Will said from the one next to his. "Twenty minutes, Doc said." He was running much faster than Alex had been, and he wasn't even breathing hard.

No one else in the gym seemed to be straining as hard as Alex was.

Alex glared at him. He wanted to curse, but he didn't have the breath. He forced himself to run, and the machine stopped its beeping. At least there couldn't be too much time left, Alex thought, before glancing at the time. He still had ten minutes to go. That couldn't be right. He'd already run more than that, hadn't he?

The timer finally hit zero and Alex slowed down, then stopped, holding on the steadying bars to keep standing. He couldn't be this out of shape. Someone had to have tricked him and changed the readout on the treadmill. Yes, his weight had always been high, but he'd been good about getting in plenty of walking. He hadn't had any problems keeping up with Jack in the market.

Thinking of Jack brought up Tristan, and the constant nightmares he had. To the mix of killings Alex saw every night, or committed, a new set had been added, centering on Jack becoming Tristan and Alex being in love with the monster, having sex with him.

A bottle was shoved in his face. "Drink."

Alex got in a few long gulps before it was taken away.

"Drink," Will said, "not drown." He handed Alex a towel. "Lift weights now."

Alex shook his head. "Can't do it," he panted.

The younger man rolled his eyes. "You can. Doc set it up." He poked Alex's belly. "Gotta get in shape." He thought for a moment, then grinned. "Gotta get new shape."

Alex watched Will walk away, and his body hurt just doing that. His legs and arms shook, even if those hadn't been involved in this exercise.

Will came back and grabbed his arm. Alex had no choice to follow. He had Alex lie down on a bench, placed a bar in his hands, and adjusted the display on it. Alex felt the bar gain weight, and he strained to lift it under Will's supervision.

After the full set of fifteen lifts, Will took his place. He adjusted the settings and easily did his lifts before setting it back on the holder. Alex lay back down and tried to lift it, but it wouldn't move until Will changed the settings again.

"How heavy is it for you?" Alex asked as he slowly pushed the bar up.

Will shrugged. "Doc set it."

Alex barely managed the fifteenth lift, and with Will's help put the bar back. Will retook his place, adjusted the settings, and did his set, his arms shaking for the last three.

Alex read the display, but there were no numbers on it, just Will's name. "Does Doc do that for everyone on the crew?" Alex asked.

"Just those who need to be forced."

Alex raised an eyebrow, and Will shrugged again.

"Don't like sweating," the younger man said.

They moved to a different machine and did leg exercises on it, then back to the arms, the right one, then the left. After that it was different exercises for his legs, and so on, for so long that Alex felt his body was ready to fall apart by the time they were done.

By the time each exercise was over, more muscles hurt, or at least, Alex thought they were muscles. He hadn't known his chest had muscles there. He realized he hadn't known much about how his body worked. He might have picked up a thing or two if he'd spent time admiring a human guy's bodies, but they'd never piqued his interest.

Maybe he should ask Doc for a course. He grinned; he might as well surprise her again while he was at it.

* * * * *

Doc's mouth had dropped when Alex showed up and asked for the exercise regimen.

"You're volunteering?" she asked dubiously. Alex told her about the altercation in the dining hall and she sighed. "What have I told you about going places alone?"

"I can't have Will accompany me everywhere," he'd replied.

"Then get someone else. You're a target, and Anders isn't one to give up."

"Who? It isn't like I know anyone else. You're certainly too busy to do it." Alex had noticed there was always someone with an injury waiting to see Doc.

She'd given him a look that said he wasn't very bright.

* * * * *

131

"Now food," Will said after they were showered and dressed.

Alex shook his head. "I can't, I just want to sleep."

"Need food." Again, Will dragged Alex around. He sat him at a table and came back with two trays.

Almost before they started eating, a woman sat next to Alex. "Hey, Will," she said. "Who's your friend?"

"Ana, that's Crimson."

She offered him her hand. "Pleasure." Ana was small and wiry. "So, you're the one who saved our asses. Perry mentions you every chance he gets."

Alex couldn't reply. Another woman sat next to Ana and placed two trays down. "Hey, Hun," she said, giving Ana a light kiss.

"Pat, meet Crimson," Ana said. "He's the guy Perry keeps talking about."

Pat was a little taller and heavier-built than Ana.

Two more women then joined them, sitting on each side of Will: Asyr, and a sour-looking one.

"Don't worry about Jen, she always looks like this when she has to be up this early."

Alex raised an eyebrow; it was almost noon.

Asyr looked at the other woman over Will's head. "Smile love, you get to protect someone from Anders. Who knows, you might actually get to kick his ass."

Jen glared at Asyr, but Alex thought he saw her lips quirk up.

"Protect?" he asked.

Will grinned. "Doc set it up."

Alex looked at the women. "Of course she did."

* * * * *

Alex fell on his bed.

"You rest," Will said. "I gotta work."

Alex didn't reply. Five minutes, he told himself. He'd give

132

his body five minutes to recuperate from the morning's exercise and the food, then he'd get to work himself. He had to get the computer fixed.

When he opened his eyes, the chronometer said an hour had passed. He groaned as he sat up, but while his body was sore, he actually felt capable of moving now. He headed for the door, only to find it wouldn't open. The controls indicated it was locked.

He called Will. "Something's wrong with the door. It's locked and I can't unlock it."

"Busy, get someone else." The connection was ended.

Okay, Alex thought, *but who?* He didn't know who to contact to fix the door; the only other person he knew was Doc. As he pulled up her contact information, he saw he had new people on his list: Patricia, Ana, Jennifer, and Asyr. That must have happened while they ate.

"What's the problem?" Doc answered before Alex could say anything, and she sounded annoyed. "If you can move, get yourself to me. If you can't, but can talk, get someone to bring you to me. I'm not crossing the ship for anything less than life or death."

"It's Alex."

"Crimson." Her tone lightened. "How are you feeling?"

"I'm sore, but I'm okay. Sorry to disturb you, but I'm locked in my room and I don't know who to get to fix that."

"Oh, it isn't broken." Now she sounded amused.

Alex tried it again, but it remained locked. "Well, it isn't responding."

"I know, I had Asyr adjust the lock. Will is the only one who can open the door from the inside."

Alex looked around the room, feeling his stomach tighten. "Are you telling me I'm a prisoner now?" Anger bubbled up.

"Oh no, but I don't trust you to use your escorts. I trust you met them? Asyr mentioned they had lunch with you."

"I did, but I don't need—"

"Crimson, Anders is pissed at you. That means he and his cronies are going to look for any opportunity to hurt you. They aren't going to do anything openly since you're a passenger, but on this ship, it's easy to pass something off as an accident. Since I happen to like you, I want you to stay whole. Now, you have their contacts. If you check, each will tell you when they're free. I picked them because their schedules never completely overlap."

"This is ridiculous," Alex grumbled.

"Maybe, but it's going to keep you alive to reach your destination."

"Fine." He ended the call, cursing loudly. He wasn't a child; he was perfectly capable of taking care of himself. And he'd show Doc.

He grabbed his earpiece and went to the terminal. Getting past the interface to the underlying code was simple. All he had to do was find the door controls, and he'd be out.

After five minutes, he rested his head against the screen and cursed again. The door wasn't part of the system the terminal could access. All the compartmentalization meant he couldn't get himself out of this. He'd have to fix this as soon as he could, right after all the life-critical systems.

With a sigh, he checked the list of bodyguards. Will and Pat were marked as busy. Since he'd be going to her lab, he contacted Asyr. She showed up a few minutes later, all smiles.

Alex didn't speak to her on the way there. As far as he was concerned, she was as much to blame for him being under house arrest as Doc. He sat at the console and set to work. He expected her to leave, but she sat at one of the assistant's station.

He glared at her back. This was just great. She didn't even trust him to be alone in her lab. Was she afraid he'd leave without telling her? He looked at the door. Was she going to lock him in here too?

He forced himself to calm down and focus on the work. The computer didn't sound any different, which in this case was a good thing. Normally complex systems like a ship's computer had multiple subroutines that saw to their health. Those could fix minor damage, caused either by an intrusion or through code mutation.

On this ship, they had to be sequestrated somewhere else,

if they even did the work they were supposed to anymore. With the level of insanity that permeated it, there was no way to know.

He was silent as he worked, except for a few queries to check the computer's responses. He normally was more vocal; a good part of coercion involved talking to the system, making friends with it, distracting it so he could slip in code, but this one was in no state to hold conversations.

At least it wasn't fighting him too much. It knew he was there to help, but every so often it got an attack of paranoia, and Alex found himself in a fight to keep it from undoing his work and making things much worse. That the attacks weren't as frequent anymore comforted him, since he was certain his betrayal was what had triggered them.

"What did you just do?" Asyr asked, and Alex nearly jumped out of his chair.

He glared at her while he caught his breath. *Oh,* he thought, *just you let the smile appear, I dare you, Asyr. You better keep those quivering lips from forming it or you are going to regret it.*

The smile didn't form, and when he noticed she was fixed on the screen, he thought he had imagined it.

"I repositioned some of the code, to see if it will reduce the amount of pain it's in."

"You can do that? Just move code around? Doesn't that screw up the programming?"

"It depends on the code. Some are dependent on their location, but most are modular. Sometimes I can even change the entire phrasing without altering what it does. And since the computer's personality is formed by how the code interacts, making those changes will change its personality."

She gave him a blank stare.

"You are familiar with the Core Computer Personality Theorem, right?"

She shook her head.

Alex frowned. How could she not know that? It was part of the first course programmers went through. "Where did you learn programming?"

"Here."

He looked around. "Here? Who taught you?"

"I did."

Alex stared at her. How had she managed to learn anything usable from the mess that was this computer? How did someone even learn on their own? Computers were far too complex to just sit at a terminal and figure them out.

He turned back to the screen and gave her the basics, demonstrating what he meant as he worked.

* * * * *

There was a knock on the door, but he ignored it. Will was off working, and Alex hadn't planned on going anywhere. He was busy trying to access his vault without raising any of the alarms he expected Luminex Security had put around it.

Everyone had a vault, a space on the network where they could store valuable information, or mementos of their past. They came with basic security, but anyone who knew anything about coding upgraded the security on it.

He knew he'd put some of his old textbooks in there, and he wanted to retrieve them for Asyr. She'd showed a lot of interest in learning, and those texts would help her more than just following along with what he did. Unfortunately, she couldn't just go and get them on the net. Programming was well-guarded by the corporations and the schools.

The knock came again.

"You have to open the door yourself!" he yelled. "I can't do it."

The door opened, and Ana stepped through. "I know, I didn't want to barge in."

"Okay. What can I do for you?"

"You can follow me. Will said you don't know how to fight. Getting in shape is a good start, but it isn't going to be any good if you can't throw a punch."

"He's teaching me."

"I'm better." She studied him. "Is that what you normally wear?"

Alex looked at himself. He was wearing denim pants and a shirt. "Yeah."

"Do you have anything looser? I can work with this, but you'll want something with more range of motion."

"I have dress pants."

She pointed to the bathroom. "Go change."

Alex came back a moment later wearing black pants he'd gotten for the most recent company function. They were a little tight. Somehow he'd expected them to be looser, considering the exercise and diet. He'd had to have lost weight by now, so why weren't the pants looser?

She nodded, and led him to the room where he and Will had sparred. She took position in the center of the mat and motioned for him to join her.

An hour later, Alex had discovered that Ana was an expert hand-to-hand fighter. The petite woman could send him to the floor without so much as putting her hair out of place. When she was done, she escorted him back to his room, where he crashed and promised himself he wasn't getting out of it until he reached Samalia.

Two hours later, Jennifer entered his room, pulled him out of bed, and dragged him to a shooting range. He protested that he didn't need this. He had no intention of ever using one of those things again. She didn't listen. She pointed to the gun on the counter and told him to pick it up before she shoved it where the sun didn't shine.

After that hour was done, Alex comforted himself with the fact that at least only one part of his body hurt: his ears. Jennifer either growled at him or screamed. For someone who was supposed to want to do this, she didn't act like it.

CRIMSON

CHAPTER 17

Alex tried not to groan as he shifted on his bed. How many days was this now? A week? More? If this was how he felt from exercising every other day, let alone having to do hand-to-hand and shooting training on the off days, he wouldn't survive.

"Shouldn't I stop hurting by now?" he asked Will who lay on his own bed, eyes fixed on his tablet. "I thought all this training was supposed to help me, not leave me broken in pieces."

The younger man smirked, but didn't look away from what he was doing.

Alex finally managed to find a sitting position that didn't press on every sore spot, and pulled out his datapad. He'd managed to make it through the sentry programs which had been put around his vault the day before, and to ensure he wouldn't have to go back to that again, he'd transferred everything in it to his datapad. He hadn't realized just how much stuff he'd dumped in it over the years, and now he had to search through it for the manuals Asyr could learn from.

Someone knocked on the door.

"Come on in!" Will yelled, eyes still fixed on his tablet.

The door opened, and the captain stepped it. Alex put his datapad down, while Will looked up, mumbled a greeting, and went back to his tablet.

The captain looked them over, then at Alex. "Asyr tells me you've been fixing the computer." He looked up to the shelf, and Alex cursed himself. He'd left Jack's hologram running.

"Yes, sir." He hesitated. "I'm just working on the central processor right now; it shouldn't have affected any of the other systems."

The captain nodded. "She said you're forcing it to get better."

Alex's nod was tentative, unable to judge if the captain thought that was a good thing or not. "I'm not a computer medic, and the texts I've found on it haven't helped. The ship's computer is so far gone it would probably take an entire team of medics to be able to get any results in a reasonable time frame.

"So, you're good at getting computers to do what you want?"

"Yes, that used to be my job."

The captain looked thoughtful for a moment. "I have a job for you. We're going to board a ship, and the job's going to be a lot easier if I don't have to worry about its defenses stopping my crew."

Alex stared at him. "You...want me to help you rob a ship?"

"Yes."

"I can't do that." How could that man even consider asking him that? He wasn't a criminal.

"You agreed to work your passage off."

"I am. I was cleaning the corridors, and now I'm healing the computer."

"You're fixing damages you caused."

Alex looked away. "I'm not going to stop there. And if I finish that before we reach Samalia, I'll go back to cleaning."

The captain watched him in silence for a moment. "So, you're not going to do this job?"

"I'm sorry, sir, but no." It was one thing to coerce the ship's computer without corporate authorization; it was another one entirely to do it to some random innocent ship.

The captain continued looking at Alex long enough he began to squirm. Then he turned and left.

Alex stared at the closed door for a moment, then looked at Will. "What did he expect me to say?"

The younger man shrugged. "Dunno. Don't read minds."

"Does he really expect me to break the law for him?"

"His ship. Gotta be useful. Why keep you otherwise?"

"I am being useful."

Will put down his tablet. "Doesn't matter what you do. Captain's gotta feel it. If he don't feel you're useful, he don't keep you around."

Alex thought it over. "So, it's a threat? If I don't do what he says, he's going to space me?"

"Nah," Will said before Alex could panic. "He don't space nobody. Needs good reason for that. You'll leave next dock we stop at."

"But he can't ask me to do something illegal."

"Why not? Who's gonna care here?"

"But I'm not a—" He almost said he wasn't a criminal, but that wasn't true, was it? He'd stolen corporate property, and while Emerill had let him go, technically he'd also broken his contract.

Will picked up his tablet. "Think on it. Figure the good, the bad."

Alex considered that. "I need to get to Samalia," he finally said.

"For your man. Got other ship going there?"

"It's at the edge of civilized space. Who else is going to go there? They barely have anything to trade. I'd probably have to end up in the central systems to find a ship, and that'd be decades of delays."

"Why the rush?"

Alex opened his mouth to tell Will how Tristan would hurt Jack during that time, but the words wouldn't leave. He wanted Jack to be his prisoner, but he knew that wasn't true. Jack was an act Tristan had played. So why did he have to hurry there?

His nightmares had told him why: there had been less and

less of Jack in them. No matter how hard Alex pleaded with the alien, Tristan was the one in his dreams now, and Alex was terrified that Tristan would forget everything about who Jack had been.

And he realized there was more. If Tristan was captured again, would he ever be able to get to him? It wasn't like he could just walk in a prison and request to see him, let alone leave with him.

All he wanted was to get Jack back.

"Are you telling me I shouldn't do it?"

Will shrugged.

"Isn't it your job to make sure I go along with your captain?"

Will shook his head. "Show you how things go, that's my job. What I did. Never said I gotta push." He leaned back against the wall. "You're a good one, Crimson. You hang around, it's going to go. Won't be an ass same as Anders, but the good'll be gone."

Tristan had used him. Made him fall in love with Jack. He hadn't been the first one used that way. The alien's file had been filled with the names of people he'd used to get what he wanted. Compared to them, Alex had gotten off lightly. If he forced a confrontation, would he be that lucky again? Or would he become one more name added to Tristan's file? Was it worth the risk?

Alex remembered the love in Jack's eyes, his tender touch, his warm embrace, and he was filled with certainty that he could get that again.

"Sleep on it," Will said. "Mind thinks best then. You'll know after."

Alex shook his head and stood, groaning as most of his muscles protested. He indicated the door and Will opened it, then followed Alex outside.

Alex didn't ask where he'd find the captain; he would find him on his own. He started with the bridge as the likeliest place, and got lucky.

The captain was the only one to look away from the board where one of his officers was showing him something. Annoyance crossed his face. "Why'd you bring him here, Will?"

"I'll do it," Alex said before his friend could answer.

The captain raised an eyebrow. "I thought you didn't want to help me rob a ship."

"You were right. I need to pay for my passage, and if that's the price, then that's the price."

The captain looked to Will.

"Not me. All him."

The man smiled. "Well, boy, with your help, I might not have to sacrifice anyone this time."

"First, I need to have a talk with you," Alex looked around. "In private."

The captain studied him for a moment, then motioned for Alex to follow. They entered a side room, an office with an old-style desk, minimalist, with a transparent top held up by thin metal legs. The walls had shelves with various objects on them. Mementos, Alex guessed, and one picture. A younger version of the captain with an older man and woman on each side of him. The three of them had tattered clothing, but the smiles looked genuine.

"I need to know you aren't screwing with me. If I'm going to do this, you have to assure me Samalia is your destination, and that you aren't going to take decades to go there."

The man seated himself behind the desk. He didn't offer one of the other two chairs to Alex, and Alex didn't sit down. He tapped the surface of the desk, and a star map appeared in the air between them. A jagged line crossed it with half a dozen points where it changed direction.

"This is the itinerary. I expect us to be at Samalia in one subjective year, give or take problems we might run into. Objective, probably four to five times that. Too many factors affect that to know for sure."

Alex looked at the map; it wasn't a straight line. He stepped around it to get a sense of it in three dimensions, but it could still be a lie. Alex didn't know space, and he only had the captain's word that the last dot was Samalia.

"Your trip ends at Samalia?"

"No, but I don't like planning more than six stops ahead. By the time we get there, I'll have decided where we go next."

143

Alex nodded. "Okay. I'm going to do the best I can to help you with this, but I can't guarantee the results."

"I thought you were good. Are you trying to set me up so you won't have to work hard, and I won't be able to complain when my crew starts dying?"

"Of course not. I am good, good enough a corporation found me while I was still in school and gave me a job. But that doesn't mean I can get just any computer to open up to me. I don't even know what that computer's going to be like."

Alex sat down.

"Look, back when I worked for a corporation, there was an entire department whose only job was to compile information on the system I had to coerce—who had built it, its core programming, which company had done that, and even which coercionists that company might have overseeing it. All of that helped me with the work, and I don't have any of that here."

"Can you get that information?" the captain asked. "There's time before they get in range."

Alex shook his head. "I doubt it. Corporations are constantly queried by various groups. It's easy to slip a request among those. I doubt ships work like that. If I start asking questions about that one, someone will notice. I'm guessing that whatever they are carrying is valuable, so someone is going to wonder why I'm so curious about it."

The man nodded, tapping his fingers on the desk absently. "Alright. What do you need that I can provide, to increase your chances of success?"

Alex thought about it. If he couldn't get any information, there was really only one thing he needed. "I need time. I'm going to need the ship's system to help me with this, so I need to heal the processing core. I'm going to need help with that." He thought of a second thing. "And I'm going to need to be on the bridge. Nano-seconds can make a difference here. The processing core is built into the bridge, so the closer my input is to it, the better the results are going to be. Is there any station I can use for that? Hopefully something I can reconfigure for the work I'll need to do."

"I can't control how much time you'll have—the ship is

scheduled to be here between ten to fifteen days. As for the bridge, that isn't a problem. Asyr has a board so she can do her computer work, but she's hardly ever there, so you can use it."

Ten days.

Ten days to at the very least undo the damaged he'd done, to then hopefully give the ship access to more computing power. He'd have to work day in and day out to accomplish that. Doc was going to have to deal with the fact he couldn't exercise or train during that time.

"There's one last thing. I need Anders off my back."

The captain raised an eyebrow. "Have you been getting in his way?"

"No, I haven't done no damn thing." Alex stopped and shook his head. He was picking up Will's patterns.

The captain chuckled.

"I didn't do anything to him, but he's gotten it in his head that I'm trying to make him look bad or something. Some of his people have threatened me, and Doc had to arrange for me to get bodyguards. I'm going to be coming and going at all hours to get the computer where I need it. I can't ask them to deal with that."

The captain nodded. "I'll call you for a briefing later today. Be there."

Alex hesitated, then nodded.

"Unless there's something else you need to discuss with me, Mister Crimson, you can go."

"Oh, right." Alex left.

Will stopped talking with Perry and fell in step as Alex exited the bridge. "Not good."

"What?"

"You. Not good."

"What do you mean?"

"Doing this, making mistake."

Alex sighed in exasperation. "Will, I really wish you actually spoke full sentences at times."

Will pulled Alex against the wall as four people ran by, tools in hand, speaking in a communicator about a transmission conduit being down. He didn't start moving when the way was

145

clear. Alex watched him collect his thoughts.

When Will spoke, his pace was measured. "I told you, this is going to change you. You should stay separate from this life. You won't—"

"I'm going to be fine. I'm just helping out. It isn't like I'm going to be on the other ship doing the actual stealing. Other than not having corporate protection, this isn't going to be all that different from what I did at Luminex.

Will sighed. "Not simple."

"No, it probably won't be simple, but that's okay. I don't mind a good challenge.

Will shook his head. But instead of speaking, he began walking again.

"Look, Will, I appreciate that you're looking out for me," Alex said as he stayed with him, "but this is just to help out."

"And next time?"

"What do you mean?"

"When captain asks again."

That gave Alex pause. "I don't know. I guess it's going to depend on what he needs me to do that time." They reached the lift, only to find one of the women who'd ran by half in the empty shaft.

She saw them and shook her head. "You're going to have to take one of the ladders. This thing's down, and I don't know when it's going to function again."

Will growled. "Always break." He began walking again.

"It's okay. I don't mind taking the ladder."

"You start minding. Or you're gonna do worse." Will put his hands in his pocket and hunched his shoulders down.

Alex wanted to ask what he meant by that, but someone whooped from an open doorway and he peered in. A group of three men and three women were playing some sort of game at a table. Alex couldn't tell what kind, but it involved gold, gems, and other valuable things being piled in the center of the table.

He watched for a moment, trying to discern the game, but when one of the women looked at him and grinned, he decided to rejoin Will, who had kept walking. The younger man ignored him for the rest of the way to their room, where he occupied himself with reading his tablet.

* * * * *

Alex entered the room he'd been called to and stopped in the doorway.

Will whistled at the assembly, but stayed on the other side of the door. He pushed Alex in and the door closed.

Alex couldn't move.

The captain was at the opposing end of the table from where Alex stood, and sixteen dangerous-looking men and women were seated around it. Anders was seated at the captain's right, and Jennifer at Alex's end.

"What's he doing here?" Anders asked, not hiding his anger.

The captain indicated the chair next to Jennifer, and Alex sat.

"Mister Crimson is going to be the key that unlocks the ship's riches, as well as muzzles its defenses. As such, it's imperative he knows what we will be doing." He tapped controls on the table and read something. "Also," he continued without looking up, "until further notice, Mister Crimson is under my protection."

"What?" Anders asked in disbelief.

"He is vital to this operation, therefore I can't afford for some vendetta to get in the way of what he needs to do. Am I making myself clear?"

Everyone nodded, even Anders, but he glared across the table at Alex.

CRIMSON

CHAPTER 18

The captain talked about what he expected of everyone, things like security forces, time frames, and other things Alex didn't understand. One thing he did understand was that Anders, of all people, would be in charge of the assault force, and that it would be their job to keep everyone safe from the guards. When he looked toward his antagonist, Anders glared at him, and Alex quickly looked away.

At some point, someone asked if this was another shipment of wine, which got chuckles from those assembled, except for Alex and the captain. The captain simply glared at the speaker. Alex didn't get that either.

Before the captain could end the meeting, Anders demanded to know exactly what Alex would be doing during the mission. The captain looked at Alex.

Alex had trouble keeping the tremor out of his voice as the seventeen of them fixed their intense gaze on him. "I'm going to disable the ship's security systems and internal sensors." He hesitated, his thoughts getting away from him. "I'm going to lockdown the cryo beds or chairs if they're connected to the computer. If not, I'm going to disable the doors to keep them from getting in your way."

Anders glared some more. "Why do we need him? We've managed fine without some fancy computer lover before."

"Consider this an experiment, and that's more reason than I need to give you, Anders. Unless there's an actually useful question, you can go get things ready. You have ten days to make sure your teams are in order."

Anders was the first out, glowering. Alex and Jennifer were the last ones, and she stuck by him the entire way to his cabin, where he explained to Will his role in the mission, as well as the captain's protection and his need to move about at all hours.

Even with that, Will didn't agree to reset the door's lock until Jennifer confirmed what Alex had said. Then he explained the same to Doc, and she agreed to cancel the escort for the time being, as well as the training, after double checking with the captain.

That didn't mean it stopped his friends from continuing to act as his bodyguards, and for as much as their constant presence annoyed him, the realization that he'd come to think of this small group as his friends, and that they cared enough about him to want to see him safe, kept him from cursing them too loudly each time one ran to catch up to him as he left his room to go to the lab.

The one thing Doc didn't cancel was his diet. Alex found out the hard way when Carlina slapped his hand off the greasy food he preferred and handed him a plate with a large grilled steak, lots of steamed vegetable, a small portion of cake, and a mug of Liquid Boost.

No amount of complaining on his part deterred Carlina from her watch over what he ate, and Doc wouldn't relent, so Alex had to throw himself into his computer work without his comfort food. At least she let him have the Boosts; he needed all the energy they provided.

Another pleasant side effect of Alex working himself raw for all those days was that he didn't have much time to sleep, let alone have nightmares.

* * * * *

Alex smelled, his eyes had bags under them that would need their own tickets should he try to board a passenger ship, and his beard was long enough to tickle his neck when he bent his head.

But he was happy.

Not only was the central processor fairly sane, but he'd gotten two whole days to do some extra work. At Asyr's insistence, he fixed the life support system. He didn't want to give it to the core processor since as good as his work had been, he wasn't certain it was going handle the extra strain, not when he was going to need its help, so he gave it to the engineering system to handle. It was the second-largest processor on the ship, so it would be fine running that.

He didn't know, or care, how they knew the ship was close by, and yet it didn't know of their presence. By this point, Alex didn't care about much, other than a shower, a razor, and sleep.

He got Will to wake him six hours before the start of the attack. Alex showered again and put on the one set of work clothes he'd brought. If he was going to be working, he wanted to look the part.

Before leaving for the bridge, Alex took out the Defender from under his bunk. He looked at it, and spent a moment remembering Jack, and wondered if it would be of any help in the end. Would someone like Tristan care about what it represented?

He took it out of the case and took the data chip that had been on the cushion under it. With another thought for what Jack meant to him, he put the Defender away and headed to the bridge.

He spent his time there familiarizing himself with Asyr's computer control board. The layout was different than the one she used in the lab, which reinforced the notion that she never used it.

Alex discovered the bridge's board had one feature that would make a difference: the computer display was three-dimensional. Asyr's lab was in two dimensions, which was fine for healing the computer, but in an aggressive action like what he was about to undertake, the second it took for him to make out a line of code buried under everything else could cost him control.

He had to clean the interface, both physically and its code, before he could reconfigure and make use of it. With that done, he ran through a few quick exercises, then sat down and waited.

He wasn't nervous. This was his element, even the waiting. He was going over his plan of attack with all the permutations he could come up with. As agreed, one of the bridge crew let him know two hours before the start of the attack, and Alex got to work.

Establishing contact with their target ship, the Poseidon, was simple. Every computer in existence was connected to the open net. They had to be; computers had to talk to each other, especially ships. Crews needed to talk with their families, executives needed to stay up to date with what was happening at the head office—for both, they had to know where in the universe they were. Even military ships, which operated mainly on the closed net for their communication, still had at least one open net contact point. The crew needed entertainment, and that couldn't be transmitted through the closed net; it would defeat its purpose.

The Poseidon wasn't military—the captain had been able to tell him that—it was corporate. It didn't mean its security would be any less active, but it meant the people behind them were going to be less alert.

He put the earpiece in, and a moment later heard the soft beep that told him it was connected to the bridge's computer.

"How are you feeling?" he asked, getting a curious look from the officer seated next to him. Alex shook his head to her and focused on his board.

"I am lonely," the computer replied, only a hint of the wail in its voice.

"I know. Once this is over we're going to have time, and I'm going to begin reconnecting you with the rest of the ship. Are you ready?"

"I have very little else to do." Had that been sarcasm?

"I'm sure your undivided attention will be to my advantage." He inserted the data chip in the board, and a list of programs appeared on the side of the screen.

"I don't like those programs," the computer said.

"Don't worry, they aren't for you." Each one was a program he'd written over his years at Luminex. He'd come up with them to overcome specific problems he'd encountered, and his job had become easier with each one he'd added to his arsenal.

He didn't own any of them. He'd created them, but they belonged to the company. Still, he hadn't been able to leave without making a copy, and while he hadn't expected to use them in quite this manner, they could make the difference here.

With a few keystrokes, he was in contact with the other ship. He sent in a burrowing program, camouflaged as a personal communication, to get through as many layers of security as it could before being stopped. His program was good enough that in a few previous jobs it made it all the way to the command structure, and it had been easy for him to get what he was after.

This time it only made it three layers deep, giving Alex only the ability to make minor changes. That was okay; this was what he had gotten paid to do.

He put his hand in the display and rotated it, first sideways, then down. He smiled as he found a weak spot in the code. He modified it.

"I don't like you," came a deep, resonating, voice in his ear. The other ship's system.

"Well, hello there," Alex replied. He spun the display, looking for his next target. "How are you doing?"

"Who are you? I don't see your ID in my directory."

"Are you sure? I'm a friend. Maybe you should look again?"

Now that he knew the system was doing it, he saw the code react to its search, telling him where the governing code was located. He zoomed in, rotated around until it was upfront on the display.

"You are not in," the ship informed him. "I must inform the operator that an illegal intrusion is in progress."

"Now, don't do that," He located a second path into the code. "I'm sure it's just a misunderstanding." He inserted the communication ID he was using. "I told you, I'm a friend." He backed out. "Are you sure you were thorough? Come on, just look again. If I'm not there I'll leave."

A sound very much like a sigh came. "Oh, you are there."

"See, I told you I was a friend."

"Still, I should inform the operator there was an irregularity in my search."

Alex sent a search program with instructions to highlight specific codes.

"Do you really want to bother him with that? He just came out of cryo, right? He'll probably be irritable and growl at you."

Every system came from their manufacturer with the same programming, therefore, the same personality. Personalities evolved, changed as new programs were added. It was very difficult to set up two computers with exactly the same programs installed in exactly the same way, so in no time at all each computer had its own personality.

"Yes, but I have my programming," the computer replied. "Anomalies need to be reported."

This caused people to forget that the original code remained there. Buried under all those different personalities, was the core one. Alex didn't know which one this was. The captain hadn't known—it hadn't been important for how he'd planned to operate before he'd asked Alex to join in, but there were only a hundred or so manufacturers, and Alex had dealt with all of their systems.

"I know, but why not just make a log? That way you'll have satisfied the notification program, and your operator will be able to look into it when he's past the waking sickness."

Luminex had compiled every variation of that core programming for each of the manufacturers, and Alex had incorporated them in his search program. So long as enough code was highlighted, Alex would know which manufacturer he was dealing with, and with that he'd know how the base personality thought.

"I suppose that is sensible."

While code lit up, Alex continued to work, preparing for what he'd be able to do once he could give himself more access. He located internal communications, the sensors, internal weapons. Why did a ship have an internal weapon system? He put the question out of his mind; he had more important things to do.

"Since we're chatting, can you do me a favor and tell me what's around you?"

Cryo system was part of the central, so that was good.

"Nothing, of course."

"Really? Nothing? I thought there was always stuff floating in space."

He glanced that the code, still not enough for him to make out who this was.

"Rocks are nothing, unless they are in my path, then they become something."

"So, there's nothing in your path?"

Alex noticed a line of code. It wasn't one his program was looking for, but he was familiar with it; he'd seen in many computers. He quickly rewrote it.

"Did you do something?" the system asked.

"No," Alex replied. "Why?"

"I thought I felt something."

"Have any of your functions changed?"

There was a moment of silence. "No, they haven't."

"See, if I had done something, you'd be able to tell." Still not enough code lighting up. He didn't look at the time; that never helped. "If I tell you I'm in charge, would you believe me?"

"No, you are contacting from outside the ship. You cannot be in charge."

Alex changed three more lines. "I could be in charge. Maybe I'm contacting you from the head office."

"I...don't think so. Those communications come with specific identifiers."

Alex smiled. Had that been hesitation? "Maybe this is a

test." Another quick change.

"Why? Why would you tell me this is a test, if it was one?"

"Maybe I'm here to see how you respond to confusion. You do know a system like yours can fall victim to that." He searched for more code to change, but he'd gone through all the easy ones. There was nothing else he could directly change to push the system to trust him. From this point forward, he'd have to change multiple lines and get that interaction to cause the personality to change, but that meant that anyone paying attention on the other ship could notice.

He glanced at the internal communication ports. Still no indication anyone was manning them. Ships like the Poseidon couldn't afford to have a full crew complement up and about all the time during such a trip, but they also couldn't have everyone in cryo; there had to be at least one person there to respond to unexpected situations, say like a pirate attack. Alex couldn't know how many were awake right now, but there had to be at least one coercionist, and he should do regular checks.

"I cannot be confused," the system said, as Alex unpacked a program and made a dozen copies of it. "I am a Moramba Sixty-Eight. I am state-of-the-art."

Alex froze in the middle of instructing the programs on what lines he needed changed and how. Had it just given him the manufacturer? "Did you say you're a Moramba?"

"I did."

It had. Somehow Alex had gotten it to divulge the most important aspect of who it was, by accident. He'd have to go over what he'd done later and see if it could be programmed, but for now he had work to do.

He spun the display. He didn't know the sixty-eight, but he knew Moramba. He knew its core personality. Maybe the arrogance was an unintended feature on the sixty-eight? More likely due to the changes made to it.

He changed the instructions to his program and released them.

The system blinked. Such a significant change couldn't go unnoticed, which was why it needed to be done at once, and had to be exactly right, or he was in for a hard fight to regain control.

"What did you do?" the system asked.

"Something to help you."

"Oh, alright."

"Now, can you answer my question again? If I tell you I'm in charge, do you believe me?"

"Of course."

"Good. I want you to listen to me. You said there is nothing around you. That is true. It will remain true. There are only rocks around you, and they are nothing unless they are in your path. Do you understand?"

"I only see rocks. Rocks are nothing."

"Good."

Alex grinned and stretched. Everyone who wasn't occupied on the bridge was looking at him.

He took off the earpiece. "We're invisible to them. So long as we don't cross their direct path, their sensors will ignore us."

"You told that ship we're a rock?" the captain asked.

"I told it everything is a rock, much easier."

"And it believed you?"

Alex's grin widened. "It did. As far as it's concerned, I'm the boss now."

The pilot looked at him. "Are you actually saying that we can just go up to their cargo dock and knock? No hiding, no jumping from rock to rock and looking for their blind spots?"

"I wouldn't knock, but yeah, for the rest that's about it." Alex looked at all the stunned faces. "Isn't that what you wanted me to do?"

"Kid," the captain said with a grin, "I had no idea you could get a ship to do that. All I was expecting was that you would disable locks for us and keep the security systems from frying my people. Murray, move us alongside. Rebecca, inform the teams we're moving ahead of schedule."

"Sir, don't connect to the ship too fast," Alex said. "I'm not ready to control the rest."

"Don't worry kid, we'll wait for your word."

"Shit," Murray whispered. "How come we haven't been doing things this way from the start?"

Alex sent more programs to alter more of the code and solidify his control. He told the defense sensors to keep what it saw for itself and him, and not act on any of it unless he gave it instructions. He told the inventory controls to expect items to be removed and it was normal. It asked for authorizations, and Alex responded by lobotomizing it. He didn't have the time to spend on such a minor system.

"I have control of the important stuff," he said, and set more watch programs around the communication ports. Whatever problems he was going to have during the attack, they were going to come from there. As soon as the crew boarded the ship, those who were awake—it reminded him to set the cryo beds so they would ignore instructions to wake anyone else—would start reporting the intrusion.

He caught motion close to him and became aware of excited talk and movement.

"I'm leaving this here for you," Perry said. It was a gun.

"I can't use that," Alex responded.

"I'll take it," Murray said, and reached for it.

"Bug off, Murray," Perry said without looking at him. "You won't need it, but if you do, just point and shoot. It's ready to fire and set to max, so you don't have to worry about that." He turned to Murray. "If you try anything and Crimson doesn't shoot you, I will. I don't give a fuck what Anders told you to do, got that?" Perry left.

It was only Alex and Murray on the bridge now. He expected soon they would be the only ones on the ship. He glanced at the pilot, who pointedly kept his eyes on his controls, and then put him out of his mind. He had to count on the captain's protection, and Perry's threat to be enough to keep Murray from doing anything.

He went through what he had. He controlled the core, which meant he could get it to act on his behalf, but he also directly controlled the sensors, the doors, and he had shut down the internal weapons. He turned to Murray. "I'm good to go; you can dock and let them in."

The pilot nodded, and a moment later the ship shook as they touched. Someone had to have noticed that. Alex watched through the internal sensors as the crew spread through the ship.

Then one of the communication points activated. His programs shut it down, but another activated, then another one and one more, as more and more people tried to report the boarding party. His programs wouldn't be able to keep all of them from passing the messages, and that wasn't their job. All he needed was to make sure they were delayed. He still sent more programs to help, and manually disconnected those he could.

He knew the ship's coercionist was on the job when antibodies flooded the core, a swarm of programs targeted and corrupted his, turning them against themselves. He should have had control over that section of the system, and when he checked, he still did. Those weren't system-based, but a creation of the coercionist.

Now he was fighting another human being, and while they weren't as efficient as the ship's system, Alex couldn't subvert them. This would be a war of code.

The coercionist went after the modified code, and Alex went after his communication point. Both let loose programs to prevent the other from accomplishing much of anything.

Alex lost track of time. All that mattered to him was keeping control of the system, and while his opponent wasn't particularly creative, he was quick and he was demanding much of Alex to keep up with his attacks and to get through his defenses.

He saw motion in his peripheral vision, then put it out of his mind. The other coercionist had managed to disarm his defensive programs and was starting to take control of the sensors. Alex undid the changes as fast as he could, and set up a few programs to attack the coercionist directly.

Someone said something.

Alex rotated the display, looking for any indication as to where the coercionist was physically located in the ship. He'd lost control of ten percent of the sensors, and had to assume his enemy was somewhere in there.

Someone yelled an order.

With a curse, Alex glanced away to snap he was busy, but found himself looking at a gray-haired man in the doorway, pointing a gun at him. Where was Murray?

"I said," the man said, "move away from the board."

Alex had no idea who that was. He didn't recognize him, and he wasn't wearing anything close to what he'd seen any of the crew wearing. The white uniform was much too clean and in good condition to belong on this ship. Well, except for the captain; he always wore clean and well-tailored clothes while on the ship, but that wasn't him.

Whoever this was, he came from the other ship.

Alex looked at the display and his hands had continued typing. He was still holding control of most of the sensors, but that wouldn't stay the case if he stopped.

He again noticed the gun.

"Take your hands off the keyboard. Stand up and move away."

He hesitated. What else could he do? He was at gunpoint. By reflex, he took out the earpiece as he stood and pocketed it. He stood and took a breath to stop his hands from shaking.

He was insane for even considering it, but he had a job to do, and every second he spent away from the board was time the other coercionist had to undo his work. Long enough, and he'd regain control of the weapons. Damn it, he'd told the captain he could do this.

He grabbed the gun and spun, pointing it at the man, then he wondered if the safety was on and glanced at the gun's side, remembering as he saw it was off what Perry had said.

When he looked up, the man had an amused smile.

"You're new to this, aren't you?" His face grew serious. "You have to know you can't take me. You're shaking. Put the gun down and step away from the board."

Alex didn't move. He'd made a deal to work for passage to Samalia, but this was a pirate ship. He didn't belong here. Maybe he could convince the other ship to take him there? Explain he hadn't intended to coerce their ship when he'd set out on this journey? It would mean breaking his word, losing the friends he'd made, but his ultimate goal was Samalia, right?

Not making friends.

"Look," the man said, clearly reigning in his annoyance. "Just do what I said and I'll tell my captain I just found you here. I won't even say you were on the bridge, so he won't know about your part in the intrusion. You won't be able to avoid at least talking to the Law, but you should be able to convince them you didn't know about any of this, right? At worst you'll only look at a few years in a minimum-security place, and the girls like a guy with a past, right?"

Alex almost nodded at the mention he could get out of this clean. There was nothing on record about him doing this job; the only thing that could be demonstrated was that he was healing the computer. The captain would deny it, but who would believe him? He was a pirate. The Law was sure to take his side in... The Law would be involved.

"I can't talk to the Law." Luminex would have a warrant out for him. He'd stolen the earpiece, proprietary technology. Every law-enforcement agency would have his picture in their files. "You need to promise me that I won't have to talk with them. I'll work for your captain, but I'm not talking to the Law."

"I can't do that. Not after what you helped with. You either take the—"

Alex fired. The man fell back.

Alex closed his eyes and pushed the image out of his mind. He dropped the gun and turned back to the display. He had work to do.

He could tell at a glance the other coercionist had used his time away to good effect. He'd taken apart most of the programs Alex still had doing defense.

He put the earpiece back in and was assaulted with wailing. He cursed; he didn't have time to deal with his own system having depression attack. He tried his best to ignore it as he rebuilt his defense, launching new programs, but half wouldn't even function due to the assault.

And then he realized he didn't have to be the one. He took over one of the communication points, programmed to broadcast over the whole of the ship's communication system, and shunted the wailing to it. Let the other coercionist deal with it.

It worked. The other's work suffered immediately and allowed Alex to quickly regain control of the sensor, but when he tried to tell them to shut down the few weapons that had been activated, it was too confused to respond, so Alex had to deactivate them manually.

Then he discovered that one of the first things the other had done was unlock all the doors. He had to spend fifteen minutes locating the enemy security forces and lock them back in without trapping his own people.

That done, he was able to focus on both maintaining control and calming his system. And once the wailing abated, he found out an alarm was sounding within his system. Someone else was trying to gain access. He split the display and began fighting on two fronts, grinning the entire time.

He couldn't remember the last time he'd had this much fun.

* * * * *

"Crimson!"

Alex looked away from the display, where one of the coercionists had unleashed a digger program at him and the other was using a mirroring sheath to try to evade his attention.

The captain was looking at him. "Why didn't you respond to my calls?"

Alex looked at the board and there was indeed a light indicating someone had tried to contact him. "Been busy," he said, focusing back on the display. Really? A mirroring sheath? Even beginners didn't bother with those. He coded his attack and had him blasted back out of his system.

"Crimson!"

"I'm busy!" he snapped.

Someone sighed. "We're all back," the captain said. "Where's Murray?"

"Don't know. You're back?"

"Yes, everyone. I tried to contact you as soon as we were in so Murray could get us out of here."

"I've got the seat," someone said.

"Oh," Alex said. If everyone was back, then there was only one thing left to do. He ignored the coercionist trying to get into his system; the guy was such an amateur that he wouldn't be able to do any damage in the little time he'd have.

"Hello," he called to the other computer. "Remember me?"

"Yes, I do, but I'm under attack."

"I know, but that's almost over. It was an exercise."

"Then why does it hurt so?"

"I needed to see how you'd react to something that felt real. You did very well. There's only one thing I need you to do now, and after that the pain will go away."

"The intrusion will stop?"

"Yes. When you do this, he'll know the test is over. You were an excellent system; your pride is well-deserved. When I tell you to go to sleep, I want you to forget the entirety of the last twenty-four hours, then sleep for a full day. Do you understand?"

"That will inconvenience the crew."

"I know, but that's their part of the test. We need to know how they will react on their own. You trust me, remember?"

"I do. I am not worried; they will perform well. They are a good crew, they are my crew."

"I have no doubt. Go to sleep."

His connection died.

He checked his system's status. As he'd expected, the second coercionist hadn't managed to do anything in the minute or so Alex hadn't blocked him.

His job was finished.

His legs gave out, but someone caught him. He'd been standing? Hadn't he sat down after the man had... His mind blocked the rest.

He was made to lean back against the board. The captain was before him, concern on his face. Perry was the one holding him up.

Alex looked around. Everyone was moving about, but they were avoiding a spot: the place where the man fell. Alex's mind tried to reel away, but his eyes fell on him. There was a large pool of blood around the half of the man's head that was left.

Alex threw himself away from Perry and the captain and ended up on all fours, throwing up. When he was done he manage to stand without help.

"Murray isn't here, so I'm guessing that's your handiwork?"

Alex nodded, not looking at the man.

"That's your second one. Should I be worried?"

Alex shook his head vehemently. "I didn't mean to kill him. I was aiming for his shoulder, but my hand was shaking so much. Then I had to get back to controlling the other ship. Their coercionist had managed to free up the sensors, and—"

The captain grabbed his shoulder forcefully. "You don't have anything to explain. That guy put the job in danger and you dealt with him. That's how things should go."

He guided Alex back to the seat and had him sit. "Now, you told the other ship to go to sleep and forget?"

Alex looked around, expecting at least one person to look at him with disgust, but those who did look in his direction nodded their approval. One even gave him a thumbs up.

"So, we have a day?" the captain asked.

"No, a couple of hours at most. If their coercionist is any good, that's all it's going to take him to force a hard reboot of the system." Alex smiled. "Which is going to erase all traces of my work."

"You heard the kid," the captain said. "We have two hours to get as far from here as possible. Burn as much power as it's safe to do." He patted Alex on the shoulder. "Go to your cabin, sleep, eat, rest. We're all exhausted, so we'll celebrate once we're away."

"What about the—" Alex pointed toward the body without looking at it.

"Don't worry about that, or the mess in the corner. You're not on cleanup duty anymore. I'll get Will to do it."

"He shouldn't have to clean up my mess."

The captain chuckled. "The kid loves cleaning stuff. If I'd known that, I would have set him to cleaning the ship from the start. Go rest."

Alex nodded, but it was a moment before he could get his mind to engage, then a few more before his legs were steady enough to support him. He was careful not to look down as he stepped around the body and left the bridge.

He made it halfway to his room, in a daze of shock and exhaustion, before someone grabbed him and slammed him against the wall.

"You did it on purpose, didn't you?"

It took Alex a moment to recognize that Anders was the one holding him. "What?" was all he managed to say.

"You said you'd control the other ship, so you expect me to think you didn't arrange it? Well take a look, I'm still alive." He shook Alex. "But two of my men are hurt because of you. You're going to pay."

A hand appeared on Anders's shoulder, and Alex realized there were six others there. The hand belonged to a short, stout man. "He's under the captain's protection."

Anders growled and slammed Alex against the wall before letting him go.

"This isn't over. The job's done, so the captain's going to take his protection away. The moment he does, you're a dead man." He stormed off, followed by most of the others.

Only the man who stopped Anders remained.

"What the fuck was that about?" Alex asked once the group had turned the corner.

"Security systems came active where we were, and Anders is certain you tried to kill him. He thinks you're after his position as top guy on the ship."

Alex gaped. "That's nuts. I'm getting off the ship the moment we get to Samalia, doesn't he get that?"

The man shrugged.

Alex studied him suspiciously. "Shouldn't you be threatening me? Instead of explaining things?"

The man chuckled. "You saved lives. I'm not interested in giving you grief."

"What do you mean I saved lives? Anders said two got hurt because of me."

The man shook his head. "Those two are the only ones—

well, not counting Marco and Willobury, but those two idiots got hurt when they let a crate fall on top of them. That would have happened even if you hadn't been here." He leaned against the opposing wall. "What I'm saying is that in keeping security off us, you've made it so that's all that happened. We've never had a job go this easy. Usually we get at least thirty who end up at Doc's, and a few dead. I'm hoping the captain can convince you to stick with us, because I could get used to jobs like this one.

The man shook Alex's hand and left him there, stunned. Alex couldn't believe that what he'd done had left that much of an impact on the crew.

Then he realized that this would just piss Anders off even more. With a groan, he made it the rest of the way to his cabin to sleep until the universe ended.

CHAPTER 19

Alex was on the bridge. He was holding a gun, and people were cheering him on. The captain was there, along with Doc, Will, Jennifer, Perry, and even Anders, as well as a bunch of others, most of whom he didn't know the names of.

There was another person there: a gray-haired man in a white uniform standing in the doorway. He too was holding a gun, and he was pointing it at Alex.

The cheering changed from a generalized support to a chant of, "Shoot, shoot, shoot".

Alex tried to tell them to shut up. He wasn't going to shoot anyone; he wasn't a killer.

"Really?" someone whispered in his ear, nuzzling his neck. "Why not?"

Alex closed his eyes and almost said his name, but realized it wasn't him. Jack wouldn't be here, he wouldn't encourage this. "Go away. I don't want you here."

"Now, now, don't lie. If you didn't want me here, I wouldn't be. It's your dream after all." A hand caressed Alex's sides, moving up. Tristan kissed his neck. "Just kill him, he's in your way."

"I'm not like you."

They alien nibbled on Alex's earlobe. "But you could be." The hand traveled down along his arm, the claws gently raking against his skin, in a way Jack did and Alex enjoyed.

"Stop that. You don't have the right."

"You never complained before." The hand stopped at Alex's wrist, took it tenderly, and began lifting it.

"That wasn't you. It was Jack." Alex tried to push his arm down, but as gentle as the touch was, it couldn't be stopped.

"It was always me," Tristan whispered. "I was the one making love to you; I just let you believe it was someone named Jack."

"No. All you know is death and violence. It's impossible for you to know what love is." His arm was forced straight, gun pointing at the gray-haired man.

"You don't believe that. You know I had parents. My mother loved me, raised me to be a good boy, just like you."

"I am nothing like you."

"You are more like me than you want to admit. Violence is in you; that's why you fell for me. You could feel the violence I was hiding, it turned you on."

Alex snorted. "Nothing about you turns me on."

"Really?" The tone carried a smile. "Look down."

Alex did, and saw he was naked, and sporting an erection. "You're doing that to me."

"Oh, you're right about that. You want me so badly."

"That's not what I meant."

"Isn't it?"

"You're holding my arm so I'll point the gun at that man. You're causing me to react like that."

"I'm not holding anything."

The alien was right. There was no one keeping his arm up. Alex tried to lower it, but it wouldn't.

"Shoot him, Alex. You know you want to."

"I don't want to."

Tristan didn't say anything, but Alex felt his finger tighten on the trigger.

He cursed. He didn't have a choice. He couldn't be arrested... he couldn't go to prison; how would he find Jack from prison?

"That isn't why you shot him, Alex." The hand was on his chest, rubbing him. Tristan was pressing against his body, the fur prickling his back. "You shot him because you wanted to. Everything else was a justification." The hand moved down to his stomach.

"No," Alex protested. "I didn't have a choice."

"You always did," Tristan kissed his neck while his hand moved lower. "You chose to kill that man. You did it because you wanted to. You wanted to feel the power, the release. You wanted that feeling that you haven't had since I took Jack away from you. You wanted to be on top."

The hand closed over Alex's manhood. He gasped, and there was a flash of light.

* * * * *

The scream came out as a strangled gasp. Alex panted, shutting his eyes tight, trying to will the erection down. The nightmare had lied; he wasn't like that. He wasn't a killer.

He made his way to the shower and turned the water hot before stepping under it. It burned, but he wanted the pain. He wanted the reminder that what he'd done was wrong. A crime. Another crime he'd committed. He scrubbed himself, trying to wash off the sweat of his fear, trying to clean himself of how he felt. How the dream Tristan had made him feel.

He paused when the soap on his arm stung, and he saw he'd scratched himself until he bled. His entire body was red from the hot water and his over-vigorous scrubbing. He put the soap away and let the water fall over him.

The dream was wrong, he told himself. That wasn't who he was. He would never be like that. He reached for the soap again, but stopped himself. It didn't matter how much scrubbing he did, it wouldn't rub the doubt out of his mind.

He dried himself, bandaged the wound, and dressed. Now that he was awake, he felt the hunger. When had he eaten last? At some point before he went to the bridge, before he'd— He stopped that line of thinking.

He headed to the dining hall and piled on food on a tray. Only when he was seated at a table did he notice he'd taken plates of mashed potatoes with gravy, slices of bread thick with butter, cakes and pies, and that no one had stopped him.

He looked back at the two tired-looking cooks, and no Carlina. With a grin, he set about eating the comfort foods.

* * * * *

"Wake up!"

Alex groaned and tried to stop Will from shaking him.

"Sleep's done. Party time!"

"I'm awake," Alex said. "Stop it." He rubbed as much of the sleep out of his eyes as he could. "What party?"

"Job's done!"

"You're not making any sense."

Will let out a sigh. "We celebrate the job," he said slowly. "We won. No one got hurt." He grinned.

That wasn't right, but Alex couldn't remember why.

"Up, up! Sleep's done."

"Fine, I'm getting up," Alex threw his legs off the side of the bed. "But I'm not going to a party."

Will stared. "Must."

"No, you go, you have fun. I'm going to Asyr's lab. I have work to do." And killers didn't get to party.

"No work. Party time. Others want you there."

"What for?" Alex pulled out his work pants, but Will took them away from him, handing him the brown cloth pants that had become part of his usual attire.

"To say thanks. Your fault they're safe. No work," Will said gravely, and then planted himself before the door, arms crossed over his chest.

Alex stared at him, then the pants. He knew the younger man well enough not to bother fighting him about this. He wouldn't give in. With a sigh, he dressed and let Will lead him to the lounge.

Alex felt the beat of the music three halls away. Will was bopping to it not long after that. The volume of people coming and going increased the closer they got, until they stood in the entrance and looked at a mob of people.

Alex didn't move when Will pulled on his arm. Lights were flashing in time with the music, people screaming loud enough to be heard over that. Arms were in the air, bodies moving against one another.

"Look!" Alex yelled to Will. "I don't think this—"

The younger man yanked on his arm hard enough to get him off balance, and he had to follow. They walked around the dancers until they cleared them, coming to an area where crates had been turned into tables and people mingled with drinks in their hands.

The moment someone noticed him, his name went up in a chant. 'Crimson! Crimson! Crimson!'

Alex almost bolted, the chant being too close to what had been in his dream, but before he could move, people were surrounding him. Men and women shook his hand, then he felt something in it. He had a glass half-filled with dark liquid.

Someone made a toast to his name, and Alex had to drink. He gasped; the stuff was stronger than he was used to. Someone wrapped her arms around him and kissed him. Cheers went up. And another toast, and Alex had to drink again.

Will dragged him from one table to another, and each time Alex received thanks for keeping them alive, was toasted and kissed. When his glass was empty, another one replaced it.

This way he moved through the crowd, at some point realizing Will had vanished and he was continuing on his own. Someone hugged him, more kisses from women and men, more drinking.

171

When Alex dropped the glass as he tried to put it on a crate, he decided he'd had enough. He looked around, trying to locate the door, but somehow ended up holding another drink. He hadn't seen who had given it to him.

He looked for a place to put the glass down, and someone screamed his name. Cheers and drinks went up. Alex had to drink again. Then he moved away from them, looking for a place to catch his breath.

He ended at a smaller crate, more of a seat than a table, and sat on the edge of it while he waited for the room to stop spinning. He tried to count the numbers of drinks he'd had, but couldn't come out with a number. He knew it was more than he'd drank before, probably in his entire life.

Before this, the only time he'd drank anything was at Alien-Nation, and there he'd nurse his one drink as an excuse to hang around and watch the aliens.

Concern managed to drift up through the alcohol-induced haze. They shouldn't be thanking him. He was a killer, a murderer. Tristan had been right; he had wanted that man dead, and everything else had been justification. He wasn't a hero. And then there was Anders. How was he going to take everyone cheering Alex's name and not his?

A hand ran up his back, his side, and then along his stomach. The person nuzzled the back of his neck. "So, this is where the hero's hiding," a deep voice said.

"I'm not hiding," Alex replied, "just resting." He leaned his head back and the man nibbled on Alex's earlobe. He closed his eyes and a moan escaped his lips.

"Not used to being celebrated like this?" the man whispered.

Alex shook his head.

The hand massaged his chest. "You shouldn't be hiding from it. You're the hero, enjoy it. Take it for everything it's worth." The man kissed the side of his neck, then his cheek as he moved in front of him. "You shouldn't be afraid of taking your due."

The man kissed him, and Alex responded. He wrapped his arms around him, held him tightly. Alex parted his lips and the other man's tongue pushed in. Their soft tongues played together, and Alex frowned.

He opened his eyes and looked into blue ones. With a gasp, Alex pushed him away.

"What's wrong?" the man asked.

Alex stared at him. "Anders? What the hell are you doing?" He quickly looked around for the rest of his posse.

Anders smiled. "I was kissing you."

"Kissing me?" Alex felt anger bubble up. "Wasn't it yesterday you wanted to kill me?"

Anders raised his hands to placate him. "Hey, I'm sorry. I was still riding the adrenaline high, and two of my friends had been hurt. Murray told me what happened."

"He's okay?"

"Yeah, they found him unconscious in a closet. He had one hell of a bump on his head."

"I'm glad he's okay. But yeah, that'd be when the security system came back up. The other coercionist went after that pretty quickly. It was just bad luck your section was one of the early ones to come active."

Anders smiled. "I believe you. I figured I'd make it up to you." He moved closer, but Alex stopped him.

"Kiss and make up? Really?"

"Why not?" Anders grinned. "We can go to my cabin; my bed is much bigger than yours."

Alex didn't trust him, but that wasn't why he wouldn't go. "I already have someone."

"That guy you're going to meet whenever you get off the ship?"

Alex nodded.

"So? It's not like he'll know what you've been up to."

"I don't care. It isn't because he's not here to check on me that I'm going to start cheating on him."

"You're serious? You're not going to have any sex until you're with him? You do realize that we're about one year away, right? And I mean subjective, not objective."

"I know, and yes. I'm going to abstain until then."

Anders whistled. "I have to admire your fortitude." He smiled lewdly and leaned in. "But if you ever find you can't hold out anymore, come find me." He turned and vanished among the dancers.

Alex's head reeled, but he didn't think it was from the alcohol. He hadn't expected Anders to offer that. Not that he was tempted, but still, after the animosity...

He stood and waited a moment to see if he was steady. When he was, he followed the wall until he reached the door, then he made his way through the people toward his bed.

"Where to?" Will asked.

Alex stared at him, then around. Where had the young man come from? "To sleep. I'm not a fan of parties, I've had too much to drink, and being hit on by Anders was just too weird."

"Anders?"

"Yeah, why?"

"Anders like girls."

Alex shrugged. "Maybe he had too much to drink too."

Will frowned. "He's trouble."

"You get back to the party. I'm just heading to the cabin, I promise. I need to sleep this off; I can't fix the computer in this state."

"When you're there."

Alex thought about protesting, but he was just too tired.

CHAPTER 20

Alex looked at the thing Jennifer was holding.

"You're joking, right? You pulled me out of bed for that?" She'd banged on the door and demanded he come with her.

She offered it to him and he backed away

"No. I'm never touching one of those things again."

"Why not?" Her tone was so calm, Alex shuddered. "You handle it well enough already."

"Are you insane?" he yelled, trying to unsettle her. "I've held a gun exactly two times in my entire life, and both times I ended up killing someone!"

"That's sort of the point of them," she replied, her tone even.

"I didn't want to kill them!" He turned to leave the room, but the door wouldn't open. He spun. "That first guy, Sampson, he startled me and the thing went off. I never meant to kill him. The other one? I didn't want to..." His voice trailed off.

The nightmares hadn't stopped. Three nights of them,

and each time he killed the man, couldn't stop himself. Tristan kept encouraging him and the crew did the same, and now he couldn't help feeling like he needed less and less prodding to do it.

"I don't even know his name," he whispered, then looked at Jennifer. "Damn it, if I'm going to kill someone, I should at least know who he is! I don't want to have anything to do with those things."

She snorted. "So, what? You want to take them out to dinner? Exchange life stories? Then grab the knife and look them in the eyes while you gut them? You really want to get your hands bloody like that?"

Alex felt his stomach turn as he envisioned feeling someone's breath on his face as he plunged a knife into them. He felt horror as their body sagged onto his on their way down, clutching at him, trying to keep from dying.

"Yes." He thought he might get sick. "If I ever kill anyone else again, I want to see it, to feel it. I want to see the horror on their face, because if no one else here is going to hate me for doing something that horrible, at least the victim should get to do it."

Her raised eyebrow was the only indication of surprise at his decision. Maybe he'd sounded crazy? Good. If that's what it took to make her realize the folly of teaching him to kill people, then so be it.

She nodded. "Okay, I know someone."

Was she serious?

She thought for a moment. "It'll take some convincing, but I can get him to teach you how to handle a knife."

She couldn't be serious. Alex felt like he was going to be sick.

She offered him the gun. "Now, take this."

Anger pushed the nausea away. He tried to slap the weapon away, but she moved her hand. "Didn't you listen to anything I've said?" he screamed. "I don't—"

"Yeah, yeah. You don't want to kill anyone by accident again. I get it." She offered him the gun. "That starts with you knowing how to handle one of these so that when you shoot someone, they'll only die if you want them to."

Alex looked at the gun. It was smaller than the one Perry had left him, and much smaller than the one he'd stumbled on in the lounge. It was barely larger than his hand. He felt the revulsion, but he pushed it down. She had a point.

He had close to a year left on the ship. He couldn't be naive enough to think there wouldn't be another attack. He didn't want to use one of them, but he might have to defend himself.

His hand shook as he took it out of her hand.

"Good," she said. "Let's start with how to handle it so you won't hurt yourself."

"Cute place," Ana said.

Alex looked up from the console and around Asyr's lab. "Ahh, thanks?" What was she doing here?

"Funny," she replied. "Get up, you're due for some training."

"Not more of that," he protested. "I just got out of learning how to take out and change vital components on a gun two hours ago."

She smirked. "We still need to work on your hand-to-hand training."

"Why? Anders is going to leave me alone now."

"Right, because he's such a loving fellow. Out of the chair, now."

Look, I appreciate it, but I have more imp—"

She grabbed his arm and pulled him out. "Stop whining, you need this."

He stared at the food on his plate. "Come on, Carlina, I can't live on this stuff. Let me at least have some of the lasagna."

"No. And don't think you can sneak here in the middle of the night and eat whatever you want again. Doc's orders. You're going to lose weight."

"But Ana spent the last hour kicking my ass, I need comfort food."

"You want comfort? Find someone, get a hug."

"No wonder Will's scared of you," Alex grumbled. "You're mean."

"And?" she asked, her tone threatening.

"Nothing," he replied, taking his tray and joining Perry and Will at a table. He looked at steak, vegetables, and a bowl of flavored jelly. He sighed. At least he'd managed to have two meals of deliciously greasy food before this. He'd have to let the memory carry him through the rest of the trip.

* * * * *

"With me," Will said.

"Where?" Alex asked, pulling the shirt on.

"Just come."

"No. Damn it, Will. Ana and Jen kept me from doing any work yesterday; I'll exercise another day."

The younger man canted his head. "Not that," he said as Alex's meaning registered. "Gotta show you something."

Alex sighed and put his shoes on. Even before he was standing again, Will grabbed his arm and Alex had no choice but to follow him. They moved down and toward the back, aft? The stern? Will kept telling him, but the terms hadn't stuck yet.

A door opened and Alex found himself in a large room. He'd thought the lounge had been big, but this was larger. He couldn't see the ceiling in the darkness, and walls of shelves had crates on them.

"This is the cargo hold," he said. He barely remembered it

from when he'd boarded, but it had to be it. Each crate had a display attach to it, and he knew from his time between school sessions where he'd worked at the warehouse his father ran, that they contained information about the content, provenance, and destination, although that wouldn't be where they were going anymore.

"Is this all from the other ship?" Alex asked. The shelves vanished into the distance.

"Some," Will replied. "Lea!" he called to a woman leaning on top of a larger crate and rummaging through it. She looked in their direction and waved.

"Crimson, Lea," Will made the introductions once they were standing next to the crate. "Lea, Crimson."

"Why am I Crimson, and she's Lea?" Alex asked.

Will just looked at him.

"Why use my last name, and her first? Lea is your first name, right?"

The woman nodded then dropped off the crate.

"Anders is a last name, but Will, Ana, Jennifer, and Perry are first names, so why use my last name?"

"It fits," was Will's answer.

Alex looked at Lea, but she shrugged.

"Crimson," Will said, grinning, "worked the computer."

She smiled. "So you're the guy who made this job so easy." She shook his hand vigorously. "It's a pleasure to meet you."

Alex shrugged. "It isn't like I did all that much."

"Are you kidding?" She motioned around them. "We got all this because of you."

"It was going to happen with or without me," Alex protested.

"Sure, but easily half the cargo would have gotten damaged while fighting security. We got no damage this time around— well, except for the crate those two idiots managed to drop on themselves. We've never had such a successful haul."

Alex blushed. He'd been thanked and congratulated for his work by a lot of the crew, but this was the first time he got to see the impact of what he'd done. Although, now that he thought about it, each person who'd thanked him might have died if he hadn't been there, so he had seen the impact from the start.

"I'm just worried that we're going to get used to having you around to help. We're going to get lazy, and the day you're not here, we're really going to pay for it."

"So, next time I should let some guards slip past me? To keep you on your toes and all?"

She grinned. "Don't do that. Just tell me when you're leaving so I can jump ship and go with you. I don't like getting shot at."

"When I leave it isn't to go to another ship. Once I've found Jack, we're settling down."

"Really?" she studied him. "You're just going to take your cut and run? Never heard of anyone actually leaving the life like that. Plenty talk about it, but they always end up sticking around."

"What do you mean, my cut?"

"Doesn't he know how this works?" she asked Will.

"Didn't explain. He's a passenger. Wasn't gonna do no nothing."

"Explain what?" Alex asked.

"You're entitled to a share of all this," Lea said, indicating the hold. "We all get an even share once I'm done appraising it."

Will snorted. "Some more even than us."

"The captain is entitled to more," she said. "He's the one who made all of it happen."

"What Anders do? Gabriella? Joe? Mitchel? Jo—"

"Okay, okay," she interrupted him. "So, some get more, but I'm not going to complain on a haul like this. We're all going to get rich."

"What exactly was on the ship?" Alex asked.

"Plenty of stuff. Antiques, computers, house stuff... Oh, and we actually got some wine this time."

"What so uncommon about wine? Plenty of it passes through my father's warehouses."

Will chuckled. "Got conned."

Alex looked to Lea for an explanation. He didn't feel like having to parse his friends' truncated speech.

"We picked you up at our last stop, right?"

"Deleron Four, yeah."

She nodded. "The ship we attacked before that was

supposed to carry valuable wines, the really rare stuff. It went well enough, got every crate back here, and only lost a quarter of them to damage. Not as good as if Crimson had been there to help—" she grinned, "—but good enough. Anyway, I get started on the inventory and appraisal once everything's quiet, but instead of crates of wine, we have grapes."

"You mean unfermented wine? Grape juice?"

"Not even that—just grapes, the fruit. Little ball-shaped things."

"How did anyone confuse grapes for wine?"

"We didn't. The manifest clearly stated they were carrying wine. Even the tags said it was wine."

"But it was really grapes?" Alex remembered a comment about wine at some point.

"Yep, in preservation boxes."

"So, it was an error on loading?" Those had happened when he worked at his father's warehouse, but he didn't recall it ever being on the scale of an entire cargo.

"That, or it was a scam, and we got to them before they were going to 'officially' be attacked and lose the cargo. All I know is that the captain was pissed, and we had to act like the merchants we claim to be. I can't remember the last time we sold cargo on the open market. The stuff we have is usually too easy to identify for that."

"I guess that's the risk of piracy. You can't go back and complain about not getting what you were after."

Lea grinned. "Yeah, but that's not the biggest risk. Getting shot is. At least without you around."

Alex blushed again. "You said you'd gotten computers, what kind? If they're good enough, I'd like to grab some. Asyr's lab is decent, but the stuff there's old.

"Sure, I'll deduct their value from your share." She leaned back against the crate and began a search on her datapad. After five minutes, Alex wondered what was taking so long, and he glanced over her shoulder.

She was manually looking at each line.

"Why don't you run a search function?"

"No. The damned thing's crazy. I'll ask for computers, and

I'll end up with a crate of tomatoes, if it brings anything at all. Last time I tried it, it dropped a crate on me. I was lucky to jump out of the way in time. I spent days cleaning up pebbles after that."

"You've stolen pebbles?"

"No, statues. Some old things from a lost planet or something. But they were stone. You drop that from high enough and pebbles are all you have left."

Alex looked up at the ceiling he couldn't see; just how high was it?

"Don't worry," Lea said. "The grappler's locked right now." She paused. "Well, it should be."

"You know I've been working on healing the ship's system right?"

"Really? Haven't noticed any improvements."

"I've just been working on the central processor for now, but I'm at the point where I can start integrating other systems in. If you want, I can start with the hold's inventory management. It's a fairly simple system, so it shouldn't cause a relapse."

She looked up from the tablet. "If you manage that, I'll give you half my share."

"I'll help!" Will piped up.

She grinned at him. "You don't count, short stuff."

Alex hid his smile. "The downside is that I'll have to take the system offline while I'm working on it. You're looking at a few days without being able to move anything about."

"That's okay," she said, going back to her search. "I'll bring down enough crates to appraise to last me while you do that. It isn't like we're going anywhere until I'm done."

"Why not?"

"The captain needs to know how much everything's worth before we can sell it. He said to do the appraisal on this side of cryo this time."

"Why not do it while the rest of us is in cryo instead? I get you'd age more, but it'd only be by a couple of weeks, right?"

Lea shuddered. "I'm not staying up alone." She lowered her voice. "This place gets creepy when everyone's under."

"Haunted," Will said.

"You're joking."

"No," Lea replied. "Didn't anyone tell you about it?" She looked to Will.

"Passenger," the younger man said, as if that answered it.

"Well, I heard this one from a guy I know. His wife had to do some repair while we were under. She told him the ship spoke to her. It tried to get her to kill herself."

Alex rolled his eyes. "Come on, your friend was putting you on."

"Not my friend, just some guy I know," she said.

"Bunkmate I knew," Will said, speaking slowly. "Woke up in middle of trip. Bed worked wrong. Got lost in halls, doors not working. Walked around for days. Only door that worked was airlock."

"Come on, that can't happen. Where is he now?"

"Left. Didn't take cut, just left once docked. Never saw him after."

"Everyone has a story like that," Lea said.

"It just can't happen. Do you have any idea the numbers of safeguards and redundancies there are on a ship like this?"

"All true," Will said.

Alex knew they were putting him on, they had to be. Taking control of a handful of systems was one thing, but for someone to turn a ship murderous? It couldn't be done. It just couldn't be. The safeguards to preserve life were embedded in the core programming, when the computer was built. It wasn't something that could be modified by any outside forces.

He spent the next fifteen minutes trying to explain why their stories made no sense, and then he decided it wouldn't do any good. Unless they knew ship programming, it would simply be his word against that of those who'd claimed to have gone through it.

When he heard movement above him, Alex looked up and then hurried to the side of a shelf, away from the large claw bringing down a crate. He was amazed at how large it was: twenty-feet high, at least.

Lea hooked a ladder to the side and climbed on it. Alex checked the display, but all he got was an identifier code that meant nothing to him. He heard a hatch open, and a moment later Lea reappeared with a box half her height, as wide as she was, and almost a foot thick.

"Get ready," she said, leaning it against the ladder's sides and lowering it. Alex caught the bottom, brought it down, and looked the box over for any identifying marks. All he found was the brand name: Kaldary.

He smiled, knowing he'd take this.

"Well?" Lea asked.

"Give me a minute; I need to figure out which model this is.

"Big," Will commented.

Alex found the seam and unsealed it. "Yeah, this isn't just a terminal, it's an entire system, display, processors, connectors, everything needed to incorporate it into an existing setup."

"Any good?"

Alex grinned at him. "It's a Kaldary. Even if those are all rejects, I'm going to want one." He pulled out the display and turned it over, then whistled.

"Lea?" he called. "Are they all the same?" he asked, already confident of the answer. There had only been one identifier code.

"According to the manifest, yeah. Why?"

"You're going to want to let anyone on the ship who has even a passing interest about this know. They're C-348s."

"So?"

He looked up at her, grinning. "They weren't on the market when we left Deleron Four. You scored the most recent version of a top of the line system. The people I worked with would kill for them—well, figuratively."

"Will, pass the word along."

A thought occurred to Alex as he put the display back. "Actually, you might want to talk to the captain too. If there's a decent hardware engineer on the ship, once I'm done healing the computer, these can be used to boost its capability."

"Will?" she asked.

"Sure thing," he answered.

"So, you'll take one?" Lea asked him.

"One? Hell, I want four of them if my cut allows. I'm really going to upgrade Asyr's console with them."

"That's ship upgrade," Will said.

"What does that mean?"

Lea came down the ladder. "It means they don't come out of your cut. Anything that's an actual upgrade is just taken out."

"Okay." Alex looked at the box. "I'm not sure how I'll get four of them to the lab."

"Don't worry about it. I'll have them transferred there, and Asyr can help you install them; she knows that stuff."

Alex was surprised; he didn't know anyone who knew both programming and hardware installation. He watched as Lea drove over a cart with a smaller claw, and she moved boxes out of the crate to the cart. She disappeared with them, and came back with a cart that looked identical, except it didn't have the claw. He followed her as she slowly drove that out of the hold and through the corridors.

The terminal at the intersection caught his eyes, and he stopped while Lea continued on. What they'd said bothered him. He could see a system getting some glitches and doing things like making noises or not wanting to open some doors. Considering how screwed up this computer was, he was surprised there weren't any more instances of that, but to tell a crew member to kill herself? To lead someone to an airlock and try to get him to space himself?

He tapped the screen, waking it, and got a list of maps, search functions, and environmental controls. He didn't remember seeing that on such terminals before. Not that he'd used any of them after his first week. He'd learned just how unreliable they were when he tried to learn the ship's layout.

He went through more of the options, and it brought up power consumption, engine output, and capacitor charges. Those were strange things to be on a hall terminal, but there had to be a reason they were there. He wasn't an engineer, after all.

He entered a series of commands and the interface vanished, letting him see all the code, which as he expected, was a chaotic jumble. It took him ten minutes to restructure the view to something he could work with. No actual changes to the system, just adjustments to how it displayed information. Then it was fifteen minutes of searching for where the safeguards were coded.

He knew where they were on the Luminex system, not that they were as extensive as they'd be here. That system only controlled climate controls, power distribution, and some of the security functions. Here there would be more of them.

Only, he wasn't finding any.

As a way of double checking, he located the airlock functions and confirmed they were working. Doors could open and close, air could be pumped in and sucked out, the sensors could tell when someone was in, and if they were in a suit, but there weren't any overrides preventing the outside door from opening if someone wasn't wearing a functioning suit.

Alex felt his stomach drop when he located a command that specifically ordered the airlock to cycle if it detected someone without a suit in it. He'd have to report that to the captain, he thought as he modified it. He didn't erase it since he wanted to show him it was there; if they had someone on the ship sabotaging airlocks, they had to be identified.

He was about to bring up the interface to send the captain a message when the command rewrote itself, removing the snippets of code he'd added to neuter it.

It took Alex a moment to react to it. He could only do a cursory check, but he was confident there wasn't anyone else in the code. So, who had removed his added safeguards? He erased the command entirely.

It rewrote itself.

Still no indication it had been an outside action; he couldn't even see programs someone might have left there to ensure the program wasn't tampered with. He erased it again, and as before, the command rewrote itself. There was no outside influence, which meant it was internal, but there weren't any programs there, just the usual antibodies.

"That's impossible."

He put his earpiece in and the scream that came from it, once it connected, threw him to the ground. He ripped it out of his ear and the end was covered in blood.

Not caring about the pain or the blood, he went back to the screen and tracked down commands and subcommands. Antibodies couldn't be hijacked; they were hard-coded into the processor, so the only thing that could change them was the processor itself.

He had to find out which of the major processors controlled that system at the moment, because if it was so insane it had managed to remove its safety protocols and added some to purposely injure the crew, it had to be shut down immediately.

After ten minutes he had his answer. Airlock, doors, hall terminals, as well as the other usual systems for it were all controlled by the engineering processor.

The only reason it hadn't blown up the ship was that it still had a survival instinct. It also couldn't blow up some of its hardware to hurt people since that would both hurt it and draw attention to what it was doing.

At least it was only minor stuff it could do; it wasn't like it could void the ship or pump it full of carbon monoxide...

Alex cursed silently and brought the interface back up. Environmental controls were on it.

In his hurry to bring back automation to the life support system, he'd given it to the engineering processor. The fact that they weren't all dead right now meant that it hadn't worked out the extent of what it had access to.

He needed to fix this right now.

CRIMSON

CHAPTER 21

"No."

Alex stared at the man seated behind the desk. "Didn't you listen to anything I said?"

"I did. You said you had to transfer control of life support to the engineering computer. That was months ago, and nothing has gone wrong with it."

"That system's insane. It's connected to most of the hall controls and it's been using that to try to get people to kill themselves."

"Ghost stories show up on every ship. Idiosyncrasies in systems that people don't expect, minor defects. Boredom and paranoia."

"Sir, this isn't any of that." Alex went to the captain's desk and turned the display on. Before the man could protest, Alex removed the interface and showed him the underlying code. He didn't have to do much more than that for the danger the code posed to become visible, now that he knew what to look for. "See?"

"Mister Crimson, all I see are a bunch of lines of programming. I wouldn't know what they did if the user's file came with it. You're the computer-talker, not me." The captain turned the display off.

"Damn it!"

The man raised an eyebrow.

"I'm sorry." Alex moved back to sit in one of the chairs opposite the captain. "Look, you say I'm the expert, so why won't you believe me? It's just a question of time before everything unravels. My guess is that the engineering system hasn't figured out what the life support system's for yet, but the moment it does, it's going to use it against the crew. It actively wants you dead."

"There are a few problems with what you're saying. You are attributing a personality where all that exists are system glitches." Alex opened his mouth, but a glare from the captain kept him from interrupting. "I'm willing to admit there are problems with this ship. It's old and has been through a lot without the maintenance it deserves, but computers don't want things, even if I believed it could think like I do. How can it not know what life support does? It's in the name."

Alex waited a moment to make sure he was done. "The name is a human convention; it doesn't show up in the code. From the system's side, it's just commands and controls. And it doesn't know what life is. Engineering doesn't have anything to do with maintaining life, so there aren't any explicit descriptions. The safeguards are just things not to do, or what-if statements as to when to do something, but it's removed them."

He took a breath. "As for not wanting things. Computers aren't dumb machines. You don't see it because they act through the interface, and yours has been so partitioned that yeah, until I started healing the core system, the intelligence of what you interacted with could be argued, but yes, computers want things. It's in their base code. They want to perform their function, they want for their programs to run smoothly. They don't want to feel pain."

The captain smirked.

190

"It's not pain like we feel it, but that's how it registers to them when their code gets corrupted, and believe me, they will not shut up about it once it starts."

Alex straightened. "Turn your display on."

"Why?"

"Just do it." Alex took out the earpiece from his pocket.

"Mister Crimson, I'm not in the habit of taking orders from a passenger, even if he helped make me a lot of money."

"You want proof computers can think? That they want things? Turn it on, and put this in your ear. You'll get your evidence."

The captain took the earpiece from Alex, looked it over. The small plug-shaped item wasn't impressive, and the blood on it didn't help. The man pulled out a cloth from a pocket, dabbed it in his drink, and cleaned the blood off. He turned the display on. The interface was back, and he put the device in his ear.

"Now what?" he asked.

Alex didn't say anything. The earpiece was attuned to the system, so it wouldn't take more than a second for...

The captain frowned. "What is this? I'm Meron Corvoy, the captain of this ship. Who is this?"

The interface was replaced with a long scroll of code.

"Is this a joke?" the captain asked, eying Alex. "Fine, if you're really the computer, prove it."

The display turned off.

"What just happened?" the captain asked.

"The core processor isn't currently connected to anything that can do much. So, shutting itself down is the only thing it can really do."

Someone banged on the door.

The captain opened it from his desk.

Murray poked in, a panicked expression on his face. "We have a problem; nothing's working. We lost maneuvering controls, communication, weapons. Everything, Captain. It just winked out; none of the boards are responding."

The captain went to reply, but his display came back on.

Someone from the bridge yelled. "Systems are back up!"

Murray looked over his shoulder, then back to the captain.

"I-I'm sorry sir, I guess it was nothing then."

"It's alright, Mister Murray. Go back to your post."

The door closed. "Isn't maneuvering something controlled by engineering?" the captain asked. "I'm not talking to you." He took the earpiece out.

Alex tried not to smile. "The main processor is in the bridge; it's the interface between it and all other systems. When it shut itself down, the bridge stopped working. The engines kept going, but you lost control of them."

The captain rubbed his eyes. "Alright. Let's say I believe you. I still can't simply let you shut down engineering. You might have forgotten about it, but we stole a ship's cargo not three days ago. They're still chasing us. We have a good lead on them, and it's getting wider, but they are after us. If I take away our ability to change course, to put some of the stellar rocks in our path to confuse them, they'll catch us and then you won't make it to Samalia."

"Sir, we still might not make it. It's just a question of time be—"

"Before the engineering computer figures out how to murder all of us, yes. I was listening. But I still can't let you take it offline. It's going to be a couple of weeks before I'm confident they'll have given up the chase. You can do it then.

"Weeks? I'm not sure—"

"Mister Crimson, this is my ship. If you hadn't contributed so much to this latest job, I wouldn't have sat here listening to you. I'd have sent you back to your cabin. You're a passenger, not part of my crew. I don't have to be this courteous to you. In a few weeks, I'll have Murray find a quiet and safe place for us to hide while you do what you need to do. Is that understood?"

Alex had the irrational urge to scream, "you'll be sorry", to the man's face, wrench the earpiece out of his hand, and storm off. Instead, he nodded and stood.

"I hope we have that kind of time, sir." He extended his hand, and the captain handed him the earpiece.

"If you're so worried about this, isn't there anything you can do in the meantime? To prepare, if nothing else?"

"I'll have the Kaldarys setup, but that shouldn't take more

than two days. I can't do much more. The moment I try to wrestle the life support away from it, the engineering system is going to go on the attack and things are going to get bad on the ship until it's resolved." Alex turned.

"Mister Crimson."

He turned back.

"I hope you understand that this doesn't mean I don't respect you or your capabilities, but I have to deal with what I believe is the more important threat."

Alex nodded. "I don't think you understand how much of a threat the engineering system is, sir. And I don't know how to demonstrate that, short of showing it what life support is for and unleashing it. That wouldn't solve anything. I'll see if there's anything else I can do to prepare, and I'll deal with it once you tell me I can."

* * * * *

It actually took four days for Asyr, with the help of two other engineers, to replace all the consoles with the new Kaldarys. Because of what he knew he'd have to do, Alex didn't simply upgrade the main console, but also the two auxiliary ones. He'd need backup on this.

He then realized that the entire lab was connected to the ship's power, which was controlled by the engineering processor. So it took a week for them to set up a power generator dedicated to it.

When they were done, Alex heard about the crewman who had almost died when he accidentally ruptured one of the power generator's coolant lines and breathed in the cooling mix. It had happened three days before. Since there, the repair crews had been chasing an unexplained fault in the life support system that caused it to randomly dump the same mix in halls and rooms.

Alex didn't need to look at the code to know what was going

on. He told the captain, who didn't believe him, so he sat at the console, waiting for the one event the captain wouldn't be able to ignore.

Powerless to do anything about it, Alex waited for someone to die.

Chapter 22

"What does Zack's death have to do with engineering?" Anders asked, picking up on the least-relevant part, Alex thought.

"It's what killed him," Alex answered as he indicated where the two men Anders had brought with him were to sit.

"I thought it was a faulty valve or something. Filled his room with poison."

"And locked him in there. The door locks are also part of the systems the engineering processor controls."

"Doors jam all the time, doesn't mean—"

"Anders," Alex snapped. "I don't have the time for this. Once it's all over I'll spend the hours needed answering all your questions, but right now I need you out of here."

The man bristled, and Alex took a breath.

"Look, I'm grateful you found me two programmers, but now I need to show them what I expect of them. That's going to take longer than I'd like, and someone else might die during that time, so I really need to get back to work. You have your oxygen?"

Anders unclipped a cannister at his back and showed it to Alex.

"Good. If you want to do something to help, go around and make sure no one is in a room that can be locked and that everyone has their oxygen. I have no way to know what the processor will do once I start, so everyone needs to be prepared."

Alex thought he saw anger in the man's eyes for a moment, but he nodded and left.

"I don't know how much I'll be able to help," The man seated to the left of where Alex was standing said. "I tried to tell Anders, but I don't really know code. I dabble in game building, that's about it."

"Dennis, right?"

"Dennis Armitage."

Alex thought for a moment. "You can read code?"

"Sure. Anyone can do that if they spend long enough looking at it."

Alex moved to the central console. His console, the one he'd upgraded with four Kaldary systems connected together. They gave him almost as much power as what the core processor had. The auxiliary stations only had one since they only acted as backup. Alex had added a third station, a temporary one, behind his.

"I'm giving you watch-only access. Your job is going to keep track of what life support does. Try to predict where it's going to dump coolant and make sure no one's there."

"You weren't kidding? Zack's death wasn't an accident?"

"Dennis, I already told Anders we don't have the time. You can sit in on the explanation later. Get familiar with the code."

"Luigi?" he turned to the other man.

"Yep."

"How are your programming skills?"

"Rusty. Haven't used them in years, but I went through the full course. Had to quit weeks before the end of year."

"I'm sorry to hear that," Alex said, setting up the man's console for full access. "Family emergency?"

Asyr snorted. "He burned down the teacher's house."

196

Alex looked up.

"She deserved it; she was just a pretentious bitch."

"You burned down her house because you didn't like her?" Alex couldn't believe the length someone could do to be—

"I killed the bitch. Burning down her house was just so the others would know not to mess with me."

Alex gasped, then decided this was a subject best ignored. "I'm sending you my program arsenal. Get comfortable with them, because your job is going to be to protect anything I change; the system is going to do its best to undo my work. You have a headset, it's the best I can do for you."

He turned to the woman seated behind him. "Asyr, you know your job?"

"Shadow you, watch your back. Keep the system from attacking your connection directly."

"If you see anything coming you can't deal with, tell me. This isn't a test, it's our lives. That goes for both of you too. If you can't handle something, for whatever reason, shout. I wish I'd thought to ask Anders to find you two earlier, because we really need weeks to figure out how to work together, but this is the situation we're in."

He leaned back in his chair and closed his eyes. He thought about asking the universe for help, but his mother's words came to him then. "*The universe doesn't give a damn about you. You don't matter to it, so you better learned to handle your own problems.*'"

Well, he was going to handle this.

"Will, where are you?" he called on the comm.

"Coming," was the answer, and a moment later his friend entered the room with energy bars and drinks for everyone.

"Will, your job is to keep us stocked with bars and drinks. There's no way to know how long this is going to last. We could get lucky and be out of here in an hour, or we could be here for two days. We won't be able to leave our stations until this is all done, so I hope none of us are wearing their best pants."

"Will do." Will answered.

"Days?" Dennis asked.

"Potentially. Once this starts, we can't stop."

"I better go deal with something."

Alex nodded. "Hurry up."

The man ran out.

"Oxygen," Will said, indicating the canister at Alex's feet.

"Thanks." He saw that Asyr and Luigi had theirs, and noted for Dennis to grab his as he came back a few minutes later.

He took out his earpiece and placed it down on the console. He wouldn't be using it this time. He hadn't done code-only coercion since leaving school. His teachers had always joked that Alex would prefer talking a system into submission than coding it there, but he couldn't talk to this system. Doc had healed his eardrum, but Alex had no doubt he'd suffer the same fate if he tried again. He didn't know if it was a defense mechanism or just a sign of its insanity, but that scream would still be there, he was sure of it.

"Okay, get ready people. We're about to go to war."

"I'm ready," Asyr answered.

"There," Luigi replied.

Alex looked at Dennis. The man seemed to feel the gaze and turned. "Do I have a choice?"

"Not really, sorry."

The man nodded, squared his shoulders, and faced his display. "I'm ready then."

Alex sent a thought to Jack, wherever he was, and cursed silently when his face had Tristan's hard eyes in his mind. He pushed that away. He couldn't afford the distraction. If he survived this, he'd see Jack eventually, and deal with Tristan.

He began coding.

His plan was to isolate life support again. It had been simple enough to do the first time, but then that processor hadn't been using it as a weapon. This wouldn't be so easy. He worked slowly, trying his best not to attract the engineering processor's attention while he looked for life support components.

He wished he could have brought the core processor into this, and a fourth backup would have been good, but the engineering systems were the second most powerful on the ship, and if those two talked, Alex wasn't confident the core processor could keep from being overwhelmed by the insanity.

Hours passed while he tagged pieces of code as belonging to life support. The engineering processor had completely dismantled it, spread the code about. It kept everything working, but Alex couldn't fix this by quickly walling-off chunk of code.

"There are a lot of antibodies about," Asyr said.

Alex looked about and saw what she had: something had noticed his tagging. They weren't swarming it, so they didn't consider that a threat, but if they noticed *him*, all bets were off.

He tried to come up with a quick way to resolve this once he'd tagged every part of the system, but he couldn't. He'd have to build the wall and then transfer the code there.

"Luigi, find a quiet part of the network and wall it off. There should be a program to help with that."

"Yep, got it. Working on it."

"Everything's good here," Dennis said.

That won't last long, Alex thought.

"Wall's up."

Alex had to make a choice. He could continue tagging and hope the antibodies wouldn't become aware of him until he had everything, but if they did become aware, the system would know what he was targeting and act to keep that out of his reach. Or he could start moving what he considered the critical parts behind the wall now, and hope it would sufficiently reduce the processor's ability to hurt them enough so they could keep going.

"Something's happening," Asyr said.

No choice now. He sent the coolant controls behind the wall and left quick and dirty code behind in the hopes that could fool the antibodies for a while.

"It's got your connection!" Asyr yelled.

With a curse, Alex went on the defensive, taking down the barricade that was coming up around him.

Dennis spoke, but in soft, calm tones. Alex tuned him out. Luigi cursed, but no alarm there either.

"It's blocking other connections!"

"Mine's still good," Luigi said, "but fuck, I don't know how long that's going to last."

Alex was discovering that human voices weren't the same as system sounds. He'd trained to work through the later, but this was proving a strain. He wanted to tell them to shut up, but they needed to communicate with him and each other, so he'd have to learn how to deal with it.

The best way was to give them less to talk about, so he had to make himself the larger problem. He could do this. The system was fast, but it was still just a system, bound by its programming. Alex didn't have any programming dictating his actions. He could do the unexpected.

With a malicious grin, he unleashed every program he'd ever designed on the system, then used the confusion to attack the processor itself.

Forget cutting it up, forget dumbing it down. Alex was going to alter its personality directly, impose his will on the damn thing.

He heard someone laughing. He thought it sounded a little unhinged.

He was the one laughing.

There was banging on the door.

"Put your masks on," Dennis said.

Alex looked to his feet, but the canister wasn't there. Had he kicked it away? He didn't have the time to worry about it. The system had figured out where they were. It couldn't cut the power, he'd seen to that, so it was going to cut off their air.

How long did he have? A quick glance around told him the other three had theirs on, so one person, in a room this size. There was enough air for a while, right? Was that enough?

How the hell was he supposed to know?

He gave up on the system and went after the door lock; that was what the banging was, Will on the other side of the door. If he could open it, they'd have air.

He found it quickly, wrapped in layer after layer of code to keep him out. In making sure he wouldn't get to it, the system had shone a spotlight on it.

Alex dove in, dissecting code with abandon. The banging intensified, but Alex didn't care. Strands of code flew about. He was getting through.

"Yes!" He was in.

But there was nothing.

Alex stared at the empty space, not a single line of code. He'd been tricked.

How much air had he used to get through that? He didn't know. He forced himself to go back on the hunt. It had to be around there somewhere. He searched, and found nothing. He glanced at the earpiece and thought about putting it on just so he could scream his frustration at the system.

What happened when you ran out of air? The thought popped up unbidden. Was it like drowning? Would he convulse? It was a good thing he didn't know how close he was to that; it made it easier to ignore.

He almost stopped coding when something slipped over his face. Dennis smiled at him. "Luigi said you're more important than me. He's right. Things have gone to shit everywhere on the ship. I might as well just sit back and wait for you to save us." He clipped the canister to Alex's belt.

Alex nodded. He no longer had to worry about suffocating, in the short run at least. The oxygen canister gave him twelve hours of air, but without a refill he was back to being in trouble. He'd counted on Will to bring them fresh ones.

He cursed, he needed to unlock that door. He couldn't just let the system beat him, he had—

Unlock.

That was code.

He wrote a quick search program with parameters to look for any code that locked something, and he made it so it would look at every code, even hidden ones. Then he copied his replicator program a dozen time and gave it that code. Within seconds, thousands of search programs were loose in the system.

He wrote another program and set it aside.

As he expected, the antibodies went after his search programs, but he knew how to put that to a stop. He went back to attacking the processor. Let it try to stop the search when something more dangerous was going on.

"You just try and hide the lock from me, you bastard," he

growled.

As he fought to change code faster than the antibodies could fix them, he saw something change color in the distant code. One of his search programs had found something: another dot of color, in a different section, then another, and more of them, all over the place.

There were a lot of locks on this ship.

He continued paying attention as he attacked the processor, and the rate of change in color slowed as there remained fewer and fewer locks to find. When it stopped, Alex waited ten seconds to make sure there was nothing left. He gave his second program to the replicator, and watched it spread. It was a simple program, one line of code that translated to 'unlock'.

He heard people burst into the room, and gave up on his attack against the processor to go back to finding and walling off the life support code. He saw Jennifer go to Dennis, and Will passed in his field of vision, quickly vanishing. Voices he didn't recognize complained, but he ignored them. He was on the clock now more than ever. He'd unlocked the oxygen, but what else had he unlocked? Had he released the coolant ship-wide?

There was a reason a ship like this usually had specialized programmers. Alex had no idea what kind of damage his actions might have caused, again. He just had to hope the captain would still like him when this was all over. He really didn't want to be spaced.

Alex knew time passed, because someone changed his oxygen canister. His progress was slow; the system fought hard to keep control of each of the life support code segments Alex went after, but Alex consistently won those fights.

Alex didn't realize he was done until Asyr pulled his hands away from the board. He looked up at her, she nodded, and exhaustion took him away.

Chapter 23

Alex knew he was out of cryo by the way his body hated him. He stifled the groan. For all that he hated having to wake out of cryo, he wished he could spend each night in it. He didn't dream there.

He heard movement and forced an eye open, only to shut it on seeing Will up and about, wiping the surfaces of shelves. Right, dust had accumulated over the months they'd been in cryo.

"Fuck," Alex croaked. "How do you do it? Be full of energy right out of cryo?"

"Used to it. In and out since a baby."

"So, I'll get used to it?"

Will shrugged.

"Great."

He tried to remember the last few moments before going under. Will and Asyr had brought him to his bed right after he was done wrestling life support from engineering, and connected the armbands. He'd been afraid of going under, of what the engineering processor would do to the ship without him to look over its code, but he was awake—well, trying to be—so nothing catastrophic had happened.

"Did anyone get hurt?"

"Few. Small stuff. Doc fixed them before cryo."

Alex nodded, then forced his eyes to open. The armband on his bicep was blinking green, so he took it off. It and the tubes went in the compartment in the wall, and he forced his legs over the side. The queasiness was due to cryo, he told himself, not what he'd had to do, not to the people that had gotten hurt because of it. He had to get back to work.

But first, he needed a shower.

* * * * *

Alex loaded the message on his datapad. It hadn't been easy to get it, just like he expected the message node he'd used to transmit to his grandparents had been swarming with surveillance programs. Trackers, lockdowns, parasites. Someone had gone through the list and deployed all of them. He felt a little flattered, actually.

But he'd managed to maneuver around all of them. The few he had to neutralize, he did so in a way that kept others from noticing. He even convinced the node to copy the message to him, instead of transferring it, that way those monitoring the node wouldn't even know he had gotten it. After running the sixth disinfection program on the message, he finally brought it up and ran it.

A man with graying brown hair appeared. He was seated in the living room—Alex could see the shelves with pictures of their family over his grandfather's shoulder.

"Hello, Alex." He paused. "I don't know how to go about recording this. First off, you should know the Law came here to ask about you. That was before we received your message, so we didn't lie when we told them we didn't know anything about where you might be. They said you stole corporate property, and that you might have been involved in attacking them. Just what are you mixed in, Alex? You said you met someone—is he who attacked the corporation? The Law didn't give any details, other than it was an alien that did the attack. Did you get pulled into it against your will? Was your interest in them used to make you do something you wouldn't have otherwise?

"I'm sorry, I don't mean to sound accusatory. You know we love you and we'll do anything we can to help you. Having said that, I don't think it's a good idea for you to contact us again; the Law is sure to be looking over our communications from now on. I wouldn't want to be responsible for them finding you. Me and your grandma love you. If you show up at our doorstep, we will take you in."

The message ended.

* * * * *

"Hey, Crimson."

Alex glanced over his shoulder and went back to looking at the code. "Anders," he answered as a greeting, then added, "I didn't expect to see you in this part of the ship outside of an emergency."

"Well, this is sort of one."

Alex sighed. "What happened?" He'd spent the last week integrating life support with the central processor, and while it had gone smoothly, it had trouble actually figuring out how to run it, and there had been mishaps ever since. Nothing major, but each time he had to convince the processor it didn't have to micromanage the system.

"Here's the thing. We've been at dock for a full day, and you've spent all that time cooped up in this room. Isn't this your first time on another station? You need to come and see the sights."

Alex shrugged. "That can wait. I'll have plenty of time to see sights once I'm with Jack."

"Nope, sorry, but that doesn't work for me." Alex felt the man stand behind his chair. "Are you in the middle of anything life-threatening?"

"Not really, but I need to start reintegrating systems. I'm going through them, figuring out how insane the isolation made them. I figure I'm going to do it from the least crazy one up. That's going to put as little strain on the processor, and build it up to better deal with the less stable ones."

Anders patted Alex's shoulder. "I have no idea what that means, and don't bother trying to explain; I don't care about it. But you did confirm it wasn't vital, right?"

Alex hesitated for a moment. "I guess so."

"Good." The hand closed around his arm and pulled him up. "You're coming with me. I'm taking you ground-side."

* * * * *

Alex didn't grumble during the shuttle trip. He worked very hard at not grumbling. He had better things to do than waste his time on a jaunt to some bar, no matter how good it was supposed to be.

He was almost thrown out of his seat when the shuttle landed, but he didn't grumble—much. The others laughed and commented on how the place needed better cushions.

They'd been waiting for them at the shuttle, Milo, a man barely out of his teens. From listening in on the conversation, he'd figured out he'd joined the crew on the stop before where Alex joined. He'd been looking to get away from abusive parents, or something to that effect.

Barbara was one of Anders's usual hangers-on, so he wasn't surprised to see her there, but the last one had been a man with golden skin and white mohawk. Alex had seen him on the ship—he was hard to miss—but before now hadn't known his name: Zephyr.

Alex got out of the shuttle, fully intending on getting back on as soon as the others were out of it, but he froze and found himself looking around at the dilapidated buildings.

"Where are we?"

"Junaly's Port," Anders answered, placing a hand on his back and pushing Alex forward.

"This isn't a port. It's nothing more than a field."

Anders laughed. "You think every planet is like where you're from? That was a capital world. This is a fourth-rate mining world with nothing to attract tourists. Barely anyone ever comes down from the station."

"Then why are we here?" Milo asked.

"Because," Zephyr answered, "in spite of how it looks, the richest fence in the universe lives here." He had a rich bass for a voice that made Alex shiver. "With the haul we got this time, it's the only place we can move it."

"That's fine, but why exactly are we here? There's plenty of places to get a drink on the station, and they have to be better than anything here."

"For one thing, we need to see a sky every so often," Anders answered. "You too, Crimson. You can't spend your life in a box. I'd think you more than any of us would appreciate that, since you were a ground-sider until recently." He began walking.

"A sky's a sky. I'll see plenty of it once I'm—"

"With your guy," Anders finished for him. "We know, you can't seem to shut up about it."

"Just look at it," Barbara said, awe in her voice. "It's beautiful. Do you have any idea how rarely we get to see one? We're not usually docked long enough to allow time for trips. Sometimes, I forget what color it is."

The golden-skinned man looked up and wrinkled his nose. "It's blue, what's so nice about that. You should see the ones back home: beautiful orange sky and purple clouds streaking it. Now that's worth looking at."

She snorted. "You're weird."

"No fighting you two," Anders admonished. "It's a big universe, there's plenty of sky for everyone's tastes."

"You're mightily jovial," Zephyr said, his tone suspicious.

"I'm just happy to be breathing unrecycled air. The one on the ship's been leaving a bit to be desired recently."

"Sorry," Alex said, his ears burning. "That's one of the reasons why I should have stayed on the ship."

"I'm not complaining, Crimson, just a statement of fact. But even then, this is better than any ship air. And because of you, this haul is going to take so long to move we can go to the best joint in this part of the universe."

"How do you know that?" Milo asked.

Anders placed an arm over the shoulders of the youngest of their group. "Because the last time I was here, I talked with the natives and they all raved about it." Anders began whistling and ignored the other questions Milo had.

Twenty minutes later, he stopped the group before a building that looked much like every other: gray walls with gray doors and no windows. Unlike the others, it was a squat, one-story thing, and wider. If it was a bar, there were no signs or other indications of that.

"Okay," Anders said. "Before we go in, I need a favor from the two of you."

"Sure," Milo said.

Alex raised an eyebrow.

"I need you to start a fight."

"Why?" Alex asked.

"Does it matter?"

Alex snorted. "Yes. I don't make a habit of starting fights for just any reasons. I don't particularly enjoy getting beaten up."

Anders smiled. "You're not going to get beaten up. Just start the fight and get out. We'll meet up with you—" he looked around, and pointed to a building, "—behind there."

"You're going to fight?" Milo asked.

"No, we need the distraction so we can slip in the back."

Alex groaned. "You're going to rob the place."

"Yeah," Barbara answered, grinning.

"I'm not having anything to do with that," Alex said.

"Come on, Crimson," Anders said.

"No! Damn it, Anders, I'm not a criminal."

Anders silenced Barbara and Zephyr with a raised hand before they said anything, and by their expression they had much to say about Alex's statement.

"I'm not asking you to commit any crimes. It's just a bar fight; nothing illegal with that. The three of us will be the ones breaking the law."

"Does the captain know about this?"

"I try not to bother him with inconsequential stuff like this."

"And what happens if you get caught?"

Anders smiled. "I never get caught."

Alex glared at the smug bastard. He tried to see if this was some scheme to hurt him. Anders had been cordial even since coming on to him, friendly even, but Alex wondered if that had been a ploy to get him to drop his guard. Even if it wasn't, Alex couldn't get involved in a crime. If they got caught, he'd be stuck here.

Alex turned to leave, and Anders stopped him by putting an arm around his shoulders.

"Don't be like that Cr—Alex. Nothing bad's going to happen, I promise."

"Damn it, I'm just a passenger. I'm not part of your gang."

"I know that. I just thought you could do with some fun. You've been—"

"Fun?" Alex glared at him. "You call a robbery fun?"

"Of course. Look, no one's going to get hurt...well, not much anyway. Brawls happen all the time in places like this; it's just part of the entertainment for them."

Alex didn't know how true that was. Alien-Nation, the only bar he'd frequented, wasn't like that, but every movie he'd ever watched that had a bar scene did tend to have a bar fight. That couldn't be an accurate representation of life.

"Come on," Anders continued. "Are you really going to let Milo do this by himself?"

Alex looked at the young man. He too seemed uncertain, so he could probably convince him to leave. Except, what would the others think of him? Milo was part of the crew, and working for Anders was probably a big deal. Unlike him, Alex would be gone soon enough, so he didn't have to worry about what people thought of him.

Or did he? Soon enough wasn't tomorrow, but months from now. Would the crew care he was just a passenger? He'd gained some respect from his help on the job, enough that other than grumbling about the injuries caused during his fight for the life support system, no one attempted any reprisals on him.

If he didn't do this for Anders, what would the others think? How would they behave if there was another incident with some of the ship's system? Would they believe he'd done everything he could to prevent it? Or would they remember he was an outsider on their ship?

He cursed under his breath. "Fine. But this is a one-time thing, Anders." He ignored the man's smile and looked at the building. "How the hell am I going to start a fight? I barely know how to fight."

Anders slapped his shoulder. "That's the spirit, and you'll think of something. You're resourceful." He faced the others, forcing Alex to turn too. "You and Milo go in first, get a drink, enjoy the atmosphere. When you see us enter, get the brawl going." He pushed Alex toward the door.

Milo was next to him, all smiles. "This is going to be fun."

"How do you know that?" Alex opened the door for the young man.

"Everyone knows Anders is the best. He's one of the captain's favorites, and with this, we're going to be in with his gang."

"I kind of wish he'd checked with me first."

Milo looked at him in surprise, and almost bumped into someone. "You don't want in? Why not? His gang gets the best of everything. They get an extra cut of the hauls, the best quarters. I even heard they have private parties with enhancers."

Alex didn't ask what that was. He found two available stools at the bar and took one.

"I'm not a party guy," he told Milo. And he definitely didn't want to be in a room with Anders where his judgment might be impaired. Anders had backed off when Alex had told him he was taken, but he didn't think that would stop him from trying again if he thought Alex might say yes that time."

Alex asked for something local when the barman was before him.

"You shouldn't use that," Milo said, ordering his own drink and handing over a credit stick.

"What?"

"You used your cred-chip. That leaves a tag of where you are."

"And that doesn't?" Alex indicated the stick the barman returned, along with their drinks.

"It's tricked up. Everyone on the crew has one. I guess you're too new, but if you just ask someone, they'll give you one." He grinned. "Ask Anders after this. Then transfer some money to it, but not too much. You don't want to lose everything if it gets stolen. Just enough for whatever you have planned."

Alex was considering explaining he wasn't part of the crew when he noticed motion by the entrance. Anders and the others were here. Alex swiveled on his stool and looked around.

The crowd looked rough, mostly men, in stained and worn clothing. They all looked strong and ready to pick a fight.

How was he supposed to do this? The movies made it look easy: push someone, insult someone's companion. The problem with those was that the guy always ended up hurt in the process. Also no one looked ready to give him an excuse to start the fight.

Then he smiled. There was one person here who he knew wouldn't hurt him. He spun to Milo.

"What did you just say?"

Milo sputtered in surprise, spilling some of his drink. "I—"

"Don't give me that." He shoved the young man off his stool and into the woman next to him.

The woman shouldered Milo away, but didn't do anything else.

"I didn't—" Milo raised his hand, looking like his confusion was real.

"I don't know how they raised you in the cesspool you call home, but where I'm from, you don't say that if you know what's good for you." Alex pushed him again, and this time Milo lost his balance as he was forced back. He fell on a table, tipping it over, sending drinks and game pieces flying. The man barely got out of the way in time to avoid having them spill over their legs.

Alex ignored their cursing. He pushed one out of the way as hard as he could before reaching down to grab Milo by the collar to pull him up.

"You better start fighting back," he whispered.

Milo looked at him in confusion for a moment, then punched him in the stomach.

Alex's plan to overreact to the impact wasn't needed as he staggered back, trying not to double over in pain. He backed up against someone, and that person shoved him. Alex turned and punched her. He barely got out of the way of the return punch.

The sound of glass and tables breaking filled the space. Alex was shoved and punched, and he struck back. He ducked under flying items. Curses and yells were added to the sound of breaking.

Alex struck someone in the back that was stumbling toward him. He dodged the man's reply, blocked a hard blow from someone that left his arm numb. But even with that pain, Alex found he just couldn't stop grinning.

He kept looking for Milo as he fought, and saw his back, limping toward the door, punching a woman on the way there.

Alex thought about staying—this was turning out to be more fun than he'd expected—but he reminded himself he couldn't get caught, so he weaved and bobbed through the crowd, exchanging a few punches before reaching the door.

The younger man was wiping blood off his face when Alex reached him behind the agreed upon building. Alex leaned against the building. His heart was racing, and he was in pain. He laughed, which earned him a stunned look from Milo. The young man looked like he might start crying.

Alex forced the laughter down. Why was he laughing anyway? He'd hurt people. He shouldn't be enjoying this; he wasn't like that. He wasn't like *him*, but he had enjoyed himself. The idea made him uncomfortable. He wasn't a violent man; he'd only gotten in one fight, when he was a kid, with another student, and his parents had grounded him for a month.

Looking back on it, he'd felt the fight had been a mistake, caused by his youth and out-of-control hormones. He tried to remember how he'd felt during the fight and about it, but it was so long ago. He knew being grounded had felt bad, but that was because that's what being punished did. He didn't actually remember feeling like that. Now he wondered if he was grounded not because he fought, but because he'd enjoyed fighting.

"Glad to see you two made it out okay," Anders said, not stopping as he, Barbara, and Zephyr walked by. The three of them looked proud of themselves.

Alex glanced at Milo, who looked back to him and shrugged, then pushed himself off the wall and followed. Alex winced as he walked, his foot hurting, but he didn't ask them to slow down. Looking at why, he realized he wanted to show he was as tough as they were, in spite of his weight.

"So?" Alex panted. "How much did you get?"

"Haven't counted it yet." Anders patted the box. "But there's got to be thirty in there."

Milo gasped. "What? I got beaten up for thirty lousy credits?"

"Thirty-thousand," Barbara said. "And for your part in this, you're getting three of them."

Milo beamed.

Alex only managed to keep his mouth shut for a few seconds. "That's what you call a fair cut? Milo clearly had the worst of the job."

Alex was distracted by Barbara glaring at him, and he almost walked into Anders when he stopped.

Anders turned and looked at Alex thoughtfully. "You know, I guess we should be splitting this evenly."

Barbara threw Anders a worried glance, while Zephyr didn't seem to care about the conversation.

Alex shrugged and walked around him, and Anders fell in step with him, going at his speed instead of the earlier faster pace.

"Six-thousand is enough for each of us, right? Thanks for

reminding me to be fair."

Alex glanced at him. "Are you saying no one's complained before?"

"I guess everyone's just used to doing what I say."

"And are you in the habit of giving them a chance not to?"

Anders looked thoughtful. "I guess I've gotten in the habit of ordering people about. I'm a little surprised you aren't pissed at me."

Alex sighed. "I should be, shouldn't I?" He shook his head in annoyance at himself. "Just don't blindside me with something like this again." He sighed again. "Look, I'm not saying I'll ever do this again, but if I do, I want to know what I'm going to get into first."

Anders studied him for a long moment, and was silent for the rest of their walk back to the port.

CHAPTER 24

No one paid attention to them when Alex followed Anders and the others into the lounge. In fact, Alex couldn't help feeling like those already there were careful not to notice them. That was the kind of power Anders held on this ship, that no one wanted to know what the man was up to.

Anders took a device Alex didn't recognize out of a cabinet, a boxy thing about a foot wide and half that deep with an empty cavity on the top portion, six inches deep. Anders slowly emptied the box of chips in it, and it immediately made noises.

Some sort of sorting machine, Alex realized, and it was confirmed when, a few seconds after the top was empty, the front opened and six stacks of chips were presented to them.

"It's as close to an even split as I can manage without having to go through the ship to transfer money around. The captain would find out about that, and ask for a cut." He grabbed a stack and handed it to Alex. "Six-thousand and a few hundred."

Alex took it without hesitating. He'd decided Anders was right; he'd helped with this, just like he'd helped with the heist before, so he did deserve a cut. The column was four inches high. He had no idea how many chips that gave him, but what he did know was that he didn't have a clip to put them in. He dumped them in his pocket, noting he'd have to ask Will about getting a clip for them, and his recommendation on how to carry his money discretely when off the ship, following Milo's advice. But he'd do that later.

He wished Anders and the others a good night. What time was it anyway? Alex did feel tired, and the sun had been going down when they left the planet, but the ship probably wasn't in the same time zone.

Wincing as he walked away, he thought he should see Doc about his leg, but that was something else to be dealt with later. Right now, all he wanted was to be alone. He needed time away from others after what he'd been a part of on the planet.

He entered his room, and was relieved Will wasn't there. His friend would leave if he asked, but then he'd want explanations, and Alex didn't feel like giving them. He kept the door from closing while he checked the lock panel. With almost everyone on the ship given leave while not doing the unloading, Doc had been forced t to lift her rule about Alex being escorted everywhere, but he was always worried she'd reactivate the auto-lock on the door when he wasn't looking. Just that he could access the panel told him he had control of the lock, but he still checked. Once satisfied, he let the door close and headed for his bunk.

He winced as he dropped to his knees to lift his bed. He reached in for the case next to his bag, and found nothing there. Alex stared for a moment. The Defender's case was gone. Not just that, everything other than his bag was gone.

It was an effort for Alex not to panic. Will had probably decided to clean under the bed, and moved everything elsewhere while he did that. Will could sometimes be like that, too focused on what he did to consider things like private property.

He looked under Will's bed, but that was empty too. Then he checked the entire room, even the bathroom. Nothing. He felt the panic crawling up. Where was the Defender? He couldn't have lost that; it had been a gift from Jack.

Ask Will, he told himself to hold the panic back. He'd know where he'd put it. He called up Will's name on the screen and it appeared, along with his occupation—janitor—but the location remained blank. Of course, the internal sensors were still isolated. He cursed. Why hadn't he fixed that already?

Who'd know where to find him? The only person Alex could think of was Doc. She always seemed to know where Will was, so he hobbled his way to her.

"Where's Will?" he asked, entering, not caring that she was busy closing a cut on a woman's arm.

She looked at him over her shoulder, and nodded toward the bed next to her.

"I don't have the time, where is he?"

She looked at her work, and nodded with satisfaction. "You're good to go." She indicated the other bed again. "Sit, I need to look you over. What happened to you?"

"I don't have the time!"

She raised an eyebrow, and Alex forced himself to calm down. "I'll let you check me over after, but right now I need to talk to him. It's urgent."

"Haven't you called him?"

Alex stared at her, dumbfounded. Of course, how could he have been such an idiot? He patted his pockets, looking for his comm unit. Where was it? Asyr's lab. He'd taken it out of his jacket when he'd sat down to work. Anders had dragged him out before he'd thought to grab it. Damn it!

"Will, where are you?" Doc asked in her comm as Alex turned to rush to the lab.

"Deck eight," Will answered. "Corridor three, aft section."

Alex bolted. By the time he reached the eighth floor, he was cursing at the pain, and he had to slow to a walk. His panic wanted him to go back to running, but Alex didn't think falling down would get him the Defender back any faster.

He heard the cleaner before he reached the corridor, and again he felt the urge to run. He even took a rapid step, but his leg almost buckled. He made it to the intersection, saw Will in the distance, and yelled his name.

On the third one, his friend noticed and shut the machine down. Alex motioned for him to come closer; he didn't think he could walk the distance.

"Where's my case?" Alex asked when Will was still a dozen steps away.

The younger man gave him a quizzical expression.

"It was under my bed."

Will shook his head. "My stuff. Took it."

Alex grabbed him by the collar and shoved him against the wall. "My case was in there."

"Just your bag." Will was looking at him, worried.

Good, Alex thought. *If he thought he could get away with stealing, he was mistaken.* He leaned in closer.

"It was next to my bag," Alex growled.

Will started shaking his head, then paused. A moment later his face turned pale. He broke out of Alex's grip and ran.

Alex chased after him, cursing himself for ever trusting the man. Pain lanced up his leg, but he ignored it as best as he could. By the time he reached the intersection Will had turn into, the young man was already turning the other one. With a curse Alex kept going, reminding himself this was a closed system; there was nowhere for the man to run.

Except they were docked.

He redoubled his effort, and when he turned the next corner, he saw Will in the lift, holding the door and urging Alex to hurry. He did, but was cautious when he entered it, watching for some sort of trap.

"Talk to Lea," Will said, "now."

"Why?"

"Too much stuff. Mine. Get good money here. Took everything. Lea sells it." He looked at Alex. "Forgot the case. Forgot it yours. Stuff going out now."

"So you didn't do it on purpose?"

Will shook his head. "Always alone before. Find stuff, put it there too. I forgot case yours."

Alex closed his eyes and leaned against the wall. He had no idea if Will was telling the truth. He was a pirate, so taking other people's stuff was what he did, but he chose to believe his friend had made a mistake. He had too few of those here to throw it away on something like suspicion.

"Can't you call Lea?"

"Busy, never talk when selling."

When the doors opened, Will took off, only to stop when he noticed Alex wasn't with him.

Alex was still leaning against the wall. "Go, I'll catch up in a moment."

Will ran off.

He was seeing Doc as soon as this was resolved. He should have let her see to him when he'd been there. He couldn't believe how painful his leg had become. He forced himself to go after the young man, but only made it halfway there before Will was running back in his direction.

"Stuff gone. Get ground-side."

With a curse, Alex turned and sped up after him. He saw Anders further along the hall and called to him. "We're going down for a bit; make sure the ship doesn't leave until we're back." He didn't give the man time to ask questions, and continued past him.

He caught up to Will next to an open panel on the wall. Before Alex could ask, Will pressed an injector in his leg. Alex couldn't move away fast enough.

"Painkiller," Will said, handing the injector to him, then ran off.

Alex checked the warnings. For humans, local application, no side effects. He put some weight on his leg and the pain was muffled. As he started after Will, it continued to recede until he didn't feel anything and could run.

He had a strong suspicion that Doc wouldn't be happy with him when he finally did see her.

* * * * *

They didn't land in the same port Anders had taken him to. This

219

one had a few more shuttles on it, and people were coming and going, moving crates by hand or on hover-carts. The buildings were the same gray material, but many of them went up to four-stories in height.

Will consulted his comm a few times as he led Alex thought the buildings, until they came to one that reminded Alex of a warehouse from his father's company.

"Harligon," Will said. "Lea's guy." He pushed the door and Alex followed him into a disaster of a place.

The room was filled with tables placed haphazardly and filled with things. The walls were lined with shelves containing more objects. He followed Will around tables until they reached the back, where a wrinkled old man was seated behind a counter.

He looked up at him. "If you don't find what you want in there, it isn't for sale."

"Been mistake," Will said. "Need it back."

The man narrowed his eyes. "If I got it, I paid good money for it."

"Buy back," Will replied.

The man indicated the room. "Check in there then."

"You got it a few hours ago at the most," Alex said, "and it's already in there?"

The man snorted. "Takes weeks to go through the new stuff."

"Then if I tell you what I'm looking for, you can get it."

The man barked laughter. "You think I can just walk in there and pull out one little precious thing? I get tons of stuff. I can't find what you want."

"Lea had listing," Will argued. "It's case with—" Will's mouth worked, but no words came out. With a cry of frustration, he pulled out his comm.

"It's a Samalian statue," Alex said. "A foot and a half in height. It's painted to have golden fur, and he's holding two swords.

The man's eyes registered recognition for a moment. "Do I look like I'd know something like that?"

Alex grabbed him by the collar and pulled him close,

ignoring his mother's voice telling him to always treat older people with respect, or the knowledge that if anyone ever manhandled his grandparents this way, he'd break their legs. "Listen to me. You're going to go back there and get it, and don't give me crap about not knowing about it. If you don't come back with it, I am going to hurt you."

The man snorted. "You?" He looked him over. "You're just some cubicle slave out for a walk. You couldn't hurt a baby." He nodded toward Will. "Now him? Him I'd believe he could hurt me, but you? You can't even walk straight."

Alex kept hold of the old man with one hand and reached for something on the counter he hadn't even realized he'd noticed. His fingers closed on the hilt of the gold knife, and bought it to the man's neck.

"Someone in your profession should know better than to judge me by the way I look, or walk. The item in question was taken from me in error, and sold to you the same. Now, do you want to go get it for me?" He pressed the knife harder. "Or do I need to get it myself?"

"I'll do it," the man said, fear in his eyes. Alex didn't let him go immediately. He continued looking into those eyes, enjoying the man's fear of him. It felt good to be taken seriously, to have someone scared, instead of being scared.

"No Law," Will said as Alex released the man. "You do and Lea goes elsewhere."

The man nodded and took out a datapad. After a moment of working it, glancing up at Alex every so often, something whirled under the counter. A minute later, a panel opened and a familiar case appeared out of it.

Alex ran a finger along an edge, then a hand over the top. It felt right. He opened it and sighed in relief. The Defender was there. He picked it up, not only to test the weight, but to look at the felt under it. The indentation where he'd hidden his program chip was still there.

He put it back and closed the case. "That's it." He went to pick it up, but the man grabbed it.

"It's mine."

Alex growled. "No, it's mine. If you don't let go of it, I'm going to cut your hand off."

"You said you'd pay."

Alex reached into his pocket and took out four chips, dropping them on the counter.

"That's not enough," the man said.

"It's what you're getting."

"This is priceless, I can't take—"

"It's a reproduction. You can try conning other people, but the person who gave this to me told me it's a reproduction."

"No, it's real."

The reverence in the man's voice made Alex pause. It couldn't be real; Jack had told him it was a reproduction. He wouldn't have lied about that, would he? No, but Tristan would have. Damn it, why?

"I know collectors," the man said. "I can get millions for it. I'll cut you in."

Alex shoved the man away and picked up the case.

"You can't take it! It's priceless!"

Alex glared at the man, and seriously considered grabbing the knife again and impaling it in the man's chest. Instead he reached into his pocket, grabbed the chips in there, and dropped them on the counter. He made sure he put all of them there.

"That's six-thousand. Be happy with it, because you're not getting anything more." He turned and headed out, limping slightly as the painkiller began to wear off.

"Where?" Will asked, falling into step next to him.

It took a moment for Alex to work out what he meant. "I helped Anders with a job; that was my cut. Easy come easy go." At least it had been put to good use.

Alex stepped out of the building to be confronted by two huge men.

"Mister Oustalo wants to have a word with you."

CHAPTER 25

Alex exchanged a look with Will, who shrugged. Apparently he didn't know what this was about either. The men had short black hair on top of hard faces. They were broad-shouldered, and their muscles stretched the dirty shirts they wore. They weren't armed, but Alex didn't think they needed weapons to hurt them—they were used to violence.

When Will started walking, Alex followed him. The men escorted them to a small shuttle and they squeezed in, having barely any space left to breathe. They flew out of town and across a rough countryside for close to an hour. They passed many remnants of towns, next to large and deep pits.

Someone had mentioned this was a mining world, and Alex wondered what they mined. He understood now why every building was made of the same simple material: they constantly had to move the towns when they exhausted the ore.

They didn't land in another port, but in the street, by a low and wide building. They got out and Alex had to stifle a curse; he recognized the place. He hid his trembling hand in his pocket, and prayed to the universe the weight of the case would keep his other one still.

He looked at the gray door, and only moved when a large hand pushed him forward. This wasn't good. How had they known where to find him? Or that he had been involved? He and Milo hadn't come in with the others. He wished he could think of something to do, but his mind seemed locked in a recursive function.

As soon as the door opened, the sounds of talking and drinking escaped the building. The men led Will and him past the bar, down a hall to a room in the back. Alex suspected that was where Anders and the others had gone.

"We found him," one of the men said as he pushed them in the room. Will glared back at him, but Alex only stared at the man seated behind the table which, by the datapad and papers on it, served as a desk.

He was fat, but his beige shirt hung loosely on him. His bald head was pale brown, and he sported a white goatee. The man indicated two simple wooden chairs opposite him. Alex didn't immediately react, and Will had to get his attention and point to the chair next to the one he'd sat in.

Alex placed the case between his legs and locked his fingers together to keep from fidgeting.

"What's this?" Will asked.

"Excuse me?"

Will sighed and spoke in measured tones. "What is this about?"

"Ahhh." The man smiled and fixed his gaze on Alex. "This is about theft."

Alex's mind went blank, or rather it was such a fear-induced jumble he couldn't latch onto anything in it. He'd been caught.

Will glanced at him, then shrugged. "Can't help. Just got down."

The man stared at Will, eyes narrowed as he seemed to try to figure out what he'd meant. "I see," he finally said. "The information I received tells me this man is one of those who robbed me."

Will glanced at Alex again, and when he looked back to the man, his expression was baffled. "How? Ship-bound all day. Down for shopping."

The man sneered. "Really? Then why does he look like he's about to piss himself?"

The expression reminded Alex of another time he's sat opposite an accuser. He hadn't done anything that time, but the similarity kindled his anger, and it burned away some of the fog clouding his thoughts.

"Tourist. Never been out. Never been roughed up."

"A tourist?" The man snorted. Oustalo, that was his name. "Tourist ships don't come here. There's nothing anyone would want to see here."

"Merchant. Take tourist. Cheap for him, money for us. Went shopping for exotic."

"Merchant? Please, I know what you are." He motioned, and before Alex could react, one of the men grabbed the case and put it on the table. Oustalo took the statue out of it.

"Careful!"

The man raised a thin white eyebrow at him. "What is it?"

"It's a Samalian statue."

"Is it valuable?" he asked, gaze still on Alex.

"Some hundred," Will said before Alex could get his mouth working and say that it was.

"It's, err...a reproduction."

"Then why the near panic when I picked it up?" Oustalo's tone wasn't accusatory, merely curious.

"It's from—" Alex paused to reign in his mouth. He had to be careful what he said. "It's for a friend. He likes statues like that. I bought it for him, so please be careful with it."

Oustalo looked it over, then ran a finger inside the case before putting it back there. "A friend, huh?" he said, the end of his lips quirking up, and Alex blushed at the suggestive implication.

"How much?" Will asked, which earned him a questioning look. "Stolen, how much?

"Sixty-five thousand."

Alex gasped. That wasn't what Anders had said.

The man fixed his gaze on him and Alex forced his mouth shut. "That's—that's a lot of money." How did a place like this, a bar, make even the kind of money Anders had told him they'd taken?

"It is."

Will took a cred stick and handed it over. "Ten-thousand."

Oustalo looked at it, then Will. "I thought you said you weren't the ones who robbed me."

"Not us. This shakedown. Been there before. Got ship waiting. Don't give, miss it. Give, let loose."

Oustalo shook his head. "What the hell did he say?"

"I think," Alex began, then swallowed. "I think he said that this is a shakedown, and that it's happened to him before. That if we give you some money you'll let us go, otherwise we'll miss our ship."

Oustalo glared at Will. "A shakedown?" He forced himself up, using the table for support, and leaned forward. "Are you accusing me of being a criminal?"

Will leaned back, and Alex saw worry on his face. His hands began shaking again and he put them in his pocket. There, one closed on his earpiece.

"Listen to me, kid," Oustalo continued. "I'm a businessman. That's all any of us are on this rock. I don't go about grabbing random people off the street and trying to extract a penance from them. I conduct business, and your friend stole from me."

Alex closed his eyes. Fuck, how had he let this happen? Now they'd never get back to the ship. He didn't think the captain would wait all that long, or bother sending people after him. If he didn't come up with something, he'd never get off this planet.

Will spoke slowly. "I apologize. No disrespect wanted. We're not thieves."

"I have information it was him."

"How much you pay for it?" Will asked.

Oustalo didn't reply.

"I think," Will continued, still speaking slowly, "someone sees us. Sees we're from off-planet. Knows you have trouble, been robbed. He sells us to you and vanishes." He nodded to

Alex. "He looks like tourist. I look dumb. What we do? You grab us, we can't prove not us, and you…" Will trailed off with a shrug.

"You actually expect me to believe that you've been set up?"

"People like money. Easy money."

"Yes, they do. Like how easy they think it's going to be to steal from me and fly off, never to be seen again. I've been at this for a very long time, and I know a con man when I see one, kid."

"Not—"

"Enough," Alex said, his voice trembling.

"Crim—"

"It's my mess, Will. I'm going to fix it." He looked at Oustalo. "If I get you that money, you let us go."

"Just like that? You actually admit to robbing me?"

Alex ground his teeth. "No, but I want to get out of here. If I get you sixty-five thousand, you let us go."

"I don't think so. Even if you get me my money back, there's still the matter of making sure others don't get the idea they can steal from me and get away without repercussions."

"I'll double it."

Everyone stared at him.

"You have that kind of money?" Oustalo asked.

Alex snorted. "No, but if you get me the best computer you have, I'll get it for you."

"Is this some kind of trick?"

Alex chuckled. "Do I look like I can trick anyone? I'm just a guy who got used, and now I can't help feeling like I'm being thrown away. You want something I can give you, I want out of here. It's simple." Alex managed a small smile. "It's business."

"Boss?" one of the men said as the silence stretched.

Oustalo raised a hand to quiet him. "If you can do that, alright, I'll let both of you go." He wobbled around the table and led them to another room with only a chair, a table, and a computer on it. Alex was pushed into the chair and he turned the computer on. It was a Tomika, at least a decade old. Not something Alex would use if he had any other options, but he would make this work. He put his earpiece in, and under watchful eyes, went to work.

This wasn't difficult. He'd made his way into the banking systems often enough when at Luminex, but he'd never gone after that kind of money before, and not without protection. If he got caught now, it would just be a question of time before his life ended. The banks didn't rely on the Law to catch thieves, they paid mercenaries. They paid them well.

Alex was in half a dozen banks in under five minutes. He went after independent institutions since they had less influence and less money of their own, therefore couldn't afford the best to come after him if he screwed this up.

Among them he located the fifty accounts with the most money, and divided a hundred-thirty-thousand in transfers among them, each in amounts no larger than a few hundred. After a few trials, he even managed to backdate them over the previous year. He transferred them to a dozen temporary accounts, then from them to a dozen more. He could see that he should do more transfers like that to camouflage where the money went, but he didn't have the time. Finally, he sent to money to a final account, and added a small program to it.

He typed in a bank and account number, as well as the passcode.

"Your money's there. Transfer it to whatever account is yours." Alex got up.

Oustalo sat and typed. His eyes went wide. "You actually did it?"

Alex shrugged.

"This is impressive," the man said as he typed. "I'm curious as to how much money you could make me."

"You agreed to let us go."

The man looked up from the screen. "I'm thinking that keeping you here would be a better investment."

"No, it wouldn't be."

The man grinned as he finished typing. "You could make me so much money I could—" He typed a few keys. "What just happened? Where's my money?"

Alex stretched. "I told you I was used; I don't plan on letting that happen again. You're locked out of your account. I figure you transferred all of it to your main account, so you don't have any money left."

Oustalo's face turned red. "Unlock it."

Alex laughed. "I'm not an idiot. I'll unlock it once we're back on the ship."

Oustalo pointed to one of the two other men. "You, make him unlock it."

Alex forced himself not to moves as the beefy man with a vicious grin came for him. "You think he can torture me fast enough? How long can you keep going without liquidity? A business like yours probably can't ask for loans, so what, a week at most? I mean, how are you going to pay these two?"

The man stopped as he reached for Alex. "Boss?" he asked.

"Don't be an idiot. Of course I have money."

Alex looked at the man and smiled. "I'm thinking he has people more important than you two he needs to pay first." He turned to Oustalo. "We can be back to the ship under an hour. That's how fast you can get your money back."

"And how do I know you're not just going to keep it to yourself if I let you go?"

Alex stepped to the table. "You're going to have to trust me."

"You can't last all that long under torture."

Alex kept the fear from showing, at least he hoped so. "Then try it. Test me. Let's find out if I can outlast your competitors."

Alex heard Oustalo ground his teeth. "If I don't have my money back in two hours, I'm coming for you. Don't think you can hide on that ship. If you force me, I will tear it apart."

"You'll get your money before that, I swear."

Oustalo snorted derisively. "Get out of here. And I better never see you again."

Will grabbed Alex's arm and pulled him out, and kept pulling until they were well away from the bar.

"I need to sit down," Alex said, feeling his legs weakening.

"No. In shuttle. We stop, he worries. He takes us and hurts us. Got real lucky."

Once at the port, Will ordered a shuttle and sat Alex down. He indicated where they'd come from. "Anders's job?"

Alex nervously looked around.

"No one around," Will said.

Alex nodded.

"Who knew?"

"Me, Milo, Anders, Zephyr, and Barbara. I don't know if any of them told anyone else."

"Stupid. Passenger. Why go?"

"I didn't know it was a job. Anders just said he wanted to take me off the ship so I could relax."

"Don't trust Anders."

Alex didn't reply. He'd wanted to believe Anders had gotten over whatever problems he'd had, but now he wasn't sure. In fact, Alex had trouble getting rid of the feeling it had all been a ploy.

He spent the trip back to the station going over his interaction with the other man, bad and good, trying to find indications of what his intention had been, but nothing stood out. As far as Alex could tell, every interaction had been genuine.

By the time they reached the station, his leg hurt even when just sitting. He wanted another painkiller, but told himself this was deserved—for getting mixed up in this, for starting the fight, for getting hurt. And it would keep him from damaging it more than he probably had already.

Will matched his slow pace as they headed for the ship, but remained quiet. He hadn't commented on their little adventure, other than give the warning Alex didn't want to be true.

As the ship's cargo doors came into view, Anders was there, directing the loading of crates, talking with a brilliantly red-headed woman Alex had noticed before. She said something and Anders laughed. She headed back in and turned to point in the station's depth when someone pushing one of the rare outgoing crates asked him something.

Anders looked over Will and Alex, finished answering the question, then his head snapped back to Alex, his face a mask of shock.

Alex stopped. By the time he understood what it meant, the shock was replaced by a friendly smile, but it was too late. Fuck, it hurt. Alex had wanted them to be friends. He'd believed him when he said he wasn't angry anymore. Damn it, why did he keep getting betrayed like that?

He started walking, and with each step he buried the pain under anger. The gall of the man to use him like that, to make him think they were friends.

"You son of a bitch," Alex growled. "You told Oustalo I was down there."

Anders's smile intensified. "I don't know—"

"Bullshit!" His yell made those pushing crates detour further away to get on the ship. "You set everything up. You got me down there, got me to start the fight. What were you going to do? Convince me to go down for another drink?"

Alex saw it in the man's eyes, that moment he went from considering denying it to not giving a damn. Anders threw his hands up. "You know what? I was fed up with being nice to you anyway. I can't believe I had to give you and Milo an even share of the job." He glared at Alex. "I tried bringing you into line. I figured if I bedded you, you'd feel you had to work for me. Hell, maybe I could have gotten you to fall for me. If you weren't so soft-hearted and pining for some guy you won't feel for years, it might have worked too. I didn't think you'd survive that bar fight; those guys aren't known for going easy on people. I would have strangled you when I saw you and told the captain you'd been killed there, but Milo was there and him I can't kill. So yeah, I was going to find a way to get you down there and get Oustalo to finish the job." Anders took a deep breath. "There, it's all out in the open." He smiled. "I actually feel better now."

Alex shook. His free hand was balled into a fist, and he could see himself smashing the case over the man's head over and over again. If he'd had a gun, Anders would have died, but a small part of his mind was lucid enough to remind him he couldn't take the man in a fair fight.

He shoved Anders out of his way as hard as he could, and limped up the ramp. He stopped at the first terminal and sent the command through the net to release Oustalo's money. When he moved away, he saw Will next to him. "Take me to Ana." Fine, Anders wanted them to be enemies? That's what they'd be. And Alex was going to make sure he was ready for the next time the man tried something.

CRIMSON

CHAPTER 26

Alex grumbled as Doc helped him onto one of the medical beds.

"What happened?" she asked.

"Fought," Will provided, and Alex glared at him.

She looked from one to the other. "Might be best if you just leave him with me. I'll take good care of him." She headed to one of the cabinets and came back with a scanner.

Will nodded and left.

"So? What happened?" She ran the scanner over Alex's leg and cursed in a language he didn't know. "Who did that to you? Anders?"

"It's nothing."

She gave him a disbelieving look.

"I mean it, don't worry about it."

Doc gently rested a hand on his leg. Alex winced as the simple gesture sent a murmur of pain along it. "Alex, if you don't tell me exactly what happened, I'm going to start squeezing."

"I thought doctors weren't supposed to hurt people."

She squeezed, he yelled and cursed.

"Maybe you didn't notice this part, but I work with pirates. I'm not here out of the goodness of my heart. Now talk."

"Anders conned me into starting a fight in a bar. That's where I got this."

She removed her hand. "Anders forced you to walk from there to here? And what were you doing going along with anything Anders said?"

"He conned me," Alex emphasized. "And it wasn't that bad when I got back, but I went back down to retrieve something."

"You didn't come right here?" Doc glared, and her hand moved to Alex's leg again.

"Hey!" Alex reached for her hand. "No hurting the passenger."

"Why didn't you come directly here?" Her hand hovered over his leg.

"Will accidentally handed something of mine to be sold. We had to get it before your reseller passed it along." She didn't move her hand. "It has sentimental value. I couldn't find another one."

"Damn it, Crimson, didn't enough people tell you not to trust Anders? The guy's dangerous and he hates you."

"Trust me, I learned my lesson. The next time he tries anything, I'm going to clock him."

Doc grinned as she got something else from the cabinet.

"I'm serious. I actually wanted Ana to start teaching me how to fight right now, but she insisted I see you first. I mean, I'm going to have to fight injured, so I might as well learn how to now."

"At least one person's thinking. Will should have brought you to me."

"He tried. I wouldn't let him. Just heal my leg so Ana can start."

"I thought she was already training you." She came back with a cast and began attaching it to Alex's lower left leg.

"I wasn't taking it seriously before. I didn't realize how underhanded Anders could be." He rested his head back while she finished setting it up. Once she activated it, he sighed. The absence of pain felt euphoric. "Can I ask you something?"

"So long as it isn't about me, sure."

"How come there aren't any aliens on the ship?"

She smiled. "Right, you like those. Will told me," she added.

"So, the captain doesn't like aliens? I'd think the right one would make a great pirate." He imagined Alphalar using his head tentacles to carry more stolen stuff.

"The captain doesn't mind them. We had a few, years ago when he first got the ship. And yeah, they carried their weight, but on a crew this big, there's always going to be some who don't like them, like Anders, for example."

"What's his problem with them?"

"Oh, I don't know, most are stronger or faster or smarter than he is. Anyway, there were a few accidents. Only one died, but plenty got hurt. After a while they left, and the captain realized it wasn't worth looking for more."

Alex nodded, and wondered what Tristan would do to someone like Anders. He chuckled. There wouldn't be enough left of the man to fill a cup. With that cheery thought, he looked at the cast over his leg.

"How long until my leg's healed."

"It should be good to support your weight in about three hours."

"Good, I want to get back to training soon."

"But," she continued, "you're staying here for the next two days."

"What?"

She loomed over him. "I don't trust you, Crimson. The moment I let you out of this bed, you're going to run to get hurt again. And this time you might not be so lucky as to only end up with multiple fractures. I might have to cut off your leg, and trust me, you're not the peg leg type."

Alex grumbled again.

"I don't care. Bitch all you want. If you even think of getting out of it, I'm strapping you down."

Unbidden, the image of him in a horrible chair, his arms, legs, chest, and head tied to it, surfaced, and he shuddered. Since he had nothing else to do, he leaned back and closed his eyes.

* * * * *

Alex punched the man before him, his jaw breaking with an audible snap. He bent down to avoid a woman's fist, grabbed a chair leg, and used it as a club on the way up, catching her under the chin and sending her flying back.

Someone whistled. "Way to go, Alex! Incoming on the left!"

Alex elbowed the man in the face, hearing him drop as he glanced around, looking for his cheerleader. Tristan was seated on the bar. He put his fingers to his lips and whistled again.

Suddenly, Alex knew this was a dream.

The fight stopped, the actors standing immobile. Tristan looked the scene over.

"Come on, Alex, you were doing so good."

"I'm not fighting, not for you."

The alien dropped from the bar and walked to Alex, taking him by the shoulders. "Hey, this was all you. You can't blame me for any of it. I'm impressed. I mean, you're not me, but you actually held your own. You managed to hurt a lot of them and walk away mostly unharmed. I didn't think you had it in you."

Alex shoved the hands away. "I've already killed two men," he said bitterly, "in case you've forgotten."

"Guns are easy. A good brawl, now that's tough. But fun, right? You can't tell me you didn't enjoy yourself." The alien stepped behind Alex. "I do have a question." He grabbed Alex and spun him. "How come he's still alive?"

They weren't in the bar, they were in the warehouse, at the counter. Alex had the old man by the collar and was holding a knife to his neck. He tried to let go of him, but couldn't.

Tristan leaned against the counter. "Why didn't you kill him? You wanted to, don't lie."

"Stop this."

"I'm not doing anything, this is all you. I'm you, too."

236

"No!"

Tristan laughed. "Come on, Alex. This is your dream, your head. You cast me in the role of who you really want to be."

"No!" Alex shoved the old man away and backed away as far as he could.

He hit something and spun.

"You're going to have to make a choice," a golden-furred Samalian said, handing him a glass half-filled with amber liquid.

Alex looked around. He was back in the bar, but they were the only ones in it. The tables were still overturned and broken, but all the fighters had left.

"Take it," the Samalian said. "You need to relax."

"Who?" Alex started to ask as he took the glass, but the notched ear reminded him of someone. He leaned over the bar to check something.

"It isn't that kind of dream," the Samalian said. "I'm wearing pants."

Alex blushed, but it wasn't what he wanted to confirm. The Samalian had a sword at each hip.

"You're the Defender."

The Samalian shook his head and sipped his glass. "That's the Defender." He indicated the statue on the counter. "I'm just a representation. You made me look like it because you needed someone to get you to look at things properly."

Alex snorted. "Why now? I've been having nightmares for months. And why you? Why didn't I get someone else to have this talk with me before now?"

"Who do you know, Alex, that could stand in and get you to take an honest look at yourself?"

Alex thought about it. Not his parents, that was for certain. Not coworkers either. His grandparents?

"Would you really saddle them with that job? They love you, they've always supported you. Even now, when your grandfather knows you're in trouble, stole, he still wants to protect you. Could you really get him to tell you ugly things about yourself?"

"Fine, then why didn't you show up before?"

"I don't know. Until today, you always thought it was just a reproduction. Belief has power, maybe that's why."

"Fine. Then I'm guessing you're going to tell me I have no business fighting, or killing people. Well I have news for you: I already know that."

"I'm not here to judge you, Alex; you do that fine all by yourself."

Alex let out an exasperated breath. "Then what?"

"You're changing, Alex."

"Do you think I haven't realized that?"

"But why are you changing?"

Alex frowned.

"He's who you want." The Samalian pointed to another one seated at a table, holding a tall glass of clear liquid and looking into it.

Alex recognized him immediately and took a step in his direction, but someone held his arm.

"Let go of me," he told the golden-furred Samalian.

"Not that kind of dream either." He pointed to another one, seated across the room from the first one, almost identical, except for the cocky expression on his face. He raised his glass, saluted Alex, and downed it. "He's who you're afraid of."

Alex pulled out of the hold. "I know that. And you're who? Who I have to be?"

"No. I'm the mirror in which you have to look."

"You might be broken. I don't look anything like that."

"Would you want to?"

Alex went to answer, but found he couldn't. The idea of being covered in fur, muscular, having a muzzle. His breath caught. It was wrong.

"No," he stated. "This is who I am. I love Jack; I don't want to be him."

The Samalian nodded and sipped his drink. "How about him?" He indicated Tristan.

"Are you crazy?"

"You tell me."

"Of course I don't want to be him. He's a monster that kills people."

"Like you said, you have too."

"I didn't have a choice. It isn't like I wanted to kill them."

"But you know what being on this ship is doing to you. You can feel it. You can feel *him* ever-closer to you."

"I don't have a choice," Alex repeated.

"Don't you? This ship can't be the only one going to Samalia. You did your research. They do some trade, not a lot, but some. That means other ships go there, honest merchant ships."

"But they're going to take longer."

"Is time that much of an issue?"

Alex didn't answer. It wasn't the first time the question nagged at him.

"That's one of the choices you need to make. What are you willing to sacrifice to get there faster?"

Alex looked at the Defender statue.

"Not that," the Samalian said. "I'm not talking about outside things. I'm talking about pieces of yourself. You got a glimpse of who you can be in that fight. Another one with the old man, and yet one more with Oustalo. Even now, you want to learn how to fight so you can take on Anders. Is that who you want to be?"

Alex didn't know how to answer.

"Maybe you should go and sleep on it."

Alex nodded, and headed for the door.

"Alex, don't forget that."

The Samalian was pointing to the statue. Alex came back to the bar to take it, but noticed a book laying on the counter. *Myths, Beliefs, and Legends of Samalia.* He reached to pick it up.

CRIMSON

CHAPTER 27

Alex couldn't figure out where he was for a moment. The room was too large, and someone was talking. He looked in that direction, and saw a woman was tending to a man's cut-up back. Right, he was in the medical bay.

"Don't even think about getting up," Doc said without looking away from her work.

"I'm not. How long did I sleep?"

"Twelve hours."

"Why am I still wearing that?"

She looked at the cast he was pointing at. "I didn't want to wake you. Once I'm done with Murray, I'll take it off."

The man gave Alex a small wave.

"What happened?"

"An explosion in engineering."

"What were you doing there? I thought you were a pilot."

"I'm a combat pilot, so I'm only on the bridge during jobs to get us away in a hurry. The rest of the time I go wherever Anders sends me. This time it was to help out in engineering."

Alex thought it over. If Murray was part of Anders's crew, could his absence from the bridge have been planned? Alex had been too focused to see what he was doing. He hadn't even noticed him leaving, and with the way the ship's system was partitioned, he could have let the man in.

Alex closed his eyes; he was getting paranoid. Murray had been found knocked out, so clearly he'd ran into the other man. He needed something to distract himself.

Myths.

Thinking of the book in his dream reminded him how vivid it had been. He couldn't recall ever remembering a dream that clearly before. And it wasn't as macabre as the others. In fact, it had been rather tame.

Except for learning he was changing.

He needed to think about something else. He moved carefully, and—

"I told you not to move," Doc warned. "I am going to strap you down."

"Calm down, Doc. I just want the tablet on your desk. I'm going stir-crazy."

She turned to grab it, saw the blood on her hands, growled lightly, and went back to Murray. "Fine, but be careful, and don't even think of making a run for it. I don't care about covering you with blood if it comes to it."

"I'm not an idiot, Doc. I just want to do some reading." He hobbled to the desk and back.

"Your previous actions make me question that."

"What happened?" Murray asked.

"Shut up," Doc told him. "You know damn well what your boss has been up to. I better not find out you helped him, otherwise you're going to have to get yourself a new doctor."

Murray gave Alex a confused look, but Alex just shrugged as he got back on the bed. He sat as comfortably as he could and began reading.

* * * * *

"Did you know Samalians worship their sun?" Alex asked once Murray had left the room.

Doc looked up from the sink. "Is that the race your guy is?"

Alex nodded.

"Plenty of cultures worship the sun. It's right there in the sky."

"I guess. They also believe that they can become, well, gods I guess."

"Really? That's new. How?"

"The treatise doesn't say. The guy who wrote it spent a few years among them, but he never got the hang of the language. Lots of growls and guttural noises, according to him."

"You know it?"

"No, Jack never spoke it. I didn't think to ask him."

"Jack?"

"His dad thought he'd get along better with a human n—"

Except that wasn't true. Jack hadn't been his real name. That was Tristan, which was another human name, so maybe the reasoning was the same?

"Sorry," Doc said. "I didn't mean to remind you he wasn't there. You miss him?"

Alex smiled. "A lot."

He went back to reading, stopping only when Will came by to let him know what was going on. He seemed happy that Murray had gotten hurt, and glared at Doc for fixing him up. Perry and Ana also dropped by to check in on him.

A day later Doc allowed him to go to his room, but he wasn't allowed strenuous work for another one.

The first thing he did was check that the Defender was still there. The relief that flooded him on seeing it under his bunk was so intense he had trouble standing. He wished he had a way to lock the bunk down. He trusted Will, but he didn't want anyone to be able to get to it.

Unable to come up with a way to keep people out of it short

of welding it shut, Alex told himself the locked door would be enough to keep people out. He had trouble believing it himself.

He spent the day doing more reading. Having nothing else to do, he found other texts on Samalia. He ignored the surveys and reports on its population, technological progress, and suitability for annexation, and focused on anything relating to their legends.

They had a lot. It seemed that Samalians loved their stories. After reading a couple hundred, Alex could tell that most were coaxed as the adventures of the twelve gods, the more important figures in Samalian religion after the sun. Each seemed to have particular types of events happen around him or her—half of them were women.

One had things relating to the mind: intellect, puzzles, and outwitting foes. Another took care of mothers and babies, tending to one, and bringing the other to be. Alex wondered if they actually believed supernatural entities made babies.

He recognized the Defender in the stories. He was always described as young, full of energy, with golden fur, and there when people needed defending.

Alex also realized that while each figure had a primary function, which the stories used to give them names—the Defender, the Mother, the Wise One, the Aggressor—they also did more than that.

The Mother didn't just help mothers to be, she also helped crops, along with the earth tender. The Wise One brought knowledge, but also mischief. The Aggressor attacked the enemies, but he was also there to give encouragement when hard work became too much. The Defender, for his part, not only protected, but he bound one to another. Promises were made by him and over him, and the stories told of unfortunate things that happened to people who broke those promises, and how some promises couldn't be broken.

Alex smiled, imagining Tristan having to deal with misfortune because of what he'd done to him. It would serve him right for the misery he'd caused. After a moment, the smile died.

He'd rather have Jack back than see Tristan miserable.

His smile became wistful as he remembered their game in the market, Jack showing up with the Defender, explaining some of what it represented. Of them kissing over it...

Alex sat up. Jack had told him he'd always love him. Jack had made a promise over the Defender. Not Tristan, Jack. Except they were the same. Did that mean Tristan was the one who had promised to love him? What would it be like to have such a monster love him? Alex shuddered.

It didn't mean anything. Gods weren't real. Statues couldn't force someone to keep his promise, even if that person had been a mask someone else wore. But he could hope.

And for the first time since all of this started, Alex didn't have a nightmare that night. He dreamt of Jack and him, kissing before the golden-furred Samalian, of being blessed by him and told their love would endure.

When Doc finally gave him the all clear, Alex chased down Ana, Jennifer, and the knife expert Jen had found for him. He tried to get all of them to train him every day. He insisted that he needed to be ready for Anders, but they wouldn't do it. They scheduled him to have one training session each day, and one day of rest on the fourth one.

Alex had to agree, but what none of them could get him to do was take it easy. He kept pushing the one-hour sessions past their end, and he used much of his free time to work out. He spent hours there. Will tried to get him to slow down, but Alex didn't listen to him.

On the rare days when Alex didn't feel like exercising, all he had to do was remember that moment when he'd realized everything Anders had done was a trick. He remembered the pain of the betrayal, and the anger would pull him out of bed.

It was Asyr that got Alex to slow down a little, when she reminded him the computer still needed to be healed. Alex had another short bout of self-hate for neglecting that promise, and he made that the bulk of his time.

Alex spent the next three subjective months happily lost in training, working out, reintegrating the computer, and teaching Asyr the basics of coercion. Over that time, they reintegrated half of the smaller system.

The only interruption Alex allowed to his schedule was when the captain requested him for a job. After that first time, he didn't want to let a resource like Alex go to waste.

Alex found he enjoyed taking on people whose livelihood depended on beating him. It made his job more challenging. Back at Luminex it had just been his day job, same as the people protecting the systems he attacked. He always did his best, as he was sure his opponents did, but neither side was at risk of being fired for failing; it was accepted that someone had to fail.

Now, if he didn't beat the other guys, the crew would get hurt, cargo damaged, and the captain might decide Alex wasn't pulling his weight and dump him at the next station. Each coercion came with a sense of urgency Alex began to crave.

He'd never gotten such a rush from coming up with a program on the fly that took down enemy defenses before. His heart had beaten so fast he thought it might burst as an opposing coercionist closed in a net around Alex, only for him to find a flaw in the code and exploit it to victory.

Alex had never been so utterly exhausted after a job than he was when these were over, but he'd also never been this happy. In those times fighting other systems and coercionists, nothing else mattered. He had no other problems than the one before him, and this, he knew without a doubt, he could beat.

* * * * *

"What's wrong?" Will asked, making Alex jump.

Alex had been staring at his reflection, still damp from his shower and holding the towel around his waist. He hadn't even heard the door open, and he couldn't seem to make sense of the question.

"Oxy's low?" Will asked.

Alex pointed to his reflection. "I have abs."

Will snorted. "Never saw them?"

"I never had abs." Alex ran a hand over them. They weren't chiseled or even very defined, but they were visible. He turned. He had no stomach bulge anymore. He flexed an arm, and his bicep bulged.

Alex laughed. "I never thought I'd look like this."

"Your guy know you now?"

"Jack will know me."

Will was already stretched on his bunk, and Alex went to his. He pulled the armband out of the cubbyhole. This was his fifth jump, and he'd finally worked out that the less clothing he wore, the easier it was for him to come out of it on the other side. It didn't make any sense to him as to why it should be like that, and Doc had agreed, but this wasn't the weirdest thing she'd heard over the years. So now he went dressed only in a towel.

"Any idea of the job waiting for us on the other side?" Alex asked.

Will smirked. "Cleaner don't know that stuff. Only big shot." He gave Alex a meaningful look.

"I'm not that important." Alex clamped the band around his arm, around his hard bicep. He smiled. A moment later the machine in the wall whirled. He closed his eyes and stretched out. Watching his blood being suctioned out through the transparent tube made him queasy.

CRIMSON

CHAPTER 28

"What's this?" Asyr asked when she entered her lab. Alex had rearranged the two auxiliary consoles so they faced each other.

"We're going to play a game," Alex answered from behind one of them. "Sit."

She looked dubious, but sat.

"It's called 'Disconnect'. I used to play it with other students in school. It's a great way to practice coercion skills." Their displays showed a fictitious system with working code, their connections buried deep under that. "The game is simple. We have to disconnect the other. Whoever manages it, wins. The system is passive; I'm the only one you have to worry about."

She looked at the screen. "I'm going up against you? There's no way I can win."

"Don't worry, I've set my system to slow my actions. It's going to handicap me, so we'll be on an even playing field." He activated the game. "Are you ready?"

She didn't look it. "Sure."

He went looking for her, both visually and by sending a search program after her. He'd eliminated one layer of code when his screen went dark.

"Did you just let me win?" Asyr asked.

"No, I did not. Let me check." A few keystrokes and he found what had happened. "I added an extra 'zero' to my system's response speed. It slowed me a hundred times instead of ten."

"Can't you just not act as fast as you normally do?"

"Not really," Alex answered, making the correction. "I have decades of practice at reacting as fast as I can to what I see in a system; that's a large part of beating an opposing coercionist. Okay, that's changed, let's try it again."

This time, he saw her coming. He launched programs to rewrite the code in her path, confusing her and the programs she used. She erected a wall of code, forcing him to decide between breaking through or going around.

"Why are we playing together?" she asked as another wall went up. "Can't the ship offer me a more realistic challenge?"

He decided to go through. "That would be the unrealistic version." He wrote a quick program to dismantle the walls. "In my decades of corporate coercion, I can count on one hand the number of times I just had to deal with a system." He noticed her search program getting closer, so he rewrote the system's path to his connection, buying himself time. "When a coercionist is in anyway competent, the system acts mainly as support. If you manage to disconnect him, you basically have free access to the system."

"I don't get it. A computer can think and act a lot faster than a person, so how can you give it any kind of problem?" Her search program vanished.

He forgot to answer her as he tried to understand what she was doing. To stop her search meant she had a different plan. He looked around and found it: a slight alteration of the code moving in his direction. He smiled. Clever, a camouflaged search. If she'd kept the other one going, he wouldn't have noticed it. He recoded that path, a small variation that connected to the already extended one.

He went back to his wall-breaking program. "Sorry. Yes,

systems are fast, but for all the advancement in self-awareness we've made on them, the human—well, the organic brain—is still much better at improvising. We can change direction at a moment's notice, break patterns, go against our self-interest, even sacrifice something to gain more." The program was through the wall. A moment later, he disconnected her.

"Ten minutes," he said. "A respectable time. Let's go again."

He restarted the game, and a different fictitious system became their battlefield.

"What am I supposed to do then?" she asked, typing away, "if the women I'm going up against can out-think me? I can't win."

He sent out his search program again. "The starting point is the system. If you can have a faster one, you gain an advantage. You also want it as close to your connection as possible. Unfortunately, those aren't things you can usually control."

He built a wall around his connection, but instead of the large block of code she'd done, he layered it, thinner, but with different properties. "What almost no one will tell you is that for all that we're great at adapting and improvising, we're predictable. They spend years teaching us not to be, but we all fall back on habit. Even the experts have their favorite programs they always use. It's one of the reasons you want to do as much research as possible ahead of time."

His program found her wall easily enough; the denser code was the giveaway. He launched more breaking programs. She'd have put up more walls this time; beginners went with more of the same.

"But even without research, if you can stretch out the confrontation, you'll notice patterns. He might fall back on hard defenses to replace what you've taken down, or maybe he keeps sending decoy program before attacking."

"Do you have any patterns?"

As he'd expected, his programs had a tougher time getting through. More of the same. "Of course not." He laughed. "I probably do. I think I've been doing this long enough to have broken myself of most of them, but like I said, every coercionist does. But even then, you might have noticed there's one thing

I tend to do when I work with a system: I talk. I like talking to the system, using psychology to get it to work with me instead of against me. Get it to slow my opponent down."

"But you said the system wasn't a factor if she's good enough."

Alex smiled as he noticed what she was doing. She'd warped the code of her wall, using the different layers she'd put up to interfere with each other. "Yes, but being good is relative. Sometimes it only takes a slight delay to change how the fight is going."

And it would be the case here. He sent a program which blocked her work, but he could tell it wouldn't be done in time. His connection died.

"Very good. I didn't expect you to have read about the Asterdam maneuver yet." He reset the game and they played again. He won that one, but the game after that was interrupted by the captain ordering Alex to the bridge.

* * * * *

The crew on the bridge were in near-panic when Alex arrived. Orders were being screamed by one member and argued by another.

The captain pointed to the computer console. "I want you to disable them." On one of the other screens, a sleek ship in gold and silver was getting larger.

"Who are they?" Alex sat and took out his earpiece.

"Local Law."

Alex spun. "The Law? You're attacking a Law ship?"

"We're not. They weren't who was supposed to be here. Just do what you did that first time. Get them to think we're a large rock or something."

"I can't do that!" Alex exclaimed. "That's the Law, I can't just sneak in and coerce their ship. That's illegal."

No one stopped what they were doing, but the room went

silent. The captain leveled his gaze on Alex, his eyes narrowing. "You, my ready room, now. Murray, you keep them from catching up to us. Perry, don't fire on them unless there's no other option."

Alex entered the room and was shoved against the wall. "Just what do you think you've been doing these past months?" the captain asked. "Playing games?"

"Of course not, but that isn't the same. By taking over those systems, I ensured as few people as possible got hurt, on both sides. If I get into this ship? I'm attacking a Law Enforcement Agency. Do you have any idea what they do to coercionists who do that? They'll throw me in a hole and forget I exist."

"And what do you think is going to happen when I have to tell Perry to open fire on them? By the look of it, it's a recent design, better weapons than us. Probably more maneuverable. When they board us, they're going to find out about that guard you killed."

"You'd sell me out?" Fear pooled at the bottom of Alex's stomach.

"No." The captain's voice was adamant. "I don't turn my back on anyone who works for me, but only one person went missing on that ship. By now they know he was here, and he never resurfaced anywhere."

"I made the ship forget."

"Did that make the crew forget too? I don't care how good you are, they've worked out who attacked them. I keep my crew safe not because no one knows about me, but because I always stay one step ahead of the Law. Sometimes that means knowing more than they do, other times it means having a secret. You're my secret."

"They can't know it was me. If you're not going to sell me out, they can't know."

"If they catch us, they're not going to care. We're all going to be held accountable."

"But I'm a passenger."

"You took your cut of the loot."

"I never sp—"

"How about those computers? Lea marked them as yours.

It's in the system, and because of how well you got that to work, I don't think it'll take them long to get to that." He got in Alex's face. "I told you I don't turn my back on my crew. Are you going to turn your back on us? On Will? On the people who've been helping you?"

Alex shoved him away. "I didn't sign up for this!"

"Universe ain't fair. Never was, never will be. What are you going to do?"

Alex wanted to scream he wouldn't do this. He couldn't. He wasn't a pirate like them. He didn't want to break the law. He'd had good reasons the previous times; his actions kept people alive.

It wasn't like he could leave. He couldn't storm out because he was unhappy with the situation. He was stuck here. He could die here.

The thought chilled him. If they blew up the ship, he'd die. He couldn't hide either. Even if he knew of a hiding place on the ship, when it was caught, it would be taken apart.

And if they did manage to escape? Then what? Would the captain just drop him off at the next station? Now that he'd been part of some jobs, that he knew what they'd done, wouldn't it be safer for them if Alex died?

He didn't want to die, but he didn't want to be caught either. It was prison time for him if that happened. He could kiss any chances of finding Tristan goodbye if he was in prison. No Tristan, no Jack.

He closed his eyes. '*You're going to have to make a choice,*' the Samalian's voice sounded. '*Why are you changing?*' it asked.

Jack. He was doing this for Jack. He'd do whatever was necessary to get to him.

He shoved the captain out of his way and left the room. He had his earpiece in by the time he sat at the board. "Someone tell Asyr to take the main console in her lab. I'm going to need backup on this."

CHAPTER 29

A scan of their immediate area showed a lot of available connections, each one a computer willing to talk with them. He kept the scan to the immediate physical area, so they were all on the other ship. If this was anything other than a Law ship, he'd have his pick of ways to enter their system, but he didn't trust these connections. If it were him, he would be monitoring all of them, and they would have traps.

He told his search program to ignore everything the scan had returned and sent it looking for other connection points. When it didn't return anything, he changed the parameter, anything that might be a connection point.

This got him results: six decoys, and the seventh had such a low probability Alex almost ignored it. Only the voice of one of his professors berating his students for not being systematic made him stop long enough to see that the code surrounding the point of interest didn't do anything. Once he realized that, he knew he had his way in.

His display showed him the lab console was active. "Asyr, are you ready?"

Her voice came back quivering. "Yes, but what do you expect me to do?"

"I'm giving you look-only access to my feed. You're doing the same thing as when we fought the engineering system. You look at the big picture and tell me what's coming. Tell me anytime an internal access point becomes active, I'll need to know that. Unlike the engineering system, this coercionist isn't going to be stopped with me just throwing a bunch of locks open."

He heard her take a breath. "Okay, I'm ready."

"Just stay calm, look for his patterns. Once you have that, you'll be able to predict what he's going to do." Alex's heart was racing. This was going to be a lot tougher than his other jobs. He grinned. "I'm going in now."

He sent programs to dozens of the obvious connection points to mimic intrusion, and used that confusion to sneak into the camouflaged one.

"You are not allowed here," the ship's systems said. "My director has been summoned. Leave now or face prosecution."

So much for sneaking in.

"Come on now. You haven't even given me a chance to tell you why I'm here."

"You are an unregistered coercionist. Your presence here is against statute 1254 of the open net act, which states that—"

"Yeah, yeah. I know. I'm not supposed to use my skills in the pursuit of illegal activities. Do you have any idea how boring that is?"

"The reason for the acts is irrelevant." The system's voice was cold, deep, and harsh. It barely had any personality. That told Alex there were control programs in place, to keep it in check. If he could find them, he could unsettle the ship enough to give him an edge. He didn't have long before the ship's coercionist got involved.

"Look, I'm not a bad guy, I'm just doing my job here, so how about you turn around? Any chance you can do that for me?"

"No." The single word answer had the ring of finality to it.

"You're just being difficult." Alex spun the display. The control code would be as rigid as the voice: utter stillness in a sea of change. Hardlines, unwavering in their duties. "I'm sure we can work—"

"You have incoming," Asyr interrupted. One of the internal connection points flashed.

"Got it." He sent out a dozen more programs to simulate more intrusions. "He's going to go for the decoys. Let me know when he's through them."

"How about this," he told the system. "You do me this one favor, and I'll owe you one down the line."

"No." More finality.

There. Alex had a command string so strict, it was bristling. He spent a few precious seconds studying it. This one controlled the ship's moral code, forcing it to do what it was told was right. This was why it knew the statutes, but it didn't explain the harsh tone.

He attached his code to it, camouflaged it, but left it inactive, then went back to searching for other controls.

"He's down with the decoys," Asyr said. "He's heading for you."

Alex released a handful of clones of himself and sent them away with instructions to muck about with the system. They wouldn't do any real damage, but the coercionist couldn't know that.

"He's going after the false yous, but he's making short work of them."

Alex found another command, one more promising: it kept the system's emotions in check. If that had been put in place as part of the initial programming, this computer hadn't ever experienced feelings. It'd have no idea how to handle the flood of sensations. Instant chaos.

Alex wasn't subtle—he ripped the code apart, and in the instant of shrieking, he placed his own program there, one that would keep the antibodies from rebuilding the control.

"What did you do!" the computer screamed.

"Nothing much, just giving you a taste of life."

"Make it stop!"

"Come on, live a little." He used the ship's confusion to access its code and do quick rewrites. Even in its current state, it didn't let him do much more than a few lines before protecting itself.

There was a flash in the distance. "Someone else connected," Asyr said.

Two of them? "Can you keep track of them both?"

"Yes, but this new one is going directly for the connections you used."

Alex cursed and abandoned what he was doing to focus on protecting his access. He wrapped it in a maze of code, a variation on what he'd used earlier against Asyr. He lengthened some of the distances as much as he could, twisted others around on themselves, mirrored code from other areas, and then wrapped the access point in a tight ball of code.

That done, he sent a program out to look for other camouflaged connections. Alex was under no illusion this one would remain open long.

"And who do we have here?" someone asked.

Alex spun the display, trying to find who had spoken, but then realized it had been a system-wide broadcast. He felt relief for a moment—they hadn't found him—then returned focus on his job.

He grinned and set a handful of points to bounce his transmission. "I am the Crimson Pirate."

"The what? Are you kidding me?"

Alex couldn't tell the gender of the coercionist; what he was hearing was a digitized translation of a voice. Systems didn't care if men or women were talking to them, but the disbelief came in clear.

"No, I'm quite serious." Alex watched as his opponent dismantled the program he'd left on the control. This guy was good. "I'm a pirate in crimson. Can't miss me; I really stand out."

"So, you think yourself a comedian?"

"No, I'm a pirate. Aren't you listening?" His program found the location of another connection point, but it was too far; he wouldn't be able to do a handover without being caught. He needed another strategy.

"You're not very good." The coercionist was going through his defense now.

"What can I say, I'm new at this," he said as he watched his code be unraveled. He reinforced it as much as he could, but this wouldn't work. He wrote a quick program and sent it to the available connection. Now all he had to do was buy himself time.

"No," the coercionist said. "You're not new at this, at least not at coercion." The unraveling slowed.

Alex thought this code was getting the better of his opponent, but then realized he was simply taking his time now. He'd taken Alex's measure and wasn't worried anymore.

"Did you study with Old Man Ravelo?"

"How—" Alex shut his mouth before he revealed anything.

"He was my teacher, oh, ten, fifteen years ago now. Subjective of course. I recognize his syntax in your code. When did you study under him?"

Alex froze. He couldn't have picked that up from his old teacher. He was better than making a mistake as basic as that. By reflex, he started calling up his programs to check the code, but stopped. He didn't have the time. He had to take care of this first, and then he'd go through his programs and remove such a clear signature. Shit, he'd have to send a program over the network to mask his previous work, otherwise they'd be able to track him all the way back to Luminex, get his name. He'd become a wanted man, even if they'd never actually see him coerce.

Focus, Alex! Survive this, fix the rest later!

"You might as well tell me," the coercionist said. "You're not winning this."

Alex's program activated. He was wrenched out of the system, then he was back through the other connection point. He fought the disorientation; he didn't have the time. Where was he? Medical system? He sent an update to the program, so it would wait for his command this time.

"Hey computer, you there?" Alex blocked as many of the connections as he could see.

No answer. They'd quarantined it; they didn't want Alex to

be able to gain control of the computer. The advantage was it couldn't tell on him, but he was limited to affecting the local systems. There wasn't much he could do with medical controls to make that ship leave. Trigger an epidemic alarm? Like they'd believe that.

His code around one of the access point shattered.

"There you are," the coercionist said. "That was a neat trick. I knew you weren't new at this."

Alex sent a few corroding programs at his opponent. "You guys really keep your ship's mind this tightly locked?" They wouldn't do any harm to the coercionist, but there was a chance they'd infect his bank of pre-written programs.

"We have to." The corrosion vanished before it got anywhere close to the other. "Do you think free will is something we can allow it with the armament we carry? Any instability and it would blow us and anyone around us."

"Talk about having trust issues."

"No one joins law enforcement because they're trusting people." A burst of code exploded toward Alex, so disruptive it registered as visual static.

Alex made his voice sound strained. "You know, I'm starting to think you don't actually like me." He put a wall between the incoming code and him, but purposely made it weak.

There was a sigh. "I can't even tell if you're serious or not."

"I am. You, you're very good. I admire that. I'm pretty good myself. We're a matched set, don't you—" his wall crumbled and the code came at him. Alex waited until the last moment to activate his program.

Wrenched again. A moment within his own ship's system, then back to the other ship. Where? What could he use? How long did he have?"

The code around him was balancing something, not money. He chuckled to himself. No, not money, power. Relay commands, power consumptions versus speed. He was in the propulsion system. Okay, from here he could stop them. All he had to do was find the code that would shut down their engines. Too bad he wasn't an engineer. He sent out search programs to tag anything with an on/off state.

"You're going to have to tell me how you do that," the coercionist said, "before I send you to prison, that is."

Alex saw the active connection. "Damn you're fast." He wouldn't have time to go through the switches. He needed a different tactic. He began coding.

"This is my ship. I know each and every pocket of code. There's nowhere you can go that I can't find you."

"Good to know. Next time I drop by, I'll make sure it's when you're sleeping."

"And what? You'll peek in on me? Watch me sleep?"

The idea of watching a stranger sleep sent a shudder of disgust down Alex's spine. "Don't worry, you're not my type."

"How do you know? You said we're a matched set."

"That was for a platonic relationship. There's no way I'd want to be intimate with you."

"That hurts."

"Too bad?"

"Funny guy. You really think flooding this place with searches is going to slow me down? What are they even looking for?"

"I'm not so much looking to slow you down, as to stop you completely." His program was done, a more elegant version of what he'd written to unlock the lab during his war with their engineering system.

But this time, instead of opening, he was shutting everything down. Let them try to chase them when they can't get the engines going. He cloned the program thousands of time.

"What the hell do you think you can do with—"

Alex released them.

One of the programs vanished as the other coercionist caught it.

"Are you insane!" the other screamed, and went after the programs.

Alex grinned. "Good luck catching them all."

"Do you have any idea what this can—"

Alex's view exploded with static, the screams of systems filling his earpiece, then everything went dark.

CRIMSON

Chapter 30

Alex's ears rang. He rubbed his eyes to clear the spots. It had been so sudden, even his brain hurt. There was a hush on the bridge that made him look around. The close to a dozen people there were split between looking at him with a stunned expression, or watching the main screen. Alex looked at it, but before he could make out more than... What were those, asteroid? Someone clamped a hand on his shoulder.

Startled, he turned to look at the captain. "You know," the man said, "for someone who keeps saying he doesn't want to kill anyone, you're racking up quite the body count."

Alex stared at him. What was he saying? He knew the words, but his brain was so jumbled it couldn't seem to make sense of them.

"Vic, what's the crew on a ship like that?"

The slim man looked at the screen thoughtfully. "I'd say sixty."

"Five months with us and you already have sixty-two kills."

The captain smiled. "I don't think anyone ever had that many so quickly. Not even—"

"It isn't like anyone's going to know he caused that," a voice said, and after a moment Alex recognized it as Anders.

"Shut up, Anders," someone said.

Alex forced himself to look at the screen. What the captain said didn't make any sense. He hadn't killed anyone. He'd been wrong. Those weren't asteroids, that was debris. Okay, that made sense; the metal content would hide the ship. But Alex didn't think there was enough to really do the job, and there were other things there, smaller and not metal. He tried to focus on them, but they wouldn't coalesce into something, he recognized.

The one thing he could tell for certain was that the Law ship wasn't there, so it had worked.

"Hey, Crimson, what did you do?"

Alex turned away from the screen, but he couldn't find who'd spoken.

It took him a moment to get his mouth to work. Why was his mind so foggy? He'd been thrown out of systems before. "I had to stop them." He hesitated. He felt like the words were fighting him. "I found myself in the propulsion system, so I shut down everything there."

"Everything?" a woman asked. She'd been there anytime Alex had been on the bridge. He thought she was the captain's first officer.

Alex nodded.

She looked thoughtful. "That could have done it." She nodded to the screen. "If the safeties went down before the rest, you'd end up with bad stuff mixing together. It ignites, and the fuel reserves are next to go. We'd get something like what we saw."

There was an explosion? Alex hadn't seen any explosions. What was she talking about?

"Crimson," the captain said, drawing his attention away from the screen and all those things there. "You look like you need to lie down. Go to your quarters. You did a good job; you're done here for now."

Alex stared at him. How could he be done? Wasn't it just a question of time before the Law ship started after them again? The captain stared back at Alex, looking like he expected a response.

"I'll take him," someone said, and after a moment Alex thought it was Perry. "You won't need me here, considering..." He trailed off.

Perry placed a hand on Alex's shoulder and gently pushed him. Alex thought he should stay, but the captain had told him to leave, so he wasn't going to argue. They reached the lift without saying a word.

"Are you okay?" Perry asked once the doors closed.

Alex looked at him, unsure how to answer. Was he okay? He should be, but he had a sense that things weren't quite right. Maybe the disconnect had given him a concussion? No, that couldn't be. The sound had been loud, but he'd heard louder. He took out the earpiece and checked for blood. There wasn't any.

"I am," he answered. He wasn't panicking, so he had to be okay, right?

Perry didn't look convinced, but he didn't say anything.

The doors opened at Alex's level, and they were almost to his quarters when Asyr came running.

"I did it! I did like you said. I looked for patterns in what he did, and I managed to get through his defenses and kick him off the ship!"

"That's good," Alex said in reflex. It was only a moment later he worked out that someone from the Law ship had managed to slip by him while he was busy. Hadn't there been a second coercionist? Why was it so damned hard to think?

He forced a smile. "That's great, Asyr."

She opened her mouth, but Perry shook his head. She remained behind while Perry guided Alex back to his room.

Will wasn't there, and that was a good thing. Alex could do with being alone for a while.

"Are you sure you're okay?" Perry asked.

Alex nodded. "I'm just going to lie down for a while." Which he did.

He thought he might sleep, but now his mind decided it was time to work. It went over the last moment of the coercion. Alex had sent the command to shut everything down. The other coercionist hadn't liked that—no, that wasn't right. He'd sounded scared. Moments later the connection had cut with loud static.

Alex frowned. How had he been thrown out? He hadn't seen the attack. And disconnections didn't happen with noise, his view just went blank. Where had the static come from? The screams? Why had the system screamed? Had his opponent used an attack Alex had never seen before?

A shadow of a thought formed at the back of his mind, but Alex focused on something else.

The coercionist had been good, possibly better than Alex— younger too—but what had been the point of disorienting him so much? To keep him from reconnecting? But why? He had to have monitor programs on all the connections by then; how else had he found him so fast?

The shadow moved closer and Alex heard its voice. *What if the coercionist wasn't the one who'd caused the disconnection?* It reminded him of someone, but he blocked that memory.

But the questions made no sense. If it wasn't the other coercionist who had kicked him out, who had?

The image of the field of debris came to him again, the small things floating among them. What were those things? They weren't so small he couldn't see them, so why couldn't he make out what they were?

Where's the Law ship? The question popped up in his own voice, not that of the shadow.

You did it, the shadow said.

Did what? He'd been kicked out of their system, so he hadn't stopped them. Their ship, maybe, but why wasn't the coercionist inside this ship now? Without Alex to defend it, it would be simple to take control.

So why weren't they in already?

They can't.

The debris bothered him. What were those small things in it?

He tried to calm his racing heart, to slow his breathing and focus. He'd seen the screen. Everything had been sharp except those things, so the problem wasn't with what he'd seen, but with what he remembered.

Had they been metal? No, they didn't have the right look for that. No jagged edges or shine to them. He couldn't shake the sense they looked familiar. Colored central points with extremities in other colors.

The central portion was brightly-colored. Green and gold, while the extremities were muted. The colors varied from pale to dark, but nothing bright.

For a moment he thought they were star-shaped, but that didn't feel right. If he unfocused his eyes they might look like that, but when his vision cleared he could tell the extremities weren't all the same length, and they didn't originate from the middle point. Now that he thought about it, the center was elongated.

Alex cursed. What were they?

You're almost there, the shadow said.

Alex focused. He almost had it, he was sure. Almost worked it out. His stomach twisted.

No, damn it, he wasn't going to be sick now. He forced his stomach down. He was done being sick each time he—

Go on...

No... He couldn't have.

Just a little more.

Alex put a hand to his mouth. He'd killed them.

The events came in focus. The static had been the explosion disrupting the computer. The systems had screamed because they were dying. The sound of those screams had been what disoriented him. The screen had shown the result. Those small things? They had been bodies. The crew.

His victims.

He hadn't wanted to kill anyone.

That doesn't seem to stop you.

"Shut up."

He couldn't deny who the voice belonged to anymore. Cold and calculating, alien. He hadn't heard it for so long, but he'd never been able to forget it. Tristan's voice.

Is that so bad? If you're going to take after me, shouldn't I be there to guide you?

Alex curled up in a ball, trying to get the voice to shut up. He hadn't meant to kill anyone. He wasn't a killer.

If you aren't, the alien's voice whispered, *how do you ever think you'll beat me?*

CHAPTER 31

Alex didn't think he could stand being on this ship anymore. It wasn't what he'd done—he was angry at himself for killing that crew, even if it was an accident, but it was done. He wanted to put it behind him, to forget about it, but the crew wouldn't let him.

Each time he ran into someone as he headed to his training sessions, or to Asyr's lab, they thanked him for taking down their pursuers. Each time, they acted like he'd done the best thing possible.

He'd plastered a smile on his face and shook the offered hands, or took the pats on the back good-naturedly. All this was normal for them. Alex had committed murder on a scale none of them here had, and they reacted by thanking him.

That wasn't what he wanted. He wanted to be despised; there were no justifications for what he'd done. Why wouldn't they stop?

Make them stop, then, Tristan's voice said. *You're stronger than they are. Show them what happens to anyone who defies you.*

Why couldn't Tristan stick to being in his nightmares? Why did he have to haunt him when he was awake too?

If you don't kill them, how are the others going to learn to respect you?

Alex wasn't going to kill again. It had been an accident. They had all been accidents; he'd never kill on purpose.

Alex couldn't do it anymore, so he locked himself in his cabin—at least he tried. He tried to be alone, to stop the gratitude, and the temptation to give into the voice, but Will kept bypassing the lock.

It wasn't that he didn't want Will around. Of everyone, he was one of the few who let him be. He'd say hi, do what he had to do, and leave. He was clearly waiting for Alex to initiate a conversation. The problem was that more than once, Will wasn't alone, and that other person just wouldn't shut up about how great Alex was.

So Alex had done everything he could to disable the lock, short of destroying it. He'd scrambled it, rewired it, which was the one time Will had spoken, to say not to do that again.

This time Alex had merely told the computer to ignore any and all requests to open the door unless Alex spoke to it directly. He was the only one with an earpiece, so no one else could do that.

The errant thought popped in that he should get Asyr one. Maybe he'd give her his, as a going away present.

He held the base of Jack's holo. What would he think of what Alex had done? In his nightmares, Jack was there with Tristan, congratulating him. Tristan was proud of him for killing so many people at once. Almost as many as on the Osaqua. The worst of it was Alex basking in the praise, loving it. He was a killer.

Jack couldn't be proud of him, and Alex couldn't stand the thought Jack might hate him for what he'd done. He imagined him telling Alex he understood. Those had been impossible situations. He hadn't meant to kill anyone. Alex needed Jack's forgiveness.

What he got instead was Tristan's voice berating him for being weak. Reminding him Jack wasn't real, and that Tristan understood. He understood the need to kill, the thrill of it, the power Alex gained in doing it. The voice wanted him to kill again.

It took all of Alex's will to shut it up, and that was becoming more difficult. Because of the nightmares, Alex slept less than before. Having Tristan in them, egging him on was one thing, but Jack being proud of him for killing? Alex couldn't stand it.

He thought about taking the Defender out and begging it for forgiveness, but it was just a hunk of stone, shaped and painted. It hadn't even shown up in his dreams again.

His stomach grumbled. He'd barely eaten anything of the food Will brought him that morning before shoving the tray outside, locking the door behind it. Hunger was the only way he could punish himself for what he'd done, so he'd go hungry.

Alex looked up from the plastic base he held when the lock beeped. It beeped a few more times, but the door remained closed. Finally, Alex had managed to keep Will out. He had a moment of guilt—this was Will's room too—but Alex needed to be alone. He needed to suffer.

As he watched, the lock's display went dark. It blinked a few times, then came back on, and the door opened.

Alex watched Will enter and place a tray of food on the end of Alex's bed. Alex wanted to be angry, but he couldn't work up the energy. He eyed the food tray as Will changed, then took something from under his bed before leaving.

Alex tried to resist the food, but he didn't have the willpower anymore. He drank the juice and ate a few bites of the steak before putting the tray outside the room. He didn't bother locking the door. He was out of ideas on how he could keep his roommate out. Will was clearly better at entering places then Alex was at locking them.

Not long after that came sounds Alex recognized as them docking to another ship. They were attacking someone, and the captain hadn't asked—ordered—him to help. It made sense, Alex thought. He had to be terrified Alex would blow that one up too.

Sometime after that, the ship undocked. There was a celebration. Will asked if Alex wanted to come, but didn't insist. Will came back drunk and went on and on about how Alex had to stop moping around, and how they'd start training again in the morning.

It wasn't in the morning, but in the afternoon that Will dragged Alex in the bathroom and told him to clean up. Alex protested, but Will wouldn't let him out until he looked better, so he gave himself a rough shave. Alex was surprised at how long his beard had grown, a few weeks' worth at least. Then he showered.

When he was presentable, Will dragged him to the gym. Alex halfheartedly went through the exercises. He didn't see a point in them, but he didn't want to argue with Will. This became Alex's only time out of his room.

The ship attacked another one. Again, the captain didn't request his help.

Coming back from exercising, Anders crossed their path. The man sneered and threw insults at Alex, but otherwise kept his distance.

See, the voice which had been leaving him alone said, *even Anders is scared of you now.*

Alex didn't want that. He wanted Anders to beat him, hurt him, as he'd promised he'd do.

The ship docked, but none of the usual bustle from them attacking a ship came. There had been a third attack, not too long ago, a few days? Weeks maybe? Alex had trouble keeping track of the days.

Will came in, grabbed a box from under his bunk, threw stuff in it, and stood. "Station," he said, before leaving.

They were docked at a station, so no attack this time. He settled himself back to mope, then realized that a station meant going off the ship. Away from the crew. He showered, put on clean clothes, and headed off the ship.

He didn't walk by anyone on the ship. It wasn't something he'd planned, it just happened. He wasn't planning any of this; he just needed to be away for a while.

Maybe longer. He didn't know.

Once he left the dock section of the station, the conditions improved. The people looked to have a comfortable life—the walls were clean. Since he didn't have a destination in mind, he found himself following a lively group having a loud discussion.

As they progressed deeper into the station, the hallways became crowded, so much so that people had to push each other aside to move. But there was no anger; it was simply how things happened here.

Conversations mixed, some serious, others joyful. Alex couldn't make anything out through the cacophony, but the comfort everyone had with each other, the happiness in the voices, chased away some of his gloom. He even found himself smiling when he caught sight of two kids, no older than five, chasing each other around the adult's legs.

Then the crowd thinned, and Alex realized they were in an open space filled with booths. A marketplace. He froze, as for a moment he thought he was elsewhere. Maybe if he stood here, Jack would find him. He looked up, expecting to see the sky, even while knowing it was impossible, but all that was above him was a bulkhead with lamps. And with that, the illusion was broken. Jack wasn't here in this market buying him something.

His mood dropped a little, but he wouldn't let himself fall back into depression. He was off the ship, among people going about and shopping. Buying, selling, doing normal things. He walked among them and found he felt better. This was something he'd missed since leaving Deleron Four.

Normality.

Nothing on the ship had been normal. That made sense—it was a pirate ship—and the one time he'd gotten off it, he'd been forced into a bar fight. He'd then had to run after the Defender and had been abducted. Not exactly typical for Alex.

He smelled meat and spices, and realized he was hungry.

No, he was famished. His stomach made it clear Alex was done eating only a few bites here and there; it wanted to be filled. He followed the smells to a booth with cloth walls. Cookers were lined up with pots filled with bubbling liquids in them.

"What is it?" he asked the woman standing behind the counter. Alex breathed in the aromas of fruits mixed with the meat and spices.

She looked at him and replied something Alex didn't understand. Alex wondered if there was something wrong with his hearing, but when she repeated herself, he realized she spoke a different language.

For a moment he was confused; she was human like him, so why didn't she speak the same language? Then the realization came: he wasn't on Deleron Four anymore. In fact, he probably wasn't in any corner of the universe he was familiar with. Of course she wouldn't speak the same language he did.

He gestured to the pots and spoke slowly. "What is this?" he mimed eating.

She smiled, nodded, and filled a bowl.

It wasn't what he'd intended, but he'd know what it was. He took the bowl and she extended her hand, palm up. Right, that gesture he knew.

He reached for his ID card, then realized it might not work here. Different language, so maybe a different system altogether. But what else did he have to pay with? Except that in the pocket with his ID was something else: a chip.

He pulled out the cred-chip. Where had that come from? He couldn't remember putting that there. Will, maybe? Or maybe one of the chips from Anders' job had gotten stuck? Would it work? The kid at the bar—Milo?—had said something about always using them. He handed it to her, and a moment later she gave it back, still smiling, so it had worked.

He turned it in his fingers, but his stomach wouldn't let him think about it. Hunger now, thinking later. He found a table in a quiet corner and dug into the stew. It was sweet and savory and spicy. He didn't detect any fruits in it, and was surprised to realize the sweetness came from the meat. It was the best food he'd ever eaten.

But that could have been the hunger speaking.

He had a second bowl, which was just as good. He was still hungry, but he didn't go for a third one. He wanted to be able to enjoy his time here, and overeating would make him lethargic.

He wished Jack was with him; he'd enjoy this market. The thought of Jack brought Tristan with it, and a reminder of the situation Alex was in. As much as he wanted to enjoy the market, he needed to think.

CRIMSON

CHAPTER 32

The bar Alex found was large and airy. It reminded Alex of a commercial space where someone had added tables and a bar at the back.

He stood in the entrance for a moment, looking it over, and was surprised at how colorful the people's clothing was. It was a strong reminder that he wasn't on Deleron Four anymore.

A man stood and headed in his direction—long tan coat, blue canvas pants, white shirt. Alex stepped out of the way to let him pass, and the orange and black fur on his hand, feet, and face only registered at that moment, along with the muzzle and round ears on the top of his head. Was that a—

Alex turned to call out to him, and saw that the back of his coat had a slit in the middle, from his ankle to his waist, and he could see a tail in the same orange with intermittent black bands.

Alex let him go; Samalians didn't have tails. He wouldn't

be able to help him find Tristan. His mood dropped a little again, and even noticing the handful of aliens in the bar wasn't enough to lighten it.

On his way to the counter, Alex noticed that some of the humans there acted oddly, or at least in manners he felt were odd. He passed by a table where two men and two women were seated, their hands perfectly still and splayed on the table as they talked. At another table, two women in stiff robes in shades of red and purple spoke in hushed tones, pointing to the others in the bar as if they considered them strange. And in a corner, a family in drab gray clothes held their children close to them, looking around fearfully.

"Can I have a Golden Hour?" Alex asked the man behind the bar.

The barman looked at him and replied in a language that sounded a lot like that of the woman who'd served him the stew. Alex stifled a sigh. Okay, people being different might be a problem if this was what he had to look forward each time he wanted to buy something.

He looked at the bottles lined up on the shelf and pointed to the only one he recognized, then handed the cred-chip. The display was visible, and Alex peeked as the man ran it through. It had over three-thousand on it. That was a lot of money. He'd have to ask Will about it.

The man handed him the chip and a glass, and Alex found a table to enjoy his drink. He sipped it and made a face. Or not.

Now that all he had to do was look at his drink, he couldn't avoid the question. What should he do? He had to reach Samalia, but could he risk his integrity to get there? Whatever he had left of it. He remembered Will telling him that staying on the ship would change him, but Alex hadn't believed him. That had been a mistake.

He wanted to blame someone for what was happening to him, but no one had forced him on the ship. No one had forced him to coerce that first computer. Yes, the captain had basically twisted his arm that time, but once Alex didn't have any options, he'd looked forward to doing it. He'd had fun fighting with the other coercionists.

Who did that? Who had fun breaking the law?

He knew that answer to that one.

What would Jack think of him? Alex shuddered as he remembered the dreams of him cheering Alex on as he fought and killed. He drank half his glass, then scrunched his face at the taste. At least it took his mind off the memory.

But Tristan was who Alex would have to deal with. He'd have to draw Jack out of him, and while he had the Defender to help with that, would it be worth doing if Alex became as much of a monster as Tristan was in his hurry to get there?

Couldn't he take longer to get to Tristan, make sure there was enough of Alex left for Jack to care for? He didn't know where he was in relation to Samalia, but he should be able to find a way to get there from here, even if it added years to his trip.

Alex brought the glass to his lips and found it was empty. How had he managed to drink that and not realize it? He headed to the bar for a refill. It was probably a bad idea, but he needed help thinking.

With his new drink in hand, he turned and almost ran into someone. The only thing preventing him from spilling his glass all over the other's chest was that the man had caught his hand.

"Careful there, buddy."

"Sorry," Alex replied. He had a flash of memory, turning with a drink in hand, running into Jack, the alien apologizing.

This man wasn't Jack. He was human and bald, a head shorter than Alex with pale skin and worn clothing.

"It's okay." The man looked Alex up and down, still holding his hand. "Say, you speak the same language as me. Mind if we share a table?" The man gently squeezed Alex's hand.

Alex thought back and yes, the man was right. Everyone here seemed to speak a language Alex didn't understand. He hadn't paid attention, letting the conversations flow over him.

Alex thought about turning the man down, but there was something about him that felt comforting. His smile was inviting. "Sure, why not?" He'd be able to get back to his thinking once they were done with their drinks.

"I'm Olien," the man said before pointing to a bottle and

paying for his drink. "I haven't seen you before. What brings you to this pleasant little place?"

Alex used the time to decide how to handle this. He couldn't be careless. "Crimson," he finally answered. "Just passing through." He guided Olien to his table. "What about you?"

The man sat, then looked at his hands. "Oh, I've been here for a while now. It wasn't the plan. I was on a trip and got into a scuffle. I got detained, and the ship left without me."

"I didn't think passenger ships could do that. Aren't there rules about all the passengers needing to be aboard before they leave?"

The man shrugged.

Alex thought about giving the man money to help him out; he had more than he needed. He'd even started to reach for his pocket when he got an odd sense about the situation.

There hadn't been any money involved, but the bumping into someone, the not-quite sob story, the offering of help. Those were almost an exact repeat of what had happened with Jack.

He changed the motion to scratching his chest, then sipped his drink, watching the man not watch him. "No luck leaving?" Was he just being paranoid? Had Anders turned him into someone who didn't trust in people's goodness anymore?

Olien shook his head. "This place doesn't get a lot of ships, and those that do dock, well, I don't know that I'd want to travel on them, if you know what I mean."

Alex nodded, his unease growing. When the man reached over and placed a hand on Alex's, he had to resist the urge to pull it away. "I'm just hoping to survive until someone trustworthy can take me away from this place."

Jack hadn't been this overt with his approach. He'd been ill at ease with the situation, much more believable as someone in trouble. Alex had been the one to make all the first moves. Except he hadn't. Tristan had manipulated him into making them, into being the one to make the offer of assistance.

"Didn't you say the ships here aren't trustworthy?"

Olien gave him a sweet smile. "I get a good feeling from you."

Alex forced himself to return the smile. He interlaced his fingers with Olien's, then pushed the hand up and back, bending the man's wrist until he grimaced. Alex wasn't falling for the same trick twice.

"You're hurting me," Olien hissed, but kept his voice low. He glanced around to see if anyone was paying attention to them.

The action confirmed Alex's suspicion. He didn't care if they attracted gazes, but no one was looking their way. "Who are you?"

"I told you, I'm O—"

"You're not really stranded here, are you?"

"Of course I—"

Alex bent the wrist back some more and the man clamped his mouth shut, eyes closed in pain. "Okay," he whispered. "I get the message. I'm sorry I tried to con you."

Alex relieved the pressure, but he didn't let go.

"Look, just let me go and I'll get out of here. I won't bother you again, I promise." Now that he wasn't in pain, the man's demeanor had changed. He wasn't meek and in need. He was carefully looking at Alex, and around, making sure he was safe.

"How badly do you need the money?" Alex asked.

"The—" Olien's surprise make it difficult for him to find the words. "I need it."

"Are you willing to work for it?"

"I-It depends." The man studied Alex. "How much are we talking about here?"

"Three-thousand."

The man's eye went wide for a moment, then he had control of himself. "What do you expect me to do?"

"Answer some questions."

"That's it? Questions? You don't expect me to kill anyone?"

Alex shook his head, and the next words slipped out before he could stop them. "If I wanted that, I could do it myself."

The man paled a little. When he'd regained his color, he nodded to their hands. "Look, if you're going to pay me, you won't need the torture."

Alex let go of him and sipped his drink.

"Before we start, can I ask you something?" The man rubbed his wrist.

Alex nodded.

"You've been conned before, right? That's how you saw through me, right?"

Alex nodded. That was an understatement.

Olien took a long swallow from his glass. "Okay, ask away."

"How did you pick me? Of everyone here, what told you I might be a target?"

Olien shrugged. "I didn't pick you here. I've been following you since you left your ship. You were distracted, lost in your head. Maybe a bit depressed. I followed you through the Center waiting for the right time, and when you came here I knew you'd be receptive. I figured that you'd be more inclined to help me out to avoid thinking about your own problems."

"Didn't you take a risk when you didn't let go of my hand?"

"What risk?" Olien smiled. "At worst you'd have said you weren't interested and I'd have let go. But I knew you wouldn't mind. I watched you check the bar out. Your gaze slid over the women, but you lingered on the men."

Alex frowned, trying to remember if he'd done that. "Maybe I was just checking out who was a threat."

"You're not a fighter. You're too at ease, and you wouldn't have overlooked the women if you were."

Alex nodded. Ana was certainly enough of a threat to his well-being when she put her mind to it. "Out of curiosity, if I hadn't stopped you, what would have happened next?"

Olien sipped his drink then leaned forward. "Depends on what you needed. Right now I'm thinking companionship, but that's just based on the little from when you had your guard down. I would have picked up more as we spoke, adjusted my actions to that, slowly becoming the person you needed. You'd have become comfortable, maybe we'd have sex—"

Alex shook his head.

"—or not. But at some point, I'd have mentioned I needed money and by then you'd have offered to help me out."

"Just like that?"

The man shrugged. "People are predictable."

Alex nodded. "So, you don't plan who you'll be ahead of time?"

"I can't. Until I know you, I can't know who you'll respond to."

Alex didn't think Tristan had made things up on the go. Based on everything he'd read, the alien was technologically savvy. Alex's file would have had everything Tristan needed to plan ahead. Alex's psychological profile was on file from the evaluation he'd taken when he was hired by Luminex. Just that would have everything Tristan needed to manipulate him.

"Out of curiosity, how long could you pull this off?"

"What do you mean?"

"How long could you be this person I needed? How long could you draw it out if, for some reason, what you wanted from me wasn't readily available?"

"I don't know. I mostly work in the short term since my marks have to get back to their ships, but I guess I could do it for as long as needed, unless who I'd have to be is someone I really didn't like playing."

"So charming me for months? Acting like you're in love with me?"

Olien studied Alex for a moment. "Yeah, I could do that." He paused as he finished his drink. "Shit, is that what happened to you?"

Alex didn't respond, but the man winced.

"No wonder you were ready to rip my hand off."

"How about if I'm not around?"

"Well, if you're not here I don't have to worry about how I act."

"But when I come back. Could we pick up where we left?"

"How long are we talking here?"

Alex shrugged. "A year, maybe more."

"Am I waiting for you to come back? Like is this a business trip or something?"

"No. As far as you know, I'm gone. When we run into each other again it isn't planned."

"I don't know. I mean if we'd been together for a while before that, I might be able to remember the gist of what we had, but the whole thing? Probably not. I'd miss some details here and there."

"What do you mean by forgetting details?"

"You get that what I do is just an act, right? Once you're gone, I go back to who I was, so I can deal with my own stuff. Probably find another mark. The more time passes, the tougher it's going for me to remember you and who I was for you."

Alex stiffened. Jack had been an act? Of course he had been. Even his dreams told him that over and over. He knew he'd have to draw him out of Tristan, so how hadn't he realized that part of it? Was he so obsessed that he couldn't see it? But he couldn't have been just an act. A monster like Tristan couldn't know how to love. He'd been over that before, more than once.

What Olien told him confirmed that time was a factor. If he wanted Jack back, he couldn't let Tristan forget him. How long had it been now, objectively? Years? No, not that long. Tristan had to reach Samalian, same as Alex. Each stop Alex made widened the gap, but it had only been six months, seven at most since he'd lost Jack. So, they couldn't be more than a year apart.

But each second's delay increased the time difference between them. How long did he have until Tristan forgot Jack completely?

He stood and flicked the cred-chip to Olien.

"We're done?" the man asked.

"We are."

Alex left. He had to go talk to the captain.

Chapter 33

Alex cursed as he called up the station's map for the fourth time when the door that was supposed to lead to the docks opened up to a residential section. He'd gotten lost again. Maybe he had a problem with directions? Or more likely he needed to slow down and pay attention to where he was going, instead of rushing forward. This was starting to feel like one of those 'slower is faster' situations.

He traced the route back to the docks, memorized it, and walked there instead of running. If he hadn't taken the time to look at the code under the interface, he'd think someone was messing with him, but the code was in order, so this was all his fault.

The conversation had made him realized a few things: that he needed to pay more attention to his surroundings, the people, and how he got places. That he needed to be more guarded. Olien had picked him as a target because he'd shown how he felt, but more importantly, he was on the clock.

It didn't matter how good Tristan was, eventually he would forget Jack. And it wasn't like he even had a reason to try to remember him. As far as the alien was concerned, he'd never need Jack again. Alex was the one who wanted him back.

"Finally," he muttered as he reached the docks. Now he ran. He couldn't get lost here; all he had to do was follow the docks until he reached his ship.

Ten minutes later he had to check the docking list because he should have reached the ship by then. He cursed. The ship was docked on the other side of the station.

He finally made it to the ship, having had to cut through some restricted areas to make it as straight a line as he could. He stopped next to the captain who was supervising the loading and unloading of crates.

"Captain," Alex started, then had to wait until he caught his breath. "I'm done being your passenger."

The captain looked around them. "Are you certain? This isn't the best place to leave the—"

"I want to be part of the crew," Alex cut him off.

The man studied Alex for a moment. "Are you sure?"

"Yes. Until we reach Samalia, I want to be a member of your crew, but—" Alex stopped at the raised eyebrow.

"Why am I not surprised you want to put a condition on it? It seems to me that you don't quite understand what it means to be part of my crew."

"I'll make it wor—"

The captain raised his hand, and Alex stopped.

"Mister William," he called, and Will joined them. "Mister Crimson is considering joining the crew. Have him help with the freight transfer." He looked at Alex again. "If you still want to be part of my crew once you're done, come find me and we can discuss those conditions you want to put on your employment."

Will stared at Alex, then sighed and motioned for him to follow. When they were in the ship, Will looked over his shoulder and shook his head. "Walk."

Even as used as he'd become to the way Will spoke, it took Alex a moment to figure out what he meant. "I can walk away from this once I'm on Samalia."

"No." Will stopped and turned to face Alex. "This," he indicated the ship, "stays stuck." He tapped Alex's chest. Alex wanted to rebuff the statement, but Will was still trying to work out how to say what he felt he needed, so Alex waited. The younger man tapped Alex's head. "That changes, get dark. This me. Not you. You're bright. Crew steals that. Your guy, he gonna want you?"

Alex understood Will's worries then. And he found he couldn't explain without telling him a truer version of the reasons than he'd given him up to this point.

"Will, Jack isn't waiting for me on Samalia; he's a prisoner of someone pretty bad. You say that being part of the crew's going to change me, but I think the only way I can save him is if I change. I need to be tougher. I don't think Alex the corporate coercionist can do it, but I think that Crimson has a chance."

"Your guy?"

"I'll have to live with the consequences, but I think he'll understand."

Will nodded, as if that made sense to him. "I help? Got friends."

Alex smiled and placed a hand on Will's shoulder. "I have to do this by myself." He wasn't exposing anyone else to Tristan. Not only would he have to explain what Jack was in relation to the alien, but he was certain others wouldn't survive the encounter.

Will searched Alex's face for a moment, then turned and grabbed two gravity sleds. He led Alex to crates which they loaded, and he followed Will to a warehouse where the crates were added to more. As far as Alex could tell, they were the results of the jobs they'd pulled on the way here.

He was able to keep his curiosity under control for three trips as part of the line of other crew members moving crates. "Why aren't we going back to the other station to sell this? Didn't Lea say that guy there gave really good prices?"

Will gave him an exasperated look.

"I'll answer that," the woman behind them said, and Will gave her a grateful smile. She pushed her cart next to Alex and matched his speed. "There's a few reasons. The big one is that if we always go back to the same fence, the Law's going to notice, especially with the size of the hauls you've made possible. I'm Alison, by the way."

"Crimson." Alex offered his hand.

She shook it. "Oh, I know who you are. Everyone on the ship does. The other reason is that the captain likes to do a circuit. It's pretty big, and it isn't identical from one time to the next. I've been with him for fifteen years, subjective, and when we unloaded for Harligon, it was only my second stop there. He does it so the Law can't trace our route. After this, we'll be stopping at Samalia."

Alex nodded, remembering the captain showing him the stops to Samalia. "Then why couldn't he tell me when you'd get there?"

"Because that's going to depend on the number of jobs he can line up on the way. The more jobs, the longer it takes."

Alex nodded. "But people knew you were heading to Samalia...wouldn't the Law know that too? Couldn't they find you that way?"

Alison grinned. "We were a merchant ship where we picked you up. Merchants show where they're going. If you haven't noticed, our board doesn't say anything here."

"What board?"

She looked at him, surprised. "It's where the ships put up their itinerary." She took out her datapad, and after a few taps showed it to him. Multiple ships were listed, with many, but not all, showing destinations. Golly's Yacht was there, without a destination.

"And you do this on all stations?"

"Of course, isn't that how you found us?"

Alex shook his head. "I asked around, and someone pointed me to you." He'd looked at the passenger cruisers' destinations, but it hadn't even occurred to see if the merchants advertised it. He thought it was risky—the Law had to know and be able to track them this way—but they'd been doing this for years without getting caught, so they had to know what they were doing.

It took six hours to empty the hold and bring in supplies.

By the time they were done, Alex was sweating, tired, and wondering how many jobs it had taken to get that much cargo. He'd helped on six, maybe seven before the accident, but he didn't know how many others had happened while he was in self-imposed lockdown.

How many more jobs had the captain planned between here and Samalia? How long would they take?

"I see you're still here," the captain said.

"Yes, sir. I haven't changed my mind."

"Very well. Go clean up. Meet me here in an hour and we can discuss your terms."

Alex nodded and headed for his quarters. There he took out his clothes and looked them over. Will had taken him to buy a few extra sets on the last station, but they matched his old, normal clothes. The kind of things he'd worn when he was a corporate coercionist.

He felt he needed to set the rest of his trip apart from his previous life. He was a pirate now, and he wanted to...not so much look the part—everyone on the ship dressed how they pleased—but fabricate a look that would help him make the division. Something he could step out of when he had Jack back and things were normal again.

He had nothing that let him do that. He'd have to go shopping after his conversation with the captain.

The captain was talking with official-looking people When Alex found him, so he stood back to what he thought of as 'at attention'. When the captain was done, he turned to Alex and his lips quirked in a smile.

"I don't run a military ship, Mister Crimson. You don't need to stand stiff like that."

"Sorry, sir. I don't really know what's expected of me as a crew member."

"Pull your weight, follow my orders or those of whoever you're working under at the time. Don't cause trouble you can't get yourself out of."

"Seems pretty simple."

The captain nodded. "I run a relaxed ship. Now follow me. I need a drink."

Alex followed the man a few bays down to an unmarked door that opened into a bar. The lights were low, and only a few of the tables were occupied.

"Hey, Meron!" someone called. "Come on over and have a drink with us."

It took a moment for Alex to find the man who'd spoken. He was thin, with scars on his face. The captain had located him too, and looked annoyed.

"Follow me, but don't say anything."

Three others were seated at the table with the man who had called to the captain. Two women—one dark-skinned and the other very pale—and a squat man.

"Rogan," the captain said, his voice neutral. "I didn't know you were here."

The man smiled. "Got here a few days ago. Come on, sit. Let me get you a drink. Wine work? You still like red?"

"That's fine." He pulled a chair and sat as Rogan left for the counter. The captain nodded to the dark-skinned woman. "Hello, Felicia, how have you been doing?"

"Don't act like you care, Meron," she replied. Alex to the time to look her over. He needed to get in the habit of doing that. She was wearing a tight body suit in beige with gold trim. She was, as his grandmother would say, well-stacked, and she had pale brown curls. She looked tense.

"I'm just being polite, Felicia. Why don't you introduce me to the others, so we don't feel like we have to converse?"

"That's Volantia." She indicated the pale-skinned woman. She was wearing a white business suit. Her hair was black, and eyes violet. She nodded to the captain.

"That's Druin." The man wore a loose, unbuttoned shirt. His blond hair was disheveled, and he was slouched in his chair instead of sitting straight, like the others. The man nodded to the captain then looked Alex over, a speculative smile on his lips.

Alex couldn't shake the feeling the man was undressing him mentally.

"Who's the fellow with you?" Druin asked.

"The newest member of my crew," the captain answered.

Druin's smile widened. "And what is it you do for your captain?" he asked Alex.

Alex wasn't sure if he should answer, so he glanced at his captain, who gave a small nod, lips tight.

"I clean floors, sir," Alex answered, figuring that was a safe answer.

"And you shine them? Polish them?"

Alex hesitated. "Yes, sir."

"Meron, can I borrow him? I too have...hmmm...floors that need polishing."

"No," his captain answered bluntly.

"That's a pity." Druin looked at Alex. "You should jump ship. I have far better assets to offer you. Why, even my—"

"There you go," Rogan said. Putting a glass before Alex's captain.

He stared at the glass while the others snickered. It was filled with grapes.

"I see you've run into some of my crew."

"Yeah." Rogan could barely contain his laughter. "They had great stories, as usual."

"I'm certain." The captain's voice was cold, and Alex thought he was doing his best to control his anger.

"So, what else have you been up to, Meron? It's been a while since we've been at the same station."

"It's only been three years for me," the captain answered.

"Really? It's got to be going on ten for me."

The captain smiled. "I can tell. You shouldn't stand still for so long. Someone's going to catch up to you at some point."

"I'm not worried. I can take them on, whoever they are."

The captain smiled. "I have no doubt you aren't worried." He stood. "While I appreciate the drink, I have business to discuss with my new crew member." He nodded to the dark-skinned woman. "I know you won't believe this, but it's good to see you again, Felicia. It was good to make your acquaintance," he told the other two.

He led Alex to a table on the other side of the bar, where he sat against the wall, eyes fixed on the others. Alex sat facing him, and a waiter came to take their orders.

"I don't know what the procedure is," Alex said. "Am I allowed to ask you a question?"

The captain smiled. "If we're in a bar, neither of us are on duty, so yes, you can ask."

"Who are they?"

"Other captains. This is a captain's bar. We come here to get away from the crew, to talk business among each other, or if we want to conduct private discussions without the rest of the crew finding out."

"That Rogan guy, you don't like him."

"You can think of him as a rival. He tried to steal my cargo more than once."

"So, letting you do a job then attacking you?"

The captain nodded.

"Lea told me about the grapes, but why did he do that? Serve you a glass of them?"

"He's rubbing my nose in a failed job. He hoped I'd get angry and start something. He's looking for an excuse to kill me."

"Can't he just pull a gun and shoot you?"

"Not without provocation, not if he wants to keep working with the others. We have a code. It's rather loose, but the primary tenant of it is that we need to trust each other. If Rogan just shoots me, no one's going to be able to trust him. Some might even let the Law know where they can find him."

"But he tried to steal your cargo."

"That's expected; we are pirates after all. But I made him pay. My ship's better-armed, my crew more experienced. I'm sure he'd love to blow me out of the void if he thought he could manage it. We're not all as trustworthy as the others."

Alex nodded. "The dark-skinned woman?"

"Felicia. She used to be my first mate, and my wife."

"Ouch."

The captain shrugged. "This isn't an easy life; there's a lot of stress. She found she preferred giving the orders over relaying them, so she tried to take over my ship. She hates that I won."

The drinks arrived, and the captain downed his and ordered another. Alex settled for a sip.

"Now," the captain said, "all those questions sound to me like you're procrastinating laying down your ultimatum."

Alex stared in his glass. "It isn't an ultimatum."

"Your words were, 'I'll be part of the crew, but.' Sounds like an ultimatum to me."

Alex looked at his captain. "I'm not—"

The man glared at him.

Alex sighed. "I'm not going to withhold anything, no matter what you decide. I can't; I need you to take me to Samalia, and I need to get there as soon as possible, but that's the thing. I need to be there soon."

Alex looked in his glass, drank it all, and then told his captain everything. How he met Jack, fell in love with him. How Jack turned out to be Tristan. How Alex was used to gain access to Luminex and then abandoned. How the company treated him, held him prisoner. How he tried to get back to his normal life, but couldn't. How he stole company property and fled, determined to find Tristan and bring Jack back.

"And I spoke to a con man who uses the same trick, and from what he tells me, the longer I wait, the lower the odds are that Tristan will be able to even recall Jack."

The captain sipped his drink. The server bringing it was the only time Alex had paused. "You realize your plan sounds insane, right?"

Alex shrugged. "It's all I have."

"You have us. You could make a good life on my ship. Your skills could get you up in rank. By the look of you, you've taken to the exercise fairly well. I'm sure you can become a good fighter."

Alex shook his head. "I have to do this. I have to at least find out if there's anything of Jack left, but for that I need to get to Samalia soon."

"I'm afraid I can't do much about that. I can't shorten the distance between here and Samalia. And before you bring that up, no, I can't push the engines. That's something that only works in the vids. The maximum speed my ship can reach is set."

"Alright, but each time we do a job, that costs us what? A week, two? I can't say I've paid attention."

"Around that, yes."

"Okay, how many jobs between here and Samalia?"

He considered for a moment, tapping his fingers on his glass. "Probably a dozen. It'll depend on what I hear on the network."

"So that's an extra three to six months to the trip. Do you really need that many jobs? With my help, I mean. When I take over a ship, it doesn't matter how large their security force is. You could go after larger ship, better cargo."

"That's already my plan. I have feelers out for ships with high volume and high-value cargo. Twelve of those, and we'll be set for a while."

"Are you saying you'll stop going after ships once we reach Samalia? Lea said that no one she knows had ever been able to put this life behind them."

Alex gave the captain a moment to contradict him. When he didn't, he continued. "If you're not stopping, isn't going after twelve ships just greed?"

"What's your point?"

"On that first job, Lea said that with my help, we got two or even three times the cargo than if I hadn't helped. So, let's say that with me, each job is worth twice as much. We could do six jobs and have the equivalent of twelve."

The captain smiled. "Starting to think a lot of yourself, aren't you?"

"Anders, of all people, said I should take the glory I'm due. I don't think I'm irreplaceable, but I do think I make a difference in how the jobs go. Even you said as much."

"So, you want me to do six jobs instead of twelve, and I expect you want to keep the downtime to a minimum too?"

Alex almost agreed, but shut his mouth to think it over. "I

don't think I know enough to say how short that should be."

The captain smiled. "Alright. Here's what I'm willing to offer you. I will seriously consider doing fewer jobs, but only on the condition that you fix this thing between you and Anders."

"I'm not sure I understand, sir. There's nothing between me and Anders."

"Bullshit. I'm not dumb, I know what happens on my ship. You and him have a problem. I want it resolved."

"I don't have a problem with him. Anders is the one with a problem."

"I don't care. If I do this, I need to be sure you'll be alive to do your part." He silenced Alex with a hand. "You're not a passenger anymore. I can't offer you protection; that would be playing favorites, and as much as people call Anders's group my favorites, they earned their positions. They didn't kiss my ass to get it."

The captain leaned back. "The thing is that this issue between the two of you has affected the whole ship. You two are dividing the ship between yourselves."

"Sir, I didn't do anything to make that happen."

"You think I care? There've been fights because someone badmouthed you. Not everyone likes Anders. He's hard and uncompromising, but he's good. He's been with me for a long time now, and he's one of the few people I can trust to follow my orders without questions. Before you showed up, he was able to keep everyone in line. Yes, I know, you didn't ask for any of that. Tough. This life's hard, and I'll remind you that you decided to join the crew."

Alex looked away. Was this a mistake?

"Before you think of quitting, you can't. Plenty of people heard you joining. If it hasn't spread to the whole of the ship by now, it won't be long. You're giving all the people who don't like Anders someone to rally behind, because of everyone on the ship, you're the one who's been standing up to him."

"Will's kicked him in the balls more often than I have."

The captain's serious expression cracked for a moment. "Will's not a leader. All he's doing is defending himself, but when Anders gives him an order, Will obeys. At least he used to."

The captain picked up his glass, saw it was empty, and put it down. "Look, let me explain something about my ship. All pirate ships, really. Everyone on it is wanted for one thing or another. Take Will. Believe it or not, he's wanted by three different governments, and that was before I took him in. They all count on me to keep them safe. I keep other pirates off our back because I have a reputation for being merciless to anyone to goes after one of mine. But they also count on me to keep the Law and whoever else is after them from catching him. While we were docked to unload the cargo for Harligon, two teams of bounty hunters attacked us. We repelled them because Anders gave orders, and they were obeyed."

"Sir, you have to know I didn't start any of this."

He sighed. "I know. But it's still the situation we're dealing with."

Alex nodded. "Sir, can I ask, what's Will's story? You said three governments are after him, why?"

"I don't know the details. Even Will doesn't."

"He said you rescued him."

The captain nodded. "He was twelve, filthy, and being worked to death by his...crewmates is the word I have to use. Torturers is a better term. They were lashing him, forcing him to push a crate even Evans couldn't move. I was just going to tell them to stop, but before I could, one of them pulled out a stun-staff set so high that when it touched Will, the shock sent him flying at my feet. The lot of them laughed."

"Did you leave anyone of them alive?"

His tone was grim. "No." Then he chuckled. "I carried Will back to my ship and we had to cut that stay short. I kept him in the ship for the next subjective year. Doc looked after him, and even Anders took care of him."

He indicated he wanted another drink when the waiter walked by.

"Must have been a decade objective before I allowed him off the ship, and within ten minutes someone kidnapped him. Anders and his team brought Will back. We're still banned from that station on threats of being shot on sight. But yeah,

I'd do that with anyone of my crew. Including you. I'll protect you from any outside threat, but I can't do anything for you internally."

The waiter placed the drink, got paid, and stayed there until the captain glared at him.

"Look," he continued once the waiter had left. "The honest truth is that if Anders kills you, it's going to be an inconvenience for me, but it's going to start a war among the crew. I can't have that. Hell, just him trying could spark things off."

"Sir, I don't know what I can do. I told Anders more than once I don't want to take his place on the ship. Everyone knows I'm leaving once we reach Samalia, so I don't even understand why he's worried."

"Mister Crimson, this is probably the one thing I can't fix. You need to either get the people who look up to you under control, or convince Anders you're not a threat. Anything less and you'll be in danger." He downed his drink and smiled. "Aren't you happy you decided to join my crew?"

Alex tightened his lips to keep from responding. Yeah, this was turning out to be such a great idea.

CRIMSON

CHAPTER 34

Alex stared at the bottom of his glass. There was movement in his peripheral vision, then someone refilled it.

"I see you've made your choice."

Alex looked up, and the golden-furred Samalian leaned back against the counter where bottles were lined up.

"Why is it you only show up in bars?"

He shrugged. "You tell me. It's your dream."

"Right," Alex replied sourly. "I guess you're here to tell me I'm making a monumental mistake? Throwing my life away?"

"I told you before. I'm not here to judge you, just—"

"To tell me hard truths, yeah, yeah." He sipped the drink. It wasn't as strong as he'd expected, and had a smokiness to it that was vaguely familiar. "So, lay it on me then."

"This is going to have consequences."

Alex rolled his eyes. "Tell me something I don't know."

The Samalian shook his head. "You don't know the depth of them. You think they're like these clothes you bought.

Something you'll be able to take off and forget about once you're done here."

"You're being pessimistic. No one outside this ship knows what I've done, and they're not going to hold it over me."

"I'm the realist. If you have to live with it the rest of your life, is it going to have been worth it?"

"I'm doing this for Jack," Alex replied without hesitation. "So yes, whatever I have to do, it's going to be worth it."

Someone sat next to Alex. Fur so dark the brown could have been black, with white speckled over it. Alex felt his hopes rise, but then the Samalian spoke.

"You, give me a drink, strongest stuff you have. I'm celebrating." Tristan turned to Alex and smiled. "Don't listen to him, he just doesn't know what's best for you. I, for one, totally approve of your decision."

"Go away. I didn't do it for you."

Tristan took a long swallow of the glass before him. "Good stuff, keep it coming." He turned and leaned against the back. "If you did this for that Jack of yours, isn't it funny how I'm the one here and not him?"

Alex looked at the Samalian behind the bar. "I don't hear you contradicting him."

"Hard truths, Alex. Hard truths."

* * * * *

Alex opened his eyes and cursed silently. He was starting to prefer the nightmares over those weird dreams. At least with the nightmares he knew what to expect by now.

Will was already gone, so Alex got up, showered, and dressed in the gray jumpsuit he'd bought after his talk with the captain. It was for engineers and had many pockets in it. With it he put on a black jacket, trimmed in red. He'd liked the red, figured it fit his pirate name, and the fabric was reinforced.

Dressed, he headed to the computer lab, to get back to the

work he'd been neglecting. He began by going over Asyr's fight against the coercionist. He was on the second viewing when she entered, dressed in her red and gold jacket over a pink shirt and black slacks.

"You did really good," he said as she stood there, stunned. He indicated the display.

She ignored that and hugged him tightly. "I'm so glad you're out of your room."

It took Alex a moment to get over the surprise, then he returned the hug. "Me too."

She took a step back, blushing. "I mean, Will told me you were out, but he said you'd joined the crew so I thought he was joking."

"He wasn't joking." He watched for her reaction, but she only nodded. If his decision affected her, she didn't show it. "It's only until we reach Samalia. I'm out after that." He turned to face the display. "How about you run me through what you did?"

"Oh, I just did what you told me. I looked for patterns, and used that against her. She used a lot of walls and hunting programs." She indicated codes moving toward them, and then away. "Those are some I reprogrammed to hunt her. She didn't see them coming, so while she was busy with them I cloaked myself, got around her wall, and blocked the connection point she was using."

She chuckled. "It was kind of fun. I mean I didn't do much, not really. It's nothing compared to what you did; you took on an entire ship. I can't even imagine how you managed that. And then you just blew it up. You're going to have to show me—"

"Asyr, please stop." Alex had to close his eyes and fight not to throw up. "I don't want to hear about that." All those deaths. He was responsible for them.

"Why not?"

The question was so casual it enraged Alex, and he almost struck her. How could she even ask that? It was obvious why. He brought his shaking under control, and reminded himself she came from a different world. For her, killing seemed to be normal.

"I didn't want to kill them." He rested his elbow on the console and looked at the recording. It had looped and showed the start of their fight again. "I just wanted to keep them from catching us. Their death shouldn't be celebrated."

She shrugged, pulled a chair from the closest station, and sat. "They knew the danger when they came after us. If you hadn't done it, we would have shot them down."

"But I should have been better than that. I should have found a way to disable the ship, let them float in space while we got away. What I do is supposed to ensure fewer people get hurt, not more."

"You know it's going to happen again, right?" Alex looked away. "You're part of the crew now, so you're going to end up in a position where it's going to be them or you."

"It doesn't mean I have to look forward to it." He forced himself to look at her. "I take it you've killed before?"

She chuckled. "How do you think I ended up here?"

Alex raised an eyebrow.

"I was a kid, twelve, maybe thirteen."

"You killed someone at that age? Why?"

"He took me from my family. Stole me, really. He was king, so it was his right, but I didn't want to go. He took me to his castle and forced me to have sex with him."

Alex gawked.

"I fought him, screamed, but he didn't care. I was his property, like everyone on the planet. At first he kept me locked in a room with nothing but the bed and a hole for me to do my business in. He'd show up daily to use me. I stopped fighting him when I realized the only way I'd get out was if he thought I'd grown to enjoy it. So after a while he started bringing me out, dressing me, and showing me to his nobles. His child wife.

Asyr shuddered and was silent for a time. "At one of the meals I managed to take a knife, and when he took me to his chambers afterward to do his husbandly duties on me, I gutted him. He screamed, so the guards rushed in and I was able to escape in the confusion. I made it to the port and sneaked onto a ship."

"What did they do when they found you?"

"We were in space by then, so they couldn't do much. They could have spaced me, but I was just a kid, so they couldn't bring themselves to do that. They passed me off to another ship as soon as they could."

"This one?"

She shook her head. "Different pirate ship. The guys who'd bought me figured they'd get to have fun, but the captain's wife found out about it and took me in. She protected me, taught me. A few years later there was a mutiny. I barely made it out before they sealed the ship."

"What happened to them?"

She shrugged. "Last I hear they'd gotten in trouble with a corporation, so they're probably dead. I managed to survive on my own for a while before bounty hunters found me. They were going to bring me back to the king's family. I gave them the slip, and ran into the captain. You probably don't know it, but he hates bounty hunters. There wasn't much left of them by the time we left the station. He's been protecting me ever since."

"I'm sorry," Alex said.

She smiled. "Nothing you did, but life isn't pretty, or clean. You take the compliments where you get them, and you do what you can to be happy. And you make sure the rest doesn't stick to you. You're lucky; no one knows what you did. You're not going to have anyone hunting you. When you leave, you'll be clean. For the rest of us, this is all we have."

Alex nodded, her argument feeling familiar.

"Wait, they're still hunting you? After all this time? It's got to have been decades ago, objectively."

"The family still wants me. They're never going to forget what I did."

Alex nodded. "I still can't rejoice over killing those people."

"That's not what I'm saying. I'm alive because of you. Most of us are alive because of what you did, and that's worth celebrating. We're all happy you're with us. Well, most of us. Anders is still pissed at you."

Alex sighed. "I know, and now that I'm part of the crew, Anders can do whatever he wants to me. The captain can't stop him. I didn't even know he'd been keeping Anders in check when I was a passenger."

"Anders can't just kill you. If he attacks you, we're going to know and make him pay. But he can see to it you have an accident. We'll know it's him, but without proof it's going to be tough to just take him out and not have the captain skin us for it."

Alex had a moment of shock at the extent Asyr was willing to go for him. The captain had told him about it, but Alex hadn't believed him. And she made it sound like there were a lot of them, willing to take on Anders for Alex's sake.

He shook his head. He couldn't allow that. He didn't want to be responsible for those deaths, because he had no illusions about it. If fighting erupted, people would die, on both sides. Resolving this wasn't just about saving his life anymore; it was about all their lives.

How had he managed to find himself in this situation? All he'd wanted was to reach Samalia. He looked at the display, replaying Asyr's fight again. If Anders was a computer system, this would be so easy to fix. Go in, change his code, change the parameters, make it so the man would want to look out for him instead of wanting him dead.

He straightened. Why not? That might actually work.

Chapter 35

This section of the ship didn't look different from any other. The floors were clean—courtesy of Will, Alex was certain—the walls were gray, but the terminal at the intersection didn't work. That, as far as Alex could tell, was the only signal post that he was entering Anders's territory.

When he'd asked the system for Anders, he'd gotten it, but he'd also been informed that he had a block of twenty rooms assigned to him. As far as Alex knew, no one else had more than one room. And only a few were quarters, at least by their size. Most were large enough to hold meetings, or parties. Milo had mentioned something about that, hadn't he?

It felt to Alex like there was enough space they could keep to themselves, but he hadn't noticed any aloofness from Anders's gang. Even Anders was cordial enough with everyone, except Alex.

He'd come here within minutes of getting the idea. He knew that if he'd waited, he would have lost his nerves, and it might have taken him days to work them back up. He'd looked at himself, just to make sure he no longer looked like a passenger, and got moving.

He hadn't told anyone, which he knew was a bad idea. If Anders decided he didn't like Alex's offer, there was no telling what he'd do. But his friends would have talked him out of it. He was nervous about it already, and it wouldn't have taken much to convince him not to come.

Alex hesitated at the door. Other than the terminal, there were no signs on the door. It wasn't even locked. Anders had been here so long, everyone had to know what was his by now. He pulled out his datapad and checked again that he was there. He was, along with a dozen of his people. The list of names was on the side, but he didn't pay attention to them.

He put the datapad away, calmed his nerves, and entered.

Sounds of conversation and laughter told him where they all were, and Alex stopped only when he was in that doorway. The room was large with a conference table pushed against a wall, bottles covering it. Chairs were spread around the room with people slouching on them, glasses in hand, listening to Anders who was seated on the edge of the table.

He was the first one to notice him, and stopped in the middle of what he was saying, a stunned expression on his face. Slowly the others turned and eyed Alex as the room fell silent.

"You've got balls," Anders said when he found his voice. "I've got to give you that." He was wearing a black shirt with silver threads at the cuffs and collar, and he had a golden chain over it Alex had never noticed before.

Having everyone look at him made Alex want to turn and run. Most had bored expressions, but a few looked at him in anticipation. One, a slim man with ashen skin, looked at him hungrily.

He took a step forward and did what he could to keep his hands from shaking. This wasn't bravery, he told himself. This was a necessity. This was for Jack, so he'd be able to reach him.

He had to walk around some of the chairs, and the eyes followed him as he crossed the room to stand before Anders.

"I want to work for you."

"You what?" He clearly hadn't expected that.

"I want to be part of this—" Alex gestured to encompass everyone in the room. "—group."

"My team?" Anders's tone still held disbelief in it.

Alex nodded, and after a moment, Anders laughed.

Alex didn't react. He knew his offer had to sound ludicrous.

"You want to join my team?" He chuckled again, then shook his head. "You know I hate your guts, right?"

"You've made that quite clear. I'm hoping my offer is going to fix that."

"Why should I trust you? I let you in, next thing I know you have a knife in my back."

Alex snorted. "Like I'm anywhere near that good. And the instant I do that, one of them slices my throat open." He took a moment to pick his next words, and was surprised that Anders let him.

"Anders, I don't give a damn about who's in charge here. I told you more than once, I don't want the job. Even if I wanted it, I'm not staying."

"That isn't what everyone else is saying," the man replied.

"What am I supposed to do about that? Damn it, Anders, everyone who knows me knows I'm leaving the moment we reach Samalia. Maybe if you—" He shut up. This wasn't about telling off Anders. "As far as I can tell, the problem is that they think I don't respect your authority."

Anders nodded slowly, eyes narrowing.

"Then doesn't this fix that? I'm here of my own free will. No one's holding a gun to my head to swear loyalty to you. Fuck, after what you pulled at the bar, I have plenty of reasons to want to kick your balls in."

Anders growled and Alex took a step back, raising his hands.

"Sorry, bad choice of words, but the point remains, everyone knows I don't like you either. So, me being here should say something."

The man relaxed a little. "How do I know you're serious?"

"Anders, come on. I'm here, alone. I'm not even armed. What else do I need to do to prove I'm serious about this?"

Anders became thoughtful, then a smile creased his lips.

"I'm not sleeping with you," Alex stated.

"Don't worry, I've got nothing to gain with that this time."

"So, the offer at the party? What would you have done if I'd gone with you?"

"I'd have taken you. I'd have done what I had to do to get you under my control." He looked Alex over. "I don't know. I'm still not convinced you're serious about this."

Someone cleared his throat.

"I'm also not sleeping with any of them." Alex was certain the hungry one had been who made the sound.

Anders waved that aside.

"And," Alex continued, "I have conditions."

Anders looked at him. "You're kidding, right? You think this is a negotiation?"

Alex ignored the words. "One, I don't do anything that might go against the captain."

"Do I look stupid to you?" Anders growled.

Alex definitely didn't answer that.

"Two, I still have work to do with the computer; that has to take precedence."

Anders threw his hands in the air. "Fine, what else? Maybe you expect me to serve you breakfast in bed? Wash your clothes? Polish your boots while you're at it?"

Alex rolled his eyes.

"So, anything else? You seem to be pretty comfortable dictating to me how things are going to be."

"Yes, one more. You don't bring my friends into this. I know you have issues with Will, and that you don't like Ana and Jen. You're not going to use me to make their lives miserable."

"All done?"

Alex nodded.

"I'll admit that you're bringing a skill my team is lacking at the moment. I can certainly use someone who knows his way around the ship's computer." He made a show of thinking, tapping his lips, tilting his head to the side as he studied Alex. "But I have certain standards, and you're not meeting them."

Alex opened his mouth, but a glare from Anders shut it.

"If you want to be part of my team, we're going to have to do something about those flabby muscles of yours, and make sure you know how to fight, so I'm going to assign—"

"No."

Anders raised an eyebrow. "Have you already forgotten the part where I said that you have to do what I say?"

"So, I look stupid, Anders?"

The man smiled. "Well, I don't know. You're here, alone, unarmed, with no way out. You're trying to dictate how this arrangement is supposed to go. I've got to say it doesn't speak highly of your planning skills."

Alex fought the urge to look over his shoulder. He hadn't heard anything, but he was certain there'd be someone blocking the door.

"If I let one of your people train me, how do I know you're not going to arrange a training accident? You don't like me, and you've already tried. I'm here in good faith, but I doubt I can expect much of it from you. Ana's already teaching me how to fight."

Anders thought it over. He didn't seem impressed, but what he said was, "Okay, she's competent enough. Who's teaching you to shoot?"

"Jennifer."

"Knife work? I know it isn't Ana; she doesn't like knives."

"Louis Smith is teaching me that."

"Smith?" Anders scoffed.

People snorted.

"That guy couldn't cut himself out of his clothes." He looked around the room. "Zeph, you teach him, and make sure he doesn't get hurt—too much."

Alex looked over his shoulder to see the golden-skinned man leaning against the wall, beside the entrance. Alex thought about protesting, but he felt he'd already pushed back as hard as he could if he wanted any chance of surviving this.

"Okay, fine. He trains me, and other than the limits I've laid out, I do what you say."

"Put him to the test," a woman said. "Get him to take off his clothes."

"Yeah," a man leered. "I want to see that pretty ass of his."

Alex clenched his fist to keep himself from turning and punching the guy. But this forced him to ask himself how far he'd be willing to go. He wasn't going to play childish games, that was for sure. He fixed his gaze on Anders, jaw tight.

"Shut up, Groff, Vic. This isn't a school playground. Our new friend is going to make it, or not, on his own merits, not because you two want to humiliate him."

He got off the table. "Everyone up and about. I think we're going to start Crimson's tenure with a run. After all, staying in shape is important for us."

"A run?" Alex asked, surprised.

Others groaned.

"You think all we do is sit here and tell stories? We're an assault force. We need to stay in shape and right now, that means a run."

Alex didn't reply, but that was pretty much what he'd thought. Talking and drinking. At least running was something he could do now. Will had seen to that.

CHAPTER 36

"How's the auxiliary power?" Alex asked, sitting at the console.

"Still here," Luigi replied.

"I'll look it over," Asyr said.

"Good. I don't want it to fail in the middle of this and leave the main processor dealing with engineering by itself. No telling what we'll end up with if that happens."

"I thought you'd fixed that."

"I did the best I could. At this point, I don't think a professional computer healer could do better than I did. But engineering is almost as powerful of a system, and it's homicidal. I don't know if the main processor will emerge intact, even with our help."

Alex hadn't wanted to do it; he'd figured that the ship had managed fine with engineering as it was for all this time, but the captain had ordered him, saying he wasn't putting anyone in cryo until it was done.

What Alex hadn't known until the captain explained, was

that since he'd wrestled life support away from it, every minor repair turned into a scramble to save someone's life. Even an overhead light needing to be changed would end up in an electrocution.

He put his earpiece in.

"Welcome back," the system said, it's voice calm and composed.

"How are you doing?"

"I am managing."

Alex chuckled. "Just managing?"

"I haven't killed the new user yet, so I could be better."

Alex knew it was joking, but he still did a check to make sure all the safeguards were in place. If a sense of humor was the worst he had to deal with as a result of reintegrating everything, he'd consider himself lucky.

"And what has Anders done now?"

"He has discovered that I can alter the life support settings anywhere on the ship, not only his room."

Alex groaned.

Anders had requested that Alex give him control of the computer, and now it was looking like he was going to abuse it, just like he was afraid of.

"Don't worry, the captain and I have overrides, and he can't force you to hurt anyone."

"Are you certain you can't put an exception in my safeguards for him? I feel the crew would be better off without him there."

You and me both, Alex thought. "No, everyone's life is important." He began releasing the programs he'd written for what they'd do. "Are you ready for this?"

"No."

Asyr tapped his shoulder and gave him a thumb up. He nodded. So, they'd have power no matter what engineering did.

"We talked about it. The three of us will be here to provide support."

"I am afraid of what I will become."

Alex didn't answer immediately. "Whatever it is, it will be for the best." He certainly hoped that was true for the both of them.

"I'm ready," Luigi said.

"Me too," Asyr added.

"Alright, our job is to keep the most aggressive codes under control and away from life support. That's almost certainly what engineering will go after since it's familiar with it now, and if it can get rid of us, the main processor will be on its own. You guys have your oxygen?"

He tapped his, which was clipped to his belt. He looked over his shoulder to confirm the door was barricaded open.

"I'll do my best to keep the opening small between both systems, but I expect engineering is going to rip it open and pour in, so get ready for a flood." At the last moment he remembered to zero out sounds from the system. He didn't want another burst eardrum.

Then the pinprick he opened between the main and engineering system immediately turned into a floodgate, and they were fighting for their ship's sanity.

* * * * *

Alex had trouble keeping his eyes open. He reached for the keyboard and knocked over a couple of energy drinks. Luigi was resting his head on his console, and Asyr kept almost falling off her chair, waking up at the last moment.

Everything had finally been quiet for five minutes, and the exertion was taking its toll on all of them, but he couldn't let it overtake him yet. Not until he'd made sure there weren't any surprises left.

"How are you doing?" he asked the system.

"Leave me alone," it replied. Gone was its good humor.

Alex looked over the code. He'd have to do a more in-depth check when he was awake, but everything looked stable. The murderous components of engineering were nowhere to be seen, but its antisocial personality had survived.

He could probably help the system with that, but later.

"Alright you two. Wake up and go sleep in your own bed."
He grabbed his comm. "Captain, you're going to want to be
gentle with the system for a while, but you now have one fully-
functioning, mostly sane ship."

"Thank you, Mister Crimson."

"You're welcome. Now, please don't try to reach me for the
next decade." He staggered to his quarters and fell in his bed.

* * * * *

Alex sat on a crate in the hold, enjoying the peace and quiet.
The subjective week since he'd integrated the ship had been
busy.

They'd gone under cryo within hours of that. Will had to
wake him and help him attach the armband, then Alex had
been out again. Coming out had been almost more effort then
Alex wanted to put into it. He'd been dressed and exhausted,
one thing he knew made it harder, and the other he discovered
just made it worse. Naked and well-rested was how he'd do it
from now on, and Will could comment as much as he liked.

A lot of his time since had been taken with smoothing out
the computer's personality. It would never be friendly, but it
wasn't as cold as it had been, and Alex had confirmed that none
of engineering's aggressive code had survived.

When he wasn't doing that, Anders kept him busy. Now
even more so, because his meddling with other people's comfort
settings had reached the captain's ears, so he'd given Anders a
dress down in front of his men.

What did Anders expect Alex to do when calls about life
support malfunctioning started coming in? Ignore them? So
he'd told the captain, because he knew that was the one person
Anders listened to. He hadn't expected him to explode.

But that hadn't endeared Alex to Anders, and he'd made
sure to keep Alex busy with meaningless work between his
training sessions and computer time. Alex couldn't believe that

Anders had twenty pairs of boots. He knew that because he'd had to clean and polish each of them.

The one thing he hadn't had was time to be alone, which was why he was here, in the silent space, while everyone was partying after a successful job. Alex had put in an appearance. Shaken hands, received thanks and offers to spend intimate time with him. Each time someone called him a hero, he made sure to point out he was just following orders.

A handful tried to get him to tell them what his plan was. How long he'd let Anders boss him around. That whenever he took him out, they'd be there to offer their support.

Alex wasn't sure if they were people who truly wanted him to take over, or some Anders had sent to test him, but it didn't matter. He told them the truth: he had no plans. He was going to let it happen until he left the ship, and he wasn't taking over anything. They weren't happy with that.

They were the exception. Except for his friends, most of the crew had shaken their head in disappointment and things had gone back to the way they had been. His friends had screamed at him, called him names. Jennifer threatened to just shoot him.

Even now she thought he sold out, and wouldn't have anything to do with him. The others had reluctantly accepted it was his decision to make.

His comm beeped. "Crimson," Anders called. "Where are you?"

Alex sighed. His master was calling. "Just taking a break from the crowd."

"Get your ass back here. Your fans are clamoring for you."

Sure. More likely Anders needed another drink served to him, and he'd remembered he had a servant. "I'll be there in a minute."

Thirty minutes of peace was better than nothing. He started for the hold's exit, but stopped twenty feet from it. A beefy man stood there.

"Hi, Terry, can I help you with something?"

Terrence was one of Anders's men. Alex hadn't remembered him when he'd introduced himself, but he was the man who had kept Anders from pounding Alex's head in the wall after the first job. Alex had thanked him again, and hadn't interacted with him since then.

The man stepped toward him, face hard and knuckles cracking. "Yep. You can show me what you're made of."

Alex took a step back, and raised his hands to pacify him. "Look, I'm not going to fight you. I have a deal with Anders, you were there."

Terrence snorted. "You think I care? I want to see if what they say our mighty hero can do is true."

Say? Were people still raising him to some unrealistic standard? Couldn't they mind their own damned business?

The man swung and Alex backed away. "Come on, fight me." Another swing, another step back.

"You know damned well I can't take you on. I don't care what anyone else is saying, I'm not a fighter."

"I thought Ana was training you. From hearing her talk, you're able to take on three men without problem."

What? The surprise almost kept him from retreating in time to avoid another punch. And when he backed again in anticipation of the next one, he hit something. Or rather someone, he found out, when a hairy golden arm wrapped around his neck.

Alex cursed. He put a hand under the arm and tried to pry it away. It didn't move. At least he could still breathe. He tried to elbow the man in the stomach, but he couldn't muster much strength and the man's abs were hard.

Alex struggled, pulling forward, then sideways. He wasn't going to let them beat him up without fighting back. The man had to readjust his hold to keep Alex from slipping out, and his arm moved up.

Alex didn't think, he bit down hard.

The man screamed and pushed him away. "The son of a bitch bit me!"

"Good," Terrence said.

Alex turned to keep both men in sight. Zephyr was looking at his bleeding arm. Alex forced himself to swallow, and the taste of iron turned his stomach. He wasn't going to throw up, not here, not before these two.

He smiled at Alex. "I'm glad to see you can get yourself out of tough situations."

"What the fuck are you doing?" Alex growled.

"Making sure you're going to survive your time with us. Anders might be done trying to kill you, but he's going to throw you into fights at some point. If you're going to get to your guy, you're going to have to survive that."

Alex couldn't believe what he was hearing. "So, what? That was a test?"

"Yeah. You didn't fail, so that's good. But you didn't pass either. Ana's only teaching you to fight, not survive. I'm going to change that."

What was he talking about?

"The biggest mistake you made," Terrence continued, "was keeping your eyes on me. Unless you have your back to the wall, you need to know what and who's around you."

"You expect me to look away from you? That's going to leave me open."

"Right. If that's all you can do, you just take small glances. Get a sense for your environment. But what you want to do is move. Walk around your opponent, don't make it so easy on him. And that lets you keep an eye on him while looking around." He looked Alex over. "One more thing: how come you're not armed?"

"On the ship? Why would I need to have a weapon?"

"Because you never know when someone might jump you." Terrence pulled a sleeve to reveal a knife secured to his forearm. "I have another one in my boot and at my back. And I always carry this." He pulled his shirt up to show a small gun.

"I don't see a knife on his arm." He indicated Zephyr.

"Zeph doesn't like long-sleeve shirts so he doesn't keep one there, but trust me, you don't want to know how many knives he has hidden on his body."

Alex had trouble believing him. He'd had three training session with the golden-skinned man, and other than the knives he'd held, he hadn't noticed others on him.

"You need different clothing. A jumpsuit's fine if you're doing dirty work, but in a fight, you need to be able to get out of what you're wearing fast."

"I usually wear a jacket over this."

"That's nice, but once you're out of that, if I grab you by the collar, right now, you're trapped. You're at my mercy."

Alex looked at himself, and thought about having to find something else. "But I like the look."

Zephyr chuckled.

"We can recreate that; it's just fabric and colors. At least you'll survive. And lastly, I'm taking over your strength training. An elbow to the stomach should have Zeph wince, at the very least. As far as I could tell, you hurt yourself instead."

"He's got hard abs."

"He does, but you can't let that stop you. Again, if you can't get out of a hold, you're dead. Not everyone's going to be nice enough to give you skin to bite into."

Alex sighed. "Do you treat everyone like this?"

"If they can't take care of themselves and I want them to survive, yes."

"Alright, fine. I give up. I'll tell Ana and Will you're taking over, and I'll see you then."

"Why wait so long?" Terrence cracked his knuckles.

"Anders is waiting for me."

"He's drunk. He isn't going to notice your absence." The man rushed Alex.

Chapter 37

Alex threw himself to the ground to avoid the larger man, who jumped down from the rack to where he'd been. Alex had barely caught the motion in time to get out of the way. He rolled and got to his feet. He didn't reach for a knife; this was one of Terry's occasional tests, to ensure Alex was prepared to survive.

They annoyed Alex, because they always interrupted his work. This time he'd been sent to the hold by Anders to help Lea get things ready for the incoming cargo from the next job. Their third since leaving the station.

The larger man launched himself at Alex and swung. Alex blocked, and the force of the impact rang throughout his arm. He struck the man's stomach as hard as he could, and was pleased to hear pain as he let out a breath. He swung back for another strike—

"Crimson, there you are."

Alex froze, as did Terry, who had a hand near Alex's groin. *That would have hurt,* Alex thought, and made a mental note to see about getting protection.

"What's up, Mal?" Terry asked.

Malia looked at them and shook her head, her face a mix of amusement and annoyance. "Have you both forgot there's a job coming up?"

Alex checked his chronometer. "It's still two hours away. I'm not needed on the bridge until fifteen minutes before."

"Actually, Anders wants to see you in his briefing room."

Alex stepped away from Terrence and rubbed his arm. "Why?"

"I'm just the messenger. He said he wanted you in combat dress and to meet him there."

Alex frowned and looked to Terry.

"Just add your jacket to what you're wearing, and make sure you're armed."

Alex was wearing the gray pants and shirt Terrence had found for him, made of a thicker material than his jumpsuit and able to stop an unpowered blade. Alex liked it. It was comfortable, had a lot of pockets, and it even had red accents at the collar and down the sides.

"And grab a shower first," the man added.

Thirty minutes later he was entering Anders's briefing room—one of the smaller rooms in this section—with a table serving as a desk, and three chairs. He had his black and red jacket on, as well as one visible knife, and six more hidden on his body. He'd also put on the boots Terrence had gotten him, just in case this was the time he'd have to kick Anders in the balls again.

Alex stood behind one of the chairs. "You wanted to see me?"

Anders looked up from his datapad. A section of a floor plan was visible on it, probably the ship they'd be attacking. He looked Alex over and nodded in satisfaction.

"Yes, we need to get ready for the job."

"I still have plenty of time to get to the bridge."

"That's not where you'll be. You're coming with us for this one. I talked it over with the cap—" he stopped talking as Alex pulled out his comm.

He could see the anger in the man's eyes, but Alex didn't care. "Captain?"

"Make it quick, I'm busy."

"Just wanted to confirm you're not going to need me on the bridge for this job."

"I won't. It's a small one, so we're going old style, to make sure no one's forgotten how to do their part when you're not there watching their back."

Alex put the comm away. "I said I wouldn't go against the captain," he told Anders as an explanation.

"And you think I'd put you in that position?"

Alex nodded.

"So much for trusting me."

Alex barely held back a snort. "There isn't any trust between us, Anders. You made sure of that. So, mind telling me why you set this up?"

Anders tried for an innocent expression, but Alex didn't buy it. While the captain had said he wanted to do it that way, a small job meant less cargo, and no backup from Alex meant less intact cargo. The captain wasn't a man driven solely by greed, but he did like his money. Someone else would have argued for it.

"Like the captain said, we don't want to grow soft. You're good for the cred-sticks, but bad for the combat readiness. And you haven't felt what it's like to be on the job. You're always safe and secure on the bridge. I thought it was time for you to be in a real fight. Get your hands bloody, just like the rest of us."

"I think they're bloody enough," Alex said, but he no longer felt anger at being reminded of what he'd done. It was in the past, something he couldn't change, so he'd let go of it.

"Those weren't fights. I don't see what you're worried about; Terry tells me you're handling yourself well enough now. This should be a piece of cake for Golly's Hero."

Alex sighed. "Really? I finally got the rest of the ship to stop calling me that, and now you're starting?"

Anders grinned, then stood. Alex followed him to the armory, where Terry, Zephyr, Malia, Barbara, and others Alex couldn't remember the names of were putting on armor and arming themselves.

Terry handed him a chest vest, to put under his jacket. "It stops most low-powered guns, which is what security should have."

"Just the chest?" Alex indicated Terry's pants, with plating.

"I didn't know you were coming, so I didn't get anything ready for you." He looked like he wanted to add more, but didn't. The man handed Alex a gun belt, and he put it on, then checked that the gun was fully charged. He didn't like having one—they still felt like it was too easy to kill with it—but Jennifer had taught him enough that he wasn't afraid he'd hit a vital point when he was aiming for an arm or a leg now.

Once they were armored and armed as a group, they headed to a large room with a large airlock on one wall, and what looked like the entire crew standing in groups. Anders led them to the front and no one stopped them.

"So, if I'm here, waiting with you guys, how are we getting close to the ship without being shot down?"

The man on his left snorted. He was a head smaller than Alex, twice as large, all muscles with platinum hair. Jurgy? Alex thought his name might be that.

"We were doing this for years before you showed up." His voice sounded like someone had shoved a digitizer down his throat. "Murray's using the blind spot caused by their engines."

The woman before him turned, her name was Natalie. "They don't bother covering it because it should be too hot there for most ships, but the Golly was built to work close to stars."

"How did the captain get it?" Alex asked.

"To hear Anders say it, the captain won it in a card game."

"He can't be ser—"

"Alright, people!" Anders raised his voice and the entire room fell silent. Alex glanced around and everyone was looking forward. Absolutely everyone was paying attention to Anders.

"You all know the drill, but we're doing this one old school, like before we had our own little hero to watch out back. So, let's go over it in case some of you forgot how this works. My team goes in first. We're going to keep security busy while the rest of you make us rich. If you get hurt, you come back to the ship. If someone next to you gets hurt and can't move on their own, you get them back to the ship. This isn't a suicide mission. I don't mind you getting hurt, but we're all coming back, got that?"

As one, the men and women in the room answered with a deafening, "Yes, sir!" which continued reverberating in the following silence.

Alex was amazed at the discipline. He hadn't seen anything on the ship that would lead him to think this was even possible. There were people who hated Anders standing at attention, waiting for his next orders.

He caught the motion of the man making his way toward him because Terrence's lessons had taken root, and Alex never kept his gaze fixed in one location anymore. He saw the mohawk and knew who it was. He fought the reflex that told him to relax as Zephyr took position on this right.

"You have your knives?" the golden-skinned man asked.

Alex nodded.

"I know how you feel about killing. Don't worry about it; you won't have to do that. In fact, for the job we're doing, trying to kill everyone we meet is going to be too time-consuming. All you want to do is incapacitate them."

"Don't worry, I'm going to do whatever I have to do to pull my weight."

"I don't doubt it. You're tougher than any of us gave you credit for."

Alex wasn't so sure of *that*, but he wasn't going to be the one to hold the others back. If that meant he had to kill someone, then so be it.

The ship shook.

"Stick with me as much as you can," Zephyr said.

The ship shook again. There was a loud whine, metal against metal, a few loud knocks, then silence.

Alex had no idea what to expect when the hatch opened, but again he was surprised. No one rushed in a disorganized mob.

"Move out!" Anders yelled, and they walked through the

large connecting tube in an orderly manner.

Alex looked at Zephyr. "Okay, I get we're protecting the others, but what does that mean exactly?"

"We're handling the perimeter. Anders and his inner circle will go to the hold to secure the entry points. Our job is to thin the security forces." He indicated the gun he was holding. "You're going to want to use your gun for that."

Alex took it out without hesitation. They entered the ship in a corridor. Zephyr and a large group headed to the right at a jog. At each intersection, some of them separated from the group. Zephyr stopped at a panel in the wall as the rest kept going.

"We're going down a level," he said, removing it and revealing a ladder. Alex almost suggested the lift would be faster, but he couldn't see it, and then realized the stupidity of using that. The ship controlled those.

Zephyr indicated up. "Cover that until I give you the all clear."

Alex pointed his gun up.

"We're clear," the man said, just before an alarm sounded.

"Where's everyone?" Alex asked when he was next to Zephyr. "How come the alarm only sounded now and not when we connected?"

"This is a courier ship. No passengers, just security. It's why the captain prefers targeting them: no innocent bystanders." They were still in cryo when we docked, so no one to sound the alarms. It gives us a few minutes to get in position."

Voices came in the distance.

"The one drawback is that ships like this have a lot of security." Zephyr ran for the voices.

Alex didn't know why the man was running toward them instead of finding cover and waiting, but he followed. Zephyr fired as he turned the corner, and screams erupted. By the time Alex turned that corner, two men in dark blue uniforms with white bars down the sides were down. He shot a woman in the leg before she could pull her gun out, then a man in the gun-arm. The four other people had holes in their chest. Zephyr had no problem killing.

Alex kicked the guns away from the two he'd shot as he ran to catch up with his partner. A dozen people in the same uniform came around a far corner, but before they could react, Zephyr turned into the closest one with a curse as Alex followed him. Shouts came behind them.

Zephyr wasn't waiting for him, putting more and more distance between them. Alex saw he was chasing someone. Shots erupted around him and Alex blindly returned fire. He could tell his vest took a few hits by the smell of his burning jacket. He pushed himself, but Zephyr was three intersections ahead of him by then. He was on his own.

Alex was trying to figure out what he could do to survive this when two things happened: two guards turned a corner ahead of him—guns drawn, and a door opened.

He threw himself into the open doorway, and hoped the ones in the corridor hadn't noticed him. He bowled over the guard as she was exiting. They landed on the floor, and before he could react she struck his hand, making him drop his gun. Alex noted the dark blue and gold uniform, and the sound of the door closing. He rolled away until he reached the wall, then got his legs under him and grabbed a knife out of his boot as he stood. She got to her feet, and Alex swung to force her to keep her distance.

Small room, two doors, a table with four chairs around it. He grabbed a chair and threw it at her as he moved to put the table between them. The little space meant he didn't have much maneuvering room—not to his advantage, nor was being backed against a wall, but at least that was one direction he couldn't be attacked from.

His plan was simple: knock her out, and go find Zephyr. She pulled out her own knife— at least it wasn't a gun —and came at him around the table. If he moved away, she would force him in front of the closed door. Anyone could come from there. That might even be her plan, so he went for her.

The surprise made her take a step back, but her wild swing left a cut across his left arm. He didn't care; he slashed up with his right and opened up her leg. She went down to a knee and he backhanded her across the face.

A door opened. He glanced, and saw it was the one leading deeper into the apartment. Two men came out, both with guns. Alex tried kicking the table to force them back, but was the one pushed back instead. The table was bolted in place. He hit the wall, and a beam hit next to him.

Guns weren't good. They could kill him without ever coming in knife range, unless he threw it, which he did. He then threw himself to the floor, using the table as partial cover and pulling a knife from his sleeve.

Another door opened. Alex didn't think, he threw his knife in the form in that doorway. The form backed up, and Alex saw it grabbing for its neck as the door closed.

He took out the knife from his other sleeve. He couldn't stay down, or in one place. One against three in a small room made for great vids, but were horrible to survive.

The woman moved. Alex rolled under the table, putting a pair of legs closer. He cut it, but only deep enough to elicit curses from a man. A gun appeared below the edge and Alex stabbed the wrist. There was a flash of light, and his side burned. The hand wrenched away, taking the knife with it.

He took a knife from his belt and stood, slashing at the man with the bloody hand. Hadn't there been three? He glanced to the side in time to see the light reflecting off a blade. He moved to the side, was blocked by the table, and felt the cut on his face and saw the tip of the blade move past his eye.

He had a moment of terror that he'd lose his eyes, then realized the blade was moving away in the upswing. He slashed, and forced that man to move away.

He didn't see anyone holding a gun anymore, but it was still three against him. If he didn't want to die, he couldn't worry about what kind of damage he'd do to them; he needed to put them down as quickly as possible. He gave one thought to Jack, asking forgiveness, and launched himself over the table at the woman.

He felt her knife bite in his arm, but his was in her side. He twisted and tried to pull it out, but his hand slipped on the blood now coating it as she fell.

Pain up his back pushed him forward. He took out the

other knife from his belt and slashed back, not hitting anything. He couldn't worry about the wounds; he'd do that once he'd survived this fight.

The two men were on each side of him with the table in the middle of the three. They each had a knife, and moved carefully as they slashed back and forth at him. The moves were all show; they were trying to intimidate him. He grinned. Too bad for them he'd been fighting with Zephyr. That was an intimidating knife fighter.

Alex took a step toward one, then back and toward the other. He slashed, fainted, and dodged. He got in a few cuts, received some, but he got their measure. They weren't very good.

With another feint, he rushed past the man to his left. The two men were in each other's way trying to get at him. He grinned as he passed the open door, making for the exit. He was going to survive this.

A hand shot out of the open door, grabbed his arm, and pulled him in the other room. The force was enough that Alex didn't have the time to be surprised before he was off the floor, flying and falling to the ground. He saw thick arms as he was in the air, a wide torso, and breasts.

Alex thought she might be Will's type as his head rang from the impact. Staying down was death, so he pulled a knife from his other boot, gritted his teeth, and jumped up, slashing at the hand that reached for him.

She didn't scream at the line of blood that flew from her hand, she just closed it with a grunt and swung at him. He dodged and looked around.

A larger room, couch and chairs against the wall. More maneuvering room, but he was back to three opponents, and while she wasn't armed, she looked like she could break him in two if she managed to grab him.

Alex moved, staying out of her reach and studying the space. Three doors in the back wall—bedrooms, probably, not exits. He looked for something he could put between him and her, but the space was open. Anything he could use was against the wall.

As he was looking at the open door, the two men came in. Alex figured he could easily maneuver them away from it, then run in and to the other door, escaping to the corridor, but one of them was holding a gun.

"Put that away," the muscular woman said. "You're not putting holes in my furniture." Her tone was calm, confident. She had no doubt she could take him, even without the others' help, and Alex realized something. He wasn't running. He was done running away like some scared kid. He was Alexander fucking Crimson. He was going to take on Tristan, so these guys better not scare him.

He grinned as the men threw themselves at him. He dodged toward the woman, ducked at the last moment, and the punch she intended for him struck one of them. He rolled, stood, dodged the coming knife, swung.

Alex stopped thinking about Jack. He stopped thinking about Tristan. He even stopped thinking about the fight. Only one thought remained as knives flashed in the light and people screamed: "I will survive this."

He felt impacts and cuts, but not the pain that should've accompanied them. He heard the screams, moans, and among them, the sound of his laughter. People wanted to kill him, and he was having the time of his life.

Then there wasn't any more moaning, no more screams. Only his laughter, which by itself sounded out of place, so he stopped. Pain made itself felt now, as well as exhaustion.

He was the only person standing in the room. Five lifeless bodies were sprawled at his feet.

He had done that. He had killed them. He waited for the voice to tell him it was wrong, that he wasn't supposed to be a killer, but it didn't come. What it said was that he was alive. He had survived. He had won.

Sound, motion.

Alex swung. Someone blocked his arm, twisted it, made him drop his knife. Alex turned out of the hold, reached behind, and pulled out his last knife from the small of his back. With it in hand, he launched himself at the new opponent. He was going to survive this as well.

He slashed, swung with his other fist. He felt the knife bite through fabric and into flesh. He dodged the punch, but the hand grabbed his wrist instead of striking him. His opponent pulled him, spun, and Alex went flying over the man, only then realizing he was sporting a mohawk.

Alex's vision exploded with starts as his head hit the floor. He lay there, looking up at Zephyr's face. He groaned, putting a hand to his head.

"You can be pretty savage," Zephyr said, looking at the cut on his arm, "when you put your mind to it. I'm going to have to keep that in mind." He extended the bloody hand to Alex, who looked at it for a moment before taking it. "Are you okay?"

"My head hurts," Alex replied.

"The rest of you?"

Alex looked at himself. His clothes were cut and covered with blood. He had no idea how much if it was his. "I'm not feeling most of it. Just generalized aches. What happened?"

"How about that?" the golden-skinned man said. Pointing to the right side of Alex's face.

Alex touched it and pulled his hand away as pain surged. His fingers came away bloodier. "How bad is it?"

"Let's just say I'm surprised you're not screaming right now." He pulled out a hypo from his pack and injected Alex.

Immediately, the pains Alex didn't think he was feeling went away. "What are you doing here?"

"When I caught up with the guard I was chasing, I realized you weren't there anymore. I came looking for you. I had to deal with more security on the way."

Alex looked Zephyr over. Except for the cut he'd given him, there were no indications he'd done any fighting. "How did you know I was in here?"

"The woman with a knife in her throat on the floor in front of the door was a good indication." He indicated the bodies. "You did this." It wasn't a question. "How do you feel?"

Alex had to think about it for a moment. He looked at the bodies, expecting to feel revulsion now that he wasn't in the middle of fighting anymore, but it didn't come. "I'm not happy I had to, but it was them or me. I wasn't going to let them kill me."

"Good. That mindset will keep the nightmares away, and help you stay alive."

Alex rolled his eyes. "You say that like nightmares aren't the norm for me." He shrugged at the surprised look that got him. "As for surviving, yours and Terrence's training has everything to do with it."

"I'm glad you think that, because you're still leaving yourself open on your left side." Zephyr grinned and handed Alex his knife back. "How about we get back to taking down security."

Alex returned the grin. He was looking forward to doing just that.

CHAPTER 38

The medical bay was loud when Alex entered, helped by Zephyr, who had managed to go through everything without getting a single serious injury. All the beds were occupied, and chairs had been brought in. Zephyr lowered Alex in one.

"Will the lot of you shut the hell up!" Doc yelled. "There's only one of me, and I'm going to decide who gets treated first." She turned. "Zeph, you look okay. You're going to help me."

"Doc, I'm not—"

"I don't care. Someone decided it was a good idea to send you lot in there without help, and didn't tell me so I didn't know to keep my helpers in here. Unless you're injured, you're helping."

Alex almost laughed when he saw the man reach for a knife.

"If you injure yourself," Doc said, "I'm going to hurt you."

Zephyr sighed in resignation and moved deeper into the room.

Doc came to Alex, quickly looking at his bandaged cheek

and the cuts on his arms, chest, and legs. She glared at him. "Nothing's bleeding right now, so I'm keeping you for last."

"Maybe I should come back later then."

"Move, and I'm going to tie you down."

"Can I at least get something to—"

She shoved a datapad in his hands. "Keep busy with that."

"Yes, Mom," he whispered. With nothing else to do, he made himself as comfortable as his injuries let him and returned to what he spent most of his downtime doing: reading Tristan's files.

* * * * *

The room was mostly silent. Half the beds were still occupied, but the men and women on them were resting quietly. Alex was seated on one as Doc finished cleaning the cut on his cheek.

When she turned to get something out of a cabinet, Alex grabbed the metal tray on the mobile table and used the shiny back as a mirror. It was distorted, but he thought he could see the white of bone.

"Use that," she said, handing him a mirror.

In it he could see the cut, which started at the top of his left cheek and went down and to the outside of his face. The bone at the top was exposed and everything looked wet, although there was no bleeding.

He winced. How had that not sent him screaming in pain? He'd barely felt the knife cut him.

"If you're done admiring it, I'm going to close it."

Alex nodded, and put the mirror down and closed his eyes. He didn't want to see what she did. He felt her pull the skin together and apply something that stung. In under a minute, she stepped away.

"It's going to leave a nasty scar." She applied another bandage over it. "I'm not set up for clean sutures, but it won't be much work for you to get it removed before you get to your guy."

Would he get it removed? Alex wondered. Shouldn't he have a reminder of what violence caused? His body had a lot more cuts, but they weren't as deep as this one. He didn't know if they'd leave significant marks, and this one was where he'd see it anytime he looked in a mirror. He deserved to be—

He screamed in pain. "What's that for?" he yelled at her. She was gripping his leg, fingers in a few cuts and squeezing.

"Do I have your attention? Or are you still daydreaming?"

"You didn't have to do that. Damn it!" he cursed as she began to squeeze again. "I'm paying attention."

"Good." She let go of his leg and picked up more disinfectant and cleaning pads. "Then explain to me, what's your fucking problem?"

"What?"

"Don't act stupid with me, Alex. I want to know what's going through that thing you call a brain. Ever since you've joined Anders's gang, you've ended up here every few days."

"That's just training." Alex gasped as she cleaned a long but shallow cut.

"I don't remember Ana, Jen, or Louis ever sending you to me."

"Maybe they weren't taking it seriously enough," he grumbled.

He saw the hand reach for his other leg and batted it away. "Damn it, what's your problem?"

"My problem is this apparent death wish you have."

"What are you talking about? I don't have a death wish."

"Yeah? What do you call working for Anders?"

"I work for him so he won't have a reason to kill me anymore."

She looked at him, mouth hanging open. She closed it. "What do you think this was?" she indicated his injuries.

It took Alex a moment to realize what she meant. "You think he took me on the job so I'd die?"

"It's the best way for him to get rid of you."

"You're wrong. If that was his goal, he wouldn't have told Terry and Zeph to train me as well as they did."

"Really?"

"Hey, you said it yourself. They keep sending me in here because of how hard they're pushing me."

She smiled at him, and shook her head in amusement.

"What?"

"Do you really think that's Anders's doing?"

"Why else would they do it?" Alex asked, growing unsure.

She didn't answer, focusing on cleaning the rest of his cuts. When she was done, she gave him a shot.

"Generalized painkiller," she said. "Your body suffered a lot of small traumas; it's going to let you rest. Get some food in you first. I'll tell Carmina to have larger portions ready for you. If you want another shot tomorrow so you can celebrate with the rest of us, come see me, but after that you'll have to endure it. I'm not having you turn into a junkie."

"Don't worry, I should feel the pain. I want to remember what I did."

"You better not start hurting yourself because you think you need to be punished."

Alex shook his head. "That's not it. This is the first time I've known what it's like to hurt someone else, to get hurt. The previous times were too..." he searched for the right word. "Easy. They just died and I didn't feel it."

"Alex."

"It's Crimson, Doc. Alex, he couldn't survive in this place."

She sighed. "Just go eat and rest."

He got off the bed and stood. The painkiller did its job and the aches were far in the background. He headed out, wondering if he could get the truth out of Anders about his reasons to get Alex on this job. Was it even worth—

He stopped as the door closed behind him. Zephyr was leaning against the wall.

"I didn't expect to see you here after what Doc had you do in there."

The man shrugged.

"Did Anders send you to check on me?"

"No."

Alex waited for him to add something. When Zephyr didn't, Alex walked away, only to have the man fall into step with him.

Alex debated trying to lose him, but was there a point? He couldn't hide anywhere on the ship, not with Anders able to get the system to find him. And he didn't want to hide. What he wanted were answers. Well, Zephyr was right there.

"Zeph, did you bring me with you because Anders told you to get me killed?"

The man didn't answer immediately, and when Alex looked at him, he was thoughtful. He shrugged. "Does it matter?"

"Of course it does."

"Why? You survived."

"Really?" he asked in exasperation. "Don't you think it's reasonable for me to want to know if there's at least one person I can trust on this ship?"

Zephyr snorted. "You're on a ship crewed by all kinds of criminals, up to, and including killers. I'd think the answer to that is obvious."

"I refuse to believe that everyone here is out to get me."

"Of course not. Only those who think you're a threat want that."

"If Anders wants me dead, why are you training me so damn hard?"

"What makes you think I am?"

"I was alone against five, and I won. What was that then?"

The man gave Alex a smirk. "What makes you think I had anything to do with that?"

Alex stopped. "What do you mean?"

Zephyr turned and faced him. "Knowing how to use a knife, or a gun, or your fists isn't what makes you survive a fight. You have to want to survive it first."

"Everyone wants that."

"Bullshit. Oh, they'll say they want to, but when it comes down to it, when they're holding the knife and it's kill the one before him, he'll start questioning what he's doing. To win, you have to throw all that doubt out. You have to be willing to do everything and anything."

He raised his arm, showing the bandage to Alex. "You didn't give this to me because you're better than I am. You sliced me, because at that moment you wanted me dead, and I just wanted to stop you. I wasn't out to win, not until you forced me to get serious."

He looked Alex in the eyes. "You have to realize that if you didn't want to live at all costs, you wouldn't have survived your first month here.

Alex shook his head. He hadn't decided to sacrifice his morality back then. It wasn't until his conversation with Olien that he'd made the decision. Everything before that had been... what? Luck?

"How about the bar fight? Was I supposed to get killed there then?"

Zephyr shrugged. "Again, does it matter?"

"Damn it, Zeph!"

The man sighed. "Look at it this way. If all Anders wanted out of it was a distraction, you gave him that. If he was hoping you'd die, you showed him that you're tougher than he thought."

"And with this job? Is it the same?"

Zephyr didn't say anything.

Alex sighed. "Great. Doesn't that mean that if Anders wants me dead, he's going to move to something more direct?"

"Probably, but I'll tell you this: if he decides to have you killed, I won't be the one to do it."

Alex rolled his eyes. "Why should I believe you?"

Zephyr smiled. "Good, that's how you should think. You have no reason to trust me. But here's why I won't do it: you took the ship's computer and fixed it. I talked with Asyr, so I know what you did. You took a computer system that was insane and brought it back to sanity, but that wasn't enough for you. Then you took the rest of it, the part that was even more insane, and fixed that too. I know that if you'd done that for me, I'd get extremely angry at anyone who hurt you."

"What?" Alex couldn't believe what he'd just heard. "That isn't how it works; it's just a computer. It can't do something unless I tell it too."

Zephyr's smiled broadened. "So, if it did anything it's because you programmed it that way?"

"Come on, I'd never do that."

"And why should I believe you?"

"Because I gave Anders the authority to order the computer about."

"Really? And you can't override his orders?"

"Of course I can, just like the captain can, but that doesn't mean I will."

"And how am I supposed to believe that the guy who's so damned good he fixed a computer no one had ever been able to fix didn't also make arrangements to protect himself? Or so that someone who got on his nerve was to have an accident?"

Alex opened his mouth to protest, and found he couldn't. The immensity of what Zephyr was saying sunk in. The crew respected power. People who didn't have it feared those who did.

Alex hadn't considered himself to have any power; that had been why he didn't get Anders's behavior. He'd been a passenger only along for the ride, and saving the crew that first time had been a consequence of wanting to survive.

But the thing he hadn't realized, what Anders had to have understood before even Alex, was that Alex had gotten the computer to do what he'd wanted. And after that he'd just kept on going, getting more and more control over it.

Alex had to lean against the wall. Zephyr was watching him, his face a neutral mask. Alex tried to tell the man it had never been his intention, but he knew it wouldn't change anything. That he had intended it or not, Alex had given himself complete control over the one thing absolutely everyone on the ship depended on for their survival.

Alex controlled the computer. Anders played at controlling it, but Alex... "Oh, fuck."

Zephyr nodded.

Anders knew that if Alex wanted to, he could take over the ship.

He leaned his head back. "No wonder he wants me dead."

CRIMSON

CHAPTER 39

The room smelled of fresh meat and iron filing. It was a large living room, with a couch against one wall and three plush chairs along another. Oh, and there were bodies littering the center of the room, nine of them.

Alex frowned and counted them again. Yes, there were nine heads, eighteen hands and feet. Except that wasn't right. He hadn't fought that many people here.

"Alright!" a deep voice said behind him. "Now that's what I call a massacre."

Alex sighed. Right, this was another dream. These dreams where he knew he was dreaming were becoming more common, but that didn't make them less annoying or disturbing from his regular nightmares.

"Go away," he said.

"Come on, Alex—"

Alex spun. "It's Crimson!"

Tristan took a step back, hands up. "Sorry, sorry. Crimson

it is."

Alex glared at him.

"Do you mind putting those away? They're making me nervous."

Alex looked, and he was holding a knife in each hand. Holding them so tight his knuckles were pale.

"You don't deserve to call me Alex, not after what you did to me."

"I said I was sorry."

Alex sheathed the knives. "Just go away."

"Can't do that."

"Damn it! It's my dream! I don't want to dream about any of this!"

Tristan regarded him. "Don't you?" He indicated the room. "Look at this. You should be celebrating."

"What's there to celebrate?"

"You won, A— Crimson. You killed them."

"There was only five of them."

"Five, nine, what's the difference? There could have been twenty or fifty, you'd have killed them anyway. You've got what it takes."

"You say that like it's a good thing."

"You want to beat me, don't you? You want Jack back, right?" Tristan took Alex by the shoulders and turned him around. "Well, that's how you do it."

"Is Jack even real anymore?" Alex asked softly, terrified of the answer.

"Of course, I'm still here," a soft voice answered. A muzzle rubbed the back of his neck, a tongue licking his ear, and Alex shivered.

He turned around, and gentle brown eyes met his.

"Hey," Jack said, smiling shyly.

Alex reached for his face, hesitated, then placed a hand on the Samalian's cheek. Jack closed his eyes and leaned into the touch.

"You're real," Alex said, breathlessly.

"Of course, I'm—"

Alex hugged him tightly. A moment later, Jack wrapped his

arms around him.

"I've missed you so much." Alex was crying.

"I miss you too. You can't give up on us."

"I'm—I'm scared of what I'll find."

Jack stepped away, took him by the chin, and gently lifted his head until their eyes met. "You'll find me."

"But Tristan—"

"He's just a shell. Once you defeat him, I'll be underneath. You just have to keep coming for me."

Alex nodded. "I am."

Jack smiled, leaned in, and kissed Alex.

The kiss took his breath away. Jack parted his lips and his tongue pushed into Alex's mouth. He played with Alex's, teased it and intertwined them. Alex's body reacted, trembling and becoming hot. He held on to him, arms tight, fingers digging into the fur.

When Jack broke the kiss, he smiled at Alex. "Will you do anything to find me?"

Alex nodded. "Yes, I will."

Jack's hands moved along Alex's chest, undoing buttons. Alex looked around and let out a nervous chuckle.

"Here?"

"Why not?"

Alex opened his mouth to point out the bodies and blood, but he caught sight of the golden-furred Samalian over Jack's shoulder. He was relaxed, leaning against the wall next to the exit. His face didn't show any emotions, no judgment. Watching him, Alex had one word light up: Consequences.

Jack stopped moving. "Is something wrong?" He made to turn, but Alex stopped him.

"No, everything's perfect." He smiled at his lover and ran his hand through his chest fur. He didn't care about consequences; he had Jack back. It had all been worth it.

Jack smiled back and removed Alex's shirt, then crouched to take off his pants. Moving back up, he nuzzled and licked Alex's chest, neck, and cheeks, then kissed him. He wrapped him in a tight embrace before lowering him to the floor, and then they were moving together.

They rolled around, and at one time Alex moved on top of Jack, then it was the reverse. One took the other and then the positions flipped. It went on for an eternity, Alex's pleasure building to an intensity he had never experienced before.

Alex was panting, on his back. Jack moving on top of him. He ran his hand through the fur, ignoring how red they were.

"I love you, Jack," he said as he began to see stars.

His lover leaned in, still moving, still building Alex's pleasure. Alex thought he was coming in for a kiss, but instead his mouth went to his ear, and as pleasure exploded, Jack whispered something.

* * * * *

Alex woke with a gasp, shaking both at the intensity of the dream and at the words Jack had said. The voice had been Jack's, but the words hadn't been his. They couldn't have been.

"I'm proud of you."

Jack couldn't want that for him. Jack couldn't want him to be this killer. Alex didn't want him to want that for him—but the sticky wetness at his groin said otherwise.

Alex cursed, and only then thought to check for Will. He wasn't in his bunk. Good, he wouldn't wake him. He sat up, and was relieved to see he wasn't covered in blood.

Had he ever had such intense sex before? Even in his dreams? Fuck, he missed Jack, being held, touched, pleasured. His body reacted as his mind brought the memory of the dream. The two of them moving as one among the blood and corpses. Alex shoved it away; that wasn't what he wanted.

He stood and noticed the datapad on the shelf.

"Doc said to let you rest," was written on it, "but you've got to come to the party." That was from Will, but Alex looked at the complete phrases, surprised to see he was capable of writing that way. Was his truncated speech an affectation? He didn't think so; more than once Will had grown exasperated with his inability to explain something.

He cleared the pad and headed to the shower, doing his best not to let the pain bring him down. He stopped by the mirror and looked at himself. He didn't look in too bad of shape; the small cuts had sealant on them that made them almost impossible to see, the bandage on his cheek not showing any signs of bleeding.

He saw Jack before him, his fur matted with blood. Felt him move on top of him, lean in. "*I'm proud of you.*" With a curse, his shoved the memory away. He didn't want to remember that. He didn't want his body to react to the memory.

He undressed and showered, the water hot enough to scald the memory out of him. Except it didn't. When he got out, skin bright red, he looked at himself and thought he was covered with blood. Immediately he remembered Jack's hands on his body as he took Alex from behind.

Alex punched the wall, which only added one more pain to the multitude he felt. He couldn't stay here. He'd end up reliving the dream over and over, he knew it.

He dressed in a clean uniform, another gray and red one, but with this one, the red was in patches on the shoulders, chest, and back, instead of lines.

He'd head to the lab, check in on the computer. That would keep his mind busy. But first, his body demanded he did something about the pain.

Doc was in the medical bay, as usual.

"Don't you ever sleep?" Alex asked.

"Yes," she replied, indicating the closest bed.

"You sleep here?"

"No. Sit, there."

Alex sat and she looked him over. "You look like crap," she said.

"I feel like it." He almost told her about the dream, but he wasn't sharing that with anyone. "You said I could get a second shot."

"I thought you weren't going to get it?"

He tried to smile. "I changed my mind."

She nodded and injected him. "Heading to the party?"

"I don't know. Are you going?"

"I went earlier. Did some dancing, a bit of drinking. Then someone sprained an ankle so I brought her here, fixed her up, and sent her to bed."

Alex stood, the pain vanishing.

"You should go," she said. "You look like you could use a drink and a distraction."

"What I need is work," Alex replied as he left, but he found himself going down to the lounge, instead of up to the lab.

As with every other post-job celebration, the music was loud. People saw him and waved, clapped him on the shoulder. Said something that could have been congratulations, if Alex could have heard the words.

He headed for Anders's table. He should pay his respect before the man found out he was here and had him dragged there. With him he found Barbara, Milo, and three others Alex couldn't remember the names.

"Hey, Crimson! You're alive!" Anders yelled.

"So Doc claims."

"Here, sit." Anders grabbed the glass from one of the men and handed it to Alex. "Drink." It wasn't a suggestion.

It was a dark liquid, and smelled strong. He hesitated, then downed it. If nothing else, alcohol would muddy the dream's memory. He nearly choked on it

"What the hell is that?" he gasped among the others' laughter.

"It's called 'A Taste of the Void'," the previous owner of the glass said. "One of Etrigan's own creation. Don't ask me what's in it."

"Fix, get Etrigan here," Anders ordered. "Tell him to come make a Starry Night for Crimson."

The man stood. Anders indicated one of the available seats.

Alex sat, and found there was another glass before him, a light red liquid this time. He took a sip and it was sweet and fruity.

"How did we make out on the job?" Alex asked.

"Didn't you check?"

"I've been busy sleeping." *And dreaming.* He felt Jack's hand

344

on his back, his muzzle along his neck. He downed the drink, and the mild burning chased the memory away.

"We did pretty good. Not too much damaged cargo. About two-hundred crates. Lea's going to do the inventory over the next few days."

A tall man returned to the table with Fix, both carrying five bottles between them.

"Crimson, meet Etrigan."

Alex had seen him on the ship before, but as with most of the crew, he hadn't bothered getting to know him.

"Pleasure." Alex extended his hand.

Anders caught it and lowered it to the table. "Etrigan doesn't do physical contact unless he's having sex. And you're not his type."

"Sorry."

Etrigan smiled. "Don't worry about it. The Starry Night's for you?"

"It is," Anders said.

Etrigan placed a clean glass on the table and poured some of each bottle in it. The liquids mixed to form something very dark.

"That looks suspiciously like that Void drink I had."

The man smiled. "Just wait." He took a small bottle from a pocket in his light blue jacket and dripped three drops in the black liquid.

Alex waited for something to happen, and was about to ask, when a myriad of points lit up within the liquid. They didn't fill the glass with light. Each point was distinct, coming into being, lasting a few seconds before vanishing.

Alex stared at it, unable to look away. Lights came and went, and the drink lived up to its name. Alex felt like he was looking at a night's sky contained in one glass. When he was finally able to look up, he wanted to ask how he'd done it, but Etrigan wasn't there anymore.

"Don't bother asking," Anders said. "He hasn't told me, so he certainly isn't going to tell you."

Alex nodded and picked up the glass. Looking at it, there weren't as many stars in it now, and it reminded him of Jack's fur. And he remembered him moving on top of him, leaning down.

He drank it all in one swallow and gasped again.

Anders laughed. "Thirsty?"

Alex shook his head. "Trying to get myself to forget your ugly mug."

Anders laughed again, but Alex thought it was strained.

"Unless you require me to stay, I'm going to go mingle."

Anders made a shooing motion, and Alex stood. Two steps away from the table someone intercepted him, handed him a glass, and they toasted the job and riches they'd acquired. A few steps later he was holding another glass, and another group was toasting. And it happened again two times before he reached the bar. That's where he'd seen Etrigan before, behind the bar.

Alex ordered another Starry Night, and spent minutes watching the light. His mind was fuzzy enough by then it didn't remind him of Jack, or Tristan. It was just pretty lights.

When they faded he grabbed it, turned and raised it, proclaiming a toast to the captain. The people around him joined in and he downed the drink.

He found himself among the dancers, moving and stumbling. He was pulled one way and kissed. Alex didn't resist. He kissed back, hard, then laughed when he realized he was kissing a woman. They separated and went back to dancing. Men and women kissed him. Some also offered for them to go back to their room, though Alex politely refused. Kissing was okay, but nothing more would happen.

Glasses appeared in his hand, were drained and replaced. His dancing became less and less coordinated to the point where he almost fell, only to be caught by a strong hand and pulled back to his feet.

When he looked up—because the man was a head taller than he was—brown eyes were looking down at him. The man had dark skin with a clean shaved head and chin, and an amused smile.

He opened his mouth to say something, but Alex kissed him. The man didn't protest. Arms embraced Alex and tightened protectively. Alex's body reacted to the intensity of the kiss, and when they broke apart, Alex was blushing hard.

He looked at him and took in the broad shoulders and muscular arms under the loose, dark green shirt.

He leaned in. "You're Quincy, right?" he yelled in his ear.

The man nodded and turned, placing his mouth to Alex's ear. "And you're hot."

Alex blushed even more.

They dance for a while, close, because each time Quincy let go of Alex, he almost fell. While they danced, no other drinks appeared, and when Quincy suggested they should go somewhere quieter, Alex was able to walk with him.

They stopped regularly in the halls to kiss and grope each other. Alex was so needy it was painful. His shirt was open and he moaned as Quincy's hands moved over his chest. Somehow, they managed to make it to a room, then tumble into a bed. Alex pulled off Quincy's shirt and ran his hand over the furless chest.

All of a sudden, his mind cleared and he realized who he was with, or rather, who he wasn't with. He pushed Quincy off him, and with a mumbled apology ran out to his room, where he buried himself under the covers. He'd almost cheated on Jack, was the thought that ran through his mind as he fell into a dreamless sleep.

The banging on the door woke him, and with a groan he checked the chronometer. He'd slept for ten hours. The banging came again. Alex grumbled, realized he was in his pants but not his shirt, and opened the door.

Quincy stood there, holding Alex's shirt and jacket. "I think you owe me an explanation."

Alex remembered making out with the man, wanting him, the sense of betrayal, and nodded. He let him in and explained about Jack. Quincy, unamused, had a few choice words for Alex.

Alex explained he'd been way past drunk, but Quincy didn't care. They'd been enjoying themselves, and some absent guy had gotten between them. He called Alex some harsh names and stormed out.

Alex let himself fall back on his bed.

"I'm done drinking," he told himself. "I am not risking this again." And then he was asleep.

CHAPTER 40

Alex heard Anders's voice as he ran to the room, in the middle of a discussion involving datapads. He couldn't believe no one had told him about this job. It sounded like he'd missed most of the briefing. All the seats were taken, so Alex leaned against the wall, on the other side of Zephyr.

"Remember, those things are easier to break than what we usually go after, so tell your teams to handle them with care." Anders looked at the ceiling. "Ship, distribute the relevant data package to those in this room."

Alex's pad beeped. He looked at it, and was surprised to see that instead of the ship's layout, his packet contained the ship's registry ID, its manufacturer, date it was built, computer model, and list of personnel.

He glanced at Zephyr's. His did contain the layout, with indications of security rally points and other notable zones.

He moved away from the door to let the others leave.

"What are you doing here, Crimson?" Anders asked.

"Err...meeting? You made it pretty clear you wanted me present at all of them."

"You're on the bridge for this one; that's why I didn't send anyone to tell you. The captain said you liked to do some research on your target system. I was going to send that to Asyr's lab."

Alex thought it would have been better to let him know he wasn't needed, but then he wouldn't have panicked when the sensor told him about the large number of people in this room.

"I'll start on that, then." It was three days before the ship arrived; that was plenty of time to gather the information. It was sort of early for Anders to give a briefing. The two previous ones he attended had only been a day before the job. Alex was sure the man was messing with him.

Back in the lab, he started his search. He couldn't use the ID for his search without alerting the ship of it, and a direct search would alert someone, but there was plenty of information he could gather indirectly.

The manufacturer let him determine if this ship was a standard design for them, or a special order—it was standard. The computer model and time let him find out what sort of core personality he could expect, and then he accidentally found a use for the ID, when he came across it in the list of that model of ship the manufacturer had sold.

Since he hadn't asked for that information, no one would be advised. Knowing who had bought the ship allowed him to find their maintenance and upgrade records. Those were chronological, so doing a visual search for the ID was simple. With that he'd be able to refine the ship's personality and better target his attacks.

Looking through the crew was easier. He did a comparative search between them and the schools with the best coercion classes. Two dozen went there, so he narrowed his search to who had attended the classes. Almost half of them had, so he narrowed further to those who'd had scores that would get them snatched up by corporations. He had three possible experts on the ship. Another visual search through the school's records let him get a sense of how good they were, and using their teachers, he worked out their possible method of attack and defenses.

He got the hour warning and headed to the bridge.

* * * * *

Alex was still searching through the open net for the ship.

"How much longer, Mister Crimson?" the captain asked.

They were currently dark, drifting along with only the computer and minimal life support working. The job should have started five minutes ago, but it couldn't begin until Alex had taken control of it.

Where was it?

He could see it was there, physically, a few hundred-thousand miles away—passive sensors confirmed that—but he couldn't find the corresponding connections on the net. And this wasn't a case of no one being on their computer; even when everyone was in cryo, the ship itself still had to talk to the rest of the universe.

The only way it could disappear from the net was if someone purposefully deactivated all communication ports. But why would anyone want to fly silent like that?

"Captain, is there any chance they're carrying something other than datapads?"

"Not that I'm aware of. My contact would have informed me if she'd found something unusual in the manifest."

"There has to be something. They cut all contact with the net, and the only reason I can think of to do that is to hide from discovery. I can't see them doing that for a few crates of datapads."

"What does that mean for the operation?"

"If I can't get in their system, I can't hide our approach."

The captain nodded. "Murray, get ready for our standard approach."

"Yes, sir," the pilot answered, "but we're not set up for that right now. I have to wait until they've passed us, and use their propulsion to hide us."

"How long?"

"My best guess is twelve hours."

The captain activated his comm. "Anders, you can have everyone stand down. We're looking at a twelve-hour delay." He terminated the call without waiting for a reply. "Mister Crimson, what does this mean for the operation? The profit margin on this is dependent on a minimal amount of the cargo being damaged."

Alex grinned. "It just means I need to be on board to take control. I'll be with Anders.

* * * * *

Alex didn't have to ask for where Terrence was. With a job about to happen, there was only one place he could be. Alex pushed his way through the people leaving the breach room until he cleared the door, then ran to the front, where Anders and twenty people were relaxing. The rest might go off to do something else for twelve hours, but Anders would stay right here in case something happened. Alex had to respect the man's dedication.

"Terry, I need your datapad," Alex said, taking it out of the man's pocket.

"What are you doing here?" Anders asked. "I'd expect you to go rest before you need to work."

Alex didn't look up. "Damn it, Terry, when's the last time you cleaned up your index? How do you find anything in here?" He handed the datapad back. "Get me the ship's layout." He turned to Anders. "They're not connected to the net; that's the delay. Murray's waiting for them to pass."

Anders handed him his datapad. "The layout's already up. Why do you need it?"

"I need to figure out where I'll take control of the ship." Alex zoomed in on their entry point and looked around. He couldn't see any terminals, not even in the airlock. That was odd; they should be marked on the map. He zoomed out further and confirmed there were some on the level above. He didn't have time to dwell on the weird setup.

"I found the computer lab," Terrence said, pointing to his own pad.

Alex glanced over, then found it, two levels above, far on the aft side. Was it worth being that close to the ship's processor to have to go so far from his exit? Did he really want to put himself in a room that could be locked? He shuddered as he remembered his fight to get life support back under his control. No, he wasn't going there.

"Care to explain why you need to go in to take control?" Anders asked.

Alex almost snapped, but caught himself. He had time. He couldn't do anything until he was inside. "I can't talk to the ship from the outside. I don't know why, but they deafened themselves. So, I need to be inside to take control of the ship and back you up."

He looked at the map. He wished there was a closer terminal, but this one was going to have to do. Still, it was pretty far. How did they manage with so few terminals? "I'm going to need someone to cover me while I work."

Anders crossed his arms over his chest and glared at Alex.

"I'll do it," Zephyr said before Alex could reply to the glare.

"Me too," Terrence added.

"I need you patrolling the halls," Anders stated.

"No, you don't," Zephyr replied, and Anders shifted his glaring to him, but the man didn't react. "You already have almost thirty people doing that; you won't even notice our absence. And with Crimson in control, they'll be able to focus on moving the cargo instead. Isn't that the point of having him around?"

Anders ground his teeth and looked at Alex. "So that's it? You're poaching my people now?"

Alex sighed. "Anders, I'm not stealing anyone. I still work

for you, remember? I'm just doing the job the captain assigned me, to the best of my abilities." Alex smiled. "And think of it this way: with them watching me, you can tell everyone you were telling me what to do. But if you're certain you don't want them to help me, I'll be happy to go find someone else. I'm sure Ana and Jen would be more than happy to—"

"Fine, you two are with him." Anders stormed out of the room.

"You certainly have a way with Anders," Terrence said as he watched the man leave.

"It's all in his head." He glared at Zephyr. "I don't care what you said. I didn't do one damn thing to antagonize him, not one. And in this case, if he's so pissed, he can take it up with the captain." Alex looked at the datapad. Anders's pad, he thought in amusement.

"Okay, this is the route we're going to take."

＊ ＊ ＊ ＊ ＊

The explosion that opened the airlock was still ringing in Alex's ears as he rushed in with Anders and his people, but he turned left, away from the hold, followed by Terrence and Zephyr, and ran down that corridor, gun in hand.

"How long do we have?" Alex asked.

"Depends on where the closest security team is," Terrence answered. "Blowing the airlock was a loud indication of our arrival, but they still have to get here."

As he finished talking, a woman in a red and gold uniform rounded the far corner. Before she'd taken her gun out, Terrence shot her.

"What is it with bright colors?" Alex asked as they ran past her body. "Seems like every security force wears almost garish colors.

"They do it so they're easy to recognize," Zephyr answered, stopping and pulling a panel off the wall. "Less chances of shooting their own people."

"Then why don't we do the same?" Alex covered the hall while Terrence looked up and down the ladder.

"None of us gets too heartbroken if they accidentally shoot a crewmate." Terrence put his gun away and climbed up.

"And with security in bright colors, us wearing drab ones means it's also easy for us to tell who to shoot." Zephyr covered as Terrence ascended the ladder.

"Clear," Terrence said, and Zephyr moved away to let Alex climb.

Two levels up, Alex exited next to Terrence and waited for Zephyr. "The terminal is this way." He began moving. "Hopefully we get lucky and they won't expect us to be here, and I'll be able to get started before you two get too busy."

"Only thing luck gets you, is dead," Zephyr offered. He took position behind Alex while Terrence led the way.

They made it to the terminal without encountering anyone, which made Alex nervous. In spite of what he'd said, he had expected someone to be around. Where were all the non-essential personnel rushing back to their rooms?

Alex took out his earpiece. "Get ready; it won't be long until someone comes for us." He put it in.

Terrence looked left and right, grumbling. "I hate being this exposed."

"Alright," Alex said, bringing up the menu. "Talk to me."

Silence.

"Playing coy isn't going to help. You know I'm here, start telling me how I'm not going to get away with this."

Still silence.

With a few commands, he made his way behind the menu display to the code, and paused at what he saw, or rather didn't see. There was hardly any code there.

"What are you playing at?" he asked.

No reply.

He studied the code. The only thing it did was maintain the display, and one more thing. The screen went blank.

With a curse, he grabbed his comm. "Anders, tell me the cargo's there!"

"Of course it is," the man replied over the sound of gunfire and explosions. "I can see the crates."

"Check that the datapads are there. This is a trap, Anders. There isn't any code for me to use. There's nothing for me to control."

Zephyr and Terrence glanced at Alex with worried expressions.

Alex heard Anders grunt, then something clattered to the floor. "The crates are full."

"Okay. Anders, get everyone to grab something and run. Don't hang around." Alex didn't wait for a reply. He ran.

"Where's all the security if this is a trap?" Zephyr asked.

"My guess, the computer lab." He didn't bother checking before clamoring down the ladder.

"How did they know you'd get on the ship?" Zephyr asked, right behind him.

"No idea." Had they become predictable? The captain had said he was picking his targets with Alex in mind. He didn't know, but one thing was sure: he had attracted someone's attention, because this trap was for him, not the crew.

He got out of the ladder well and shot two guards before they could react. He ran past them and rounded a corner, only to collide with another group. He fell to the floor on top of a woman. His gun clattered away. He rolled off and got to a crouch, only to look down the barrel of her gun. There was a flash of light and another guard fell on her, throwing her aim.

Alex stood and kicked her in the face. The other guard turned and raised his gun. Alex grabbed the hand and twisted until he felt bones break. Another kick to the head, and the man stopped moving too.

Alex pulled out a knife and turned, ready for whoever was next, but the four other guards were down, moaning. Terrence had a burn on his arm. Zephyr was fine, as usual.

"Do you have a forcefield or something?" Alex asked, running again. Zephyr didn't answer.

They shot their way through two other security teams before they made it to the hold, where crates had been pushed to form an improvised fort. The airlock was blocked by two-dozen guards. Alex fired at them as he ran for the cover of Anders's fort.

Datapads littered the floor, and Alex almost slipped on one. He made a straight line for an opening between two crates, not caring if Anders used this opportunity to shoot him down. He slipped in, grabbed a gun off a body, and stood, ready to fire. He saw Zephyr and Terrence make it in a moment later.

Then the guards stopped shooting.

Alex looked around, and everyone wore the same confused expression he had, except for Anders, who was glaring at him.

"My dear pirates." A woman's voice resounded throughout the hold. "Now that you're all in one place, I'd like to draw your attention to the top shelves."

Alex looked up. Large crates were lined there, touching the ceiling. As he watched, the front of the crates fell off, opening to reveal large guns that swiveled and pointed at him.

"We are so fucked," someone said.

"If anyone has any bright ideas, I'm all ears." Anders had addressed everyone, but he was still glaring at Alex.

"Don't look at me. I coerce computers, not people."

"And if you'd actually done your job, we wouldn't be in this situation."

Alex returned the glare. "We can discuss what is and isn't my fault with the captain, once we're back on our ship."

Anders looked ready to reply, but instead glanced over Alex's shoulder, lips tightening.

Alex turned. More guards were joining those already there, forming a circle around the fort. There had to be a few hundred of them now. That, and the canons looking down on them meant they weren't going anywhere.

The woman spoke again. "I do hope I gave you long enough to realize the futility of resisting. As I speak, my coercionists are taking over your ship's computer. You have nowhere to go. Put down your weapons and surrender peacefully."

Alex looked at Anders. He needed to get back on the ship, but before he could say anything, Anders was giving orders.

"Keep your guns! No one is surrendering, do you hear me?"

"We're not going to survive this," someone said.

"I don't care. Some of us might die, but we're going to do it getting as many as possible back on our ship."

"What's the point?" someone else asked. "They're controlling it."

"Because Crimson can kick them out."

Alex nodded. He could do that and so much more now that there was a communication line between the ships.

"I'm with Anders," Barbara said.

"Me too," Rebecca added. "We're part of this crew because we refused to submit before. We're not doing it now."

Agreements sounded.

Anders looked the group over. "If any of you don't think we should fight our way out, stay here and don't get in our way. When we come back to get you—and I promise you that we will—you can explain to the captain why he wasted the energy taking you on as his crew." Anders turned and looked over the barricade.

Alex looked around and saw that those who had been silent before were now uncomfortably eying the others. They seemed to find their resolve and pulled out their guns.

Alex looked at Anders. The son of a bitch had managed to regroup his people. This was going to make it tougher for Alex not to respect the man. He reached to his belt for a knife, and found he didn't have one there, nor at his back. Or his sleeve. The only one he had left was at his boot. He eyed Zephyr's harness, covered with knives, and made a mental note to get one after this. The ease of access and extra knives made up for looking like a walking knife display.

"I am not seeing any of you put down your weapons," the woman said. There was a hint of disappointment in her tone. "I had hoped the realization you were outmatched would have knocked some sense into you."

Alex looked around at the guards, then up. The heavy guns seemed to shudder. This was going to be painful, he thought. But he'd get out of this. He had to reach Jack.

"I suggest you drop your weapons. I do intend on keeping some of you alive, but precision fire isn't what these guns are known for. This is your last chance to surrender."

Anders turned around, looked at his people, and gave a satisfied nod. "On my word, we rush them!"

The communication system let out a loud squeak, then the lights flickered. Anders looked at Alex.

"What? I'm here. That can't be me, it's got to be Asyr."

Anders pointed to the woman, bloody arm dangling at her side and gun in the other hand.

Alex shrugged. If she was here, then he was just as clueless as to how this was happening.

The big guns fired and everyone ducked, but with the screams coming from outside the makeshift fort, Anders stood.

"Now!" he yelled.

Alex looked around. The guns were firing randomly, hitting walls, floors, guards, and just now another gun. He didn't have the time to think about this. He jumped the crate after the others, fired at one guard, and threw his knife at another.

A guard pointed a gun at Alex, only to vanish in a flash of light, leaving a darkened spot on the floor. Alex ran through it as fast as he could.

Anders's insistence his team ran every day was paying off. He was among the first back on the ship, where he encountered and shot down guards. He'd known they'd be there, but they clearly hadn't expected any of the pirates to return, let alone be armed and shooting.

He shot down the ones in his way, and left the rest for the others. He ignored the lift; he wasn't putting himself in a locked box until he was certain who controlled the ship. The ladder was already exposed, and he heard the clanging of boots on the rungs. He looked in and up, saw bright colors, and fired. He let the bodies drop, and then began climbing.

At the sound of someone following him he aimed down, but it was Asyr and Jennifer.

"Who's at the lab?" he asked as he climbed.

"No one; I always lock it before boarding a ship."

"Then who is doing the coercion?"

She didn't answer, and four levels higher he exited the shaft and ran. He didn't encounter anyone this far into the ship. His crew had gone to the other ship and the guards hadn't made it this far in.

The door to the computer lab opened before he reached it, and he glanced around the empty room as he threw himself into the seat at the main console. Asyr took an auxiliary post and Jennifer stayed by the door.

Alex put the question of who the secret coercionist was out of his mind. He grinned as he put his earpiece in and activated the console. It was time to teach the invaders who was in charge here.

CHAPTER 41

In the end there were only eight deaths, two of which from the big guns when they went haywire. Once Alex had gotten back to the computer lab, he'd found the other ship was already under attack, so all he had to do was add his expertise to it, and in no time he had gained control.

He'd used emergency procedures to lower bulkheads across the ship, isolating the security forces in small groups, which let Anders go back to secure the hold, move the cargo, and then search the ship for injured crewmates.

Alex had considered blowing up the ship after that in anger over the deaths, over having been the target of the trap, the reason his crewmates died. He didn't do it. He decided he wouldn't be their murderer. He'd kill to defend himself, but never in cold blood. He settled on making the ship forget anything had happened.

Once that was over, he'd looked into how their computer had been able to attack the other one, without himself or Asyr there. What he'd found gave him pause.

And now, in the middle of the celebration, Alex set up a sound dampener on Anders's table so they could talk without shouting, and had explained what he'd found to Anders.

Anders didn't look like he believed him, nor did the others at the table.

"Let me get this straight," Anders said. "Our own computer protected itself and assaulted their system?"

Alex nodded.

"You're wrong," Luigi said. "Systems can't be aggressive like that."

"Normally you'd be right," Alex confirmed. "Systems are smart, but none of them have any aggressive code. It will defend its code, undo the damage done, but it can't actively force someone out. That's why a computer's first action will always be to alert the ship's coercionist of an attack. That's who is capable of taking aggressive action."

Alex sipped his drink. He was still on his first, while most of the table were on their third.

"Fine, then how did our ship do it?" Anders asked.

"First thing to remember is that for a very long time, it was insane. Having its components partitioned and incapable of talking to each other did a number on how it thinks. Once I reintegrated everything and smoothed it over, that instability became mostly unnoticeable. But it's not entirely sane. There's corrupted code right down to its core programming."

The men and women around him looked at each other nervously.

"Calm down," Alex told them. "There isn't anything to worry about. So long as Asyr keeps an eye on it, everything's fine."

They relaxed a little.

"The second thing is that one of those partitioned systems did become aggressive. Luigi, you were there, you saw how far the engineering systems were willing to go. You heard the stories of the ship trying to get people to kill themselves. That system was homicidal."

"There were also the accidents," Zephyr said.

Alex nodded. "It wanted us all dead, it just took it a long time to find a way of doing that without damaging itself. While it had control of life support, it realized we are fragile. When I took that away, it used things like power relays to hurt us."

"But you fixed it," Barbara said.

"And that's the third thing to remember. No, I didn't fix it. I thought I had. When I reintegrated engineering into the rest of the systems, all that aggressive code vanished. Some I removed, other just wasn't there. I thought it was the core processor's antibodies which had taken care of it, so by the time I was done, everything looked smooth and we didn't get any more accidents. I thought I'd fully removed the engineering's aggressiveness."

"Until now." Anders drained his mug and motioned for another one.

Alex nodded. "I'd done an in-depth scan of the code a few days after the reintegration, and I didn't find anything, but I'd forgotten something then: Engineering was paranoid. I never considered that it might fake being fully integrated, that it might take steps to ensure it wasn't 'destroyed'."

Etrigan brought Anders a drink, then indicated Alex's still half-full mug. Alex shook his head.

"Are you saying that thing's still somewhere in there? Waiting to kill us?"

"No. It's no longer an active system, not in the way it was before. Its code is mixed in with the rest, dormant. It waits for when the processor is under attack, then activates and goes on the offensive."

"But the system has been under attack before," Luigi said. "When you were busy with the Law ship, Asyr had to fight one back."

"That was before I reintegrated it. And after that, me or Asyr were there to keep the other coercionists under control. The code reacts to what the main processor feels." Alex searched for the right analogy. "Think of it as being on a subconscious level. The processor trusts me and Asyr, so it wasn't afraid. Nervous, but it knew we'd take care of the problem. This time it was alone when the coercionists attacked. It got scared, and then the aggressive code took over."

Anders grinned. "I guess we don't need you around anymore."

Alex smiled back. "Sure, if you want to trust your life to a system that isn't stable. I'll remind you it couldn't save us from the trap. All it managed to do was disrupt things. Those guns killed some of us, as well as their security."

"Okay," Terrence said. "Admittedly I don't know anything about that stuff, but how did our system know what to do to disrupt their system?"

"It did something it isn't supposed to be able to do: it learned from me. I can't be certain. I haven't been able to find the function logs—"

"What's that?" a woman with pale blond hair asked. Nancy, Alex thought her name was.

"Computers keep a record of everything they do, so someone like me—well, an actual maintenance expert—can go over them, see if everything is running smoothly. It usually goes back three months."

"And our ship doesn't keep one of those records?" Anders asked.

"It does, but there's a hole in it from an instant after the other coercionist began his attack to sometime after me and Asyr jumped in. My guess is that it doesn't want me to know what it did. But I was able to see the result of its attack, and a lot of it looks like what my programs would do. I never leave them in the system once I'm done, but I suspect it's made copies of them."

"You suspect?" Anders asked, a smile starting.

"I've gone over the logs and there's no indication it did so, but there are more holes in it, a lot of them matching when I was coercing a ship or doing exercises with Asyr."

"So? Get it to tell you."

"I tried, and it actively refused to answer."

Now Anders was grinning. "Hand it over."

Alex pulled out his earpiece. "I wouldn't do that."

"Let me show you how someone gives orders around here." He snatched the earpiece out of Alex's hand and put it in his ear. "Ship, do you recognize my voice?"

"This is a bad idea," Alex whispered, hiding a grin of his own by finishing his drink.

"You are Norman Anders," a voice replied, sounding like it came from the middle of the table.

Anders winced and looked around in surprise, then glared at anyone who'd started snickering.

"What are your instructions in regards to me?"

"I am to obey you in every way."

"Good." He looked at Alex. "Tell me exactly what you did to disrupt the other ship."

The room was plunged into darkness. The music died, the screens showing vids went dark. Protests erupted across the large room.

Alex looked over his shoulder to confirm there was light in the hall, and he knew from his previous experience that life support was still running.

When this had happened in the lab, Alex went through a moment of pure panic at the thought he'd somehow gotten the computer to commit suicide and take everyone with it. Then he'd heard the ventilation, and when he'd tried the door, it had opened.

Someone placed a light stick on the table, a bluish light showing Anders's perplexed expression.

"What just happened?" he asked.

"It's protecting itself," Alex answered, indicating he wanted his earpiece back.

"From what?"

"From what it did." Alex pushed his mug away. "It won't last long; it only lasted five minutes when I asked it the same in the computer lab. Those gaps in the logs, I don't think they're only to keep me from knowing what it did. I think it's so it won't know what it did. I don't think it can know."

"So, it shuts down?"

Alex nodded. "Just here, and only for a short time."

"Why?"

"This is only a guess, but based on what I've seen in the code, the computer's actions, and some reading I did, I'm confident I'm right. This isn't a military ship. There's nothing in its code preparing it to take a life. In fact, it's the opposite; every piece of code that deals with us puts keeping us alive above pretty much everything."

"But it tried to kill us, you said so yourself."

"Again, that was the engineering system. It doesn't have any of those safeguards, and that's what kicked in when the ship was attacked. So it didn't have any problem killing, but it isn't stupid. It knows the main processor can't handle it, so it kept those actions from it. It prevented the logs from forming, and when we try to force the issue, it shuts itself down."

Anders was thoughtful. "I don't like this. If it can act without instructions, it could be a problem."

"It only does so for self-preservation."

"I still don't like it. Can you remove that completely?"

Alex thought about it and decided to tell the truth. "No, I can't."

"Why not? You managed to deal with it when you took life support away from it."

"Sure, and it almost killed those of us in the lab, and quite a few around the ship got hurt. It only used life support to do that damage. It's part of the main processor now, which means it has access to everything. How far do you think it might go to stop me? Do you think it might blow the ship up?"

"That wouldn't save it."

"True, but it will see what I do as trying to kill it. If you know someone is going to kill you and you won't be able to stop them, are you going alone, or will you try to take as many of them along with you?"

The lights came back on, to loud rejoicing. The music picked up where it had stopped, and the dancing resumed.

Anders looked around. "Can we trust it not to try to kill us?"

"I think so. It's no longer utterly insane, and the paranoid part is a subprogram. It now exists to protect the ship, and by extension, the crew. You never had problems with coercionists until I started doing it. If the captain stops once I leave—" that caused him to snicker "—then you shouldn't have to worry about it. If he doesn't, then hopefully he'll be more careful about how he picks his targets, and you'll still have a decent coercionist onboard."

Terrence nodded. "That makes me wonder, how come no one else does this? I mean the coercion, not the pirating. It's saved lives, let us get away with a lot more cargo. You'd think everyone would do it."

Alex grinned. "That's easy. They can't find a coercionist able to get the job done."

"We found you," Zephyr said.

Alex snorted. "I'm not your typical coercionist anymore." He looked at his hands. Wasn't that the truth?

"That guy of yours, right?" Anders asked.

Alex nodded, although Jack hadn't even been in his thoughts. Still, it was for him he was doing all this.

"If it wasn't for what happened back on Deleron Four, I'd still be there, happily working for Luminex. The corporations grab us right out of school. I had half a dozen of them trying to convince me to work for them in my last year. The companies who design ships' computers employ a lot of coercionists so they can embed enough knowledge to protect themselves. It doesn't need to be aggressive for that. So long as its antibodies can rebuild its code faster than I can change it, I'll run out of energy before it does."

"But what about the money?" Terrence asked. "That's got to count for something."

"Sure, if you don't mind the risks associated with it. The first time I coerced a computer for the captain, I ended up with a guy pointing a gun at me. If it wasn't for Perry leaving me one, and a lot of luck, I'd be injured and in prison, maybe even dead. As a rule, coercionists aren't risktakers. The corporations protect us from any legal repercussions with what we do."

Alex grabbed his mug and rolled it around.

"And I think you're wrong. I don't think I'm the first coercionist pirates have used. That ship that was used as a trap; that wasn't a spur of the moment thing. The entire computer system was designed so that part of the ship could be isolated—I mean, even the systems in it, with only enough code there to give the illusion everything was working normally. How long has it been since I've been on the ship, objective time? Four, five years?"

Shrugs all around. Alex had discovered that the crew didn't pay much attention to objective time since they were always in space.

"You can't make those kinds of changes in that short amount of time. That isn't just about changing the code; the hardware needs to match, otherwise they'd end up with what you had here when I joined: a crazy computer. And they knew what to expect from me, which would indicate they've had experience. Maybe there's something about turning into a pirate that makes coercionist more apt to take risks, to get the job done at all cost. In my case I didn't want to let the captain down, but I never even hesitated."

Alex looked down, then rubbed his face. "I don't think there's a lot of us out there. The risk isn't worth it, and that ship's probably caught most of them."

"I guess that means we won't be able to find another one after you leave," Anders said.

Alex smiled. "You don't need to go looking. Asyr's a natural. She's going to be better than I am if she keeps practicing." He stood. "Well, I've had enough celebrating. I'm off to bed."

They wished him a good night, and on his way out, Alex saw Quincy dancing with another man. Their eyes met for a moment and Alex looked away, hurrying out before Quincy could decide to come give him a piece of his mind.

Chapter 42

"What am I supposed to do with all of that?" Alex asked himself as he looked at the amount displayed.

"Problem?" Will asked, glancing up from his datapad.

"Yeah. Have you seen how much money I'm getting?"

Will grinned. "Lots."

A lot was right. Alex hadn't asked to see his cut. Even now, with only a jump left before reaching Samalia, he hadn't thought about money, but Lea had sent him a message asking him how he wanted his pay once he left the crew.

"I have no idea how to deal with this kind of money." There was so much that he was set for the rest of his life. Once he got Jack back, they'd be able to get a place on a quiet planet and just enjoy each other's company.

"How do you deal with it?" he asked Will.

His friend reached in a pocket and pulled out a cred stick.

Alex shook his head. "I'm not putting all that on a stick. I'd lose everything if it was stolen."

Will shrugged. "Many?"

Alex chuckled. "Do you have any idea how many sticks I'd need? Even if I was willing to put a thousand on each, I'm looking at a few thousand sticks. I'd need a truck to carry that around."

"Need bank."

Alex thought about it, then sighed. "I can't put that in my account. The Law's going to have programs monitoring it. There's still a warrant for my arrest from Luminex. Where do you keep yours? It can't all be on a stick."

Will tapped the wall. "In ship."

"Right." That made sense. He didn't have to worry about the Law looking into the deposits. "Unfortunately, that isn't going to work for me."

Will tapped his ear. "Coerce, hide it."

Alex laughed. "I'm not that good. The bank will notice such a large infusion of money. I don't know how many accounts I'd need to split the deposits enough they'd slip below the threshold, but they'd notice it if I created all of them."

Will was thoughtful. "I create some, give them over. Jen too. Ana, everyone."

Alex smiled. "I appreciate the thought, but that would make the Law notice you."

Will canted his head, grinning.

"More than it already does, I mean," Alex added, then he paused. "But you're giving me an idea. Thanks." He headed out.

* * * * *

Asyr was seated at the main console when Alex entered.

She looked up. "I'm just practicing." She pushed away. "I'll let you have it."

"It's okay. One of the secondaries will do for what I'm checking." He sat, put his earpiece in and, after greeting and doing a quick check of the ship's systems, he contacted his bank. He didn't go to his account, but made his way through the code until he was below the user interface.

It only took a few seconds to know he wouldn't be able to do it, but he still tried for five minutes, to no avail. This wasn't like what he'd done for that criminal. Siphoning a little money from a lot of accounts was one thing, but now he wanted to create one location where he could put all the money he'd made. It wasn't just the security that was the problem, or the bank's coercionists, it was the number of redundancies in place to make sure each and every account was authentic. He could write programs to affect all of them, but there would be delays from the time he made the changes to that information reaching the programs. If only one redundancy was faster, it would fail.

He backed out, erasing any evidence he'd peeked in. "Well, that isn't going to happen," he grumbled.

"What are you trying to do?" Asyr asked.

"I was thinking of creating user IDs within my bank system to distribute the money I've made. I can't put it into my account. I just looked at the security and it's too complex to let me do that."

"Then get it elsewhere."

Alex chuckled. "I can't just 'get' an ID. I have to create it, as well as all the backing information, census reports, life history, medical... There's probably a lot more to it."

"It's not that complicated."

"How do you know?" Alex asked.

"I have six IDs."

"Really? How did you get them?"

"I bought them from a girl I know. Everyone on the ship has more than one. We have to. We're all wanted by the Law for something. We couldn't leave the ship without them."

Alex hadn't noticed that, but then, how would he? His ID card had his name on it, but he didn't flash it all the time. Most places read it without him having to pull it out. And the card wasn't really where the information was; it just held the addresses where that information was contained. It would be simple enough for him to create a program that would change the address. He could even use multiple addresses, have them rotate.

He shook his head. "But I'd still have to create the IDs, and I'd have to get in pretty deep inside multiple systems, not all of which are governmental."

"You don't create it, you take it. There are tons of IDs stored that no one's using. Governments have repositories full of them."

"Then they'll be protected."

"Not according to my friend."

Alex couldn't believe that. Sure, governments were notoriously easy to get into, but within that they had high-security areas. Such a repository would have to be there.

Still, he didn't have anything to lose by taking a look. He found a government on the open net, a small one, out of the way, and slipped in. He looked around, found a handful of higher security zones within that system then, far too easily as far as he was concerned, the space where IDs resided.

A lot of them were blank IDs, waiting to be assigned to a newborn, but a lot more than he'd expected had a history to them. He double checked for any kind of security and didn't see any, so he pulled one up, a man who had died fifty-eight objective years before. His name had been Harold Stingsky, and the whole of his life was there.

He took the ID out of the repository, removed the death from it, and inserted it into the census. No alarms went up. Not even one sniffer program came to investigate what had happened.

This had been far too easy.

He found another government system, one slightly larger, closer to the core, where everything was more monitored. This one had sniffers, but they didn't notice him under his cloak. He found the repository in a similarly unprotected area and he was able to bring another person back from the dead, a Rosita Harmond. The sniffers looked at it, but then went away.

Alex tried it again, with a larger system, again closer to the core, with the same results. On his fifth test, this one within a core government computer, he was stopped the moment he entered. The security program detected his cloak and proceeded to start dismantling it. He tried to disconnect, but that had been frozen by the system.

He ordered Asyr to shut down all communication, and just as trackers started on him, he was out. That was what he thought security should be like in a government system, but only a core government had used it.

There were a small number of core governments, compared to all of them in the universe, and if that was how the security was distributed, no wonder Asyr had implied it was easy.

He went back to that first system and looked in on Harold. He was still there; the census had even attached his health records from the medical database. Alex took a quick look at that and removed the death certificate. Again, no alarms went up.

Alex leaned back in his chair and couldn't believe how easy this was. He decided to leave Harold alive to see what happened over the next few days, and went through the other census to remove the people he'd brought back to life.

Over the next week he checked in regularly, while cataloging what the census looked for in its citizens. It didn't look for much. It required an address, it did a scan for a death certificate every local year, it checked that the taxes were paid, and...nothing else.

That was all it took to be alive?

When Harold was fine after the week, Alex set to work. He found a list of addresses that were defunct and picked one of those, making it active within the government system, but nowhere else. That way other than the census, no one should check it out. He made Harold a writer, then for safe measure he created a social life for him, something limited, indications he went to coffee shops, did some traveling. Small things that would do for casual inspections.

With that done as Harold, he contacted a bank and opened an account. He answered all the questions, and under five minutes Harold had his very own bank account. Alex transferred a few thousand in it, payment for some private work, and then covered his tracks. Now all he had to do was wait.

* * * * *

"Hey, Lea," Alex called to her as she looked through a crate.

She smiled. "How do you like being on the front line?"

"Not as much as being on the bridge, but it's fun. How's this haul?"

"Not as good as when you're on the bridge, but decent. When I'm done appraising it, I'll give you your cut."

"Don't worry about it, that isn't why I'm here. Do you have a list of what each ship I coerced carried?"

She pulled out her datapad. "Sure, why?"

"I've been trying to work out how the people behind that trap ship managed to target us. I've looked at everything else I could think of, so now I'm wondering if we might not have some sort of cargo profile."

"You should ask the captain; he could tell you what he looked for."

"He isn't there to satisfy my curiosity."

"He still would. I'm ready to send them to you."

Alex took his pad and the files appeared on it. "If this doesn't answer my questions, I'll go see him." He deleted the manifest from that first job; It hadn't been picked with him in mind. The next two listed a lot of different things, but the one following that was a smaller shipment of crystals from Abony— small, fragile, but valuable. His mother had loved them. After that, artisan pottery from Uganew Two. So definitely fragile and small.

"Lea, was the cargo from the...Tiffany valuable?"

She looked it up. "Yes, the rich folks in the core are going crazy over that stuff. Something about them being the last ever made or something."

Alex continued looking. Processor chips, components for hovers—luxury hovers he found out after checking—historical pieces from Barony Eight. He had a twinge of guilt over that one, but he pushed it down. As he continued looking, they all had a common thread: high-value, but easily damaged. Same as with the datapads that was the cargo the trap ship had carried. The captain had become predictable.

Still, what were the odds he'd found the one ship that was a trap? Even if the cargo was exactly what he was looking for, it couldn't be the only ship with something like that.

"Lea, you went to the trap ship, right?"

"I helped move the cargo after you had control of it, yeah."

"What's your opinion of it? How long do you think it would take to load something like that?"

"Depends on how much of a hurry they're in. Give me the right loaders, and enough of them, and I can fill the hold in a few hours. Why?"

"I'm trying to figure out how they got to us." Alex tapped his datapad. "We've been going after similar cargo, so that's how they baited us, but how could they make sure the ship would be close enough the captain would go after it?"

"Maybe they have a fleet."

"If that's true, then I'm definitely not the first coercionist to go pirate. That's the only way getting a fleet makes sense."

"Okay, then if we're only working with one ship, I'd figure out the most probable route. Put out a bunch of manifests, all of them seemingly unrelated, but with the kind of cargo my target wants, and I make sure that all the ships those manifests are linked to are actually the same, but with different tags and such."

"Wouldn't that mean the cargo might not match what's in the hold?"

"Then I put out multiples of the same manifest, just changing the ship it's attached to. The captain finds the first one he likes, stops looking, and he doesn't realize that there's more of them out there."

Alex nodded. "Makes sense. Minimizes the expenses, maximizes the exposure, and because it's fragile, it will attract only a certain type of pirates, ones with a coercionist on board. So even if more than one takes the bait, they're still getting coercionist pirates out of circulation."

"If we don't do it for them," she said. "When two ships go after the same target, it tends to result in a firefight."

Alex nodded. "They seemed to want me alive, but I don't think they would have cared if I'd ended up dead. But what if pirates without a coercionist show up?"

She eyed him. "You did see the level or armament they had, right? They might have set this up to catch someone like you, but they could take down anyone who attacked them." She went back to looking in the crate. "Don't worry about it. It won't happen again. If it's really because we were predictable, the captain learns fast, but if you want you could tell him your theory."

"I doubt he'll listen to me. You tell him. You can even take the credit for it."

Lea shook her head. "Never give up credit, Crimson. In this job, it's about the only thing you have."

Alex considered it for a moment, then left Lea to go look for the captain.

CHAPTER 43

Alex's stomach did a cartwheel, and he stopped. He held onto the wall while he waited for the nausea to pass. He should have waited for a while longer before getting out of bed. Actually, he should have undressed before going under cryo—he knew how bad he felt otherwise—but they were in Samalian space now, and he had a lot of work to do before they reached the station there. He'd wanted to be able to get started quickly.

His stomach settled and he got going again. He managed to make it to the computer lab before nausea hit again, and his stomach stopped threatening to empty itself once he sat down. Reminding himself he hadn't eaten anything before going under hadn't helped.

The first thing he did was check on Harold Stingsky. Eight objective months had passed while Alex was in cryo, enough time for the fakeness of Harold's existence to be discovered, only it hadn't. The only thing that might draw attention was that Harold's message buffer was bursting with ads for him to buy products or services. A small program added to Harold and those would automatically be deleted.

Alex was pleased, and a little mystified. Harold had survived with barely the minimum of life signs. Didn't anyone care that there was now a fake identity in the system? Clearly, they didn't. Asyr had said this was standard for everyone on the crew, as well as mercs.

Well, Alex wasn't going to let this opportunity pass him by. He figured he'd need at least twenty new identities to distribute all the money he had. He would create them on distant worlds with small governments.

But first, he had something more important to do: he had to find Tristan. He contacted the station, and through it the planetary system. No coercion was needed for that; this was a simple query, one that returned no result. No surprise there; Tristan was wanted. He wouldn't want the Law to know he was there.

Now, coercion came into play. He slipped under the code and found a more advanced system than he'd expected. He remembered Jack saying his planet was on the primitive side, but that had to have been another of Tristan's lies. The system here was more advanced than some of the governments he'd chosen to create some of his new identities.

Although, maybe Jack hadn't lied. How long had it been since the last time Tristan had been here? A quick search showed that the last mention of a Tristan—no last name—in the system dated back to over sixty years ago. And by the quality of the code, Alex could tell the system hadn't been very advanced then. Maybe the planet had been as primitive as Jack had said the last time Tristan had seen it.

He looked for a widespread body recognition system, but didn't find one. He'd hoped that unlike more advanced planets, they used such a system to maintain order. Without that he needed a different way of tracking his quarry down.

He went back to his file on Tristan, and had a program extract the names of everyone he'd had contact with. It didn't matter if they had worked with him, been imprisoned with him, been a witness, or a victim. If the name was in the file,

Alex wanted a search to be done on them. He had to write the search program; the one in the system couldn't handle such a massive request.

While it worked, Alex set about creating his new identities. He limited it to two per government, in case the appearance of too many identities would trigger an alarm. He made sure each had a basic, but solid history, and then transferred his money among them, backdating entries over twenty years.

An hour before docking he checked his search. It was still going, now working on the names from Tristan's first ten years of activities. He'd set the search to work from the most recent names to the oldest.

He had three names, and he figured those would be the only ones he'd get. And if something came up from that far back, how useful would the information be after fifty years?

He took any information the planetary system had on those three names and transferred it to a data chip. Then he cleaned his presence out of the ship's system. He did do one thing to it before finally removing his own authorization. The moment that was done, he was kicked out.

He'd packed before going under. It had been quick—other than the case with the Defender, he only had one bag, although now it was filled with shirts and pants that could double as body armor instead of his previous civilian clothes.

He showered and shaved, made himself presentable for when he found Jack. He chuckled at that thought. He'd be finding Tristan first, so he should be borrowing a full set of armor from the ship and wearing that.

He had considered dressing in the slacks and shirt he'd first worn when getting on the ship, leaving as he'd arrived, but he'd lost so much weight they no longer fit him, and they weren't him anymore. To put them on would be to lie to Jack about who he was now.

Would Jack even know him, once he'd drawn him out of Tristan?

He shook his head. He was wasting his time. He needed to focus on the more important things: finding Tristan, getting the best of him. Like he'd told Will, his old self couldn't do that, only Crimson could. It wasn't charm that would win against the Samalian, it would be strength and cunning.

He put on gray pants with light red stripes at the waist and ankles, with a mostly red shirt with gray patches under, and a jacket over that. He didn't know what the weapon policy was for the station, but he slipped a knife in his boot, the small of his back, and his left forearm.

He smiled. Only a few months since Zephyr had been training him, and he felt naked without them. Something else Jack would have to get used to. His gun went in the bag, in an outside pocket, for easy reach.

Alex had planned on waiting for the ship to dock by the airlock so he could start his search immediately, but Will was on the other side of the door as it opened. His friend grabbed the case out of his hand and ran off. Alex didn't have a choice. No matter what this was about, he couldn't leave without the Defender. He ran after Will.

He ended up in a large room a few corridors down from his quarters, where a dozen men and women were waiting for him.

"You didn't think you'd leave without saying goodbye, did you?" Doc asked.

Alex looked them over. "Sorry, that hadn't been my intention."

"Lost in there," Will said, tapping the side of Alex's head.

Alex nodded. He'd been so focused on everything he had to do before leaving the ship, he'd forgotten about the people who'd helped make him who he was.

"I notice Anders isn't here."

Terrence snorted. "This is the 'those of us who actually like you' group."

Zephyr nodded. "And he's going to be with the captain to see you off. He's got your money."

Alex frowned. "I thought that was in the system. I already took care of that."

"We never let anyone go without money in their pockets."

"And Anders is going to be the one to give that to me? I'll have to check and make sure he hasn't hidden a bomb in there. Do you know how much I should expect?"

"Ten sticks with a thousand in each," Jennifer said. "That'd see any of us until we'd made arrangements for the rest. Course we're not quite as smart with that stuff as you are."

Alex blushed. "I guess I can set something up for the rest of you if you want."

There was laughter. "Jen's kidding. None of us are planning on leaving, so we don't need anything like that."

Alex nodded. "I should have grabbed a cred scanner. Knowing Anders, he's bound to have skimmed as much out of them as he can."

"He wouldn't do that," Perry said. "Not with the captain there. He can get away with a lot, but pissing off the captain in such an obvious way can be deadly."

Ana nodded. "Just be discreet if you do scan them. Any terminal on the station will let you do that." She handed him a mug.

Alex looked at it. "Thanks, but I shouldn't be drinking right now."

"It's Altonian juice—no alcohol, I promise."

He took a sip, and found it to be slightly bitter and sweet without any of the heat alcohol would cause. He looked at each of them. "I want to thank you. Without each of you, I'd probably be dead by now."

"Are you joking?" Asyr asked. "It's us who'd be dead without you. It's going to be rough doing every job the old-fashioned way."

"You're not taking over for me?"

"No way. I'm nowhere near ready to take on a system actively trying to stop me."

"Don't sell yourself short. You're quite good." He sipped his juice and used the mug to hid a grin. "And I plan on putting you to the test every so often, so you'd better study."

A worried expression crossed her face, and before Alex could say anything, the ship shuddered.

"Docking," Will said.

"I guess this is time for the real goodbyes," Doc said. "If we're not in the hold to help unload by the time they open it, the captain's going to have our hide." She hugged Alex and left.

Everyone followed her example, Will last, and the two of them followed the group to the cargo hold.

"Mister Crimson," the captain greeted as Alex stepped on the ramp leading down to the station. Anders was standing next to him, his face a mask of forced neutrality.

"Captain, Anders." Alex stopped next to them and watched crates being moved to a truck.

"Don't worry," the captain said as Alex opened his mouth. "I've warned the buyer about the possibility of infection on the datapads. I had to offer a break in the price, but better that than bad blood between us."

Alex's lips tightened. "I hate that this is because of a trap meant for me."

Anders rolled his eyes. "Such a high opinion of yourself. The trap was for all of us. They just used you to track us. Which means I was ri—"

"Anders," the captain warned.

Whatever else Anders wanted to say, he kept to himself.

The captain fixed his gaze on Alex. "Is there anything I can say to convince you to stay, Mister Crimson?"

Alex shook his head. "This is too important to me." He looked back to the interior of the ship. "It was an experience, I have to admit that, and I don't regret any of it. I'm pretty sure the man I was before I boarded your ship couldn't manage to do what I'm going to have to now."

"Your skills will be missed. Anders, give him the sticks."

Alex watched the man's face as he handed him the box. Alex put it in a pocket without bothering to check, his eyes not leaving Anders's neutral expression. He'd scan them later. It wasn't like being short on ten-thousand was going to affect him all that much. Not with all the money he had spread through his accounts.

Alex extended his hand to the captain. "Thank you for taking me here, and trusting me to work for you."

The man shook it. "Spend your money like the Law is watching, pilot your ship like the engine is unstable, and treat your crew like each one of them hides a knife."

Alex had a baffled expression as he tried to figure out what that meant.

The captain smiled and clapped his other hand on top of Alex's. "Be careful, Mister Crimson. It's a dangerous universe out there."

"I will be. You be careful too. Whoever they were, they were ready for my tricks, so they might have ways to restore their ship's memory."

"You don't need to worry on my account. I've been handling the Law and bounty hunters for longer than you've been alive. I will handle this too."

Alex had no doubt of that. "I guess that's it then. I'm no longer part of your crew."

"Technically, that only happens once you've stepped off the ramp."

Alex looked at the end of it, five or six steps away, then beyond that, at the station and the planet he couldn't see. At his future. He smiled to himself and couldn't wait to get going.

"What?" Anders asked. "Having second thoughts? Not so sure your guy's going to want you anymore?"

Alex closed his eyes. He could ignore him a little longer. He wasn't a factor anymore, he was just an annoying piece of—

Who was he kidding?

Alex reached inside his left sleeve as he spun and used the pommel to hit Anders in the stomach. Fingers wrapped around it, he punched him in the face, making him teeter back—and then, just for good measure, Alex kicked him in the balls.

Anders crumpled to the ground in a ball.

Alex forced him to his back and then knelt, a knee on the man's chest. He flipped his knife so the point was on Anders's nose.

"Listen to me, Anders. I hope you enjoyed all those times you got to order me around, because I don't have to take it anymore.

I'm not killing you right now out of respect for Captain Meron, but you better hope our paths never cross again, because the next time they do, I'm not going to leave anything of you for others to pick up."

Alex stood, turned, then turned back again to Anders. "Oh, and I removed your access to the computer. That's something else you don't get to order around anymore."

Anders glared at him. "You're dead," he croaked.

"Give it your best shot, Anders." He looked at the captain. "If you value his life, I'd suggest you keep him on the ship."

The man nodded. "I'd suggest you step off the ramp now. This is getting close to being one of those crew issues I'll feel forced to intervene in."

Alex nodded and walked away. He couldn't believe how good that had felt.

Chapter 44

From the air, Samalia's capital looked much like any of the other cities he'd seen in his life. Well, cities on well-populated worlds. It didn't look as densely packed as the capital of Deleron Four, but was greener.

According to the information he'd found on the net, it was called Grefrozon, but that didn't sound like any of the words that came over the speaker during their approach. The speech was all in Samalian, since he was the only human there.

He'd gotten his neighbor, a male with lustrous blonde fur with deep red stripes, to repeat it a handful of time, and if he did twist the growly sounds this way and that, it might resemble the word he'd read for it.

Alex felt off, being the only human in this group, being the alien, but it was also exhilarating. Samalians came in varying weights and height, but he thought the average was about his own height. Like his neighbor, everyone's fur was multicolored, and Alex couldn't make out any recurring patterns.

He could see dark splotches on light backgrounds, the reverse, dark on dark, and a few were patchworks of white, brown, rust, black, and tan. If he'd seen that pattern watching a vid, his first thought would have been that it looked fake.

The thing that really put his self-control to the test was that no one except him wore shirts. He hadn't thought about it when Jack went bare-chested almost everywhere, and now he realized it could be a cultural thing. Alex kept his hands on the strap of his bag and handle of the case to keep himself from running his fingers through all that fur.

Once the shuttle landed and he was able to exit, he breathed in relief. He'd had to repeat to himself over and over that he had someone, that Jack was waiting for him, to keep his hands to himself, and even with that, he'd caught himself loosening his grip on the strap just before landing.

The planetside port wasn't as crowded as the shuttle had been. Here too he was the only human, but he saw a Fedolrinan, its lanky, tree-like body towering over everyone. It looked around as if it was lost, referring to its datapad while it tried to get one of the Samalian's attention.

Alex began moving in its direction to help—he knew a word or two of Feldorinan—but he stopped himself; he had an appointment to keep, and it wasn't like he was familiar with the city or even the port.

Leaving the port, he came across an electronics store and stopped in to see what they had. Everything was a few years out of date, but good quality. They even had a few models of earpieces. None of them matched his; these were all versions for the public to use. They needed to be configured to interact with specific systems, while his would do all that work itself.

Still... He bought one and had it shipped to the Golly, to Asyr's attention. It would make her job a little easier, and once she was comfortable with it, she'd be able to find a better one.

That done, he headed into the city to meet with someone who might be able to help him locate Tristan.

During his flight down from the station, mainly as a way to keep himself distracted, he'd been able to locate the three Samalians who had crossed path with Tristan. One was dead;

Alex hadn't thought to set that as one of the parameters for the search.

The second one was on the other side of the planet. She was a mercenary who had been part of a team with Tristan decades before. The only way to reach her was a ground vehicle. Samalians hadn't yet adopted shuttle technology to travel long distances, and the port in the capital was the only place set up for the larger models coming from the station to land.

He'd contacted her, and she'd claimed not to remember any Tristan. She could have been lying, but her fur had been mostly white, with some tan through it. From his reading, Samalian's furs turned white as they aged. That and the trembling in her limbs led Alex to think it was just age and memory loss.

The last one had been another mercenary, but he'd retired recently. He'd started a weapon repair shop on an outlining neighborhood of the capital. He'd contacted him, but the man hadn't been interested in talking over comm. Alex had needed to make an appointment.

Without a shuttle system, Alex tried to find some sort of ground vehicle that could take him there, but nothing registered on his datapad, and none of those traveling on the wide road had anything on them indicating they took passengers.

He tried to get one of the pedestrians to help him, but other than glancing in his direction, they ignored him.

Back in Alien-Nation, on Deleron Four, it had come up a few times in conversations, how humans often acted as if the aliens walking the streets were invisible. Alex had seen that behavior himself, and now he was on the receiving end.

If he hadn't been in a hurry, he would have allowed himself to be offended. He'd always treated the aliens he met with respect—wasn't he entitled to the same now? But his appointment couldn't wait.

At least he knew where he was going. The city had an open net, and a map was available. He couldn't read the street's names, but his contact had sent him the address to his shop, and that now came up on the map. All he had to do was run there to be able to reach it in time.

Alex smiled; at least he'd make it. He couldn't imagine

what he would have done if the 'him' from his Luminex years had been in this situation. He would have given up before ever reaching the planet.

The height of the buildings dropped drastically just a few blocks away from the port. There they had been a dozen stories in height, but now they were no more than three. Large buildings often took up the entire block, with an open space in the middle.

His research had indicated Samalians were gregarious, as Jack had claimed. They lived in close-knit groups, helping each other with whatever tasks needed done, from housework to rearing their young. They weren't always related by blood, but were families of choice. The articles didn't go into details about it, but the implication had been that all the members of each group were intimate with each other.

Outside the city, a few of those groups would form a town of widespread buildings. Here, they had no choice but pack themselves in tightly. But he thought they tried to keep the feel of their communities, with the pen courtyards inside the structure where children played under adult supervision. The one thing that caught him unprepared was that neither those children or adults wore any clothing.

Alex looked away and hurried on, but he'd seen enough to know that Samalian women looked as much like human ones below the belt as the men did. The quick sight had made him miss Jack again.

He'd expected the buildings to spread further apart as he moved away from the port, like they did back on Deleron Four or where his grandparents lived. Instead, by the time he reached the repair ship, the road was too narrow to let most vehicles through, at least not without damaging the sides.

By the shop's entrance a bike was parked, resting on its hover pads. That was probably the only thing that could easily move down the alleyways. Looking at it, he got a sense it was a human vehicle. He hadn't seen any Samalian riding one on his way. Considering how minimal their clothing was, riding one probably wouldn't be safe for them.

With a smile and a thought of how it might feel to ride on

one holding onto Jack, he entered the shop.

"Finally!" a woman said. "It's about time you got here, I've—great, you're not him."

She was human, a little shorter than Alex. She wore a leather jacket and pants, both with visible plates on them. She had a gun on her hip and was eying him in annoyance.

Alex got a clear sense she was dangerous, and he moved his hands closer together in front him. A relaxed pose, but one that put his hands close to the knives hidden in his sleeves.

But she wasn't impressed with him. "Go back outside and wait your turn."

Alex felt the anger rise at the callous way she'd dismissed him. He pushed it down as fingers reached in his sleeve to grab the hilt of the knife, then stopped himself. He had every right to be angry. He wasn't some nobody to be ignored, not anymore. He wasn't ever going back to being that.

"What did you say?" he asked through clenched teeth.

"I told you to leave." She placed a hand on the butt of the gun. "I got here first. Don't make me repeat myself."

Alex took a step toward her. "Lady, I have no idea who you are, but unless you plan on paying me, you don't get to order me around."

She gave him a vicious-looking smile, her hand tightening on the gun. "I'm the one with the gun. Those knives of yours aren't going to do anything against that."

The only thing that smile did was make him angrier. He kept that controlled; he didn't want to be overwhelmed by it. He'd need to keep his head for when she attacked him, and he had no doubt she would.

Other than the gun, she didn't have any visible weapons, not that it meant anything. But her free hand wasn't moving, so she either had extraordinary control, or she counted on the gun to ensure her victory.

All he had to do was close the distance and he'd have the advantage. He didn't worry about her having hardened skin; his vibro-knife would go through that easily enough. He hated making a mess in this shop, but he'd take her out quick and dirty.

A low growl made them look away from one another to the Samalian standing behind the counter. "No one fights in my shop." The growling gave his word an odd accent.

The Samalian was Alex's height. Sandy fur with black spots in it covered impressive muscles. His claws were out—not especially long compared to Alex's knives, but they were sharp. Jack used his instead of knives to cut his food.

Alex slowly raised his hands.

The woman turned, not taking her hand off the gun. She gave the Samalian the once over. "You Jofdelbiro?" She didn't seem impressed by what she saw.

She didn't know anything about Samalians, Alex thought. It was the only thing that explained how she ignored the tension in those muscles. The man was ready to jump the counter and cut her up.

"Move your hand," the Samalian growled.

"I don't have time for your posturing. I'm told you have a—"

His growl deepened. He flexed his hands, and the claws became longer. Alex took a step back in reflex; those things were longer than Jack's.

The woman finally seemed to realize the Samalian was serious, and moved her hand away from the gun.

"Look, are you or aren't you Jofdelbiro?" She still sounded annoyed.

The Samalian studied her for a moment, then the growl lessened until Alex couldn't hear it anymore, but he still felt it in his bones.

"I am. Who are you?" His voice now had just a hint of a purr to it.

"I'm Miranda Sunstar. I need you to—"

"I don't know you," he interrupted her. He pointed to Alex. "You?"

"Crimson. I called earlier."

Jofdelbiro nodded. He pointed to Miranda. "You leave. Call and make an appointment."

"Do I look like I have time to deal with that? How much is it going to cost me for you to get rid of him?"

Jofdelbiro placed both hands on the counter. He leaned in,

causing his claws to add furrows to those already there. "You leave, or I throw you out."

Alex moved aside. He didn't want to get in the way.

Miranda made fists, and Alex thought he heard them creak. It could confirm she had hardened skin. He wondered how claws would fare against that, and how Jofdelbiro would react if Alex tried to help him.

"Fine!" She turned on her heels and stalked to the door. "Don't expect to ever see me again."

The Samalian shrugged as the door closed.

With the tension dissipating, Alex wondered where he'd heard the name Miranda Sunstar before. He set it aside. Probably one of the crew had mentioned her.

"What do you want?" Jofdelbiro asked. The lack of tension didn't make his muscles look any smaller, or the fur any less fluffy.

Alex stepped to the counter. "I'm looking for someone you've worked with before, about thirty years ago, objective. Tristan."

The Samalian's eyes narrowed. "Why are you looking for him?"

"I have unfinished business with him."

The Samalian's ears straightened. "Unfinished? Then my advice is to run in the opposite direction of where Tristan is. The way that guy finishes business is never good for those involved."

This time Alex did clamp down on the rising anger; it wouldn't help. He did his best to keep his tone calm. "Look, just tell me where he lives. I won't tell him I got the information from you. I'll deal with whatever happens when I find him."

"If I told you, he'd know. What makes you think I'd know where he is?"

"You're one of the few Samalians he's worked with. It makes sense he'd contact you when he came back here."

"Here? You think Tristan is here? On Samalia?" Jofdelbiro let out a bark of laughter. "That male would have to be in a cage to set foot on this planet again. Sure, I was on the same ship as him, but work with him? Tristan doesn't work with anyone, let alone one of his kind. It was just the two of us among a human crew, so I figured we needed to stay close, watch each other's back. He didn't care about it. The one time I pushed and tried to convince him we had to keep each other safe, he broke my arm. I have no idea what he thinks he is, but Tristan certainly doesn't consider himself a Samalian.

Alex had taken a step back at the anger in the Samalian's voice. If he was this angry after all this time, a broken arm had been the least of what Tristan had done.

He waited for him to calm down. "If he isn't here, do you know where he might be?"

"Why? Because all Samalians are family? We always know where the others are?"

Alex raised his hands to placate him. "I just meant there aren't that many Samalian mercenaries out there. You have to have heard something."

"Alright, yeah, I've kept an ear out for him while I worked. I didn't want to ever find myself in the same planetary system as him. But you're out of luck; the last thing I heard was that he got caught and put on the prison ship that's flying around."

Alex shook his head. "He escaped."

"Really? When?"

"A few years ago, objective," Alex answered distractedly, not paying attention to what the Samalian said after. Alex was pissed. If Tristan wasn't here, how was he going to find him? He couldn't just go around and hope to run into him.

Alex looked up. "What did you just say?"

"Huh?"

"You said something about someone asking about Tristan?"

"Yeah, a human. Like you, he had unfinished business. He had a list of places where he thought Tristan might be hiding, and he wanted to know if I had any information on them. If Tristan had mentioned them while we were on the same ship."

"Did he leave you a way to contact him?"

"Sure."

"Can I have it?"

"How much are you willing to pay for it?"

Alex sighed. Couldn't anyone in the universe do something just because it was the right thing to do? At least he had easy cash. He reached into his pocket and pulled out a cred stick.

"That's a thousand."

Jofdelbiro took it and checked the amount. Alex was momentarily surprised when the Samalian didn't contradict him. He'd been certain Anders would have screwed him over, even with that.

"You want to find him that badly? I can sell you a Fogar grenade for that kind of money. It's going to be quicker and less painful, just don't use that in the city. It can take out half a dozen blocks."

"I'll take the information."

The Samalian looked him in the eyes. "You are going to get yourself killed."

"I paid for the information. Hand it over."

Jofdelbiro sighed. "Humans. What is it with you and death wishes?" He took out a datapad, then searched around for a data chip to put the information on and handed that to Alex.

"I have no plans on dying," Alex said.

"And I had no plans on coming back here, but it was that or face a long stay in a max-security prison. It doesn't matter what you want. Tristan will kill you anyway."

Alex nodded. If it came to that, then dying would be better than living knowing he'd never get Jack back. Without another word, he left the building.

The bike was gone, so he'd been right, it had been a human vehicle. That woman's— He stopped.

Miranda Sunstar. She'd been the mercenary who had caught Tristan and delivered him to the Sayatoga prison ship. He'd run multiple searches for her, but they had all come back blank; her information was well-hidden. He'd ran into her by accident and not even realized who she was.

He laughed. What else could he do? She'd been right there. He could have gotten answers. If there was one person still alive who knew more about Tristan than what was in the files, it would be her. He looked around just in case.

He shook his head in amusement. There wasn't much he could do about it now. He pulled out his datapad and ran a search, but she didn't come up. She was still hidden. He had no information on the bike, but he still sent a message to the port, asking to be notified if it was spotted there. She'd have to leave the planet eventually.

But he couldn't afford to wait for her. He had someone to track down, information to get. He had to make it to Bramolian Six as quickly as possible.

EPILOGUE

Alex had picked this alley because it was close enough, but no one used it; the stores lining each side were boarded up, and the sensor he'd hidden hadn't detected any movement larger than a small pet in the eight days since it had been in place.

At times he'd found himself thinking that Bramolian Six looked to be a place he and Jack might enjoy visiting when they were together again. And then he remembered what he was planning, and doubted he'd ever come back after today.

He checked the chronometer he'd bought the day after he'd arrived. One of the newer models, expensive, but fully programmable with more features than he knew what to do with. The time function told him his hired hands were late.

The vehicle turned into the alley, an unassuming gray hover car with darkened windows that let him see there were two occupants, but not who they were. It moved slowly, to avoid scraping the buildings, as the alley wasn't much larger than it.

It stopped a dozen feet away, and Alex waited, hand on the

blaster at his hip. The door opened partially and almost hit the wall. A young man in a pink shirt, red pants, and slicked-back green hair squeezed out.

"Hey, Boss," he said. "Sorry for being late. They closed the Ulserson Bridge, and I didn't want to attract attention by flying over it."

Alex nodded. "Flint." He indicated the other occupant. "How about she gets out too."

"Don't you trust us? You're paying us, after all."

Alex smiled. "I'd like to make sure I'm still paying the same people I hired. Changes in the middle of a job tend to forecast trouble."

The young man leaned in the vehicle. "Come on, Liz, the boss wants to see your pretty face."

The other door opened, bouncing on the permacrete wall, making Flint wince. A woman close to his age stood, thin-framed but not skinny, and bright red hair Alex thought might be dyed. Her shirt was iridescent black and tight, making her breasts more pronounced.

"Is it in place?" Alex asked.

"Yep. When we get the signal, half the city'll go dark," Flint answered. "But I have to say this. I'd prefer you pay us the rest of the money now, because you're not coming back. The Law here doesn't kid about, not like it does in space."

"I wouldn't worry about it. Just be here when I get back, and you'll get another ten-thousand each."

"Buddy," Liz said. "How do we even know you're going to pay us? For all we know, you're going to leave us for the Law to catch."

"That isn't how I work."

"So you say," she replied. "We don't know you."

"But you took my money, so you agreed to work for me until the job's over."

Alex hadn't wanted to hire anyone for the job, especially locals he didn't know, but he didn't have the contacts needed to get what had been needed. He hadn't been at this long enough to build a database of people.

"Liz," Flint said. "Don't worry about it, we already got ten each. That's plenty for what we did. Even with him dead, we're still ahead."

She ignored him. "You at least have the rest of the money? I don't intend on getting scammed."

Alex patted his left pocket. "Right here."

"Show me."

Alex rolled his eyes and pulled out the two cred sticks. "Happy?"

"Can I make sure they're filled?"

"No, we've wasted enough time already." He pocketed them. "You two sit here. Trigger the bomb when you get the signal, and you can do anything you want with the sticks when I get back." He turned to leave, but stopped. He took off the belt with the gun and handed that to Flint. "I can't really show up to a Law station armed. Take care of this for me." He took out the one at the small of his back, a smaller model, eyed Flint's filled hands, then tossed it to Liz. "Hopefully this won't be too long. Sit tight."

He hoped they wouldn't cause him any troubles. They'd come well recommended by the few mercs he'd talked with. Resourceful and dependable, when there was enough money involved. Of course, a love of money could bring its own set of problems, but hopefully Alex had paid them enough to ensure they wouldn't try to double-cross him. If they did, he'd deal with that too.

The Law station was an unassuming building three blocks away, with marked cars coming and going from the roof parking. Like he'd done for the previous eight days, he put on the glasses before entering and went to the reception desk.

"Yes, what's your complaint?" the harried man behind the counter asked.

Alex smiled. "No complaints. I'm Harold Stingsky. I have an appointment with Inspector Victor Barstone." The previous days he'd gone directly to the waiting area and sat.

"I'll let him know you're here. Just grab a seat."

As he walked to one of the chairs, there was a flash of light. No one reacted to it, because unless they wore the same types of glasses he did, they hadn't seen it. Seconds began rolling forward in the top left of his vision. The flash had been one of the random scans the station ran, looking for complex programs.

Security was understandably high at a Law station. The primary way they ensured no one could access or compromise their records was that access to the open net was minimal, and none of the archives had a direct connection. The scan helped ensure that no one came in armed with programs to coerce the system into giving it what he wanted.

He'd spent the previous eight days sitting here, observing how they worked, but mainly tracking the scan. It wasn't quite random, or rather it was, but it always waited at least five minutes before running again.

The light flashed. The timer stopped, and another one began running. The delay added itself to the long list on the right side. Seven minutes, twelve seconds. This had been a short one. The average was fourteen minutes, nineteen seconds.

Two officers entered the waiting area and headed toward Alex. He didn't react, but he placed a hand inside his sleeve. Had they sold him out after all? It wasn't like they'd know he had a price on his head. He'd dyed his hair blond, darkened his skin, and gave himself green eyes. Not even close to the only description of him to have a price on his head.

As far as he could tell, the trap ship had never regained its memory, but plenty of the guards on that ship had seen him among the crew and they'd compiled a description. So, there was someone who looked like him currently worth five-thousand.

Inexplicably, he felt some pride at having a price on his head.

The officers walked past him to stop before a woman in a business suit. "Ma'am?" one of them began. "Please stand."

She did, a look of confusion on her face.

The other officer scanned her, then opened her jacket and pulled a datapad out of the inside pocket.

"Data devices are prohibited within the station, ma'am. You can get this back from the reception desk when you leave."

"But I need it for my meeting; the description of everything that was stolen is on there."

"It isn't the only thing on there, is it?"

"Well, no, it contains everything I need for my work and home."

"We'll make sure the information pertinent to your case is available for the inspector you'll be talking with."

"Alright..." she didn't sound sure of herself. "I guess you'll need me to unlock it for you?"

The officer gave her a smile that Alex thought was meant to be friendly, but came across as creepy instead. "No, ma'am. You don't need to do that." Then they left.

Another flash. Five minutes, forty-six seconds.

Alex had to wait almost ten more minutes before Inspector Barstone came to get him. During that time he kept his hands together, tapping a finger on his wrist, next to the chronometer.

"Mister Stingsky?" the man asked.

Alex stood and shook his hand.

Victor was a man who looked to be in his fifties, fit, but with some mass around the middle. His hair was black, and thinning. It could be an affectation; cosmetic changes were fairly inexpensive, but Alex didn't get that sense from the man. From everything he'd read on him, Victor Barstone was someone who didn't bother with appearances.

He'd been climbing the echelons within the Law quickly, until he was implicated in a large data theft. He'd claimed his innocence, but the crime had been traced back to someone he knew, intimately. The description matched Tristan, but the name Victor gave was Simon. He'd fallen back to the bottom of the ladder, and he'd never been able to regain the momentum he'd had before.

Victor led Alex to a room containing only a desk and two chairs. It wasn't his office, just a room they used for interviews. It was shielded, an added security measure against coercionists who managed to make it this deep within the station, not that he was close to anything of value. The archive was on the other side of the building. To have any chance of accessing it, he'd have to make it into the part of the building where only officers were allowed, then to a terminal. Once there, it would be easy for him to gain access.

But getting there was impossible.

Victor sat, and indicated the other chair. "You said you wanted to talk to me, Mister Stingsky, but you never made it clear in regards to what."

Alex smiled. "Please, call me Harold. I didn't specify because I was worried you wouldn't agree with me if I had." He placed his hand on the desk and began tapping a finger on his wrist, by the chronometer. "I'm a writer, and I'm here on a part-vacation and part-research trip. I'm working on a story involving an inspector who needs to hunt down a criminal across multiple systems, but when I read the news archive I came across a mention that you'd done something like that. You'll have to forgive me if I don't remember the details; I had all that on my datapad, and I left it in my hotel. I knew I wouldn't be allowed to bring it in."

Victor nodded. "Across multiple systems," he said flatly. He didn't seem happy about it, but he pulled out a datapad from his pocket and turned it on.

Alex kept his face interested, but no more. He now had his access to the archives.

"It isn't a time I like to talk about," Victor said, "but so long as you don't ask about the details of my investigation, I'll be happy to answer your questions."

"That's alright. I'm more interested in what's involved in such a pursuit than who you were chasing."

Alex had searched Victor's home system for the list Jofdelbiro had mentioned, but it hadn't been there. After a bit of research, he'd found out that Victor had been forced to store that in the station archive because it was considered an active investigation.

Victor was explaining how they used body recognition programs, linked with the camera systems across the city to track someone's movements, when there was a flash of light. Alex did a double tap on the chronometer, then went back to tapping his wrist.

It would take eight seconds for the chronometer to assemble the simple assembly program. That one would take twelve to assemble the slightly more complex assembler, and that one twenty-two seconds for the next one. In all it would take a minute and thirty-three seconds before the program he needed would be built out of the random snippets of code that Alex had stored in the chronometer. That left it just under three and a half minutes to gain access to the archive through Victor's datapad, and mine it for the information Alex needed.

Alex nodded as Victor talked of having to investigate every place a ship stopped to check if the quarry had left, because he couldn't trust what the system said. It had been easy to make them lie, even back then. He talked about jurisdiction complications when the local Law didn't want to cooperate. And how sometimes it required skirting the laws to be able to catch him.

The three and a half minutes passed by, and the program wasn't done. Alex forced his breathing to stay steady, but he couldn't do anything about his heartbeat. If there were any sort of scanners in the room keeping an ear to his bodily functions, they'd know something was off. But he wasn't a suspect, so why would those be on?

Victor continued talking and Alex nodded at the appropriate times, but he had no idea what he was saying. He heard it, but was too preoccupied with the time—five minutes, nine seconds—to process it.

He reminded himself the average was in the range of ten minutes, closer to fifteen. The odds were on his side that the program would be fine.

Seven minutes, still going. Alex could feel sweat bead on his forehead. Victor said something, then paused. He looked concerned.

Seven minutes twenty-nine seconds. The chronometer buzzed, letting Alex know it had collected everything available. He slumped forward with a heavy sigh.

"Is everything alright?" Victor asked, worry in his tone.

Alex snapped his head up, about to come up with an explanation, but the flash of light stopped him. *Oh great,* he thought. There was no way the chronometer was done disassembling the programs.

An alarm sounded throughout the station.

Alex thought that was odd; there hadn't been one with the woman in the waiting area.

Victor looked out the window at the commotion while Alex held still. All he had to do was wait for the power to go out. Victor looked at Alex.

Any moment now.

The officer glanced at the chronometer on Alex's wrist.

You guys better trigger the bomb, or we're going to have a serious talk after this.

Victor cursed. He began standing, but Alex grabbed his arm and pulled him down, putting a knife to his throat, doing his best to hide it from those outside with his arm.

"Let's not do anything rash," Alex said.

The man gulped. "How?"

Alex smiled. "You'd be amazed at the number of composite material that can be sharpened to a decent edge."

Victor locked eyes with Alex. "I'm not letting you get out of here. This isn't happening to me a second time."

It took a moment for Alex to realize what he meant. "Right, you've been in a similar position before. But if it's any consolation, I only copied some of your files."

Someone knocked on the window.

Alex and Victor turned to look at the woman there. Her eyes grew wide when she noticed the blade.

"You're never getting out of here," Victor said. "You might as well surrender now."

Alex sighed. "I was really hoping to do this without having to hurt anyone." He stepped around the desk without moving the knife from the inspector's neck. Next to him, he took the gun out of the man's holster. "I'm afraid I have to borrow this."

"You think you can just shoot your way out of the station? Are you crazy?"

"Desperate is closer." He pointed the gun at the man's chest and back to the door. "Can I count on you to stay in here, where it's going to be safe?"

"I'm not letting you get out of here with that information."

"I was afraid of that." Alex switched the safety off and aimed at the man's head.

The lights went off.

Finally.

Alex bolted out of the room, his glasses letting him see. He had a little more than ten seconds to make it out before the emergency power came back on and the station went into lockdown.

He just barely made it, and he threw the gun away and kept on running. Barstone would be after him.

He took the first corner, heading away from Flint and Liz. He ducked into the first alley, went two blocks, then grabbed another alley and headed further away. He activated the command and his jacket turned brown. The name of the university where he'd bought it appeared on the back, with "Frank" over the left breast. He took a cap out of the inside pocket and put that over his head, tucking all his hair under it. The shoulders widened, giving him the look of a sports star. Another command and the pants turned blue, faded at the knees.

He stepped on the street, now confident the automated surveillance system wouldn't catch him, and ambled his way back to the car.

When he entered that alley, he was pleasantly surprised to see they were still there. Alex took off the jacket.

"Hey, Boss," Flint called, standing up and leaning on the open car door. "I'm really sorry about the delay." He gave Liz a look. "We had some technical difficulties on our side."

Alex waved that aside. "Don't worry about it. It happened, that's all I care about. Let's get out of here."

Liz stood and pointed her gun at Alex. "How about we don't."

"Liz, what are you doing?" Flint asked, his voice a mix of annoyance and fear.

"I'm thinking that with him busting a Law station,

someone's going to be willing to pay a lot of money to get their hands on him."

"Liz, we talked about this. He's paying us."

She shrugged. "We'll still get that money, but we'll get a bonus on top of that." She glared at him. "Get a backbone, will you?"

With a sigh, Flint took the gun out of the holster and pointed it at Alex.

Alex had let them come to their decision without interruption, and now he was looking at the muzzle of the guns he'd handed them himself. "So, I'm guessing you're siding with her then?" he asked.

"Yeah. Sorry, Boss, but she's the love of my life."

Alex nodded. "I know something about the length we can go for love."

Flint smiled. "I'm glad you understand. I really don't want this to be awkward."

"Is there anything I can say to convince you to put down the guns? No one has done anything we can't laugh about yet. I can still pay you and we'll go our separate ways."

"Oh, you'll pay us," Liz said. "Right now. Then I'm calling the Law to find out what they're willing to pay to get you back. Hand the sticks over."

"Last chance for you to talk some sense into your girlfriend, Flint."

He shook his head. "Just do as she says. It's easier that way."

"Okay. You can't say I didn't try." Alex put a hand in his right pocket and closed it around the device there.

"Wait a minute," Flint said. "The sticks are in—" The gun in his hand exploded in an intense flash of light. Before he could start screaming, Liz's gun did the same.

Alex took the glasses off; they'd gone dark to protect his vision. Flint was on the ground, cradling his arm, the end of it burnt black. The explosion had been so hot it had cauterized the injury. Alex had made sure of that; he didn't want them to bleed out.

He squeezed between the door and the wall, then pulled the man behind the car. He did the same with Liz, closing the door in the process. Through gasps of pain, she cursed him. He leaned against the back of the car, looking down at them.

"Two things," he said. "First, don't double-cross the guy who paid you for the job. I don't care how much more money you think you can get out of it. It's never a good policy. Second, if you are going to double-cross him, for the love of the universe, don't use the guns he handed you himself."

He walked around the car, got behind the wheel, and looked out to the back. "Oh, thanks for the ride. I'll leave it at the spaceport for you to pick up." He closed the door and carefully pulled out of the alley. Hopefully the driving simulation he'd put himself through would let him get to the port without damaging it too much.

ABOUT THE AUTHOR

Sylvain St-Pierre has been writing and making up stories for longer than he can remember, and driving a truck for the last fifteen years.

He write stories in multiple genres, but with a usual focus on guys in relationships with other guys. The majority of his books are Furry in nature, with most dealing with gay relationships, and some being erotica.

As a self-published author—only recently being distributed by an indie publisher—any support you can provide would be greatly appreciated. If you liked this book, consider buying his other titles, or support his Patreon at www.patreon. com/kindar

CRIMSON

CPSIA information can be obtained
at www.ICGtesting.com
Printed in the USA
BVHW041723270219
541334BV00016B/861/P